MW00561441

A GRAVE ROBBERY

ALSO BY DEANNA RAYBOURN
Killers of a Certain Age

Veronica Speedwell Mystery Series
A Curious Beginning
A Perilous Undertaking
A Treacherous Curse
A Dangerous Collaboration
A Murderous Relation
An Unexpected Peril
An Impossible Impostor

Lady Julia Grey Novels

Silent in the Grave   *Dark Road to Darjeeling*

Silent in the Sanctuary   *The Dark Enquiry*

Silent on the Moor

Lady Julia Grey Novellas

Silent Night   *Twelfth Night*

Midsummer Night   *Bonfire Night*

Other Works
For a complete list of Deanna's titles,
please visit *deannaraybourn.com*

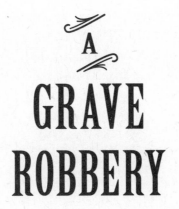

A
GRAVE
ROBBERY

A VERONICA SPEEDWELL
MYSTERY

Deanna Raybourn

BERKLEY
NEW YORK

BERKLEY
An imprint of Penguin Random House LLC
penguinrandomhouse.com

Copyright © 2024 by Raybourn Creative LLC.
Penguin Random House supports copyright. Copyright fuels creativity, encourages diverse
voices, promotes free speech, and creates a vibrant culture. Thank you for buying an authorized
edition of this book and for complying with copyright laws by not reproducing, scanning, or
distributing any part of it in any form without permission. You are supporting writers and
allowing Penguin Random House to continue to publish books for every reader.

BERKLEY and the BERKLEY & B colophon are registered trademarks of
Penguin Random House LLC.

The Edgar® name is a registered service mark of the Mystery Writers of America, Inc.

Library of Congress Cataloging-in-Publication Data

Names: Raybourn, Deanna, author.
Title: A grave robbery / Deanna Raybourn.
Description: First edition. | New York: Berkley, 2024. |
Series: A Veronica Speedwell mystery
Identifiers: LCCN 2023028930 (print) | LCCN 2023028931 (ebook) |
ISBN 9780593545959 (hardcover) | ISBN 9780593545973 (ebook)
Subjects: LCGFT: Detective and mystery fiction. | Novels.
Classification: LCC PS3618.A983 G73 2024 (print) |
LCC PS3618.A983 (ebook) | DDC 813/.6—dc23/eng/20230707
LC record available at https://lccn.loc.gov/2023028930
LC ebook record available at https://lccn.loc.gov/2023028931

Printed in the United States of America
1st Printing

Book design by Kristin del Rosario

This is a work of fiction. Names, characters, places, and incidents either are the product
of the author's imagination or are used fictitiously, and any resemblance to actual persons,
living or dead, business establishments, events, or locales is entirely coincidental.

For Angèle Masters. Thank you for giving Veronica her voice.

A GRAVE ROBBERY

CHAPTER

1

London, October 1889

I draw the line at monkeys," Stoker said with considerable severity. "I will have no monkeys, Veronica."

Stoker was usually amenable to animals of every description, but the fact that the creature in question was currently sitting atop his head in a posture of nonchalance had doubtless contributed to his irritability.

The monkey in question was a golden lion tamarin—*Leontopithecus rosalia*, to be exact—also known as a golden marmoset, a description which is far more enticing than the creature itself. It was small, weighing no more than a pound and a half, and of modest proportions. Its quizzical expressions and the bright orange hair that circled its head in an exuberant impression of a lion's mane might have been charming, but the effect was spoilt by its naked face and downturned mouth. It was scarcely a year old, but it studied everything around it with the sour judgement of a wizened old person. Occasionally, when it looked at me, it tipped its head to the side and pulled its mouth further down, as if it could penetrate my secrets and found me wanting. It was unpleasant in the extreme, and the fact that it had taken to Stoker with an affection that bordered on the aggressive was a welcome development. It had been a gift to our aged friend, Lady Wellingtonia Beauclerk, from a Brazilian admirer, and in a moment of lunacy, I had agreed to care for it until Lady Wellie could make permanent arrangements. Unfortunately, there were few listings for callitrichines in the Situations Wanted advertisements in the London papers.

"It is hardly my fault the little beast prefers you," I said serenely. "Lady Wellie assured me it would be no trouble. A dish of tea, a spoonful of fruit, and a secure little nest is all it requires for its comfort, I am informed. And you must admit, it does not ask for much beyond that."

"Much beyond?" Stoker's voice took on a distinctly strangled note. "Veronica, she drinks out of my teacup. She purloins food from my fork. And the least said about her unhygienic sleeping arrangements, the better."

He might have been grumbling, but I observed with a smothered smile that he had already assessed the monkey's gender and applied the correct pronouns.

"It is adorable that the little beast dotes on you so," I assured him. "You are a very large, strong man. Surely you do not begrudge food and drink for such a tiny creature."

"I do not begrudge her the food and drink. I begrudge her the fact that she sleeps upon my pillow, and this morning she tried to join me in the bath." A delectable rosy blush tinted his cheeks.

"One can hardly blame her," I murmured, delighted to see the blush deepen to crimson. Stoker and I had, for some time, enjoyed a thoroughly satisfying and thrilling personal relationship, a meeting and mingling of minds and bodies that was as successful as our working partnership. We were both of us natural scientists, Stoker with an affinity for large mammals and extensive taxidermic skills whilst I preferred lepidoptery. We were employed by the Earl of Rosemorran—great-nephew of the monkey-riddled Lady Wellie—with cataloguing, repairing, and arranging his vast store of artefacts, art, and other agreeable treasures for eventual display in the Rosemorran Collection, the museum he planned to open for the edification of the general public. We had initially anticipated that his lordship's possessions, including the hoards inherited from his ancestors, a wealthy and acquisitive group, could be organised and ready for installation within a few decades. But as his lordship was an incorrigible haunter of auction houses, showroom sales, and other people's attics, the amount we had to sort seemed to increase on a frankly alarming basis.

The benefit to this, of course, was that Stoker and I could rely upon our employment to extend into extreme old age. The drawback was a tendency towards melancholy when contemplating exactly how much remained to be done. It did not help matters that we were, all too frequently, called away from our endeavours by the crime of murder and occasional instances of grand larceny. More times than would seem probable, Stoker and I had been prevailed upon—or had chosen, if I am honest—to involve ourselves in the investigation of the most heinous crimes. We had thwarted villains, saved innocent men from the hangman's noose, and restored priceless jewels to their rightful owners. We had masqueraded as royalty, foiled ancient curses, and evaded certain death. Our escapades were as invigorating as they were unlikely, and I had adored each and every one.

But I was conscious that morning, as a brisk October wind teased russet leaves from the branches of the trees, of a certain restlessness. We had, only the month previous, concluded a successful investigation that had imperilled both of our lives. Stoker had scarcely healed from the dislocation of his shoulder, and our dogs—five at last count—had just begun to accept that we were at last home and settled. Without the benefit of marriage, Stoker and I naturally occupied separate quarters at the earl's Marylebone estate of Bishop's Folly. A series of small, perfectly appointed pavilions had been built by one of the earl's ancestors—a Roman temple, a miniature pink Scottish castle, and so forth. I had claimed the French Gothic chapel for my own use whilst Stoker slept in the Chinese pagoda. Next to these charming buildings was a pond of significant size and depth to permit swimming, and bordering this pond was a shrubbery where the earl's Galápagos tortoise, Patricia, frequently upended herself, legs waving woefully in the air and giving lamentable cries until a rescue party could be formed to put her to rights.

Beyond the shrubbery was the Belvedere, a freestanding ballroom of sorts which held the bulk of the collected artefacts. It was workroom, office, laboratory, and club, furnished with such oddities as a decaying camel saddle, a collection of caryatids, the workings of a Sicilian puppet theatre, and an Egyptian sarcophagus which served as our sideboard. Busts of emperors jostled with mediaeval weapons, and paintings of dour Madonnas looked down upon Wardian cases filled with creatures of every description. Upstairs, the snuggery provided shelving for acres of books and periodicals along with Napoléon's campaign bed—a surprisingly comfortable spot to nap. A porcelain Swedish stove provided tea-making facilities and a handy cloisonné cupboard was always stuffed with tins of biscuits, gingerbread, and assorted sweets. There were cushions for the dogs, and an entire wall of cubbyholes crammed with papers, waxes, inks, brushes, pens, paints, glues, filaments, furs, wires, and every other supply we might require. The roof was sound, the walls thick, and his lordship's numerous—and frankly anarchic—progeny were strictly forbidden to enter without adult accompaniment.

It was, in short, the happiest place on earth, in my estimation, and I was never more contented than when engaged with a new batch of Lepidoptera. I had meant to spend the forenoon writing up the talk I had been invited to deliver to the Aurelian Society, but the morning's deliveries had distracted me. They included a pair of elegant cases of French design, each holding a pristine sample of the Madagascan moon moth.

I had sat for several minutes, admiring the elegant sweep of their hind-wings and the vividness of their eyespots before Stoker and his monkey interrupted me.

I turned back to my magnifying glass and my enormous silk-spinning beauties. "I have every faith in your ability to cope with one of the smallest primates in existence," I assured him.

"I have *work*," he muttered. It was with an heroic effort at restraint that I did not point out he was interrupting my own work. It has been my experience that the male of the species, though often thoroughly il-logical, can—when encouraged to sit quietly and think hard—be guided into a position of sense. I applied myself to my moths whilst Stoker con-sidered his options. He had just begun to feed the monkey bits of honey-comb from the paper twist in his pocket when a discreet cough sounded from the doorway.

"I do hope I am not come at an inconvenient time?"

I looked up at our employer with sincere pleasure. "Your lordship! It has been an age since you have visited the Belvedere," I said, laying down my magnifying glass. "We have made real progress since your last inspection."

"I have no doubt," Lord Rosemorran said. He seemed a trifle uncom-fortable, tugging at his collar. His fingers, as usual, were begrimed with ink and left a grubby mark upon the linen. It did not matter. His cloth-ing already bore traces of encounters with his children. His garments were streaked with the acids, inks, and paints of their various activities. I was only glad to see no traces of Lady Rose's latest endeavours. Her attempts to dye her aunt's white Persian cat the same colour as a peony had resulted in the entire household's linen turning a virulent shade of pink. She was the youngest, and by far the most villainous of the earl's brood, and I made a point of avoiding her whenever possible. I do not care for children even when they are biddable, quiet, and clean, and Lady Rose was never any of those.

As if intuiting my thoughts, the child in question bounded in behind her father, her eyes dancing with an unholy light. "Have you asked him, Papa?" she demanded.

The earl shifted uneasily. "I was just coming to that, my dear."

She hopped from foot to foot. "Do it now, Papa. You must!" Her tone was imploring, and she gave him a look only an indulgent father would interpret as winsome.

"What is it you wish, Lady Rose?" I asked.

Her expression turned baleful. "Nothing from you, Miss Speedwell. I need Stoker," she said. The very sound of his name was adoring on her lips. Like females of all ages and most species, Lady Rose harboured a tender spot for Stoker. Whether it was the courtly manners which had been bred into him by his viscountess mother or the juxtaposition of those manners with his staggering appearance—one need only say the words "Elizabethan buccaneer" to conjure tumbled witch-black locks, an occasional eyepatch, and a wealth of tattoos and golden earrings— most feminine creatures found themselves utterly beguiled by him.

"Oh," Lady Rose breathed as she looked at Stoker properly. "You have a monkey on your head. Did you mean to?"

"Yes," he told her solemnly. "I hear it is quite the fashion this year. Even the queen has one—a chimpanzee, I am told. It sits on her head in place of a crown and sleeps in a golden bed in the palace."

Lady Rose grinned. "You are very *silly*," she informed him.

Stoker returned the smile and gently removed the monkey from its perch, depositing it into the marble embrace of a handy caryatid. "Now, what can I do for you, my lady?"

Before Lady Rose could reply, there was a commotion at the door. Porters arrived bearing an enormous and obviously weighty crate. Lady Rose danced around it. "She's here, Papa! She's here!"

I looked in some alarm to his lordship. "She?"

The earl hurried to explain as Stoker directed the porters where to place their burden. "It is a trifle complicated. Perhaps it is better to show you."

The porters eased the crate to the floor and left, their pockets weighted with the earl's generous gratuities as Stoker applied a pry-bar to the lid. It was the work of moments to have the thing opened, and as the wooden sides of the crate fell flat, we stared in frank astonishment.

Inside the crate was a long glass box, a crystal casket, and inside lay a waxwork figure on a satin pillow. It was a young woman with long dark hair, rippling unbound over her shoulders. She wore an old-fashioned dress of heavy red velvet edged in fine lace, four inches deep. The neckline was deep and square, revealing an unblemished décolletage the same pale hue as the graceful hands. They were not, as one might expect, folded at the breast in a posture of stiff repose. Instead, they rested at her thighs, palms gently curved, the fingers tapered and relaxed. Her face was singularly beautiful, each feature moulded with grace, from the arch of the dark brow to the delicate line of the jaw. The complexion was pale except for the flush across the cheekbones and rosy lips which were softly parted. The whole effect was one of a maiden captured in enchanted slumber, a fragment of a fairy tale translated from the page to our workroom.

"She is exquisite," Stoker said hoarsely. His gaze rested dreamily upon her face, and I suppressed a flicker of irritation. One cannot be envious of a waxwork, I reminded myself firmly. I turned to our employer. "Where did you find her?"

"There is a warehouse in Shoreditch that currently holds a few items I haven't had the chance to transfer here," he said. I looked around at the already crowded Belvedere wondering precisely how much more his lordship intended to bring us. We could scarcely move about the place as it was. He must have seen something of my thoughts in my expression, for he hurried on. "Only a few items," he assured me. "Very small.

You will hardly notice them when they arrive. But I happened to stop in to deposit a quite modest collection of—"

"My lord, you are not only keeping things in Shoreditch we knew nothing of, you are *adding* to them?"

He had the grace to look abashed. "Well, one sees things and one simply cannot resist them." He spread his hands helplessly. "In this case, I had purchased a full set of German tilting armour—very fine, fourteenth-century—from an auction house quite near to the warehouse. It seemed easiest to take delivery there and leave the armour until we had cleared space here in the Belvedere. Whilst I was there, I happened to notice the adjoining warehouse was clearing out items that had been left and never claimed." He nodded towards the figure in the glass casket. "When I heard there was a waxwork for sale, it seemed the happiest of coincidences. Rose had asked for one for her birthday."

"Had you?" I asked his daughter.

She was hopping from one foot to the other, fairly vibrating with excitement. "Oh, yes. Sidonie takes me sometimes to Madame Tussaud's." Their mother long dead, the earl's children were left frequently in the care of his sister. Since governesses left the house as frequently as the soiled laundry, the lady's maid, Sidonie, was occasionally pressed into service to lend a hand. I was not surprised that her notion of an appropriate outing for Lady Rose was a trip to the waxworks. The excursion was cheap and thrilling and conveniently located a quick walk away in Baker Street. "I am particularly fond of the Hall of Horrors," Lady Rose went on. "But Sidonie thinks I am too young to see them, so I made a point of escaping her to see the murderers. She found me in front of Burke and Hare," she said, pulling a face. "They robbed graves, you know. A *nasty* thing to do. So then we went to see something nicer and she showed me the Sleeping Beauty."

"Ah," I said, suddenly understanding. The figure was one of the most famous of Madame Tussaud's works, although likely not sculpted by her own hand. Unlike our waxwork, that lady was gilt-haired and rested on a chaise longue in a posture of exhausted abandon. There was the faintest whiff of the erotic about her, the way one arm had been thrown above her head, revealing the delicate, naked skin of her wrist. It was said she had been modelled upon the luscious form of the Comtesse du Barry, the last mistress of Louis XV, a commission to memorialise the lady's artful charms. Others said she was a noble widow put to the guillotine for resisting the advances of Robespierre. But whether royal courtesan or victim of vengeance, the true attraction of the figure lay in its refinements. The torso had been fitted with a clockwork mechanism to simulate the motion of breathing. To stand and watch her was an extraordinary experience. She ceased to be a waxwork and became instead a fairy-tale figure, a *belle au bois dormant*, drifting into dreams, and it was not uncommon to see visitors to Madame Tussaud's whispering and tiptoeing away, leaving her to undisturbed repose.

"And you wanted a waxwork of your own?" I asked Lady Rose.

"Not just any waxwork," she said, her eyes gleaming again with that devilish light. "I want one that *breathes*. My very own Sleeping Beauty."

"For what purpose?" I demanded. She was only a child, of course, lacking the maturity of an adult, but surely she could not think the finished waxwork would be a suitable plaything.

She rolled her eyes heavenwards. "For the purpose of charging admission, of course. Papa says I can keep the proceeds." The brightness in her expression, which I had mistaken for childish excitement, suddenly revealed itself as keenly entrepreneurial, and I experienced a dart of something akin to respect for her.

She turned to Stoker. "Can you do it? Will you?"

Stoker circled the glass casket, scrutinising the figure inside. "You want me to modify this waxwork to make it breathe, as Madame Tussaud's Sleeping Beauty does?"

"Is it too much trouble?" the earl put in, a line furrowing its way between his brows.

"I do not think so," Stoker said slowly. "The mechanism itself is simple enough. One would only need make an incision here—" He indicated the side of the mannequin and sketched an elliptical shape with his hands. "Then around in order to make space for the chest to rise. With the proper gears and rods and a bit of luck, it will run indefinitely." He bent swiftly, peering through the glass. "We shall have to be careful removing the gown if you want her to wear it again. It will not be easy to manipulate it over the limbs. The wax is flexible, but it will have been sculpted over armature." Lady Rose shot him a puzzled glance and he explained. "A sort of skeleton, a framework of metal. It gives structure and strength to the figure."

Any other father might have blanched with horror to hear his daughter discussing a subject as inappropriate as *limbs* with a man, but his lordship had no such qualms. He had never shielded his children from any topic of learning or conversation for which they had a sincere interest.

Lady Rose pursed her lips thoughtfully. "No, I think she would look well in blue. We shall have a new gown made. I will pay for it out of my pocket money," she assured her father.

He smiled kindly. "Never mind that, Rose. We will tell Stoker thank you and be on our way now," he urged.

"Oh, yes," she said, turning to Stoker, face suffused with gratitude. "Thank you ever so much! When do you think she will be finished?"

"Rose," her father said in a warning tone. "Stoker has other work, you know."

She gave Stoker a graceful curtsy by way of apology. "Whenever you can then, Stoker. Only do make it soon," she urged.

Stoker grinned and tossed her a piece of honeycomb. She snatched the candy out of thin air and skipped from the room, tugging her papa by the hand. I could hear snatches of her enthusiastic conversation as they went.

"You indulge that child," I began mildly.

He shook his head. "I would have done this for anyone. It is a singularly thrilling piece of work. The figure will require a little refurbishment, I think, as well as the mechanism. And I think I may learn a thing or two about sculpture. This is an extraordinary piece of art, quite unlike anything I have seen before in its delicacy. If I could figure out how it was done and translate that to the swan I have been working on . . ."

His voice trailed off as he bent again to the waxwork figure, running adoring eyes over her from tip to toe. He murmured to himself as he circled her, making mental notes on his planned improvements.

"If it is so educational, you ought to make a point of inviting Lady Rose to watch you work," I told him.

He reared back, the blush once more in evidence. "I hardly think so."

"Whyever not?"

The monkey apparently took umbrage at my tone. It chattered rudely and leapt off the caryatid to take a perch on Stoker's shoulder, where it began to run its little claws through his hair. Stoker ignored it as he began to explain.

"There are two types of waxworks," he said. "There are those created for the purposes of entertainment, the sort put on display at Madame Tussaud's and the like or hauled about the country in travelling shows."

"And the others?" I watched, mesmerised, as the monkey held up a lock of his hair at a time, examining it closely.

"Created for the purposes of teaching anatomy. It used to be that corpses served the purpose," he said, pulling a face.

"Burke and Hare," I put in, remembering Lady Rose's interest in the grave robbers at Madame Tussaud's.

"Just so. But robbing graves is a nasty business, not to mention highly unethical. So, artists in Italy began to sculpt them. They were already in the habit of making human forms out of wax because they had been doing so for the purpose of sacred statuary. It was a small step from fashioning saints for churches to sculpting educational aids for medical studies. They were called Anatomical Venuses, and they were quite popular for a century or more, particularly in university cities like Bologna."

"What does that have to do with our lady?" I asked. The monkey sniffed one lock of hair deeply and began to rub its face on Stoker's head in apparent ecstasy.

Stoker looked deeply uncomfortable, but I suspected it had little to do with being molested by a monkey and more with the waxwork figure lying before us.

He gestured towards her midsection. "Well, if she is an Anatomical Venus, she would be complete. Thorough. Intact, as it were."

I stared at him for a long moment before understanding dawned. "You mean she would be—"

"As detailed as an actual woman. In every particular."

"All the more reason to include Lady Rose," I said. "The child is on the cusp of puberty and heaven alone knows if anyone has prepared her for it."

"That is hardly within the purview of our work here," Stoker protested in a horrified voice.

"No, I suppose not. And certainly not anything you ought to be concerned with," I told him. All the same, I made a mental note to invite Lady Rose and her elder sisters for a comprehensive examination of the wax figure should she prove complete. I had little doubt it would be instructive even if the Beauclerk children had been tutored in the rudiments of reproductive biology.

"Of course," Stoker went on in a bleak voice, oblivious to the monkey's antics, "I have no doubt Lady Rose will turn up on her own as soon as she suspects I've got to work. I shall have to think of some means of bribing her to stay away."

I looked up at the monkey and saw it had wrapped a lock of Stoker's hair around its head like a bonnet. It gazed beatifically at him before turning to me and baring its teeth as it made a sound that could only be described as a hiss. I gave Stoker a consoling smile. "Leave it to me, dearest. I know exactly what to do."

CHAPTER

2

After dinner that evening, I finished the last of the day's tasks, stacking articles to be sent, wiping pens, directing letters into the proper pigeonholes—*actual* pigeonholes since our correspondence was sorted into an antique dovecote—and generally bringing tidiness to my desk. Stoker thrived in artistic chaos, but I preferred a more regulated environment. We had bickered, gently but often, on whether or not an orderly space was indicative of a regulated mind.

After a final polish of my magnifying glasses, I joined Stoker in the rear of the Belvedere where the waxwork had been left. Stoker had made preliminary efforts at organising the work—clearing a large table and laying out an assortment of tools and supplies. My own contribution to the effort was to bribe Lady Rose to stay away by offering her an evening with the monkey.

"Keep it for the whole night," I urged Lady Rose as I plucked the creature from Stoker's shoulder. "You needn't return it anytime soon," I added as it nipped me smartly upon the thumb, drawing up a bead of blood.

"I shall let it sleep in my bed after I've given it a bath," Lady Rose

A GRAVE ROBBERY

replied, eyes bright with mischief. "And I will put curlpapers in its hair to make it pretty."

Anyone else might have feared for the child's safety with such a little beast, but I had no doubt Lady Rose could hold her own. Any doubts I might have had upon that score were firmly dismissed as they left, Lady Rose describing in detail to the monkey the doll's clothes she meant to dress it in.

"You would look very nice in lace," Lady Rose said seriously. The monkey glared at me over Lady Rose's shoulder as it was borne away, and if I believed it capable of such higher-order thinking, I might have said it was plotting a reprisal against me.

But dealing with vengeful primates was a task for another time, and I smoothed out my skirts and donned a fresh working pinafore before joining Stoker at the rear of the Belvedere.

He had spent a considerable part of the afternoon rigging up assorted lamps and mirrors to illuminate the glass casket, and the effect was as theatrical as it was scientific. A bright halo of light cascaded down upon the glass, creating a sort of nimbus about the figure within as well as Stoker. He was bent over the casket, fingertips resting lightly upon the lid, expression thoughtful as he studied her. He must have heard my footstep, but he did not turn, and after a moment, I gave a dry cough.

"Would you care to be alone?" I asked waspishly.

"Hmmm?"

"I was offering you and your lady friend some privacy," I told him.

He straightened. "Veronica, you cannot be serious. You are not jealous of a wax doll."

"Not jealous," I assured him. "But a trifle concerned. You do seem preoccupied."

His lips twitched as if he were suppressing a smile. He came near to

15

where I stood, folding his arms across the breadth of his chest as he looked down at me. "You think me distracted by the beauty of the wax-work?" he inquired.

"Distracted. Intrigued. Obsessed," I muttered. "You appear thoroughly enchanted with her."

"Veronica, if I am enchanted with her, there is a very good reason," he said, moving closer. "Take a look at her. Intently."

I huffed a sigh and regarded her with a scientist's scrutiny. "Yes, a compelling project, I grant you, but—"

He interrupted me. "You mean you do not see it?"

"See what? That you find her beautiful? Yes, I do."

The twitching lips curved into a full smile. "I find her beautiful, my irrational beloved, because she is the very image of you."

I peered more closely at the figure in the casket, running my gaze from the tumbled black hair to the pale skin and rosy lips. "I cannot say that I see it. There may be a superficial resemblance, I grant you."

"Veronica, you cannot be serious. She might be your twin."

"No," I said firmly. "I am already in possession of a doppelgänger in the form of the Hereditary Princess of the Alpenwald. A second would be a coincidence too far."

I paused, briefly recalling the events of the previous spring that had led to my impersonating Her Serene Highness during one of the unlikely and enchanting adventures upon which Stoker and I so often and so unexpectedly embarked.* Being dressed up in tiaras and ballgowns and priceless parures had been tiresome—jewels are *extremely* heavy, being rocks after all—but I drew the line at being abducted and nearly murdered at sea. The fact that our detectival endeavours frequently ended in our near-demise was unfortunate and unavoidable. Peril was not our business, but it was most definitely our vocation.

---

* *An Unexpected Peril*

I drew my attention back to the slumbering waxwork. "Will it be much trouble to fit her with the clockwork mechanism?"

Stoker shrugged. "It depends entirely upon what sort of figure she is. If she was created as an anatomical model, then she will be hollow and fitted with models of various organs which may be easily removed."

"And if she was intended as a fairground attraction?"

He stroked his chin as he considered. "Then she would be solid wax. A more difficult task, but straightforward, I think. It should be a simple enough matter to incise around the torso to create a panel that will float freely," he explained, sketching the actions with his hands. "In either case, when the mechanism is installed, the panel comprising the belly will be replaced and secured but not tightly fixed so it may move with the action of the clockwork. That is how Curtius fashioned the Sleeping Beauty of which Lady Rose is so enamoured. It is a rather ingenious design but not a complex one."

"When do you mean to begin?"

He shrugged. "No time like the present. I shall have to open her up to take measurements for the mechanism." With my help, he lifted the lid from the casket. It was a single, remarkably heavy sheet of glass banded in brass. Tarnish had turned the gilt colour of the metal to a sickly greenish hue. "I shall give that a polish when I am finished," Stoker observed. We put the lid aside and worked together to lift her out. She was heavier than I had anticipated, and I was panting slightly when we shifted her to the worktable. The velvet of her dress rippled in the lamplight, creating the illusion of movement, and I shivered a little in spite of myself.

I bent and gave a deep sniff. "What a curious odour. I cannot place it. Do you think mice have got at it? Or perhaps it is the wax?"

I looked to Stoker, but he did not reply. He looked decidedly uncomfortable. "I don't suppose you would—"

He gestured vaguely towards the figure's clothing.

"You want me to undress her?" I asked.

"Well, yes. It hardly seems appropriate for me to do it," he said, his colour rising adorably.

"Stoker, you are a naval surgeon. Surely you have seen the female figure in a state of undress."

"There are precious few female sailors in Her Majesty's Navy, Veronica," he reminded me. "I know it is irrational, but it somehow feels impolite. Perhaps because she is so unnervingly lifelike."

I considered the figure on the table. "I know what you mean. I almost expect her to open her eyes and speak."

He gave me an imploring look. "Indulge me."

"Oh, very well," I muttered. I carried out the task with brisk efficiency. It is no easy thing to remove garments from a stiff wax figure, and I was surprised to find her clad in undergarments as well as the elaborate dress. A peculiar dampness clung to the garments, and I draped them over various things—a camel saddle, one of the caryatids—to air out. At last she was dressed in a pair of bloomers, and these I removed only to give a quick exclamation of surprise.

"It seems she was indeed created for the purposes of anatomical instruction," I said, peering at our waxen friend. I pointed to where the sculptor had seen fit to ensure that she was completely and comprehensively intact. I gestured towards the thicket of curls at the juncture of her legs.

"An Anatomical Venus," Stoker said, choking a little.

I studied her elegant profile and the pretty details of her appearance—buffed, pointed fingernails, a slender black ribbon tied at her throat. "But why such a glamorous, feminine sculpture for medical purposes? Surely a more neutral figure would be more suitable, something more *clinical.*"

"That is the thinking now," he agreed. "But the Venuses were sculpted by artists, not physicians. They were fashioned by hands that were schooled to create beauty above all else, that had been trained to make beautiful things, elaborate statues of holy women."

I thought of the waxen effigies I had seen of sacred ladies on my travels in Italy, dressed lavishly and adorned with flowers and jewels and carried out in triumph on their name days by the worshipful. It was, I supposed, in the nature of the Latin to make beautiful that which was merely necessary.

Stoker went on. "There used to be hundreds of these models, if not thousands. Every medical school in Europe and beyond boasted a selection of them. Eventually, professors and lecturers began to prefer actual cadavers, and textbooks were drawn to reflect the change. That is when these ladies went out of favour, and many were destroyed or shut up in storerooms, but some people collect them."

"How do you know so much about them?"

"I once knew a man who travelled about, displaying his," he said somewhat absently. He had bent to examine the figure and as he scrutinised her, his brow furrowed. "Odd. A proper Anatomical Venus would have separate panels that could be removed to display the different layers of dissection. This one is intact."

"Then she is a simple waxwork," I suggested.

"But that does not explain the—" He gestured vaguely towards her lush pudenda. "Although, I have heard that some gentlemen . . ."

I raised a brow as he trailed off, his complexion of so combustible a shade, I thought he might suffer an infarction.

"Some gentlemen?"

"Commissioned such figures in order to enjoy them in solitude," he rattled off quickly.

I blinked at him for a long moment before comprehension dawned. "Oh, for *purposes*."

"Of amusement," he said quickly.

"To assuage their loneliness, I imagine," I added. "But in that case surely she ought to have a few more accoutrements. An opening that would approximate a vag—"

"I beg you not to finish that thought," he pleaded.

"I am simply pointing out that if the intention of such a figure is to provide sexual gratification, she really ought to come fully equipped for such activities."

"I think we should stop speaking," he said in a faint voice.

He took up his scalpel and gently probed the smooth, hard surface of the figure, running a fingertip along the edge of the torso as he assessed her with an artist's eye.

"Just here might make the most graceful place to create the panel," he said. He bent, pressing the blade into the waxwork. It stuck almost immediately, and he waggled the instrument back and forth. "Good god," he muttered. "What sort of additives did they put into this wax? It is a good deal harder than I expected. I shall have to use a skinning knife."

Stoker turned to his tools again, selecting a knife with a curved blade. He used it frequently in his taxidermic efforts, careful to keep the edge honed to a wicked, gleaming sharpness.

He plunged this blade carefully into the figure and gave a nod of satisfaction. "That's better," he murmured as he made quick work of the job, his hands moving in slow, graceful arcs around the torso. When he was finished, he laid the knife aside and slid his fingers beneath the waxen flesh to pull the panel free. It took a bit of effort, that much was apparent from the corded muscles of his forearms.

"Heavy?" I inquired.

"Stuck fast," he replied. "Almost as if there were some sort of suction involved." He braced his feet and pulled again, his jaw set in grim determination. With a great and terrible sound of yielding, the matter in his hands came free and the waxwork was opened.

We looked inside, and for a long moment neither of us spoke. After a pause that might have lasted entire minutes, I posed a question, my voice sounding distant above the roaring in my ears.

"Stoker, is that—"

"Yes. Yes it is. Would you mind holding this?" Without waiting for a reply, he thrust the portion of the torso into my hands and turned away to be lavishly sick upon the floor.

I waited calmly for him to finish, and as I waited, I wondered exactly how an actual human body had come to be disguised as an anatomical waxwork and who precisely the dead woman might be.

I like to think it was an innate sense of justice that posed these questions, but there was undoubtedly the flicker of something else. Once more, adventure had sounded its siren's call and we were compelled to answer.

It was beginning.

CHAPTER

3

Lord Rosemorran, hastily summoned from a cosy evening with his stamp collection and gluepot, stared at the figure on the table. We had invited him to the Belvedere to explain our findings to him. Lady Rose would no doubt have included herself, but we had chosen the hour well, making certain she was being forcibly bathed by her governess at the time. The dogs, sensing a heightened atmosphere, had arranged themselves quietly in a row, watching politely as the earl gave us a dubious look. "Are you *entirely* sure?" Uncertainty coloured his tone. "It does seem most unlikely."

"I am sure," Stoker confirmed. "If you would care for me to explain, I could point out the cross-section of the blood vessels—"

His lordship backed away, hands raised in a posture of defence. "Oh, no. Quite unnecessary." He shook his head, his expression mournful. "Oh, dear. This is distressing, I must say. I cannot think how Rose will take the news that her waxwork is not to be."

I suppressed a flicker of impatience. The earl was a kindly man, but he had the misfortune to be both easily distractible and born to wealth, both of which—in my observation—are deleterious to the powers of intellect.

"My lord," I said gently, "I rather think there is a more pressing matter to hand than Lady Rose's reaction."

He roused himself in obvious surprise. "Really?"

"The matter of the dead woman," Stoker said. "Who is she? How did she end up in a warehouse in Shoreditch? And *whose* warehouse?"

"Ah, that was Raby—John Raby," the earl replied with unexpected promptitude.

When immersed in his various researches, he had been known to forget the occasional detail such as where he had acquired parts of the collection, whether he had eaten, how many offspring he had. His forgetfulness was part of his vague charm, I often thought, when it was not maddening to the point of vexation. But we had apparently caught him on a good day, and I pressed him gently.

"And where in Shoreditch might we find Mr. Raby, my lord?"

"That is the difficult bit," he said with an air of gentle apology. "I am afraid the fellow is dead."

"Dead," Stoker echoed.

"Thoroughly. You see, the warehouse was his, but the contents were being sold by his widow. A very good woman of business, but hard, I thought. A very pinched mouth and quite small eyes, although a truly lovely pair of ears. One seldom sees such nice lobes." He drifted off into his thoughts again and I coughed gently.

"My lord. Mrs. Raby?"

"Oh, yes. As I was saying, she seemed determined to wring every penny she could from the sale, but one can hardly blame her. Emigrating to the Argentine does require a little capital."

"The Argentine? You mean to say that Mrs. Raby is no longer in England?" I asked.

"No, I am afraid not. She was leaving directly the sale was finished, she told me. The warehouse had already been sold, you see, and she wanted cash on the barrel for the contents. She had in mind to purchase a nice little finca for herself and grow—what was it again? Pomegranates? Pineapples?" He broke off, turning his gaze heavenwards as he searched his memory.

Stoker held up a hand before his lordship could divert the conversation into the comparative merits of fruits. "Did Mrs. Raby provide any sort of documentation?"

"Just the bill of sale," the earl replied. "But she'd run out of paper, so she scribbled her signature on my handkerchief," he added, rummaging in his pockets. Like Stoker's, his garments were a repository of the unexpected. He pulled out a penknife, a piece of honeycomb—unlike Stoker's, the earl's honeycomb was not candy but *actual* honeycomb, seized from a hive and wrapped in a piece of waxed paper—a tin whistle, a ball of catgut, and a pocket edition of Coleridge before brandishing a wadded bit of linen with a grin. "Rather surprised to find it still in situ as it were."

He handed over the grimy cloth. It was marked with various pencilled figures, a streak of custard, and what might have been jam or blood. Stoker scrutinised it for a moment, then shook his head. "I can only make out a vague signature and possibly a date. Nothing more."

"As I say, it was scribbled," the earl said, taking back his handkerchief.

"And she said nothing about what it was, where or how her husband had acquired it?" I ventured.

His lordship thought for a moment, then shook his head, the lamplight picking out the threads of silver in his thick, dark hair. "Nothing whatsoever. We fell to discussing her worries about the voyage out. She suffers from mal de mer, you see, and I was making a recommendation to her of a few remedies that have served me well upon my own travels. Fresh ginger, grated into boiling water, is just the thing," he added.

"I find it goes down best with a spoonful of whisky," I agreed.

"Oh? I have not tried that. Perhaps on my next voyage! Have you any experience with oil of peppermint? One suspects it would be efficacious. It is so very *bracing*."

Stoker made a growl deep in his throat, clearly annoyed at our conversational detour. "My lord," he said tightly, "is there nothing you can think of that might help us to identify this unfortunate young woman? Did John Raby keep records—a ledger perhaps—of the contents of his warehouse?"

The earl shook his head. "Raby had a prodigious memory, kept all of his records under his hat, as it were. I am afraid it made no end of trouble for his widow. She hadn't the slightest idea of what half the contents were, so she simply sold everything for the best offer and took coin in hand."

"A slipshod way for Mr. Raby to run a business," I observed.

"But not unusual," his lordship replied. "And far more discreet than keeping written records."

"Yet it does little to answer our purposes," I reminded him. "We have no idea where this waxwork—this *person*—came from or who put her there."

"Of course," the earl said in a subdued voice.

"The police will want to know everything about the acquisition," Stoker began but Lord Rosemorran shied like a frightened pony.

"The police! Oh, no, no. That will never do."

"But this must be investigated," Stoker told him.

His lordship's expression was stricken. "Certainly, certainly. But is it possible to do so discreetly? Without involving the police? As soon as the police are involved, the press are bound to discover the story. There will be no keeping it quiet."

"You are concerned about possible scandal?" I asked gently.

"Most concerned," he said. "I can see the lurid headlines in those filthy rags now, trumpeting the fact that this," he waved his hands about vaguely, "was a gift to my daughter. The way they embroider and embellish! Poor Rose. It will follow her forever, the association with this distasteful situation."

Stoker and I said nothing, but the earl hurried on, pressing his point.

"And the crime involved here is not a hanging offence," he pointed out. He paused in obvious confusion. "Or is it?"

"No," Stoker assured him. "This sort of tampering with a dead body is reprehensible, but there are no signs of violence."

"There you are!" Lord Rosemorran said happily. "You can investigate and discover this young person's identity, the story behind how she came to be in this state. And," he said quickly, "if it becomes apparent that there was any question of foul play, I will of course agree to bringing in the proper authorities. But until then, perhaps we might do without the intrusion and the scandal? Would that be acceptable to you?" He finished on a hopeful note, and Stoker gave a gusty sigh.

"Yes, my lord."

Lord Rosemorran turned to me with an appealing look.

"Yes, my lord," I told him.

"Very good. Most grateful to you both." He paused, his expression stricken. "What shall I say to Rose? She will be terribly distressed at losing her treasure. I must find something to ease the blow, some new amusement."

"I have made Lady Rose a loan of the tamarin," I told him. "Tell her she may keep the creature as long as she wishes."

"Oh, you are kind," the earl said. "Are you certain?"

"Quite," I told Lord Rosemorran firmly.

He took a deep breath, rubbing his hands together briskly. "If there is nothing else I ought to be getting back to my stamps. I received a packet from Mauritius today," he finished with an air of pleased contentment. "They have palm trees on them, you know. Most charming."

"Of course, my lord. Go back to your stamps," I told him, not unkindly. Stoker said nothing, but I could perceive a tiny muscle at his jawline jumping.

I showed the earl to the door, returning to find Stoker standing over the slumbering beauty, his expression serious.

"Veronica—" he began.

I held up a hand. "Let us not brangle, my love. This is the point in the proceedings when I insist something must be done, and that we are the persons who must do it. I will make an impassioned plea for justice. I will point out that this nameless creature deserves a proper burial. Now, I will allow she might have been handed over to some medical authority with all the necessary procedures being followed, but if she were not, then some misadventure may have befallen her, and a villain must be held accountable. I will further remind you that we have been, upon several occasions, the instruments of such justice, and that we are uniquely gifted in the requisite qualities for carrying out an investigation of this nature. Furthermore—"

I was warming to my theme when Stoker spoke up, clipping each consonant sharply. "Veronica, do be quiet."

I blinked. "I beg your pardon?"

"I am not arguing with you. In fact, if you did not insist upon investigating what horrors befell this young woman, I would."

"You would?"

He shrugged one heavily muscled shoulder. "Of course. Whoever she is, however she came to this state, she ought indeed to be laid to rest with respect. And, as you say, there is a possibility she may have met with misfortune at the hands of some blackguard and if so, he must answer for it."

He paused and canted his head, regarding me closely. "Veronica, are you quite all right?"

"I do not know," I replied. "You are agreeing with me. It is a curious feeling."

A ghost of a smile touched his lips. "I shall not make a habit of it."

"Don't," I begged. "It is distinctly unsettling."

CHAPTER

4

I ought not to have been surprised by Stoker's insistence upon embarking on this adventure. He had shown similar sensibilities during a previous investigation regarding an Egyptian princess.* Whether he felt protective of comely corpses *only* was a question I did not consider. (Stoker, I had no doubt, would be equally considerate of the dead dignity of the lowliest gutter urchin. He was one of Nature's true aristocrats.)

Having decided to undertake the matter properly, I took up a fresh notebook and began a record of our efforts—the culmination of which you hold now in your hands, dear reader. I had used the time between our previous escapades to record them in detail for the purposes of science. Memory is an unreliable, meretricious hussy, and I have always found that setting down events whilst they are fresh is the surest defence against her depredations. These records filled several notebooks, and I kept them locked in a glass bookcase on the upper floor of the Belvedere in an area we referred to with great affection as "the snuggery." I could view them through the glass panel, each volume hand-

---

* *A Treacherous Curse*

somely bound in dark red leather with gilt-edged pages and filled with the carefully transcribed notes from our investigations. I spared nothing in the process, no foible or failure of mine was omitted, but neither was I circumspect regarding the mistakes of others. Scientific observation, after all, includes fact, and although fact must be interpreted through the lens of experience, I thought a few artistic flourishes might engage a potential reader's attention.

"What reader?" Stoker demanded late the next day as he saw me settling to scribble notes about our waxen corpse.

I flapped a hand. "Any reader. I am making a record of our investigations for the edification and perhaps entertainment of posterity."

"What sort of record?" he asked, narrowing his gaze.

"An unvarnished account of our actions, hypotheses, stratagems, et cetera. I thought it of interest to anyone undertaking similar activities."

"Veronica, who? Who but *us* would undertake such activities? Do you really imagine London is full of natural scientists repeatedly and relentlessly distracted from their work by felonies and mayhem?"

"It might happen," I said absently. I dipped my pen into the well and scrawled a title upon the frontispiece in a swirl of violet ink.

He bent forwards to read it. "'The Case of the Sleeping Beauty.' Veronica, no. I must protest. It is enough that you insist upon keeping a diary of our most sensational activities—" He broke off, an expression of horror spreading over his handsome features. "You do not record our *most* sensational activities, do you?"

"If you are referring to the odd foray into violence, I cannot refrain. They are an essential and inevitable result of our investigative efforts, my dearest. If, however, you are referring to the refreshing and healthful sessions of physical congress in which we frequently engage, I refer to them only obliquely, I assure you."

"You needn't refer to them at all!" he thundered.

"There is no call for indignation," I assured him. "Whenever I am called upon to describe your physique or your prowess, I am complimentary in the extreme. Accuracy demands it."

He made a vaguely scornful noise which set the dogs to howling, and it was some minutes before he settled them again by way of sharing out a pocketful of cold sausages. When he had done, I passed over a fresh tin of Cook's best peppermint rock, knowing the sweet would have the same conciliatory effect upon him as the meats had upon the dogs.

He took it with ill grace and subsided into a leather porter's chair, legs slung carelessly over one arm as he pillaged the tin for the choicest bits.

"How should we begin?" I inquired. In past cases, I had often driven our efforts towards justice, but I had to admit that in this instance, I was at a bit of a loss. Without the Raby connection to explore and with no distinctive markings upon the clothing or person of the corpse or the glass casket, there were few threads to unpick. We had scrutinised her from top to toe in an attempt to discover some helpful clue, but there had been nothing. If this were a proper detective story, there would have been a maker's label pasted beneath the base of the casket or a scrap of letter in the dead woman's pocket with a cryptic but solvable bit of address leading to her next of kin. But our slumbering victim yielded no information whatsoever. The gown and undergarments were of fine quality but considerable antiquity. Whatever labels or laundry marks they may once have borne, they were long lost. Her body boasted no curious moles or memorable birthmarks, and the casket itself was all it appeared to be—a brass box fitted with panels of clear glass.

Stoker sucked on a piece of peppermint rock and considered. Suddenly, a light kindled in his eyes and he sat up. "Of course. Veronica, put on something warm that you do not mind being dragged through mud and other unspeakable things."

He snatched up his own greatcoat, scattering dogs as he pounded down the circular staircase, thrusting his arms into the sleeves as he went.

I snatched up my own cloak. "Where are we going?"

He looked up, gentian-blue eyes gleaming with intention. "To a place I vowed never to return."

I stopped, my fingers curled around the narrow iron balustrade. "Oh, no."

"Oh, yes, my dear. We are going to the circus."

F or most people, a pronouncement of one's intention to visit the circus is a simple and straightforward thing. Stoker, as I hope I have conveyed to the attentive reader, is not "most people." The third—and least-favoured—son of a viscount, Stoker had run away from his family's stately home on numerous occasions. During one such excursion, he had joined up with a circus, Professor Pygopagus' Travelling Curiosity Show. It was called such because the proprietor was a gentleman born with a conjoined twin. (A much nicer twin, which would lead us quite neatly into a discussion of the effects of inherent nature versus nurture, but that is for another day.) The professor specialised in what are unkindly called "freaks," those folk whose appearance or abilities somehow set them apart from the average human. He commercialised them, touring them from town to town and taking the lion's share of their earnings, but he also provided them with a family of sorts, the company of others who understood them far better than their own blood kin. It was here that Stoker had worked a variety of positions in the show—rigger, magician, featured fighter. He learnt the intricacies of ropes and legerdemain as well as a considerable fluency with a weapon called a rebenque, a sort of whip commonly used by gauchos in the Argentine. In the course of our first adventure together, Stoker and I had taken refuge in the travelling show although we had, in the end, been forced to flee under circumstances which left Stoker thoroughly enraged with the professor and considering a little light vengeance should they ever meet again.

For my part, I was delighted at the opportunity to visit the travelling show once more. My own work as a lepidopterist had taken me on journeys around the breadth of the world more than once, and the members of the show, whilst not natural historians, were likewise wandering souls. We carried within us the yearning towards sights yet unseen, peoples yet unmet. We thrilled to the dawn chorus of birdsong, the crackling of the campfire, and the steady clip-clop of the pony's hoof was the rhythm of our heartbeats.

My pleasure at the proposed visit did not distract me from the necessity of dressing appropriately. I took a few precious minutes to exchange my working gown for my favourite garments—my hunting attire. I had designed several of the suits myself, refining the variations with each attempt. First, narrow trousers of fine tweed and a pure white shirtwaist with neat pin tucks worn under a fitted jacket. Over the trousers went a skirt of clever construction, also narrow and fitted with an arrangement of buttons that permitted it to be opened at the sides and fixed out of the way, thus freeing the legs for greater mobility. Flat boots that laced to the knee were essential, as was a collection of subtle weapons. A pair of slender stilettos were secured in my boot and another in a channel stitched into my corset.

Into my cuffs went minuten, the headless pins that are an essential tool of any entomologist's kit. They were handy for all sorts of emergencies, not least fending off importunate men who tried to hold one's hand without invitation. Stoker, infinitely more skilled with a needle than I thanks to his work as a surgeon and taxidermist, had fitted my seams with deep pockets, the better to hold handkerchiefs, a pencil and tiny notebook, a miniature magnifying glass, sturdy hairpins for picking locks, a sandwich in greaseproof paper, and a tin of sweets for Stoker in case of emergency. The last addition to my ensemble was a flask filled with aguardiente—a potent South American liquor—which I strapped to my thigh. Its revivifying effects were not to be underestimated. Thus attired, I was prepared for any eventuality. With the addition of a large jar of cold cream of roses and a simple gown of black silk, I could have traversed the globe twice over.

Stoker had no cause to change, being already dressed in similar fashion. He invariably chose country tweeds over a town suit, although even the most fashionable of Bond Street tailors would never make him look like a creature of the city. His hair was always a-tumble, his ears glinting with small golden hoops acquired, like the tattoos upon his torso, from his time in Her Majesty's Navy. And even if these nuances were overlooked by the casual observer, the black silk eyepatch and narrow silver scar running neatly from brow to jaw would have made him remarkable. These were mementos of the time he struggled to the death with a jaguar, narrowly emerging victorious. The cat had not taken his eye, but it had been a near thing, and the experience left him with eyesight that was intact but subject to fatigue. The patch permitted him to rest the eye, but the greater benefit, in my opinion, was the dashing air it lent him. No matter what he wore, he resembled a privateer who might have graced the court of Gloriana herself. It was a sight to thrill the heart of any susceptible maiden—and a good many other of her parts as well.

We rendezvoused at the gate of Bishop's Folly, dressed and ready for battle, grinning at one another as we emerged onto the street, leaving the seclusion of the earl's estate behind. We hailed a hansom and drove as far as the Duke of Hamilton pub before alighting to finish the rest of the journey on foot. Hansom cabs are a necessary evil when one lives in London, but Stoker and I were in agreement that there are few things as essential to good health as a bracing walk in the fresh air.

Unfortunately, the air of the city is less than salubrious, the line of the horizon marked as far as the eye could see with chimneys belching endless quantities of black smoke into the air to descend as low grey clouds softening the edges of the buildings. We found ourselves wheezing slightly as we climbed the heath, a fine powder of soot settling on our faces.

"Hell's harpies, even my teeth are gritty," Stoker grumbled. He spat onto the grass and reached into his pocket for a violet pastille.

"The air is clearer the higher we climb," I consoled him. "Onwards! And whilst we walk, you can tell me who it is we are meant to be meeting."

"Branzino," he said shortly. "Or Signore Branzino, as he prefers to call himself. He has been on the travelling show circuit for some years with his waxwork—a pretty blonde thing that has definitely seen better days."

"I do not recall him from our time with Professor Pygopagus," I told him.

"His appearances were always intermittent. He travelled with the same waxwork, but every year he changed out her costumes and gave her a different name. It wore her to bits, and he was forever making repairs to her with candle wax and portrait wire," he added. "The professor used to make rather pointed remarks about the quality of his work, and Branzino would scream the place down and leave in a rage. He always came crawling back when he needed money, and the professor would allow him back for a smaller cut of the proceeds each time. The last I saw of him, he was working for pennies—all of which went towards drink. I never liked him. He was a nasty little vermin," Stoker concluded. "If he happens to be back with the show, mind you give him a wide berth."

I snorted. "One cannot possibly be afraid of a man named for a fish."

We fell to silence then as we moved ever upwards, emerging at last on the top of the heath, the freshening wind scouring the sooty clouds away and whipping colour into our cheeks. Paths crisscrossed the expanse, copses dotted here and there, the trees shedding their autumn colour in bursts of scattered leaves that rustled like taffeta. The smell of woodsmoke rather than coal hung in the air, the delicious fragrance of countryside, the sweetest refreshments after the malodorous city. I plunged ahead, eager as a hound, my steps quickening to a run. The way was deep in shadow, but I heard the rustlings and scrabblings of squirrels gathering hazelnuts and acorns in paws tufted with red fur. No doubt there were berries as well, the deep crimson of bittersweet and black bryony and the brighter orange-red jewels of rosehips. Elder, beech, and yew all offered up their fruits, as did the hawthorn and the sloe. At our feet, the caps of sleepy mushrooms nestled in the slumbering woods. It was an enchanted evening, walking in that glade, and as Stoker entwined his fingers with mine, I marvelled—not for the first time—at the whims of Fate which had drawn us together.

I was still lost in my musings when we spotted the picket of horses, the furthest reach of the travelling show's encampment. I remembered from our last visit that the wagons would be sited just beyond, huddled together for protection rather than privacy. Strangers were held at arm's length amongst show folk. Like the Roma, they relied upon one another and mistrusted outsiders with good reason. Cooking fires would be kindled inside the warm circle of caravans, lines of washing strung, and an air of contented if makeshift domesticity enveloping all.

The westering sun had long since dropped below the horizon, and a brisk breeze whispered through the treetops, sending the temperature plummeting and causing folk to gather close about the fires. We skirted the edge of the shadows, making our way through the assembled wagons towards the line of show tents. Of assorted shapes and sizes, the tents were where the public were welcomed for the price of a ticket, and it was where the professor held court in his own pavilion where favoured visitors might be admitted if he deigned to receive them.

As we crossed the campground, no one made direct eye contact, but I felt the tickle between my shoulder blades that said our arrival had not gone unnoticed. Wandering folk have a nose for trouble, an instinct which thrums in the blood, warning them of the approach of strangers. I had no doubt that even before we gained the edge of the encampment, word of our imminent visit had gone round. We walked on, neither challenged nor welcomed, our presence unremarked. We might have been phantoms, shadows moving through the campsite, past caravans whose curtains twitched and clotheslines whose flapping garments hid curious eyes.

Stoker had taken a circuitous route, moving slowly past the assorted caravans and tents, but none of them sheltered Signore Branzino. There were several acts I remembered from our stay with the troupe, but a few new ones I did not know. The elderly Madame du Lait—whose claim to fame was being the wet-nurse of Napoléon—had billed herself as being one hundred and fifty-three years old, but there was no sign of her, and I wondered if she had failed to make one hundred and fifty-four.

Across the camp, I saw a shadow of great enormity, larger than three huge men, detach itself from one of the caravans. I poked Stoker gently in the ribs.

"Do not look now, but Colosso has noted your arrival," I murmured.

Stoker did not break stride. "He will not trouble us," he assured me decisively.

"Are you quite certain? Only the last time we saw him, he seemed a trifle put out with you."

"He was entirely furious, and I don't blame him," Stoker agreed, a tiny smile of satisfaction playing about his mouth. Due to the professor's machinations, Stoker had been forced to fight Colosso, and the weapon of choice had been the rebenque. Colosso, not content with the advantages of strength, girth, and height, had cheated, weighting the handle of his weapon with enough lead to have killed Stoker with a well-aimed blow. But Stoker had proven more than a match, thrashing the giant with such dexterity and skill that Colosso had not been entirely the same afterwards.

"I believe he threatened to murder you and pick his teeth with your femurs," I reminded him.

Stoker's little smile deepened. "Let him try. It has been a while since I had a good fight."

"For a civilised man, you are entirely too comfortable with demonstrations of violence," I said. "I blame your education. Boarding school does seem to bring out the worst in boys."

Stoker glanced to where Colosso was standing, arms folded over his massive chest, glowering. Colosso drew a finger across his throat, smiling a dreadful rictus grin that resembled a death's head.

"Perhaps you were right," Stoker said mildly. "He does seem put out. Well, we shall have to deal with him later. We've arrived."

CHAPTER

5

We stopped outside one of the tents, a striped affair of red and white with blue pennants fluttering from the top of the centre pole. A sign, painted with flourishes of scarlet and gilt, proclaimed that this was PROFESSOR PYGOPAGUS' TRAVELLING CURIOSITY SHOW. From within there was a murmur of conversation, a low buzz of anticipation. I flicked Stoker a glance and saw his jaw tighten. The prickle between my shoulder blades grew stronger, and I hazarded a look behind to see figures emerging from the shadows and drawing near, but not near enough to see properly. They were not incautious enough for that. They would wait to hear how we were received before extending either an open hand of friendship or a fist.

"Into the mouth of Hell we go," Stoker muttered. He drew in a deep breath and stepped into the tent. Inside was arranged the most interesting and unique gathering of people imaginable. In an armchair large enough to accommodate a family of four sat a very pretty lady of frankly tremendous proportions. Behind her stood a man in uniform—remarkable as much for his height as for the fact that his entire face was covered in lush golden fur. On the other side of the tent, a girl with Titian-red hair flowing to her hips reclined upon a chaise longue of blue velvet. From the waist down, she was draped in a sort of coverlet, and at the bottom, where one might have expected to find toes, there peeped the edge of a fish's tail, the scales shimmering in the lamplight. Perched atop her head was a slim crown of coral and pearls with matching gems adorning her ears and arms. Next to her stood a lushly sensual woman with rather fewer garments than propriety might demand. Her bronze velvet robe was not equal to the task of constraining her exuberant décolletage, nor did it manage to conceal much of the exquisitely formed legs clad in black stockings. She was heavily painted, and her rouged mouth was curved into an enigmatic smile.

Between these two extraordinary sights was a pair of elaborately carved chairs placed almost exactly back to back with the arms between them cut clean away. This was to accommodate the elderly twins seated there, conjoined as they were at the ribs and shoulder. One held an accordion with which he produced a Baroque tune I had heard only once before. His brother sat wreathed in smoke from a Turkish cigarette resting in a long ebony holder. He greeted us with a smile, gesturing magnanimously with the cigarette holder and its plume of acrid smoke. For a long moment, no one spoke. The etiquette of the travelling show is as rigid as that of a royal court at times. They were all awaiting the professor's reaction as a guide to how we were to be received. They were motionless, no doubt taut with expectation and interest to see what would happen.

"Stoker! And Mrs. Stoker! What an unexpected delight," the professor crowed.

It had entirely slipped my mind that the last time we had joined the show, we had been travelling under false pretences. It had seemed prudent at the time, and there was little point in correcting the misapprehension now.

I smiled at the silent twin. "Good evening, Otto. It is pleasant to see you again."

He added a few more flourishes to the Baroque melody before ending on a high note. Otto had never spoken, but I understood him well enough to know he was happy to see me. Forced to the periphery of conversation by his inability—or unwillingness—to speak, Otto was both highly observant and fluent in musical commentary.

"Hello, professor," Stoker said coolly.

"So good of you to come, my boy," the professor said, his gaze bright with malice. "I rather thought you were angry with me after our last encounter." Their last meeting had involved not only the rebenque fight but our hasty departure as we fled from possible arrest thanks to the professor's meddling.*

Stoker bared his teeth in what might have passed for a smile. "The encounter where you forced me into a rebenque fight with Colosso and nearly got me killed for my trouble whilst revealing my whereabouts to the public when I was wanted by the police for murder? I haven't thought of it at all, I assure you," he said tightly.

"I am delighted to hear it," the professor replied. "These things do happen." He turned to me. "And how are you, my dear? I must say, your association with Stoker agrees with you. You are positively blooming! Although, it is not 'Mrs. Stoker,' is it?" he asked, canting his head and wearing an expression alarmingly like that of Lady Wellie's tamarin. "It is lovely to make your acquaintance properly, Miss Speedwell."

"You have been making inquiries," I observed.

He gestured, sending more smoke into the air. "One collects scraps of information, rather like a magpie collects bright and shiny things." Otto's thread of melody took a slightly sinister turn. The professor went on. "We are delighted to have you both amongst us again. I think you know the others."

He waved a languid hand, and the rest of the little group became

---

* *A Curious Beginning*

animated in their greetings. First, the lion-faced man and the portly woman beamed at us, and Stoker went to shake hands and bestow a kiss upon the pink cheek of the lady. These were Tilly, billed as the Fattest Woman in England, and her husband, Leopold the Lion-Faced Lord. They sent friendly nods my way which I returned with cordiality. Then the figure upon the chaise longue put out her arms.

"Stoker!"

"Hello, love," he said in a tone of real affection as he went to her. She was young—perhaps not twenty—and her expression shone with genuine happiness. When he bent to her, she clasped him close.

"I have missed you," she said softly.

"I have missed you too, petal," he returned. "How is the tail holding up?"

She grinned and flung back the drapery to reveal a mermaid's tail. It was a glorious thing, glistening in nacreous shades of green and pink and burnished with the glow of old silver. I realised suddenly that she had no legs, only the tail fitted to her torso, replacing the missing limbs. She made a sort of undulation with her body, and the tail rose in a graceful movement. It was as elegant as any ballet in Covent Garden, and she fluttered it a second time before letting it settle once more to the chaise longue. Stoker watched it with careful attention. "Still working well then. Perhaps a bit of paint to touch it up," he added kindly.

"With a bit more lustre?" she asked hopefully. "To make it more like a pearl!"

"If you like." He motioned for me to come forwards. "This is Veronica. Veronica, this is Sirena, the Princess of the Seven Seas."

She put out her hand and grinned. "It is Alice, really."

I shook her hand. "Hello, Alice. You are the very first mermaid I have ever known."

Her laugh was light and merry. "Thanks to Stoker. I used to be billed as Baby Alice, the Adult Infant, but Stoker thought of this," she said, gesturing to the elegant tail. "Far nicer than sitting around in a baby's bonnet and sucking a false teat," she added with a dark look at the professor.

He spread his hands. "My child, we must work with what Nature gives us."

She pulled a face and stretched one hand towards her tail. "This is much nicer," she repeated.

I agreed with her, but I was vaguely aware of a heightened atmosphere, and I turned from Alice to the statuesque woman whose bosoms had suddenly seemed to take on a personality of their own. She had thrown her shoulders back and thrust her rib cage forwards, and the effect caused Stoker to make a choking sound.

"So, you have returned!" she proclaimed in ringing tones that might have suited Siddons herself. "Have you come to break the heart of Salome once more?" she demanded, striking one of the bosoms with a closed fist. Her accent was some hideous amalgamation of assorted and nonspecific Mediterranean intonations.

"Good god, Salome, do be careful. You might rupture something," I advised her.

"I was not speaking to *you*," she said, rolling her eyes towards Stoker. She had lined them heavily with kohl. Studied theatricality was one of her specialities.

"But I am speaking to you," I said firmly. "When we parted, I thought we had become friends." *Friends* might have been a slight exaggeration. The fact that she and Stoker had enjoyed a somewhat frenzied physical relationship once upon a time would prevent Salome from being an intimate friend of mine, but I had a healthy respect for any woman who could be born a Sally from Dunstable and make of herself a Salome of the travelling show.

"Friends! When you have stolen the love of my life!" She rolled her eyes again and made a few more gestures of high drama whilst the rest of us looked on. "I am a woman bereft!" she cried before launching into a vaguely unintelligible soliloquy.

"Do you think she is winding down?" I asked Stoker in a loud whisper. "Only I am feeling rather peckish, and if she means to go on much longer, I might have to ask Tilly for a cream cake."

Something of what I said must have penetrated Salome's fugue of despair, for she picked herself up from the carpet where she had flung herself and dusted off her hands.

"What do you think?" She rose smiling, her accent dropping once more into plain Bedfordshire. "I'm trying for a part in the proper theatre. I fancy being a tragedienne."

"So you are not pining for love of me?" Stoker asked in a bewildered tone.

Her laugh was raucous. "A likely thing," she scoffed, "when I've a husband now." She waggled her left hand in front of his nose, the ring on her finger glowing softly gold in the lamplight.

"Hearty congratulations to him and best wishes for your happiness," I told her.

"Thank you, Veronica." She gave me a narrow look, then assessed Stoker before turning back to me. "Made an honest woman of you yet?"

"No, thank god," I replied fervently.

"If we have concluded the preliminaries," the professor put in smoothly, "I think we might move to the business of why you have come."

Stoker and I exchanged glances. We had discussed our approach on the journey, and we were in agreement. The professor was a clever fellow who had been born without advantages. In his experience of the world, it was necessary to hide one's motives, to cloak one's goals in mystery. Every movement was that of a chess piece, shrouded in stratagems and secrecy. He trusted no one, not even his own twin, and the only possible approach in this situation was one of obliquity.

"I spent some years travelling with this show," Stoker pointed out quietly. "Can a man not indulge in a bit of nostalgia?"

"Nostalgia?" The professor's slender white brows rose. "My dear Stoker, you possess as many soft emotions as a cart horse. Fewer, I should think. A cart horse may demonstrate loyalty."

Beside me I felt Stoker bristle, and I hurried to take the reins of the conversation before matters galloped wildly out of control.

"I am afraid the intrusion is entirely my fault," I said, offering a winsome smile. "I have become quite interested in the subject of anatomical models, and Stoker informed me one used to travel with your entourage."

The professor's lips thinned in an expression of mild reproof. "Entourage? Family, my dear! We are a family."

Tilly snorted into her cream cake. "That's a laugh, that is. Turn any one of us out on our pretty arses if we didn't bring in the brass, and that's the truth."

The professor gave her a sour look by which she seemed blithely unbothered before turning back to me. "You were saying, my dear?"

"The Anatomical Venus," I reminded him.

"Ah, yes! Signore Branzino. How could one forget? Well, if you meant to visit him, he is long gone from here. He grew too old for the traveller's life," he said, spreading his hands. They were elegant, long-fingered and graceful, and he used them to excellent effect.

"Where might we find him now?" Stoker inquired.

The professor shrugged. "Your guess is as good as mine. He left us with little fanfare and less notice."

"Is his name really Branzino or is that a *nom de cirque*?" I asked.

He shrugged again as a tiny smile played about his malicious mouth. He was enjoying this entirely too much. Whatever his reasons for disliking Stoker—and I had no interest in rummaging through the doubtlessly unholy chaos of the professor's mind—he relished the opportunity to toy with him. Of course, one might just as unwisely poke at a bear with a sharp stick, but the professor would have his amusement.

I could sense Stoker's irritation rising. I had no fear he would harm the professor—Stoker would never strike a man older or smaller than himself—but the resulting ruffled temper would be tedious to endure. He could often be soothed back into good humour with sweets or a rousing bout of physical congress, but this was hardly the place for amorous couplings and Tilly kept a close grasp upon her cream cakes.

"Come now," I said firmly to Stoker. "The professor has no wish to help us, and I am not surprised. He has not improved with age."

The professor gave a sharp bark of a laugh, like a fox, and his eyes gleamed with satisfaction. "Come again whenever you like," he said with a broad smile as he threw his arms wide. "It is always so amusing to see you."

I tugged Stoker out of the tent before he gave vent to the worst of his spleen. As it was, I had to endure several minutes of fluent profanity before I rummaged in his pocket and extracted an old rock cake wrapped in a scrap of greaseproof paper. I stuffed it into his mouth. "Eat that, and do stop raging. I shall have a headache soon if you carry on."

He chewed and swallowed before speaking, and when he did, his tone was somewhat mollified. "Sorry. I forgot what a thoroughgoing *bastard* he is—"

I held up a hand and followed the cake with the tin of honeycomb from my own emergency stores. "If you do not hush, I will be forced to feed you something much less tasty. Like my cold cream."

He counted to twenty—in a particularly challenging dialect of Portuguese—and blew out a sigh. "There is one possibility," he said, his gaze resting on the sole pavilion we had not yet visited. "Come along."

He strode off and I trotted to keep up as he led the way to the tent, this one pitched in a far less prominent location. The canvas had possibly been white once. Now it was begrimed by age and the vagaries of the road, and a threadbare banner hung over the flap. MADAME ARACHNE, THE HUMAN SPIDER was painted in sprawling letters embellished to resemble spider's legs. A few webs had been daubed in the corners. Outside, a small boy stood assessing us with a narrow gaze. "Come to see Madame Arachne, have you? She is the greatest marvel of the modern world, alive and living for all to see!"

"'Alive' and 'living' are synonyms," I told him.

"And it's tuppence to see her, missus," he replied, putting out his hand.

Stoker put a pound coin into the grimy palm. "Here. Put that in your pocket and keep anyone else from coming in until we leave. We shall only be a moment."

The boy looked down at the coin and gave an exclamation. "That's a bit of flummery, that is," he accused.

"I assure you it is not counterfeit," Stoker replied.

The boy bit the coin before giving us a grudging nod. "Feels right enough to the tooth. But if I find you've palmed me off with a gimmick, I'll have my brothers on you, I will," he said fiercely.

Stoker's nod was grave. "I am duly fearful."

"Mind you are," the urchin said, slipping the coin into his pocket and waving us on.

There was no point in remonstrating with Stoker over the amount he had just bestowed upon the child. It was not the first time I had watched him hand out the equivalent of a year's earnings to a boy on the street, and I had little doubt it would not be the last.

He pushed onwards through the dirty tent flap and I followed, pausing a moment to let my eyes adjust to the dim light. All of the tents had poor illumination, for the tricks and sleights of the various hucksters would never bear the scrutiny of proper daylight. But this was murkier than most, no doubt to heighten the atmosphere of creeping horror. Two large poles, stout as Scottish cabers, had been planted in the middle of the tent. Between them, ropes of black silk had been woven into a web as complex and beautiful as that of the most skilled Araneidae. In the centre of the web perched a being unlike any I had ever seen with the head of a beautiful, dark-haired woman, and the body of a spider, black and menacing. Where the body met the head, a neat ruff of black velvet framed the face, and as we approached the narrow legs jerked, making a horrible chattering sound and causing the web to ripple. I stared in fascination as the red-lipped mouth curved into a smile.

"Stoker! It has been a long time," the woman said, her voice low and as melodious as an angel's.

"It has."

She turned her dark gaze to me. "I do not know you, but I think you must be Miss Speedwell."

"You are very well informed, madame," I replied.

She inclined her head gracefully, causing the web to shiver. "In my business, it is good to know things."

"So either you are the professor's confidante or informant," I suggested.

She gave a full-throated laugh. "Both. Neither. You spent time here a little while past. You must have seen how precarious our lives are. We exist on the fringes of society, my dear. We must seize whatever advantages we can."

"You were not here when I was with the show," I pointed out.

She tipped her head with a little smile. "I find the work taxing. I take a little time each year to sit by the seaside and stretch my limbs." She flexed the velvet spider legs for emphasis.

I took a step nearer, surveying the silken web and the array of legs with the human head settled in the midst. Only with the closest scrutiny could one detect the mechanics of the illusion. A large box had been constructed and painted to imitate the canvas walls of the tent. With the silken web laid over the top, the box completely disappeared from view. The velvet ruff hid the neat hole which provided a place for her head to emerge whilst the box concealed the rest of her body. An elaborate arrangement of almost invisible filaments had been attached at one end to the spider's legs, then disappeared into the box.

"Ah, so that is how it is done," I murmured. "You manipulate the legs with the filaments. Clever."

She smiled. "You are more observant than most. The box is in plain sight to any who care to see, but most prefer the illusion of Madame Arachne, the Human Spider!"

"But I can see why you enjoy a seaside holiday," I continued. "It must be devilishly cramped in that box."

"I was a contortionist as a younger woman. I am no longer what I once was, but I am still able to manage the box," she admitted. "At least for a few months at a time. Then it is a nice rest beside the sea."

"Brighton? Bournemouth? Blackpool?"

She grinned. "I prefer Deauville or Trouville. I have a fondness for French cuisine."

"And for a little flutter in the casino in Monte Carlo," Stoker put in dryly. "Hence madame's practice of trafficking in information."

"You are clearly a lady of unconventional thought and resourceful thinking," I told her.

"Like recognises like," she replied graciously. "You want to know something."

"We do," I admitted.

"Then you have come to the right person. I do not know why you wasted so much time peering into every little corner of this camp before seeking me out." The reproof was gently delivered.

"How do you—" Stoker broke off. "The urchin outside. He is your eyes and ears whilst you are bound to the box."

"You speak as if I have only one set of each! My dear fellow, Argos himself would envy my little collection of eyes. Now, ask, before I tell him to let in the next group of punters."

"You trade in information," I reminded her. "Do you not wish to be paid in advance?"

"The boy outside was dealt with generously, if I know Stoker," she said.

I looked to where Stoker stood, blushing furiously. "He seems a hardworking lad."

"The brightest I have taken into my employ," she agreed. "He has seen the backside of an open hand too many times in his life. I think a little kindness in return for yours is not inappropriate. Unless you would rather pay me in cash?" she asked with the arch of an imperious brow.

"Signore Branzino," Stoker said hastily. "You recall him?"

She gave him a frankly disgusted look. "You think I forget anything? A name? A face? Madame Arachne remembers all. Yes. Who could forget him? A curious little man with his glass coffin."

"What became of him?"

Her gaze narrowed. "Why do you wish to find him?"

"We don't, actually. But we desire information about glass caskets," I explained. "They are rather rare, and we have come into possession of one. We have questions. We thought perhaps the signore could help answer them."

"How disappointing," she said. "One hoped for a more interesting story than that. But I am not surprised. Branzino was, apart from his pretty wax Venus, a thoroughly boring man. He is not the sort who would attract interest, although"—she paused, her expression thoughtful—"come to think of it, how he left the show was rather intriguing. He was ailing. Too many years of quietly drinking away his earnings. His liver had begun to pain him, and he wished to retire to Calabria. That is where he hailed from, you know."

"I didn't," Stoker told her. "I am not certain I ever really spoke to the fellow."

"He kept himself to himself," Madame said. "But he liked to come and talk to me once in a while. I think it amused him to believe I could not get away when he wanted to converse, rather like his poor Beauty in the box. He would come and talk to me of Calabria, the stony poverty of it, the hunger of his childhood. He longed to return and die amongst his own, but he hadn't the money. Until the gentleman came."

"The gentleman?" I asked. "What gentleman?"

"A very handsome one. Distinguished. A collector of anatomical models. He pointed out to Signore Branzino that there were one or two unique features of his Beauty and said he would pay handsomely to acquire her. Branzino sold her without a second thought."

"And the coffin?" Stoker pressed.

"Went with her, of course. What use has a dying Calabrian for a glass casket unless he wished to be buried with it himself," she added with a laugh.

"So Signore Branzino took the money and sold his Beauty to this gentleman," I said. "Could you describe him to us? Give us some clue as to his identity?"

"I could," she said solemnly. "Or I could just tell you that he lives in Holborn, Lincoln's Inn Fields." She cocked her head for a moment then supplied the house number.

I gaped at her. "And his name?"

"Lord Ambrose Despard. The younger son of the late Marquess of Harwich."

"That is most helpful indeed," I told her. "Thank you, madame."

She inclined her head, as gracious as an empress. "The pleasure,

Miss Speedwell, was entirely mine. Should you ever find yourself in Monte Carlo, I do hope you will call."

The gathering noise outside indicated a crowd was assembling, and I heard the young lad begin his patter. "Come and see the wonder of the natural world, Madame Arachne, half woman, half spider!"

We thanked her again and took a hasty leave, emerging to find the boy cheerfully collecting coins and directing punters into the tent. Without a word, Stoker took my hand and we made our way across the encampment. When we came to the edge, we paused. This was the very top of the heath, where heaven and earth met. London glittered in the darkness below, the gaslights shimmering like stars spangled on the night sky. It was seldom that I stopped to appreciate the wonders of the city, but it was impossible to ignore them on a night such as that with the wind still rustling crisply in the trees, the fragrance of the leaves still mingling with the campfires.

Stoker, who was given to quoting Keats at romantic moments, did not disappoint. His delicious baritone shaped the phrases of mellow fruitfulness before passing on to some decidedly more direct passages, and I responded as any red-blooded lady with any claim to human emotion might have done. It required little effort to persuade him to avail ourselves of a handy deserted copse, the ground heavily shadowed and thickly carpeted with moss and fallen leaves. When we had finished, we spent some little while bringing order to our disarranged clothing and plucking pine needles from our hair, but the effort, I assure the gentle reader, was entirely worth it.

CHAPTER

6

Having concluded our work the next day in a timely fashion, we fell into gentle disagreement about how best to beard the marquess's son in his den.

"We cannot simply appear at Lord Ambrose's door unannounced," I pointed out. "It is not done."

"When," Stoker inquired in a tone of exaggerated politeness, "has that ever deterred you?"

"Shall I remind you now or later that we are undertaking this investigation for your benefit, dearest? This is our one and only course of inquiry just now, and if we offend Lord Ambrose by imposing our attention on him without warning, he may dismiss us at once as frauds or fantasists."

"I suppose it does seem a trifle unusual to ring a man's bell and ask to see his doll collection," Stoker admitted with ill grace.

"Anatomical Venuses," I corrected him. "Shall we prevail upon Lord Rosemorran to write us an introduction?"

Stoker shook his head. "He has gone to Cornwall. Something about trouble with the tin mines, and he wants to look things over. He expects to be gone the better part of a week."

"We could wait until his return," I suggested. "Or . . ."

Stoker put up a warning finger. "Do not say it, Veronica."

"Or," I went on as if he had not spoken, "we could apply to some other person of influence to provide an introduction."

Stoker flopped backwards into his chair with a groan.

"I shall take that as agreement," I said cheerfully. "Put on your coat. We are going to see your brother."

S toker had, in point of fact, three brothers of whom he was fond in varying degrees depending upon geography. Generally speaking, the further away one was, the more Stoker liked him. At that particular moment, the eldest—Tiberius, Viscount Templeton-Vane—was amusing himself by turning his considerable talents to the management of his country seat in Devon. The youngest of the brothers, Merryweather, was currently engaged in consoling a bereaved gentleman who had featured heavily in our last investigation.* That left Sir Rupert, the second-born and most conventional of the Templeton-Vanes. Whilst Tiberius had acquired his title through inheritance, Rupert had been knighted by Her Majesty—ostensibly for the translation of Chinese poetry, but really for the successful completion of several delicate diplomatic missions. He was a paragon of discretion, privy to my own secret status as a semi-legitimate member of the royal family and virtuous enough to keep that confidence unto the grave.

But where I saw stalwart loyalty, Stoker perceived priggish intractability. For his part, Rupert would forever deplore Stoker's refusal to conform to the expectations of his class—namely that he should settle down to one of the few occupations open to gentlemen and starch his collars.

---

* *A Sinister Revenge*

Managing the various quarrels and grudges amongst the Templeton-Vanes was a task for which I had neither time nor inclination. I bullied Stoker into a half-decent town suit and hat although he refused to put on any sort of necktie and wore his dustiest boots by way of rebellion. He grumbled all the way to Rupert's house where, as it was a Saturday, we expected to find him settled comfortably by the fire. Rupert was a creature of habit and a lover of home comforts. He never strayed far from hearth or tea table if he could avoid it, and that particular afternoon was cloudy and unseasonably cold, the lowering skies threatening rain at any moment.

We were ushered into the drawing room where we were greeted with genuine warmth by a tall and graceful lady of middle years, although there was no sign of Rupert.

"Veronica! This is an unexpected pleasure, my dear. And Stoker as well, how lovely. Come, sit by the fire. It is grown chilly, and you are just in time for tea." Lavinia, Rupert's wife, urged us to chairs, deep, comfortable, and upholstered in heavy glazed chintz. A fire screen needle-pointed with the Templeton-Vane arms shielded us from the heat of the fire, softening it to a homely warmth, whilst bowls of potpourri steamed gently upon the hearth, sending fragrant drifts of rose into the room.

"Are you certain we have not interrupted you?" Stoker asked, nodding towards the open book she had clearly just abandoned on the sofa.

"Indeed not," she assured us. "One can only read so much before the eyes begin to tire and the mind wanders apace."

I leant near to peer at the title. "Mary Somerville's *Connexion*." I was as impressed as I was surprised at her choice.

"Have you read her?" Lavinia asked eagerly. "I confess I know precious little of mathematics or astronomy so I find it slow going, but it is so intriguing I am determined to finish. She proposes a planet that may lie beyond Uranus. Astonishing."

"I will send you a copy of her *Personal Recollections* to read. Marvellous stuff. One wonders what she might have accomplished if she hadn't been distracted by the business of bearing and burying children."

"Indeed," Lavinia replied dryly. "Rupert was called away on business, but he ought to be returned any moment. Don't let's wait tea for him. It is far too foul a day to put off the pleasures of the tea table."

The tea things appeared then, and we applied ourselves to refreshment, Lavinia and I taking modest portions of sandwiches and cakes whilst Stoker happily consumed the rest of the sandwiches, seven jam tarts, scones with jam and cream, and the better part of a chocolate cake. The plates were almost empty of anything but crumbs by the time Rupert arrived, soaked to the skin and shivering. He punctuated his greeting with several heavy sneezes in succession.

He greeted me with cordiality and dropped a kiss to the fair cheek of his wife before looking in dismay at the wreckage of the tea table. A lone and very tiny chicken sandwich reposed in solitude on the platter. "My god, Stoker, you have the appetite of an anaconda. I think there is a leg of lamb in the larder. Shall I fetch you the bone to gnaw upon or would you rather suck the marrow directly?"

Stoker gave him a lazy grin and held eye contact as he reached for the sandwich and popped it into his mouth. "Oh, dear. I seem to have finished it all."

Lavinia rose smoothly. "I am so glad you enjoyed it, Stoker. That is a new receipt, and I have worried there might be just a touch too much tarragon in the mayonnaise. I shall tell Cook you approve. And I will order a fresh plate of sandwiches for you," she told her husband with a meaningful look. I understood her intention at once. *Be courteous, dear. They are guests.*

Rupert flushed a little and grunted. "Thank you, my dear. But I think just toast if you will send for bread and hand me the toasting fork."

We conversed politely of the weather and the state of the pound until the tea things had been refreshed. A stack of newly cut bread arrived with more sandwiches, whole plates of cake and tarts along with a kettle of boiling water for the pot. I toasted the bread whilst Lavinia occupied herself with the business of serving, handing out cups topped with a lavish spoonful of whisky this time.

"For the chill," she murmured. The maid left at last, and as Rupert applied himself to a stack of buttered toast, Lavinia turned to us.

"So with what fresh adventure can we assist today?" she asked brightly.

Rupert choked a little, and it took several swallows of tea before he recovered himself.

"My dear," he managed at last. "I think the safest course in our dealings with Stoker and Veronica is never to ask questions about their deviltry."

Stoker raised a brow. "What deviltry?"

Rupert gave him a pained look. "Stoker, I have, as you know, the confidence of the Government at the highest levels. Kindly pay me the compliment of not underestimating what I know about your exploits."

"Exploits?"

Rupert waved a hand. "Very well, your *shenanigans*."

"Shenanigans?" Stoker was clearly outraged. "I will have you know those *shenanigans* have resulted in—"

"Your near death and Veronica's by drowning, stabbing, shooting, garroting, and—have I left any out?" Rupert asked pleasantly.

"I was going to say they have resulted in the exposure of several murderers, the saving of an innocent man from the hangman's noose, and—oh, yes, how quickly we do forget—the successful signing of a treaty between Britain and our allies that has preserved the peace against German encroachment," Stoker thundered back.

"Should we speak *quite* so loudly about the treaty?" I asked. "Perhaps it is best if the entire domestic staff do not know the details of matters of international significance."

"It is quite all right," Lavinia assured me. "They are all hired through

Rupert's office and thoroughly vetted. The upstairs maid used to work at the Palace."

"Oh, that is nice," I told her.

"Yes, she has given the laundress some extremely useful tips on how to get Rupert's cuffs white. He is forever scribbling on them in pencil. Usually secret codes," she added with a tap of the finger to the side of her nose.

I nodded in understanding, and Rupert made a strangled noise deep in his throat. "My dear, do you think it is possible that we might omit any discussions of my precise work with people who are not altogether—"

"Not altogether what, Rip?" Stoker asked as he set his cup into its saucer with an audible crack. The use of Rupert's nickname ought to have been a signal to him of Stoker's mood, and if not, the tone certainly was. Stoker was edging into a dangerous mood, one which might well result in a bit of fraternal unpleasantness. He was always sensitive to slights from his brothers, and Rupert's perpetual conventionality would never fully appreciate Stoker's more unorthodox talents.

Rupert sighed. "Please do not break the crockery, Revelstoke. The tea set was a gift from the Khedive of Egypt and it's rather a favourite."

"It is a most attractive pattern," I put in kindly.

"Thank you, my dear. Now, if you do not mind, I have had rather a trying day, and my feet are wet. I am starting a cold. I want a hot bath, my slippers, and a proper dinner on a tray in bed, followed by a glass of port that is older than any one of us. I do not believe this is an entirely social call, so I should take it as a personal favour if you would state your business and let me get on with slowly dying."

"People hardly ever die of colds," I told him.

"I shall mark that as a consolation," Rupert replied. He paused and looked at us significantly. Stoker had lapsed into mulish silence, and I realised it was left to me to explain our errand.

"We have indeed come to ask a favour, a very small one," I assured Rupert. "We would like an introduction to Lord Ambrose Despard."

"Despard! What do you want with that eccentric?"

"Is he eccentric?" I asked, widening my eyes. It had occurred to me that anyone who collected waxwork Beauties might well be rather out of the ordinary, but the less we shared with Rupert the better, I decided.

"The whole of the Despard family are," Lavinia put in. "The late marquess was a bit of a fanatic with regards to health—always following the latest fads. I remember a time when he was obsessed with body temperature. He believed it had to be strictly regulated, so every morning he dressed in seven coats, and as the day went on and he became warmer, he would discard them one at a time."

"A trifle unusual, I grant you," I said. "But not entirely unhinged."

"Except that he simply dropped the coats wherever he happened to be. On a train, walking across a field, in the middle of church—he just tossed them aside. The children who lived near his house knew they could earn a ha'penny for each one returned to him, so they took to following the marquess around and waiting for him to discard his coats. Of course, the oddness didn't end with him," she went on. "The new marquess, Lord Ambrose's elder brother, courted me briefly when I first came out. A frightfully good dancer, but he would only waltz with his left hand held above his head. Something about blood flow. I tried to overlook it—one doesn't like to be impolite, and he was a wonderful conversationalist."

"And your mama never lets me forget you might have been a marchioness if I hadn't paid court to you myself and let Harwich get on with it. You'd have married him and gone on to be mother to a new generation of hypochondriacs," Rupert put in dryly before turning to us. "Again, what do you want with Ambrose?"

"It is rather difficult to explain," I said with a smile. "And we have taken up so much of your valuable time already."

"Oh, do tell," Lavinia urged. "I hear so little interesting gossip."

"Very well," I began. "Apparently Lord Ambrose is a keen collector of teaching mannequins, wax models of the female form that are completely correct, as it were. As intact as a human woman. They are sometimes known as Anatomical Venuses. I am told the level of detail is extraordinary even to the inclusion of pubic—"

Rupert surged out of his chair and made directly for the writing desk in the corner. "Say no more." He dashed off a few words on a sheet of writing paper headed with his name and arms, then signed it with a flourish before stuffing it into an envelope. "There you are. An introduction."

I took it with a smile of real affection. "Thank you, Rupert. Very good of you, I am sure. Do get some rest, and try a mustard plaster on your chest before that cough gets worse."

He nodded and thrust the envelope into my hands. "I shall. In fact, I think I will go upstairs this very minute. Good afternoon," he said, herding us into the entrance hall. He turned back into the drawing room and banged the door closed as Lavinia walked us out.

Stoker took an affectionate leave of his sister-in-law and thanked her handsomely for the tea. He started down the front stairs to the pavement as Lavinia leant down to me, pitching her voice low.

"Entirely anatomically correct?" she asked.

"So I am given to understand."

She paused, her expression thoughtful. "Do come again for tea when you know for certain. I should love to hear all about it."

"I will," I promised her. I kissed her good-bye and turned to go.

"Oh, and Veronica?"

"Yes, Lavinia?"

"Ask if there is such a thing as an Anatomical Adonis, will you?"

CHAPTER

7

In deference to the baleful weather and the unsociability of the hour
between tea and dinner, Stoker and I chose to postpone our visit to
Lord Ambrose and retreated to the Belvedere where we enjoyed our
evening meal amongst the comfortable chaos of dogs, books, paintings,
natural history specimens, weapons, sculptures, and the occasional
mummy. Given the eccentric and eclectic nature of our surroundings,
the glass casket with its waxen figure did not seem altogether out of
place. We had replaced her after Lord Rosemorran's visit—as much for
her dignity as to preserve the state of her. Changes in temperature and
humidity could only cause her to decay, a thoroughly unappetising
thought when one considered that we took most of our meals in the
Belvedere.

"I do hope we shall discover her name," I said as Stoker applied himself to the last of the apple blancmange Cook had sent up to follow the
roast duck and trimmings.

He looked up, his gaze resting upon the slumbering form. "More to
the point, I hope we discover who did this to her."

"You are convinced it was some act of violence that led her to being
thus preserved?"

"How can it not?" he asked. He laid aside his spoon—a sure sign of his preoccupation. "No young woman of respectable family would have gone missing without some hue and cry being raised."

"What makes you think her family were respectable?" I put in. "She may well have been an unfortunate wretch who made her living by her wits. We have seen enough of those women in the course of our adventures." I paused and in the silence which followed I knew we were both thinking of the audacious Elsie—"From Chelsea, loves!"—the irrepressible lady of the night whose path had crossed ours in the course of two separate investigations. And any thought of Elsie must conjure a memory of the brief time we had spent with her friend, Mary Jane Kelly, a pretty, generous girl whose life had been snuffed out at the hands of a fiend.*

Stoker shook his head slowly. "I cannot say why I am certain she was not a creature of the streets, but I am."

I shrugged. "You are an observant man by nature and your skills have been honed by experience. No doubt you saw something in your brief examination of her body from which you drew subtle conclusions."

"Perhaps." He dropped a hand to ruffle the ears of Betony, Lord Rosemorran's Caucasian sheepdog, who—like most females who encountered Stoker—had fallen completely under his spell. She responded by rolling her eyes back ecstatically in her head. Beside her, Nut the pharaoh hound and Huxley the bulldog awaited their turn along with my newest acquisition, an Italian greyhound that shivered in spite of the tiny sweaters Stoker had knitted for her.

"Et tu, Al-'Ijliyyah?" I asked repressively. Of all the animals in our menagerie, only Vespertine the deerhound preferred my company, often resting in noble composure at my feet. The greyhound, naturally, did not answer my question, and I turned back to Stoker, following the

---

* *A Murderous Relation*

train of thought to its logical conclusion. "If the cursory examination you made led you to draw inferences about the Beauty—"

"The what?"

"The Beauty. We must call her something, and she is, after all, a sort of Sleeping Beauty, is she not? In any event, the Beauty revealed some small part of her secrets to you during your first encounter with her."

"And?" His hand continued to stroke Betony's ears but his gaze was wary.

"I think you should examine her again—properly this time. We may learn a good deal."

His hand stilled. "I don't want to." His voice, a strong and resonant baritone, rumbled soft and low with a note of something akin to pleading.

"Whyever not? Death is your trade," I reminded him with a broad gesture towards the dozens of taxidermic trophies scattered about the Belvedere.

"Animals," he countered. "I work with animals, and the purpose of my work is to make them seem lifelike again, to restore dignity to what remains of them. Prodding that poor girl would feel wrong. Disrespect-ful." I remembered then a similar discussion on the subject of mummies during our third investigation. Stoker had held forth with considerable passion on the inherent dignity of the dead and our responsibility as the living to respect it.

"I understand," I told him gently. "She is no longer a fairground at-traction, fashioned of wax for the masses to pay a tuppence to gawk at. She was a person—*is* a person. And that person deserves justice if she was mis-handled. What if you are correct and there is a family that grieves her still? Do they not deserve answers? And even if it is not possible to find them, does she not deserve our best efforts at justice?"

I could see my words were beginning to sway him. A tiny muscle worked furiously in his jaw as his hand tensed on Betony's head. She nuzzled nearer to him, and he lowered his face to the thick fur.

"Stoker?"

When he raised his head, he wore an expression of resignation. "I suppose if I refuse you will carry on, making appeals to my emotions?"

"I am making sound logical arguments in appeal to your intellect," I corrected. "You know as well as I do that the first step of any scientific inquiry is observation. Everything else flows from that."

"And you will continue posing these logical arguments until I capitulate?"

"I will. I have just eaten a hearty meal, and I enjoyed an excellent sleep last night. I can do this for hours," I promised him.

He heaved a gusty sigh of surrender. "I am well acquainted with your stamina, Veronica. Very well. If we are going to do this, then let us get on with the thing and have done with it."

It was the work of some few minutes to prepare. Although the unfortunate Beauty was already dead, we instinctively wished to preserve some semblance of modesty in our researches as well as affording her every possible respect. To that end, we sent the dogs to the mews with the stable boy and made our preparations. The examination would require greater care and more intense observation than Stoker's previous efforts. Every lamp that could be found was brought along with a selection of mirrors to illuminate our makeshift mortuary.

Stoker collected various implements of the surgeon's trade—and the taxidermist's, although that was not an altogether happy thought—and we moved silently to our task. I helped him remove the glass lid of the casket. In the lamplight, her skin glowed, gilded alabaster with a rosy hue that lingered just below the surface.

"Extraordinary," I murmured. "One almost expects her to speak."

"I hope to Christ not," Stoker muttered in reply. The nearer we came to the crucial moment, the darker his mood, and I did not hold it against him. Men are seldom cheerful when they have been persuaded out of an emotional state into rationality. They are, in my experience, creatures of feeling rather than thought, and one must make allowances.

I carried on, ignoring his lowering mood, and helped him to gently lift the Beauty once more onto the worktable. Her limbs were neither entirely pliable nor did they exhibit the stiffness one associates with corpses of some age.

"I noted before that she is lighter than one might expect given her height and her apparent state of health at her death," I observed. "She was not undernourished."

"It is to do with the water," Stoker said in an absent tone. "Whatever method was used to preserve her must first have removed the water from her tissues. Water is the author of destruction, hastening decomposition."

"Hence the Egyptians' use of natron salts to desiccate the mummies," I replied.

"Just so." He bent near to her skin, observing the texture closely through a magnifying glass. "But natron has not been used here. It is a harsh method, drawing out every drop of moisture from the body and leaving only the withered husk behind. Mark the nature of her skin. If she had been treated with natron, it would have the texture of old leather. But she is fresh and dewy as a flower."

A less robustly confident woman than myself might have issued a sigh of irritation at his obvious admiration of her charms, but I am nothing if not entirely secure within myself.

"Did you say something?" Stoker raised his head.

"Nothing whatsoever," I told him firmly.

We removed her clothing a second time with a slow, almost religious reverence, putting the garments aside for further inspection after we had finished with the Beauty herself. Following this, Stoker scrutinised her from head to toe with the glass, prodding and peering, and making occasional sotto voce remarks to himself.

"Anything of note?" I asked dryly when he had finished his extremely thorough examination.

"Nothing obvious to indicate a cause of death, if that is what you mean," he said. "There are no marks of violence—not a stab wound or garrote mark. No markers of poison either."

"Would they be detectable?" I asked.

He shrugged. "The most common and lethal poisons, yes. Discolourations of fingernails or skin are the most common. Burn marks around the mouth for corrosive acids, that sort of thing. I shall take a small sample of her hair to perform a Marsh test for arsenic, but I suspect it will prove negative."

"There are other poisons," I suggested. "Botanical toxins such as monkshood or foxglove. They can be found in any garden, and their effects would not be immediately apparent in death."

"True," he agreed—reluctantly, I fancied.

He moved to her head and beckoned for me to hold a lamp closer. With infinite care, he tugged gently upon one eyelid, revealing an iris of such delicate sapphirine colour, it might have belonged to a Renaissance angel. The pupils were wide and black against the pale irises which themselves were ringed with a much darker blue.

Suddenly, he bent swiftly to the eye, motioning with impatience for more light. I obliged, realising he had caught the scent of something of importance. He examined first one eye, then the other, peering closely at the eye itself and then the eyelid. When he finished, he did a most curious and unexpected thing. He turned back her lower lip and gave a smothered shout of satisfaction.

"What is it?" I demanded.

"Look there," he said, pointing to a collection of dark spots inside the lip, clustered like a constellation. "I have seen it once before, on the *Luna*. One of the cabin boys went overboard in a storm. By the time we sailed back to find him, all we could do was recover the body. He had marks just such as those inside his eyes and lips. The ship's surgeon said it was a common thing in those who drowned."

"So the Beauty may well have drowned. But accidentally or by the hand of another?" I asked.

His expression was grim. "That is what we must discover."

He bent once more to his task, scrutinising the flesh of her limbs. The skin was smoothly, unsettlingly perfect.

"The effect is so odd," I observed. "She is so lifelike, one expects her to speak, and yet there is something utterly cold about her."

"Whoever did this to her robbed her of her humanity," he replied grimly. "It is monstrous—" He broke off, bending even closer to peer intently at her right hand, then her left. He said nothing as he studied her, but it was apparent he was forming a conclusion of some sort.

"What do you see?" I asked.

"A moment," he murmured, moving quickly to her legs and examining them before giving a little growl of satisfaction. He straightened and faced me with a grin. "Whatever processes she has been subjected to have smoothed and plumped her flesh, but with close observation it is possible to see three things: a set of distinctive calluses on her hands, knees whose skin is thickened and slightly discoloured, and telltale swellings below the kneecap."

He waited as I assembled the pieces. "A maid!" I exclaimed.

His smile deepened. "Precisely."

He pointed out the features he had described and I nodded. "Not just a maid then," I told him. "A maid-of-all-work. See here? The faintest of scars at her wrist, too precise and narrow to be anything but the edge of an iron. But those calluses and kneecaps speak to scrubbing brushes and time spent on hard floors, not a laundrymaid's purview."

He was thoughtful. "She is a little old for a maid-of-all-work, but not by much. Poor girl."

He did not elaborate, but I knew we were both thinking of those unfortunate children, plucked from workhouses and orphanages and put to work at the most menial of jobs, hauling and scrubbing, cleaning, cooking, and laying fires, tending linen, mending, sewing, and any other chores expected of them. Most were employed by the age of twelve and mercifully only toiled for a few years before moving on to slightly less arduous employment. Theirs was the lowest rung on the ladder of domestic service, found only in households which could not afford a proper complement of staff. It was inhumane to expect a single girl to do the work of at least three indoor servants, but there were many who could afford the pittance of their wages and counted themselves too proud to stoop to the emptying of slop jars and hauling of water cans. It was little better than remaining in the workhouse, but not by much. That the Beauty had once undertaken such employment meant that she had at some point found herself in a desperate situation. Had she been orphaned? Left friendless and without family until some enterprising soul took her into service, exchanging her youth for drudgery?

"She died before they could rob her entirely of her beauty," I mused. "A few more years and she would have been worn to ribbons."

Stoker did not reply as he moved to her torso. He removed the section of her abdomen he had already loosened, putting it gently aside. I did not wish to look at the panel of flesh, but in the interest of science I forced myself. It seemed like that of any young and healthy individual, with a consistent distribution of fat below the skin and no marked imperfections.

The first time the Beauty had been laid open to our gaze it had been so unexpected a thing that we had no chance to examine her properly or even notice anything of interest within the abdominal cavity. This time was different. This time, one could clearly see the machinery of digestion in its various and gory glory.

"No blood," I observed.

Stoker shook his head. "There wouldn't be. The first task of preservation is to remove any fluids which might contaminate the process. Ordinarily, the organs of digestion would have been removed as well, but whoever did this wanted to preserve her perfectly as an anatomical model," he told me, pointing out the stomach, the pale grey tangle of intestines.

I think he meant to say more, but he stopped abruptly, his mouth slack. "Oh, no, no, no," he managed in a hollow voice.

"Stoker, whatever is the matter?" I demanded. "Surely you can tolerate the sight of a little viscera. You are a man of science," I reminded him.

He said nothing else, only lifted a finger and pointed, and I noticed his hand was not steady when he did so. He was indicating a place below her large intestine, the place where the organs of fecundity repose.

I lifted the lamp near and saw the unmistakable swell of the womb, an enlargement that could have only one cause.

"The Beauty was with child," I said in horror.

CHAPTER

8

S toker, dearest, the American beaver has cause to grind its teeth in order to fell trees for constructing its habitat. From the sounds you are making, I can only think you intend to build a dam of your own," I said with a curve of the lips to provide a touch of levity to the mild reproof.

In fact, I was feeling less than cheerful myself. My invitation to address the Aurelian Society had been abruptly withdrawn on the grounds that the gentlemen issuing the appeal had not realised the "V. Speedwell" who had authored the article which so enraptured them—"Observations on the Hand-Rearing of Rare Lepidoptera"—was female. I chafed against their stupidity and briefly considered boxing up and posting them the steaming pile that Vespertine had deposited under the shrubbery that morning, but in the end, I chose to accept the disappointment with dignity and apply myself to the conundrum at hand, unravelling the puzzle of the Beauty's life and death as well as the source of Stoker's discontent. He had been making unholy noises for the past quarter of an hour and my nerves could stand no more, hence my gentle gibe about beavers.

He did not return the smile. "I am not grinding my teeth. I am chewing boiled sweets." He crunched down hard upon another and the aroma of aniseed filled the carriage. We were bound for Lord Ambrose Despard's house, and in light of the smart new town dress I had donned—violet silk with a luscious trimming of black passementerie—I had insisted upon a carriage to save my hems. I was beginning to regret that decision. Stoker had been decidedly not himself since his examination of the Beauty the night before. A walk to Lincoln's Inn Fields might have worked out some of his overwrought emotions.

"It is not like you to chew them to bits like a piece of industrial machinery," I told him. "Are your nerves unsettled?"

He turned to me in frank astonishment. "My nerves? Unsettled? I cannot imagine why you would suggest such a thing. I have only performed a thoroughly illegal postmortem on a pregnant woman I am quite certain has died of violence."

"You did not cavil at the legalities of the situation last night," I reminded him. It was true that he had not undertaken the investigation with quite as much enthusiasm as I had, but the results of the examination had distressed him. He had been withdrawn and silent as we restored the Beauty to a semblance of propriety, replacing the panel of her abdomen and dressing her once more. I had been a trifle surprised at his reaction, but it was not his fault that his courage was failing him. Men require, in my experience, considerable bolstering of the spirits in order to carry out any activity requiring imagination or fortitude. It was a source of tremendous satisfaction to me that Stoker required less bolstering than most and usually of the physical variety. A comprehensive session of sensual congress was often enough to rouse any flagging spirits, and when coupled with a warm toddy and a good night's sleep, it ensured he was always right as rain the following morning.

In this instance, however, my usual remedies had failed. After concluding our examination of the Beauty, Stoker had said little as we placed her in a position of repose in her glass case. He found a tapestry—Flemish, fourteenth-century, and depicting the Judgement of Paris—to drape over the coffin in an attempt at concealment. We did not discuss the need for such precautions, but neither of us would have wanted any member of the Beauclerk household, least of all the irrepressible Lady Rose, to have stumbled upon the uncomfortable truths we had observed. Lady Rose had been distracted enough by her guardianship of the tamarin not to have missed the Beauty, and the children were strictly forbidden unaccompanied access to the Belvedere, but I trusted them as far as I could ride Patricia, the Galápagos tortoise.

When Stoker finished his camouflage of the casket, it still looked too starkly coffin-like, so I heaped a stack of moth-eaten silk cushions atop the tapestry along with a pair of light lithographs and an enormous stuffed albino peacock. In front of the casket I arranged stacks of an incomplete collection of Napoléon's *Description de l'Égypte*, the encyclopaedic survey of the Nile and its environs. Atop these I placed a selection of blown ostrich eggs, precariously enough situated so that anyone would think twice about exploring further in that particular corner of the Belvedere.

Afterwards, Stoker refused my invitation for an interlude in the Roman baths, preferring instead to retire alone to the cold, chaste bed in his little Chinese temple. I was not in the slightest perturbed at this, of course. Good manners dictate that one must receive a refusal with as much grace as one welcomes an acceptance, and I was the last person to press my company where it was not greeted with enthusiasm. I buttoned up my nightdress—I had discarded it in my haste to get to the business of things—and apologised for tearing his trousers. (It is possible I misunderstood the nature of his refusal and at first thought he was simply playing at being coy. It was necessary for him to issue his rebuff a second time and then a third, with a stern removal of my hands from his person, before I comprehended his sincerity. I make no apologies. Stoker had, during the course of our previous investigation, made it quite clear that he wished to be seduced upon occasion, and I was simply taking him at his word. Once he had found new trousers and staunched the bleeding, we had a comprehensive discussion on the subject of initiating congress and came to a cordial and necessary understanding that a first refusal is to be honoured immediately and without resentment. I offer this bit of digression as a piece of instruction to the gentle reader that it is worthwhile to have such discussions, albeit perhaps *before* the fact rather than when one has been forcibly removed from an attempt at a complicated position known to ancient Romans as the Vines of Venus.)

By the time I appeared at breakfast in the Belvedere, Stoker was immersed in his labours, and we spoke little as he applied himself to the refurbishment of a charmingly posed maned sloth, *Bradypus torquatus*. The tamarin was still evidently in Lady Rose's clutches, for it made no appearance—a circumstance for which I was heartily grateful. I applied myself to the correspondence that never seemed to diminish no matter how many letters I sent, and the morning passed swiftly. After luncheon and another few hours of work, we decided to refresh and smarten ourselves for our call upon Lord Ambrose. At least, I decided. Stoker would have happily appeared in the Drawing Room at Buckingham Palace in a half-open shirt stained with glue and ink, but I pointed out to him that at least a modicum of civility was required when calling upon the son of a marquess. He took the news with bad grace but appeared some little while later, hair still damp from his ablutions, wearing a town suit and an effort at a necktie. My violet silk was set off handsomely by a fetching black velvet hat with stiffened peacock plumes.

"My god," Stoker said, rearing back. "You will put out someone's eye with that bloody thing."

"It is," I informed him loftily, "the height of fashion. I have no doubt Lord Ambrose will appreciate the effort."

He snorted by way of reply and threw himself into the carriage where he remained, crunching on boiled sweets and grumbling under his breath as I mentally reviewed our points of discussion with Lord Ambrose. We had agreed that no mention was to be made of our Beauty. The fewer people who knew of her existence, the better. We would inquire about the casket only, and any general information about Anatomical Venuses he might care to impart. The world of their admirers must be a small one, I reasoned, and it was not impossible that Lord Ambrose could have heard rumours of someone who was inclined to dabble in something far darker.

Such thoughts occupied my attention until at last we drew up in front of the house. A footman, powdered and liveried in pale amber, took in our cards and the letter of introduction Rupert had provided, leaving us to wait in the vestibule. The house, like all in that particular quarter, was a model of quiet elegance with the regular symmetry one associates with good Neoclassical lines. Inside, it was an example of breathtaking originality. The floor was chequered in a traditional pattern, but the tiles were emerald and grey marble, both subtly veined in gold. Recesses around the room which might have held pretty vases or arrangements of hothouse blooms in other homes, instead sheltered an assortment of black marble busts of Roman emperors.

I was just admiring a particularly attractive head of Hadrian when a gentleman descended the stairs, smiling in welcome.

"Mr. Templeton-Vane! How do you do? And Miss Speedwell, a pleasure to make your acquaintance," he said. He grasped my gloved hand and came within a breath of touching his lips to the back of it. He turned and shook Stoker's, giving me a chance to study him briefly. He was well above average height, topping Stoker by some three inches or so, and his slenderness only augmented the effect. He had a nose as sharply modelled as Hadrian's, and he was dressed quietly but at obviously great expense. He was not yet forty, I surmised, and in excellent condition with a fencer's physique. His hair was a pale, burnished gold, and his eyes a decidedly warm spaniel-brown with a slightly mournful expression although his manner was kind.

I recalled myself to find him scrutinising me with equal candour. He smiled in obvious approval. "Any friend of Rupert's is entirely welcome here. It is too early for tea, but would you care for some refreshment?"

"Perhaps later," I told him.

"We have many commitments," Stoker said sulkily. I resisted the urge to pinch him. If I had realised he was still quite so distressed about the postmortem on the Beauty, I would have left him at home. The coaxing of information from gentlemen was a particular speciality of mine, and it would only hinder the cause if Stoker's sullen mood dampened the cordiality of our conversation.

"Then I must make it my mission to persuade you," Lord Ambrose told him. "I am afraid Sir Rupert's note did not state a purpose to your visit. Have you come to see my collection?"

"Your collection?" I asked.

"Oh, yes. I often receive visitors. I have amassed quite an interesting assortment of oddities and artefacts."

"What sort of artefacts?" I inquired.

"Egyptological, Grecian, Roman. And of course the natural history specimens. I have a number of butterflies, which is how I know the name Speedwell. You must have some connection to the author of the recent article in the *Journal of the Aurelian Society.*"

"On sexual dimorphism in *Trogonoptera brookiana*? I wrote it. I am V. Speedwell," I told him to his obvious delight. "You read it?"

"Read it? I was riveted!" he assured me. "And whilst your theory about the purpose of the dimorphism is entirely original, I must say your argument was sound. I found myself entirely persuaded. And perhaps I could impose upon you enough to ask a question. I have recently acquired a case of *Meandrusa payeni* from Sikkim and wonder if they are all that they should be. I fear they have been misidentified by an unscrupulous seller, and I hope you will be kind enough to lend me your expertise."

We had come for information about the Beauties, but the invitation was too intriguing to pass up. A Yellow Gorgon was not a thing to be denied.

"You may depend upon it," I promised.

Behind me, Stoker gave a low growl, which I attributed to a bout of indigestion courtesy of too many boiled sweets.

Lord Ambrose led the way to a narrow staircase descending from the principal floor.

"The entomological collections are down here with the Egyptian things—and the Roman, although my collection of Roman antiquities is paltry at best."

His protestations were those of false modesty. His assortment of Roman antiquities were, to my poorly trained eye, of the highest quality. Further, they were so perfectly assembled, so beautifully displayed as to bear proud, silent witness to the delicate taste of their collector. His entomological specimens were of the same impeccable quality. We made polite noises about the various beetles and arachnids, but there is only so much one can say about a spider. I was far more interested in the lepidoptery, and though his collection was modest in size, it was exquisite in its contents. In a small alcove between two of the rooms, cases had been hung from floor to ceiling, each holding a pair of butterflies, exemplars of a single species. Most lepidopterists preferred a few dozen of each species in order to convey the breadth of variation in colouration or markings or size. But not Lord Ambrose. He had chosen perfection instead, selecting one male and one female of each in order to present the most complete and ideal version of the imago.

Propped against the wall was a case containing the promised Yellow

Gorgons. They were hooked swallowtails, their sweeping ochre wings spotted with cinnamon. The female was duller than her companion, but her shape was every bit as elegant, suggesting a child's kite that would ride the wind with delicacy and grace.

"They are lovely," I told Lord Ambrose truthfully.

He smiled, his eyes a trifle less melancholy than before. "Oh, do you think so? I am glad. Although I hardly know where to put them, the wall is already quite full," he added, gesturing towards the arrangement of cases. "I suppose I ought to be more selective about larger pieces, but I cannot resist a thing of beauty." He gestured towards a statue upon a raised plinth, a young woman fashioned of alabaster, the material giving the figure a sort of luminosity, a quality of being lit from within. Her garment flowed behind her as if she had been captured in motion. Her arms arced gracefully overhead, but where the fingertips ought to have been there were only leaves, so delicate one might have imagined them butterfly wings. Her forearms bore the faint striations of bark, and her feet, which ought to have been high-arched and light, instead were heavy, rooted things boring into the churned earth.

Stoker was busy inspecting a case of dermestid beetles as Lord Ambrose and I went to stand in front of the statue. He raised a hand to trace a fingertip along the length of one branching arm. "You recognise her, of course?"

"Daphne, the poor nymph who refused Apollo and was turned into a laurel shrub for her trouble."

"It is dangerous to spurn the love of the gods," he said in a low, pensive voice.

"Apollo has always seemed to me the most petulant of the gods," I told him briskly.

"Apollo—you cannot mean it!" Lord Ambrose cried in mock horror.

"I do," I assured him. "Every ill-fated creature he encountered—goddess, maiden, nymph—seems poorly done by him. We are given to believe he was radiantly handsome, and yet he was forever chasing women who had no interest in him. Why? Because like most overly handsome men, I suspect he was a tremendous bore."

"And yet it is thanks to his amorous pursuits that we have this glorious creation," Lord Ambrose replied.

"Apollo was also the patron of sailors," Stoker put in from across the room. I had thought him occupied by the industry of the beetles—they were nasty little creatures, busily engaged in gnawing the flesh from a chicken bone with gusto—but he turned, folding his arms over his chest as he went on. "And medicine. Apollo protected herds and invented music and mathematics. He wrestled Mars into submission. Perhaps those accomplishments might go some way towards softening your opinion of him."

"Not in the slightest. There was no mercy in him," I insisted.

"Apollo persuaded Zeus to free Prometheus," Stoker reminded me. The Titan who had challenged the gods and brought the gift of fire to the world had paid a heavy price for his daring. He had been chained to a rock, a living sacrifice for an enormous eagle who tore his liver out each day. Being immortal, he never died, but suffered the eternal agony of having his liver grow anew only to be plucked out the following morning.

"I will grant you that was a kindness," I said. "Prometheus ought never to have been punished in the first place. It was no crime to bring fire to humanity, do you not agree, Lord Ambrose?"

Lord Ambrose's complexion seemed a trifle paler than it had been, and when he spoke his voice was taut. "I think playing with the powers of the gods is a dangerous business, Miss Speedwell."

He had not looked away from the immobile face of Daphne, but he shook himself suddenly and summoned a smile. "Come. I have other treasures to show you."

CHAPTER

9

I played the wide-eyed ingenue for the better part of another hour, making all the appropriate noises of appreciation as Lord Ambrose guided us through room after room of paintings, coins, arms, and pretty bric-a-brac that would have done justice to a municipal museum of a good-sized town. I praised his taste, his intelligence, his vision, and by the time we reached the third floor of the house, I had all but admired his trousers.

Through it all, Stoker's demeanour swung between silent contemplation and grudging admiration. He did not thaw until he came face-to-face with a curious creature whose skin seemed composed of plate armour. It was small with a thick tail and a pointed, almost quizzical nose. The scales caused it to resemble a tiny dragon, if one believed in such things, but this was no creature out of myth. Stoker recognised it at once. He leant towards the little creature in obvious excitement.

"*Phataginus tricuspis.* Lord Ambrose, how does it come to be that you are in possession of a tree pangolin? I believe they are exceedingly rare in this country."

"Few indeed have made it to our shores," Lord Ambrose told him. "I admit, I find him a winsome little fellow, although I am troubled by a bit of damage he sustained in his journey from West Africa." He pointed out the curious angle of one ear. "You see how inelegantly it sits compared to the other? I would dearly love to have it corrected, but I am afraid I do not know a taxidermist of sufficient skill."

Stoker remained silent. He would never put himself forward, but I seized the opportunity to sing his praises. I related Stoker's recent successes with a quagga and a Tasmanian tiger—both as rare as this creature—and Lord Ambrose regarded him with delight.

"But I have seen that quagga!" Lord Ambrose replied happily. "A Mr. Pennybaker invited several patrons of the Royal Society of Mammalian Scholars to view it, and I must say, your work is first-rate, sir. I wonder, would you be at all interested in applying your talents to my little project here?"

Stoker fairly choked in his haste to accept.

"Splendid!" Lord Ambrose said. "I shall have him crated up and sent over to you, shall I? Now, would you care to see the most extraordinary part of my collection or shall we stop for tea?"

He had paused at the door to the next room, his hand on the knob. I was seething with impatience at this point. "Oh, do show us more, I beg you," I urged.

Lord Ambrose smiled. "Very well. Give me a moment to remove a few dust sheets and turn on the lamps."

He disappeared into the room, and Stoker turned to me with a whimper. "No tea? I am famished."

"When we have finished," I told him firmly. "The Anatomical Beauties must be in that room."

"I hope for your sake they are," he said. "I could perish of malnutrition for all the time it has taken us to get this far, thanks to your insistence upon seeing every last eyelash in his collection."

"We want to find Signore Branzino's waxwork and gain information,"

I reminded him. "And information is more easily dealt to those with whom one has a rapport."

"And the fact that he is a handsome, wealthy gentleman with exquisite taste and a collection of Yellow Gorgons would have nothing to do with it?"

"I shall not dignify that with a response," I said in lofty tones.

Before he could reply, Lord Ambrose reappeared with a smile. "Come. I would like to introduce you to the prize jewels in my collections." He gestured for us to precede him into the room.

Whatever I might have expected after inspecting our own Beauty, I was thoroughly unprepared for the experience of finding myself in an entire room of wax figures. Each was encased in glass, like so many sleeping maidens. Each was beautifully formed, elegantly shaped, but amongst them they represented many facets of feminine appeal. One, resting on a crimson satin drape, had raven hair fanned out across her lace pillow, pearls at her throat. Next to her, a blonde maiden reposed, hair neatly plaited with blue velvet ribbons. In the casket on the other side lay another, this one on her side, her features distinctly Japanese, and her robe of pale pink silk folded back in pleats as elaborate as the pillowy rolls of her coiffure.

On and on it went, coffin after coffin, figure after figure, each so perfectly moulded, so exact in every detail, I would not have been surprised if they had rubbed the sleep from their eyes and risen from their slumbers. I had offered Lord Ambrose considerable flattery during the course of our visit, but in this room, my praise was fully sincere if slightly aghast.

"How did you come to acquire so complete a collection?" I asked as I bent to study one particularly ravishing Venus whose sensual pose suggested more of the courtesan than the anatomical teaching aid.

He shrugged. "How does one acquire any collection, Miss Speedwell? Patience and passion."

"And money," Stoker put in dryly.

Lord Ambrose was generous enough to smile. "That as well. I am fortunate that my share of my mother's fortune has permitted me to indulge my interests to the fullest."

I recalled what Lavinia had related about eccentricity in the Despard family and observed to myself that the fine line which marked peculiarity from madness was often simply a matter of wealth.

As if intuiting my thoughts, Lord Ambrose turned to me, still smiling. "No doubt, if you are acquainted with Sir Rupert's wife, you have heard tales of my family. We are a notoriously eccentric lot."

"She may have mentioned your father's interest in matters of health," I temporised.

"Did she tell you about my mother?" he asked. "A thorough original, obsessed with pigs. Lives in the country with her porkers and refuses to have a single one of them butchered for meat. They are pets, you understand. With the run of the house. You cannot imagine what they have done to the floors."

He turned back to his waxworks. "My Venuses are rather less destructive. Lying in perpetual slumber, they are a constant invitation to view, to learn, to admire the fullness of human anatomy."

"Female anatomy," Stoker said blandly.

"Yes." Lord Ambrose's voice was smooth. "The female human is far more complex and therefore more interesting than the male, but then that is true of most species, don't you think?"

Without waiting for a response, he moved on, pointing out the various features of several of the models. One was crafted specifically for the teaching of obstetrical arts, fitted as she was with an infant, fully formed and actually crowning. Lord Ambrose presented this with the detachment of a physician, but I looked swiftly away. When one has no intention of giving birth, one cannot be entirely delighted by the carnage of birth, I had found.

The next figure was more gruesome but somehow less alarming. Lord Ambrose opened the casket and demonstrated by lifting out assorted pieces how she might be configured for teaching. "You see here? Seven levels of dissection for close study. She is a marvel, is she not? Only look at the detail on that pancreas."

"Yes, it's very nice," I said faintly. "I notice several of your Venuses have labels written in Italian."

"Oh, indeed. The Italians were at the vanguard of their creation, and examples of their craft have always commanded the highest respect and prices," he added with a wry look that did nothing to damage his attractions. "They were once the crown jewels of the collections in Padua, Pavia. And then the Germans began to see the merit in them. The use of them spread to Leiden, Berlin, Heidelberg. At one time, there was not a university worth the name that did not have at least one to boast of."

"But surely these ought to be in teaching hospitals," I protested with a sweeping gesture.

"Their day is past," he told me regretfully. "With the creation of Dr. Grey and Dr. Carter's textbook on anatomical study, the fashion for the Venuses was finished. Students prefer the cold and clinical words on the page to the allure of a lifelike model." He paused with a melancholy sigh before shaking off the gloom as a dog will shed water. "Still, it is an ill wind that blows nobody good. If they hadn't fallen from favour, then I should never have been able to acquire so many first-rate specimens, and mine are among the most perfect ever constructed."

He fell to silence again, and I darted a meaningful look at Stoker. It was time to draw Lord Ambrose further out, if possible, on the subject of the Venuses. With a subtle flick of his finger, Stoker indicated which of the Beauties had formerly resided with Professor Pygopagus's show. I moved near, making appropriate noises of admiration as I surveyed her long blonde tresses and pretty blue eyes.

"This glass coffin is a particularly fine example of the art, I think," I ventured.

"Oh, indeed! A happy marriage of the Venetian glassmakers' efforts with the metalsmiths of Florence. Frequently the caskets are damaged or missing entirely, so it was a real coup to discover this lady with her original place of repose."

"Wherever did you find her?" I asked, widening my eyes in curiosity.

"A thoroughly disreputable travelling show," he confided. "I should never, in the course of regular events, have been seen near such a place, but I had been advised that a particularly fine example of a Susini wax-work was to be found there. Clemente Susini was one of the masters of this particular genre, you understand. Having one of his sculptures to add to my collection was a spectacular coup. I could hardly credit finding her in such a place, but she is thoroughly genuine. I offered a generous price to the owner, and he was content to part with her that very night. She has been with me ever since."

"But your other Venuses, you had to find caskets for them?" I pressed.

"Yes, it is rather more difficult than finding the waxworks themselves, but I am nothing if not resourceful," he said.

"You must be so very clever, Lord Ambrose. I cannot imagine where one would begin to look for such a thing," I said with my best attempt at a simper.

"How kind of you to say. I search out specialist dealers," he said. "There is an agent on the Continent who is always scouring the various markets and private collections for additions to my assembly."

"As it happens, we have come into possession of such a casket—at least our patron, Lord Rosemorran, has. Perhaps you could offer a little insight as to where it might have come from?" I suggested.

"Indeed?" His ears, like those of a hound on a scent, seemed to prick and his nose lifted. "Has it any special markings?"

"None, unfortunately."

"That is a pity. And without a specimen inside, it is difficult to attribute the coffin to any particular workshop." He paused, as if searching carefully for his next words, and when he spoke, his voice was almost too casual. "Do you know what his lordship means to do with it?"

I shrugged and answered in an offhand manner. "Use it to display bibelot, I suspect. He is forever in need of cabinets for his collections."

"And he has no interest in a Venus?" Lord Ambrose's gaze was narrow and intently focused. I suppressed the inclination to roll my eyes heavenwards. Collectors are a competitive lot, and there is nothing like the hint of rivalry to stoke the fires.

"None," I assured him. "But if we should encounter one, you would be the first to know."

Lord Ambrose murmured something courteous and moved to escort us out. I was a trifle piqued he did not repeat his offer of refreshment, as I had a line of questioning I intended to put to him over the genial intimacy of steaming cups and slices of cake. But the invitation was not forthcoming, and it was with some impatience that I realised we were being politely shown the door.

We said all the correct things—he thanked us for coming; we thanked him for receiving us—and hands were shaken. The footman in amber livery opened the door, and I fancied Lord Ambrose's parting smile was tinged with relief.

Stoker followed me over the threshold, but paused and turned back just before the door closed.

"I nearly forgot, Lord Ambrose," he began.

"Yes?"

"Your waxwork Beauties are extraordinarily lifelike. Is it possible, I wonder, to preserve an actual human body to such exactitude?"

Lord Ambrose paled and seemed to waver slightly. For one terrible moment I thought he might faint, but instead, he recovered himself enough to utter one word in a hoarse voice.

"No."

With that he stepped sharply back and made a violent gesture towards the footman who shut the door firmly in our faces. Our visit was at an end.

CHAPTER

10

The rest of the day proved thoroughly unprofitable. First, we engaged in a robust debate on the wisdom of tipping our hand to Lord Ambrose. The existence of a perfectly preserved corpse in our workroom was not a fact I cared to have bandied about.

"We are notorious enough as it is," I reminded Stoker as we arrived back at the Belvedere. "Do you really want polite society to tattle about this particular tittle? Look around you, beloved," I urged, throwing my hands wide to encompass the whole of the space. "We live and work surrounded by a pack of unlikely dogs, a motley collection of such oddities and curiosities. We must appear the least desirable acquaintance in all of London."

"I have never known you to care for the opinions of the madding crowd," he said, tearing off his neckcloth in a gesture of frustration. He tossed it aside and it landed atop the death mask of a pope, giving the cleric a rakish air.

Stoker turned back to me, enfolding me in his arms. I permitted it, laying my cheek to the place where I could best feel the slow, deep pulse, as steadying as any prayer.

"Is this because your invitation to speak to the Aurelian Society was rescinded?"

"Perhaps," I said, my voice muffled by his shirt.

"I am sorry," he murmured into my hair.

"When the invitation arrived, you called them a pompous bunch of horse-faced numpties," I reminded him.

"And so they are. But they are *your* numpties, and I know it meant something to you to be invited to address them."

I sighed and pushed away. "It was the first real recognition I have had from my peers that I have made contributions of significance to our field."

He put a finger under my chin and tipped it up so that my gaze would meet his. "If you think those wool-wits are your peers, you are very much mistaken, Veronica. They are not fit to hold the tip of your butterfly net."

I rose on tiptoe and pressed a kiss to his nose. "Thank you for that. I will make every effort to throw off this fit of the morbs. Now, perhaps we ought to address yours."

"Mine?"

"Stoker, I am well acquainted with your face in repose. It is solemn, sometimes to the point of grimness. I confess, it amuses me to watch otherwise confident men entirely lose their self-possession simply from being in the same room with you. But there was something of rancour in your manner towards Lord Ambrose. Is it envy?"

"Envy?" He reared back in surprise. "Of your flirtation with him?"

"Heavens, no. You know me well enough to understand when I am employing a stratagem in order to gain information. And you also know me too well to suppose I would ever entertain a moment's admiration for such a man when you are in the world. No, when I said envy, I was thinking of his pangolin."

"I would not mind owning one," he admitted.

"Not mind? I suspect your feelings run deeper, perhaps to the sort of covetousness that caused Moses to carry down the tablets from Mount Sinai. But I think it is not simply the pangolin?"

I paused and he gave a slow exhalation, as if setting down a burden. His hands, warm and broad of palm, ran up and down my arms, eliciting such sensations as made it difficult to concentrate upon his answer.

"It is because we are at a dead end," he said finally. "What if we cannot discover anything about her? Or her child? She was a maid-of-all-work, and she drowned whilst pregnant. What does that suggest to you?"

"Desperation," I said softly.

"Precisely. Hers or someone else's. There were no marks of a ring upon her finger, and we know exactly how vulnerable such girls are. She was, at best, seduced—and most likely something far, far worse." He paused. "A maid-of-all-work has no such protection, no housekeeper to look after her, to guard her from men in the household or neighbour lads or the barrow boys delivering from the colliery and the costermonger."

"And no matter the situation, the girl would always be blamed for her fall," I said. "Our poor Beauty must have been so terrified. No household with any pretence of respectability would have kept her on. She would have been turned out as soon as her state became obvious."

"To go where? The workhouse? The gutter? Her prospects would have been worse than grim."

"If she did take her own life, one can hardly blame her. She must have felt she had no choice."

"Indeed. And it is a story so common as to be unremarkable," he said in some bitterness. "But she ought not to be forgot. We should have a name for her, a grave to put her in. And whoever is responsible for despoiling her corpse ought to be held accountable."

I took his hand. "I am entirely in agreement, my love. I do not argue with you about the necessity of this investigation, only your state of mind. You seem disheartened."

He said nothing for a long moment, then said, in a small, low voice, "What if, this time, there is no justice for us to deliver?"

"How can you think so?" I cried. "When have we *ever* failed to uncover the plots that surround us? When has any villain eluded our efforts?"

He opened his mouth—no doubt to enumerate the miscreants who had in fact escaped our attempts to bring them to account—but I pressed a hand over it. "Never mind. Our ledger may not always have us in the black, but on balance we have succeeded far oftener than we have failed. Do you really not believe we can do so again?"

"I do not know," he said with a weariness I had not heard from him before.

"Piffle. Your lack of spirit alarms me. Do you require building up? I could ask Lady Rose's governess for a dose of iron tonic."

"You are all the tonic I require," he told me. (The interlude that followed does not bear upon the narrative, so I shall include no further comment except to say that it was gratifying indeed.)

The following day we had no sooner set to work than Lord Rosemorran's porters appeared with two crates, one large and one small. The smaller bore my name but no other markings. I set to it with a pry bar and very soon had the lid away. I breathed in sharply at the sight of the contents.

Inside the crate, nestled on a bed of excelsior, was an elegant glass case. Inside this was a branch with a flower, both so cunningly crafted as to appear more lifelike than the real thing. Hovering on a slender filament of wire just beyond the petals was a familiar butterfly with glorious goldenrod wings.

"A lone Yellow Gorgon," I breathed. There was a note inside, but I did not have to read it to know the name of my benefactor. The paper was heavily embossed with the Despard arms and the handwriting was an elegant swirl of grey ink.

My dear Miss Speedwell,

Seldom does one encounter another collector with such exquisite taste, and it seems entirely wrong that I should possess more than my share of these beauties when a lady who appreciates them with perhaps even more fervour should have none. Also, I heard with some dismay that you will no longer be presenting a paper before the Aurelian Society. I hope this small token of my esteem for your professional accomplishments may dull the edge of what I can only imagine to be a keenly felt disappointment. I assure you, whatever unhappiness your absence causes you, it will be nothing to my own.

Your devoted servant,
Lord Ambrose Despard

No sooner had I come to the end of this pretty missive than Stoker gave a roar of unmitigated delight. The larger crate, as I suspected, contained the pangolin. The dogs circled it, sniffing curiously. Stoker stared, eyes gleaming with the same expression I have observed in the faces of newly made fathers.

"Well, it seems Lord Ambrose was not as put off by our questions as I thought," I said.

"Indeed." Stoker roamed around the little animal. It was far smaller than many of the other beasts that had had occasion to populate Stoker's workshop. He had exercised his considerable skills upon Russian black bears, American bison, and even—on one remarkable occasion—an African elephant. But the size of these impressive creatures could not compete with the winsome charm of this specimen. His expression was frankly comical, the wide eyes being set at such a quizzical angle, it lent him the air of a curious and slightly worried Pierrot. In spite of its armature, its figure was not calculated to strike terror into the hearts of men. It was too modest in size, too oddly proportioned with its broad tail. One could easily imagine him rolling about as he assumed a defensive posture, short, stubby legs and pointed snoot tucked carefully away from view.

"I have seldom beheld a mammal so interesting," I said. It was almost enough to make me give up lepidoptery altogether. Almost. I returned to my elegant Gorgon, gloating a little as I set him in a place of honour. He hovered over my desk, arrested in perpetual flight, a glowing beacon of perfection. It was a rare pleasure to keep a butterfly for myself. I seldom retained my trophies, even those I reared myself in the vivarium Lord Rosemorran had established for my use. Rather than hunting in the field, I restricted my efforts to breeding various species in this hothouse environment, only mounting them once they had perished from natural causes. They were then sold on to collectors, providing a healthy supplement to my income from his lordship who would not even accept a peppercorn rent for the use of his glasshouse.

His lordship's generosity in this—and in so many other matters—meant that I seldom refused him when he asked a favour. That afternoon he requested we entertain Lady Rose as the governess had tendered her resignation that morning after her wayward charge had seen fit to pillage the governess's dressing table in search of accoutrements for the tamarin. Lady Rose arrived bearing the little monkey, who looked decidedly harried. A multitude of tiny satin bows had been tied into its hair, it positively reeked of perfume, and it bore a streak of dull white along its back.

"Lady Rose," I inquired with determined cordiality, "did you *powder* the tamarin?"

"Of course," she said offhandedly. She had just helped herself to a piece of cake from the tea tray and spoke through a mouthful of crumbs.

"For what purpose?" I asked.

"Miss Fforde said she smelt. I thought she might withdraw her objections to keeping her in the nursery if she weren't so noisome. I tried to give her a bath but she didn't much care for that. She did something nasty in Miss Fforde's bed, and Miss Fforde was *most* upset. She packed her bags before luncheon." I unravelled this tangle of pronouns to understand that it was Miss Fforde, the governess, who had objected to the odiferous little pet and the monkey who had protested at having a bath. In any event, another governess had been cowed by the Beauclerk establishment—this one before I had even made her acquaintance.

"No, I imagine the tamarin would not care to be bathed. Monkeys do not, as a rule, disport themselves in water," I told Lady Rose.

Stoker raised a finger in protest. "The Japanese macaque—*Macaca fuscata*—has been known to bathe in the hot springs in the cooler climate of the uplands."

Lady Rose gave me a triumphant look. The child was rather too quick to enjoy any error or omission on my part. "Well," I said smoothing my skirts, "then they are the exception that prove the rule. Have more cake, Lady Rose" I insisted, thrusting another slice towards her. With another child I might have feared instilling habits of overindulgence and perhaps bringing on a bout of indigestion, but Lady Rose had the dilatory powers of an anaconda and the cast-iron insides of a steam engine.

When she had finished her tea, Stoker mercifully took her off my hands to introduce her to the pangolin whilst I applied myself once more to my correspondence. The tamarin, perceiving Lady Rose's distraction, took the opportunity to slip away to the snuggery by means of brachiation. I watched it a moment, admiring its nimble ways, and feeling a certain softening of my sentiments toward the creature until I discovered the small deposit of excreta it had seen fit to leave behind on my favourite hat.

Between the cleaning of the hat, finishing my letters, labelling a case of rosy maple moths—*Dryocampa rubicunda* is an exuberant little moth with unlikely pink and yellow colouring—and penning a handsome note of thanks to Lord Ambrose, the afternoon passed away quickly. Lady Rose was soon handed off to the ministrations of her aunt, Lady Cordelia, who remonstrated firmly with her about the resignation of this latest governess, and who refused to be moved by the child's tears when the tamarin eluded her attempts at retrieval.

"I think," Lady Cordelia said in tones that were dry and kind in equal measure, "we ought to give up the notion of keeping a monkey in the house. She is not yours, after all." Lady C. turned to us. "I am selling tickets for the event at the Curiosity Club," she told us, invoking the name of the establishment where women of ideas and daring gathered to exchange thoughts, celebrate one another's accomplishments, and rest from the obligations of domesticity.

"What event?" Stoker inquired, darting a nervous eye to the railing of the snuggery where the tamarin was perched, watching his every move with a beady sort of possessiveness.

"An evening of tableaux vivants," Lady Cordelia said, and I suppressed a groan. Tableaux vivants had been at the zenith of their popularity in the middle of the century, but had fallen from favour as more exciting modes of entertainment had been invented. There was little thrill to be had in staring at ordinary people garbed as figures from literature and assuming stiffly theatrical postures. I had often been keenly aware of the urge to stick one with a pin just to see what would happen.

Lady C. went on. "It is to benefit the fund that underwrites the studies of talented but impoverished young women. It shall be scenes from antiquity—the Bible, mythology, and so forth. We have a particularly fine set of Greek heroes for the siege of Troy. Surely you will both come? Tickets are eleven shillings, ninepence."

"To watch some poor devil stand around, shivering in his underwear?" Stoker demanded. "Thank you, but I am afraid I must decline. I am already engaged that evening."

"I haven't told you when it is," Lady C. replied coldly. "Upon which evening are you engaged?"

Stoker grinned. "All of them."

She sighed and turned to me, but I shook my head. "I am happy to contribute to the cause, but we have undertaken a new endeavour which I fear will keep us otherwise occupied for the foreseeable future," I advised her.

Lady Rose had taken advantage of her aunt's inattention to attempt to scale the nearest caryatid with an eye to snatching the tamarin. At the last moment, Lady Cordelia reached up and plucked the child down, setting the girl on her feet with a finality that brooked no opposition. "I said *no monkeys*," Lady C. told her with a firmness I had never heard.

Lady Rose reared back in surprise. Lady C.'s newfound resolve must have startled her, for she went with her aunt quietly enough, and after a hasty dinner, I instructed Stoker to make himself a trifle more presentable—mostly through the application of soap and water to remove the considerable filth that adorned his person. Sawdust, glue, ink, excelsior, cotton—these are merely a few of the substances I noticed had left their mark upon his clothing and hands.

"You needn't dress formally, but clean raiment is desirable," I told him.

"Why?" he demanded. "What tortures have you planned for me?"

"I have invited guests to come and drink wine with us," I told him. And when I told him the names, he groaned by way of response.

"J. J. I can just about bear, but *Mornaday*." He groaned again.

J. J. Butterworth was a lady reporter of our acquaintance. Intrepid and enterprising, she was one of the few females I counted as a friend, although the relationship could be decidedly prickly. J. J. knew the truth of my parentage and had not revealed it in the pages of the gutter publication for which she wrote, but I harboured a fear—unjust, I suspected— that the day might dawn when her ambition would overrule her affection and my identity would be broadcast far and wide. After all, revealing the existence of the Prince of Wales's semi-legitimate daughter would be the story of the century. But J. J. had proven herself loyal thus far, and I found myself growing increasingly fond of her.

Mornaday was a cat of a different colour. Dogged and very nearly clever, he was employed by Special Branch of Scotland Yard as a detective inspector. He had excellent powers of recall and a merry disposition, but he was rather too inclined to speak his mind to his superiors. The head of Special Branch, Sir Hugo Montgomerie, tolerated and occasionally even indulged him, but few others in the Metropolitan Police force were as motivated to favour him. Both of them, J. J. and Mornaday, thirsted for recognition. They shared an almost palpable ambition and it was a source of considerable irritation to me that they had never made a match of it—not least because it would prevent Mornaday's outrageous flirtations with me and cure J. J. of her occasional tendency to make cow's eyes at Stoker.

At my insistence, Stoker took himself off to make his ablutions and when he returned, his hair waving damply about his collar and his fingernails scrupulously white, it was at the precise moment that J. J. and Mornaday appeared.

I greeted them cordially, and Stoker poured a delicate Sauternes we had been given by a grateful client. There was even a plate of wine biscuits to be offered, and whilst Mornaday took one with relish, J. J. regarded us over the rim of her glass.

"You want something," she said flatly.

"The company of our friends," I said with a smile.

Mornaday raised his glass. "Hear, hear." He drained it with gusto and held it out for more.

"My god, man, it is a wine meant for sipping, not guzzling as if you were at the Portly Pug in Shoreditch," Stoker remonstrated. But he poured, and Mornaday took it, sipping with an ostentatiously raised little finger.

"Better, your lordship?" he asked in a voice thick with sarcasm. "I forget how much of an aristocratic prig you can be."

"And I forget how much of a tiresome son of a—"

I held up my hand. "Gentlemen. Let us not quarrel. J. J., do tell us how you got on at the asylum. You have returned to London rather earlier than expected, and I have seen nothing of your story in the newspaper."

J. J. had, upon the conclusion of our last investigation, been admitted at her own instigation to a facility for the care of demented ladies. She had been inspired by Nellie Bly, whose own incarceration in such a place had brought considerable acclaim. Bly had written frankly of the horrors such women faced at the hands of their attendants. Doused with icy water, deprived of food and drink, physically mistreated, and confined to their beds by means of restraint whilst rats and other vermin made free with their persons—it was unthinkable. The circumstances, harrowing enough for those deprived of their senses, were compounded by the frankly criminal practice of perfectly sane women being committed by their own relations solely for the purpose of keeping them out of the way. Bly had done much to draw attention to the abuses found in these establishments in America, and J. J. had thought to follow in her worthy footsteps. With the aid of Stoker's eldest brother, she had spent a fortnight locked inside an institution in Devon.

J. J. put down her biscuit, or at least the pieces of it. She had reduced it to crumbs with the force of her grip. "It will not be published."

"Not this week?" Stoker asked kindly.

"Never," she replied, her usually attractive features settled into a grim mask. "I cannot write it."

"Whyever not?" I pressed. "Are the conditions at Milverton House so dreadful that you cannot put them into print? Is the British reader so much more delicate than the American that they cannot be exposed to bitter truths?"

"There *are* no bitter truths," she said irritably. "The facility is situated in the lea of a pretty valley, with grounds as neatly kept as any gentleman's country seat. The house itself is fitted with every comfort to ensure privacy and solace. The food is wholesome and good. The prescribed treatments are rest and the refreshment of enticing views. The women are encouraged to paint or sing or do needlework, and whatever their chosen occupation, they are provided with all necessary supplies. Improving literature is stocked in the library, and musicians are engaged to come once a week to hold concerts of pleasant music so the patients may be inspired to calmness and good cheer. The physicians are attentive and kind, and not a single woman there was held against her will. In short, the facility is a marvel of humane treatment and consideration," she added gloomily.

Stoker handed her a fresh biscuit. "Surely that is a good thing?" he suggested gently.

"Of course it is," she acknowledged with a sigh. "But it doesn't do me a bit of good, does it? I planned a piece so extraordinary, it would expose the maltreatment of the insane and garner me a place in the history of journalism. Instead, I have learnt to paint watercolours and play a tolerable hand of whist. Worse still, I returned with considerably refreshed spirits and a liking for handwork. I very nearly knitted last week. It is not to be borne."

I turned from her morbid visage to Mornaday's equally downcast one. "Tell us something cheerful," I urged. "How are things at the Yard?"

"Things?" He downed his second glass of wine as swiftly as the first.

"Things are not good, Veronica. Not at all good. Sir Hugo is gone to Bath for his health due to a particularly nasty bout of gout."

"Bath! No one has gone to Bath for gout in half a century," J. J. protested.

"Well, Sir Hugo has, and I am left at the mercy of his second, a man whose smallness of mind is equal only to the vigour with which he persecutes me. I shall count myself lucky if I am still employed this time next week."

"Well, you are a pretty pair," I told them with a touch of asperity. "But perhaps you will be diverted by our little conundrum. We have a puzzle for you."

Mornaday covered his face with his hands whilst J. J. gave me a level look. "I swear before the almighty god, Veronica, if this is another of your ridiculous and outlandish investigations—" she began.

"Oh, nothing like that," I put in hastily. "It is just that we seem to have acquired a body."

Mornaday peeped through his fingers, clearly intrigued in spite of himself. "A body?"

"Whose body?" J. J. demanded.

"That is what we were hoping you could help us discover," Stoker said.

"But *how*?" J. J. asked. "How does one simply acquire a body?"

"Ours was purchased at auction," I told her.

Mornaday groaned again, and Stoker passed him the decanter as I rose.

"Come along," I said briskly. "Let us introduce you to the Beauty."

CHAPTER

11

It was the work of a few minutes to uncover the casket and arrange proper lighting, but when we had done, J.J. and Mornaday came near, mouths agape. Suddenly, Mornaday reared back as if burnt.

"You said you had a body," he accused. "That is a waxwork." He continued to move backwards as he spoke until his back hit the wall, slightly upsetting the suit of mediaeval German armour as he did so.

"You don't care for waxworks?" I inquired.

"I do not," he stated roundly. His face had gone quite pale and tiny beads of sweat pearled his hairline. "They are unnatural, they are. Looking a bloody sight too real for my comfort."

J. J. grinned. "So we shall not find you whiling away a rainy afternoon in the waxen amusements at Madame Tussaud's?"

Mornaday swore fluently but had the courtesy to do so under his breath. He swayed a little, and I put my hand to the back of his neck, shoving his head between his knees.

"Breathe," I commanded. "Slowly and through the nostrils. Exhale at the same pace through lightly parted lips until the giddiness passes."

He nodded and did as I instructed.

J. J. shot us a look of annoyance. "It is a low trick to promise us something as interesting as a body only to present us with a waxwork."

"But she isn't wax," I said. I turned to Mornaday. "Do not distress yourself. She is a human corpse, I promise you."

He brightened. "Is she indeed?"

"I have performed a rudimentary postmortem," Stoker put in. "She is entirely human—or at least she was once. What remains has been heavily tampered with."

"I shall pretend I did not hear you confess to an illegal act," Mornaday said dryly.

Mornaday, slightly more accustomed to dealing with the dead than J. J. circled the figure, scrutinising her closely whilst J. J. demanded information. Every detail must be answered—how, why, where, when. Stoker and I answered to our ability, having already established the who was unknown. The story was swiftly told and although J. J. questioned and cross-questioned every particular, there simply was not much detail to be related, only the fact of her pregnancy and our theory as to her employment as a maid-of-all-work.

"Extraordinary," J. J. said at last. Her eyes were bright, and her hair, never tidy at the best of times, had begun to make a concerted attempt to escape its pins. Her colour had risen, and I was pleased to see the change our challenge had wrought in her demeanour.

"She wasn't half-lovely, was she?" Mornaday asked no one in particular.

"A little respect," Stoker warned him. "Or I will see you have a proper burial before she does."

Mornaday bristled a little. His relationship with Stoker had begun in hostility and settled into a gentle state of armed neutrality with occasional outbreaks of bellicosity. There were rare moments of real amity between them, but this was clearly not to be one of them.

"I am simply saying, she was a young lady blessed with considerable charms," Mornaday protested.

Stoker said nothing but continued to watch him with a wary expression. J. J. was scrutinising the Beauty from top to toe. "What do we think? Eighteen years old or thereabouts?"

"Something like that," I agreed. "No older than twenty, I should think."

She peered at the hands. "I see the calluses and the scar, but there is a strange quality to the fingers," she pointed out.

Stoker nodded. "It seems as if whoever preserved her like this put considerable effort into the face and hands. The flesh seems plumper there, somehow."

Mornaday shuddered. "I cannot endure it. Do not speak of the wax, I beg you."

J. J. turned to him. "You are a singularly odd creature, Mornaday, that you can more easily bear the sight of a dead woman than countenance the fact that she has been dipped in a bit of paraffin."

"Hardly paraffin," Stoker corrected. "If she were, she would go up like a Roman candle near a flame. I think it a different substance, although I am not altogether certain what. It seems a complicated formulation based in beeswax, perhaps."

J. J. was thoughtful. "Have you ever seen anything like it before? With Egyptians, perhaps?"

Stoker shook his head. "Egyptians removed the internal organs and dried the flesh by burying the body in natron salts. It was preservation by desiccation. This is something entirely different. The nearest thing that resembles this is a form of Spanish mummification I've read of."

J. J. looked thoroughly intrigued. "How was it done?"

"Most likely via reserving solutions circulated through the capillary system. Later, any voids in the body, say spaces in the abdominal cavity, are filled with wax, and the entire body is later enrobed in wax. That seems a likely starting point for this job," he said, nodding towards the Beauty, "but I cannot imagine how the person responsible for this was able to retain the organs. The rates of decomposition would dictate—"

Mornaday held up a hand, his complexion faintly green. "No more. I beg you. But answer me this: Do you know anyone capable of that sort of work?" he asked with a gesture in the Beauty's direction.

Stoker furrowed his brow a moment, then shook his head. "No. It is an exceedingly complicated procedure."

"Not the sort of thing you could do?" Mornaday asked with narrowed eyes.

"Are you accusing me of something?" Stoker asked in a deceptively quiet voice.

"I was simply *wondering—*"

"Well, you clearly haven't the skill for it, so don't tax yourself," Stoker returned.

"Now, see here—" Mornaday was clearly squaring up for a fight, and Stoker drew himself up, nostrils flaring.

"Oh, do shut up," I told them. "Stoker, Mornaday does not really think you are responsible. Do you, Mornaday?" I asked him in a governess's tone.

He looked as if he would have liked to continue tweaking Stoker, but one glance at my arched brow and he dropped his gaze to his shoes. "I suppose not."

"To answer the gist of your question," I went on, "most natural historians are familiar with the general principles of preservation. Lepidopterists have no need for such procedures, but almost every other branch of science—zoology, anatomy, et cetera—requires specimens that have been treated with formalin or other such chemicals. This is far and away beyond that."

I looked to Stoker, who joined the conversation with a sigh. "As I was saying, the internal organs present unique challenges, particularly those involved in digestion. With circulation, everything in the human body works on proper cycles, filtering out impure matter. But as soon as death occurs, the various systems shut down. Undigested food and other waste material, cooling blood, unfiltered urine—all of it sits, stewing away. And without the fresh blood to bring oxygen to the tissues, everything becomes so much rancid meat, a study in decay. From the moment of death, it is a race against time to preserve any semblance of life, of wholesome tissues."

"Fascinating," J. J. murmured whilst Mornaday looked greener than ever.

"So who is she?" Mornaday asked. "And why have you shown her to us?"

"Because we do not know her identity," I replied. "There is nothing to explain how she came to be in this state or who is responsible. And we thought, perhaps, the pair of you might be able to lend assistance."

Mornaday's brow shot heavenwards. "I don't believe it."

J. J. fairly crowed. "You are asking us for *help*. How many times have you resisted our efforts to assist you? How many times have you pushed us away when we wanted to work in partnership?"

"If you will recall," I replied icily, "I enlisted your help only last month at Cherboys."

J. J. snorted. "Only because I was already there and you thought you could use me to get information."

"Well, perhaps," I admitted.

"I want to know her name," Stoker said quietly. "And I want to see her buried properly. With dignity."

J. J.'s expression softened. "I cannot make a mockery of that," she said. "It is a noble motivation." She canted her head as she looked at me. "What is yours?"

"The same," I assured her. "But there is something else. She may have met with an accident. Or, in light of her pregnancy and facing disgrace, it is possible she took her own life. But we cannot rule out the possibility that she may have been murdered."

Mornaday brightened. "Indeed? Were there signs of violence upon her?"

"Not the kind you're thinking," Stoker told him flatly. He related the details of the rest of his examination as J. J. took out her notebook and a stub of pencil. She licked the tip and began scribbling as Stoker talked. When he had finished, she skimmed her gaze over the pages, her brow furrowing in concentration.

"No outward signs of violence, apart from the tiny haemorrhages in her eyes and lips, suggesting suffocation," she read back.

"Or drowning," Stoker added. "With what they have done to her lungs, it would be impossible to say if they were once full of water."

"What have they done to her lungs?" J. J. asked with a malicious look at Mornaday.

Stoker described the process in lurid detail, explaining that the organs of respiration had been pumped full of the preservatives that filled the rest of the body, giving even her machines of mortality the same waxen appearance as her exterior.

Mornaday groaned and dropped his head between his knees again.

"If you swoon, I shall write about it," J. J. promised.

"You would not *dare*," Mornaday said through gritted teeth.

J. J. and Stoker exchanged grins whilst I reached under my skirt for the flask strapped to my thigh. I poured out a tiny measure of the liquid inside and held it under Mornaday's nose. He reared back in protest, but I pinched his nose closed until his mouth opened, upon which I poured in the liquid and used the end of my forefinger to force his chin upwards. He swallowed involuntarily, then opened his mouth, gaping like a landed carp.

"Aguardiente," he rasped. He knew I always carried the potent liquor upon my person for just such occasions. There was nothing like this distillation of essence of sugarcane to clear the nasal passages and stiffen the resolve.

He blinked several times in rapid succession. "I see stars."

"It will pass," I promised. I turned to the others. "Do stop tormenting Mornaday. He cannot help his aversion to wax dolls."

J. J. snorted and Stoker smothered a smile.

"It is not *dolls* I take issue with," Mornaday protested. "But there is
something distinctly uncanny about that," he finished, pointing at the
Beauty.

"She still deserves a proper burial," I reminded him.

"And justice," Stoker put in.

Mornaday retrieved a spotted handkerchief from his pocket and
ran it over his damp brow. "Why have you not reported this to the police? Properly, I mean," he said. "You would never have summoned us
here if you hadn't meant for it to be off the official record."

Stoker and I exchanged glances. "It is Lord Rosemorran," I explained.
"He is fearful of any potential scandal." I glanced narrowly at J. J., who
batted her lashes in feigned innocence.

"I would never abuse his lordship's good nature," she promised. "So
long as I have the exclusive on the story, I will keep the Beauclerk name
out of it."

We turned to Mornaday who was wearing a thoughtful expression.
"And if there was indeed foul play involved and we find the villain responsible?"

"Then the arrest as well as the full credit for the investigation is
yours," I said.

He grinned. "All right then, let us take this thing from the beginning. We must work from the smallest circumstance to the widest."

"Meaning?" J. J. demanded.

"Meaning, we begin with the body. Stoker has made certain observations which are not conclusions, but which are suggestive. We have a
young woman bearing signs of domestic service—and not at the highest level. This was no lady's maid or governess, judging by her hands. But

neither was she born to the lower orders. Her features are too refined for her to have come from the workhouse or the gutter."

"You cannot be certain of that," Stoker protested. "Darwin himself in his studies on physiognomy—"

Mornaday made a gesture as if strangling himself with a hangman's noose. "Have over with your theories, man! I am telling you, this was no prostitute or beggar girl. You can infer as much from her bone structure."

"You bloody well cannot," Stoker retorted.

I held up a hand. "We can at least agree that she worked for her bread. Her body bears the signs of her labour. And we can further agree she was most definitely not gentry," I added.

J. J. was quick to catch my meaning. "Because if she had been from that sort of family, her disappearance would have been noted far and wide."

Mornaday nodded. "Exactly. At some point this young woman vanished. Someone must have missed her. If her family were highly placed, the story would have become a cause célèbre."

"But if she had been turned out of service for an illegitimate pregnancy, who would have noticed? Or cared?" J. J. asked. It was a sobering thought, but not an uncommon story. A slip, the threat of a scandal, and a girl's life over before it had truly begun.

Mornaday stroked his chin. "Is there any indication of when she died? How long ago this may have been done to her?"

Stoker shook his head. "Without knowing the particulars of the process, I cannot begin to hazard a guess. All I can tell you is there is no strong smell of preservatives, which suggests the processes were not completed recently."

"And there is no indication given to his lordship of how long the casket had been in the warehouse?" Mornaday pressed.

"No," I told him. "But I conclude it must have been a few years at least. The casket had apparently been in the warehouse for some time before the payments fell into arrears and Mrs. Raby felt obliged to sell it on."

"Well, that's a beginning," Mornaday said. "So, we are looking for a young woman who most likely disappeared at least two years ago, but likely some time longer."

"If her employers turned her out, they would not have reported her missing, but perhaps she had friends who asked questions," J. J. said thoughtfully. "Mornaday, will you look in the archives?"

Mornaday groaned. "I suppose, but do not think it is a small thing you ask of me. The archives are not easily accessible, you know. They are located in a series of warehouses along the river, each damper and more dismal than the last. And there are rats."

J. J. flashed him a rare and radiant smile. "I believe you are more than equal to any challenge presented by a rodent," she assured him.

He was not mollified. "They smell of mould and despair," he grumbled.

"But they may hold a clue to the identity of our Beauty," I reminded him. "Besides, J. J. has archives of her own to search."

J. J. blinked. "I beg your pardon?"

I offered my most winsome smile, a perfect parody of the one she had just given Mornaday. "The *Daily Harbinger* has archives of its own, has it not? And surely newspaper archives are just as rich a mine of information as those of the Metropolitan Police."

"But they are also in warehouses," she said feebly. "In Rotherhithe. With mildew. And black beetles."

"Then neither of you shall have an advantage over the other," I said happily. "And if Mornaday is more than a match for a rat, I have no doubt you are more than woman enough to triumph over a black beetle." She whimpered in response, and Mornaday gave her a look of pure triumph.

"Touché," J. J. muttered.

They left us soon after, and Stoker turned to me with a knowing glance. "You told them nothing of our friend Lord Ambrose."

"Do you suspect him of anything untoward?"

He shrugged. "He has an affinity for Anatomical Venuses, and he behaved with excessive peculiarity when I suggested the very possibility that a human might be preserved like a waxwork."

"But he sent us such charming gifts!" I protested.

"He sent you a gift," Stoker replied. "He sent me a commission—one I clearly wanted. Together, those have the hallmarks of a man bent upon keeping us thinking well of him."

"Which is how most human beings conduct themselves," I reminded him. "Not everyone shares your tendency to scorn the company of others."

"Scorn the company of others! Thanks to you, I speak to entirely too many people, entirely too often."

"Exactly. You were practically a hermit when I met you."

"I was not a hermit," he said through gritted teeth. "I was a professional man with work that I was actually permitted to do rather than being dragged into murder investigations because I had not yet met a woman whose very raison d'être seems to be falling over dead bodies."

"That is hardly fair. This one," I said with a nod towards the Beauty, "was none of my doing." He muttered a few profanities which I chose to overlook. I went on. "I still do not agree with your assessment of Lord Ambrose. He is eccentric and a little shy. I think perhaps he has been disappointed in love."

Stoker stared at me in disbelief. "You cannot be serious. There is no possible way for you to have inferred that from the time we spent with him."

"Of course there is," I replied coolly. "I have a scientific mind, which means I have applied observation and logic to the situation. He is an attractive and wealthy man of refined tastes and good fortune. He has amassed a collection of beautiful female figures, in wax, alabaster, stone. Everywhere you look in his house, you are met with feminine beauty. He surrounds himself with it in art because he does not have the pleasure of experiencing it in life."

"That is the most preposterous load of plangent poppycock I have ever heard."

I grinned at him. "Care to wager on the matter?" Stoker and I had a long tradition of wagering a guinea on various subjects, often the outcome of our investigations, but sometimes over matters as inconsequential as the weather.

"Very well. I say Lord Ambrose is harbouring some nefarious secret."

"And I say he is a gentle soul with some tragedy in his past which haunts him still." I put out my hand. "The wager is struck. Shake on it?"

He moved past my outstretched hand to slide an arm around my waist.

"I have another idea." He dipped his head to my ear, murmuring details of that idea in a delicious whisper.

"Very well," I said in a hoarse voice. "You fetch the feathers, and I will join you as soon as I have warmed the oil."

In the end, I was forced to agree that Stoker's idea was a much more satisfactory means of sealing a wager than a handshake. Much more satisfactory indeed.

CHAPTER

12

O f necessity, some days passed before we heard news from either of our would-be colleagues. J. J. had been assigned a story about an outbreak of influenza in Poland, and Mornaday, in retaliation for some perceived slight by his acting superior, was relegated to copying reports. As for Stoker and myself, we covered up the Beauty once more and turned our attentions to the work at hand. I was involved in cleaning and remounting a particularly valuable set of *Papilio aristodemus*—I had a soft spot for Schaus' swallowtails as they have the rare ability to fly backwards to elude predators—whilst Stoker applied himself to the restoration of a great horned owl. It was not an especially remarkable specimen, but the pose was interesting enough to make the work a challenge. It had been mounted in flight, the wings fully outstretched into the full width of the four-and-a-half-foot span.

At last, it was Mornaday who turned up trumps. He scribbled a note with a scant few lines:

Body of a young woman, aged approximately eighteen years, pulled from Regent's Canal. No identifying marks

and never claimed. Taken to Plumtree and Son Mortuary.
February 1873.

I stared at the note, frowning. "1873. Surely that cannot be our Beauty."

Stoker, streaked with glue, the odd feather tucked in his hair, shrugged. "It is possible."

"Fifteen years! I hardly think so," I protested. "She is in exquisite condition for a corpse of that age."

"Drowning produces little immediate disfiguration. If she were pulled from the canal quickly after death and the process of preservation begun at once, it is just possible. Particularly as the method used upon the Beauty is so singular. She was fixed in an attitude of life by an artist's hand with the brain of a scientist. He has employed techniques of which I was entirely unaware, and I am in the business of restoration," he reminded me with a gesture towards the completed owl.

"I suppose," I said reluctantly. "At least we have a clue in the name of the mortuary, albeit a slender one."

"So slender as to be nearly invisible," Stoker replied. His expression was sombre, and I did not care for this solemnity. I longed for him to be surging once more with vitality, eyes agleam with the fire of the chase. And I vowed then to do whatever necessary to see that he was restored to his customary high spirits.

"Do you know this firm?" I studied the few lines again. "Plumtree and Son?"

He shook his head. "Never heard of them, but there are hundreds of small establishments in London. They mayn't even be in business after a decade and a half."

"We shall soon see," I said with an air of perfect decisiveness. "Conclude your intrusions upon that *Bubo virginianus* for now, my love.

Tomorrow morning we shall take ourselves off to call upon the good Mr. Plumtree and his son. And if they have knowledge of our Beauty, we shall discover it."

I dressed for the visit in my smartest town ensemble, a well-cut affair of blue silk trimmed in astrakhan. The dressmaker had suggested a matching toque of astrakhan, but I could not be dissuaded from a black velvet tam-o'-shanter with a modish pair of black and white spotted feathers. The weather was chill enough to require a cloak and muff, and it was with a sense of rising anticipation that I set out with Stoker on a jaunt from Marylebone to Chelsea. Mornaday had not provided the particulars, but a few inquiries had revealed the firm was still in trade at its original location and founded nearly thirty years before. It required little imagination to suppose the business had been established during the height of the mourning hysteria surrounding the death of Prince Albert. The loss of the queen's beloved consort had plunged the capital— nay, the country itself—into a paroxysm of public grief the likes of which the Empire had never seen before. Public buildings from Caithness to Canberra, from Prestonwick to Pondicherry, had been draped in black bunting. Mirrors were covered in crêpe and society figures in bombazine, every inch of fabric designed to dull the lustre of the living. The richest caparisoned their horses in ebony ostrich plumes whilst the poorest managed a scrap of black pinned to a sleeve in acknowledgement of the prince's passing. Even jewels were not spared, rubies and emeralds laid aside with the bright silks and sumptuous feathers in favour of jet and obsidian. Miniature portraits of the consort had done a roaring trade along with various mourning jewels and even imitations of his hair, curled into lockets and sold as genuine souvenirs to the gullible. Not a single sphere of public life, from the presentation of debutantes to the reception of ambassadors at the Court of St. James, was spared the weight of Victoria's grief.

But misfortune often brings opportunity to the bold, and a number of mercers and mortuaries had sprung up like mushrooms. The fashion for lavish mourning had taken hold, and those who were clever and quick had learnt to profit from it. Some even went so far as to rent the essential accoutrements of a fashionable funeral in order to satisfy expectations without sending a grieving family into insolvency. Full warehouses had been established for containing everything from casket palls to the apparel for mourning mutes, but it was apparent upon our arrival that Plumtree and Son was no such vast endeavour. The building stood in sober dignity on a quiet street suited to the sombreness of its purpose. The sign above the door was handsomely lettered but slightly faded, Time having clearly worked a little wear upon the edifice. The door cried out for a fresh coat of paint, and if the brass fittings could speak, they would have doubtless complained of being polished indifferently and infrequently. Whatever the circumstances of Plumtree and Son's establishment, however much it may have prospered to have built such an edifice in years past, it had clearly come down a little in the world, although its shabbiness was not so much off-putting as endearing, as when an old friend appears in a twice-turned frock.

We were admitted to the premises by a robust, harried-looking young man with an extremely pleasant bespectacled face and a demeanour of such bonhomie that one was put instantly in mind of a genial and shambling sheepdog.

"Do come in," he urged, ushering us into an interior office and shutting the door firmly behind us. "Only a little chill seems to be rising, and I do so hate to be cold." The atmosphere inside could best be described as sultry. The windows were firmly shut, each heavily curtained and fitted with draught extruders. The floors were covered in layers of carpets, and every door was hung with a set of portieres to keep out any particle of fresh air. In the corner, a fat iron stove was throwing off an extraordinary amount of heat. In spite of this, the young clerk—for such I supposed him to be since he had greeted us at the door—was wrapped in a series of shawls and mufflers, each one a different testimony to the knitter's art. Seed stitch, cable stitch, herringbone stitch—the garments had been fashioned with great care and dexterity, although I wagered from the young man's use of all, he favoured them more for warmth than the elegance of their designs.

He settled himself behind his desk, propping his feet upon a tiny brazier that smoked gently from the heap of coals inside. Stoker, who could never bear being cooped up when fresh air was to be had, gave a soft wheeze at the close atmosphere.

"How very cosy," I remarked with a smile.

The young fellow nodded. "Oh, yes. One can never be too careful of a draught, you know. Killing things, draughts."

"You ought to know," Stoker remarked.

The young man blinked behind his spectacles, as if considering whether to take offence, and I hurried to make amends. "My colleague merely means that in your line of work, one must be well acquainted with death."

"Oh, indeed!" he replied with a quick smile. He plied us then with hot tea and offered a selection of biscuits, each handsomely wrapped in crisp paper sealed with a wafer of black wax. "The seal features a memento mori," he pointed out. "A winged skull. Do you like them? I rather wondered if a cherub wouldn't have been nicer, but Mamma thought the skulls very smart."

"They are most appropriate," I assured him. Stoker had already unwrapped his and was sampling the biscuit inside.

"Caraway," he said in obvious approval. Stoker reached for another as our young host settled back into his chair, raising his feet to the brazier once more. "How can I help you today?" he inquired with all the expected solemnity of a gentleman in his profession.

"We wish to speak with Mr. Plumtree," I said. I handed over our calling cards. I carried both in a neat case in my reticule as Stoker could never be bothered to remember his, and even if he had, they would have been so begrimed and streaked with sweets and dirt from his pocket, they would never have been fit to offer.

"Or son, if Plumtree senior is not available," Stoker said, reaching for another funeral biscuit.

"Oh, I am sorry, but that is impossible," the clerk said.

"We ought to have written to make a formal appointment," I said by way of apology, "but the matter is of some urgency to us, and we require only a few minutes of either Plumtree's valuable time."

I added a winsome smile to which the young clerk responded with an audible gulp and a charming blush to the tips of his ears. "I am heartily sorry to disappoint you, Miss Speedwell. Sorrier than I can say! But I am afraid the Mr. Plumtree referenced on the sign is no more."

"And son?" I asked.

"Dead also," he told me.

"Then who," Stoker asked with exaggerated politeness, "are you?"

"Oh, I am a Plumtree, to be sure. Wilfred Plumtree, at your service," he added with a tiny bob of the head.

"But you are not a mortuary Plumtree?" I inquired.

"Not at all, although I hope to be," he said with some pride. "I am newly come from Kent—a pretty little village called Appleden. Perhaps you know it?" he asked with a hopeful expression.

"I am afraid I have not had the pleasure," I told him. "But then I have travelled only a little in Kent and am the poorer for not being well acquainted with its many beauties."

This seemed to please him, for his blush deepened, and he ventured a shy smile. "It is truly the loveliest corner of England, but the village is a small one, you understand. Very little scope for a man to make his way in the world. I did try," he added anxiously. "I read law. Only as it happens, I don't much care for it—the law, I mean. And even if I did, no one in Appleden has much need for a solicitor. I spent many a lonely hour in my rooms, waiting for clients whilst Mamma knitted in the corner. She's very careful of my health, is Mamma. I am an only child," he added with a self-effacing little gesture. "When I inherited my uncle's business, I came straightaway to London to seize the reins, as it were. Mamma did protest most vociferously, but I insisted." He looked frankly delighted at his own initiative, and I was not surprised. It was easy to imagine what he had been—a bored and rather lonely young man, overly cosseted by a domineering mother—but it was too soon to see what he might become. At least he had had the bottom to take up this opportunity, and I wished him joy of it.

"Do you mean to carry on the practice of undertaking?" Stoker asked.

"I do," young Plumtree said stoutly. "That is, I will, if I can bring myself to—"

He broke off, his complexion taking a faintly green tinge. It was not difficult to hazard a guess as to the source of his discomfort.

"Mr. Plumtree, are you a squeamish fellow?"

"I do not mind the selling of coffins or the arranging of services. I am happy to display the mercer's wares and choose the hymns, although my mother thinks it the most dreadful comedown for a man who has read law. I think in time it might make me happy if only I could get past . . . It is the dead," he said quietly. "I do not care for the *bodies*. They are uncanny, Miss Speedwell. When one is here alone, one can almost imagine them about to rise."

He took a deep draught of his tea and that seemed to settle his nerves.

"If you've no love for the trade, why not sell the business, man, and buy another? One you are more suited to?" Stoker demanded.

I darted him a repressive look, then turned to young Plumtree with sympathy. "I quite understand. I am a lepidopterist by trade. Handling dead things requires a steady hand and a steadier nerve. Perhaps you are simply too heavily blessed with imagination for this line of work."

Wilfred Plumtree brightened. "I suppose that is possible. Do you think I could learn to be less imaginative? To be a *steelier* sort of fellow?" He darted a look at Stoker, and I wished he had not. Stoker was, by any standards, a fine specimen of manhood, tall, broad of shoulder, and beautifully muscled. After insisting he dress the part to call upon Lord Ambrose, I had said nothing when he presented himself that particular morning attired in a variation on his work costume—stained suit, shirt open at the neck and missing its collar, cuffs grimed with ink and glue. Gold rings glinted in his ears, and his eyepatch was in evidence. The effect was one of almost aggressive masculinity, and I could easily discern young Plumtree was finding himself lacking in comparison. I was only grateful he could not see Stoker's tattoos.

But it occurred to me that the lad's longing to play a more heroic role might serve us well.

"I certainly think you capable of it," I told him without a flicker of remorse. "More than capable," I assured him. "But to do so, you must practice, Mr. Plumtree. Seek out some danger and test your mettle. Now, we have some questions regarding work that was done here some fifteen years ago. I realise you were a mere child at the time, in Kent, as you say. But perhaps there are records?"

He nodded. "Oh, yes. My uncle and his father kept extensive notes on all their clients. It is just that these papers are not as precisely ordered as one might hope. Follow me."

Taking up another muffler to wrap around his neck, he led the way across the corridor and into a suite of rooms packed to the ceilings with boxes. Each box was crammed with ledgers; papers spilled to the floor. Stoker groaned, but I quickly realised matters were not quite so bleak as they first appeared. Each box was marked with a year.

"Let us try 1873," I said promptly. To his credit, Wilfred Plumtree did not inquire why we wanted information or, indeed, even what information we required. He simply set to work finding the correct box and presented it to me with the air of a puppy dropping a favourite bone at the feet of its mistress.

"1873," he said happily. Stoker rummaged in the box, extracting a series of purple clothbound ledgers, each stamped with the device of a tree bearing fruits and the name of the firm. As he made his way swiftly through them, young Wilfred sneezed heavily, several times in succession, and I blessed him. "Thank you—the dust, you see. Mamma always says I should be careful of dust."

I noticed then that the modest effort required to carry the box had resulted in sweat dampening his hairline. "Mr. Plumtree, I do hope you will forgive the impertinence of so personal an observation, but would you not be more comfortable without quite so many layers? Perhaps three shawls are one too many?"

He blinked, as if encountering a possibility he had never before even suspected. "You mean leave off one of them?"

"Just to see if it suits you," I said.

With an air of great daring, he stripped off the outermost shawl. He drew a tentative breath, then pulled himself up to his full height. "It feels rather good, actually," he said in a tone of wonder. In rapid succession, he shed the other two shawls and one of the mufflers, exclaiming as he unwound each one at the lightness, the ability to breathe more freely. "Perhaps Mamma was wrong," he said in a tone heretics might once have used to utter small blasphemies.

I gifted him another smile, this one of sincere approbation. "You will make a man of yourself yet, young Plumtree," I assured him.

He fairly preened under the praise. "You are very kind, Miss Speedwell. I do not think I have ever met another lady quite like you."

"There are not many of us about," I explained.

Stoker interrupted us with a dry cough. "If the pair of you are quite finished approving of one another, I have found what we are looking for."

Young Plumtree and I turned as one with rapt expressions to listen to Stoker as he summarised the information within the ledger.

"This contains information on the first quarter of 1873. According to this, on the fourteenth of February, the Metropolitan Police retrieved the body of a young woman from Regent's Canal. With nothing to identify her, she was removed here with the understanding that Plumtree's would commission a death mask to be inserted into the appropriate newspapers along with pleas to the general public for information."

"Death mask?" I asked. "Surely a photograph would be more useful."

"Oh, photographs are never taken in such cases," Wilfred Plumtree said. "It is too upsetting for actual likenesses to be captured and displayed. Most undignified for the dead. I remember my uncle Plumtree speaking of it—only in general terms. Not with this young lady, of course, given the year. I was, as you say, a child still in Kent at the time."

"What became of the death mask?" I inquired.

Young Plumtree shrugged and looked to Stoker. "Is there a note on its whereabouts?"

Stoker skimmed the page, frowning. "Not that I can see. The handwriting is devilishly crabbed."

"What does it say about the disposition of the body itself?"

Stoker's frown deepened. "A series of numbers and letters following her entry."

He passed the ledger to Wilfred Plumtree who took it under scrutiny. "Why, she was buried. In Plumfield."

"Plumfield?" I queried.

"The small cemetery in Berkshire that was the exclusive burial ground for Plumtree's clients."

I felt a dart of irritation. Surely this was our Beauty! And yet if she were buried in Plumfield, how could it be? I looked up to find Stoker's expression echoing mine. The annoyance stirring in my breast surged at the resignation in his eyes. He was so bent upon securing justice for the Beauty that it was essential to chase every fox down every hole, I decided.

"Mr. Plumtree, we have trespassed entirely long enough upon both your time and your good nature," I began.

As I anticipated, the young man protested effusively, insisting it had been his great gratification to do so and that he considered the experience both unique and unexpected. He finished by saying that he could not do enough to assure us of his esteem.

"In that case," I said, laying a coaxing hand upon his arm, "perhaps you would be good enough to take us to the grave."

He blinked rapidly, his spectacles fogging from his exhalations. "It would be my acute pleasure, Miss Speedwell."

He led the way from the room, throwing off another of his shawls as he did so. The last one he wore with the rakish air of a privateer bent upon adventure, and any feeling I might have had of taking advantage of the fellow was swiftly smothered by the conviction that he was enjoying himself enormously. He guided us through various doorways and corridors and through rooms dedicated to the business of death. Two of the rooms were fully tiled, with drains in the floor that suggested nasty doings, and a wall of shelves held assorted implements of the funerary arts. Beyond these lay a doorway leading to a flight of steep stairs that gave on to a wide stone-arched cellar.

"Well done," Stoker murmured in my ear. "I think that puppy would follow you to the gates of Hell itself. Mind you don't choke him when you tug on his lead."

I had just shaped my mouth to issue a tart reply when the words stilled on my tongue. We stood in silence as young Plumtree opened an enormous steel door, wrenching it back upon its hinges. It gave way with a groan of ancient metal and a grinding that sounded almost reluctant. Beyond lay a short passage of such cobwebbed antiquity one might have been entering a tomb of a lesser pharaoh. Blackness beyond blackness stood before us, not a speck of cheerful light lessening the Stygian gloom.

"Gates of Hell indeed," I murmured. And I stepped forward to put my hand in his.

CHAPTER

13

My initial discomfiture intensified as Wilfred Plumtree lit a lantern and coaxed us into the darkness. Charon himself could not have asked for a more suitable setting, and I half expected to hear the rushing waters of the black-waved Styx as we moved beyond the feeble comfort of the mortuary cellar. The walls were lined with more shelves, these packed to the top with dusty glass jars of various chemicals and embalming fluids of some antiquity.

"What is this place?" I asked as my eyes became accustomed to the tenebrous passage. The lantern sent a brave circle of light, but it did little to penetrate the atmosphere beyond. I had a sense of an arching ceiling some distance overhead, but as to the width of the passage itself, I could not begin to imagine.

"It is the necropolis railway," Stoker exclaimed suddenly.

Young Plumtree turned back with an excited grin. "Indeed, it is, sir!"

"What is the necropolis railway?" I demanded.

"Precisely what it sounds," Stoker replied. I was happy to feel the sudden reassuring weight of his palm pressed to the small of my back as he explained. "It was established some thirty years ago to carry the dead to Brookwood Cemetery in Surrey."

"Not just the dead," Plumtree corrected. "Mourners as well. It was thought more convenient and discreet to establish a means of transporting those who have passed and those who grieve them to the cemetery without the vexations of modern travel or the curiosity of passersby. No crowded streets or prying onlookers. It offered the greatest privacy and discretion for mourners. It was a sound enough notion— so sound, in fact, that at one point a few other mortuaries decided to emulate the project. Plumtree's was the first, and this is the result."

He raised the lantern high enough to illuminate a narrow track laid upon the ground and resting on that track, a miniature train comprising a tiny engine and two small cars. One was just large enough to admit a coffin, the other fitted with two long benches to accommodate a party of mourners.

"Fascinating," I breathed.

"Not half so grand as the original necropolis railway, and even still, expensive enough almost to bankrupt the mortuary," Plumtree said ruefully. "My grandfather and uncle took a terrible gamble in building it. They believed if they could offer some service most other mortuaries could not, they would secure the lion's share of funereal custom. And since Brookwood is in Surrey, they thought an opposing effort in Berkshire would be just the thing."

"And they were wrong?" I asked.

Young Plumtree nodded, the lantern light warming the lenses of his spectacles to oblique golden discs. "Exceptionally, comprehensively wrong. They forgot that the great and good of fashionable society are laid to rest in Highgate or at their country seats. Grandfather and Uncle Plumtree borrowed heavily to build the thing and would have lost the entire mortuary if it were not for a stroke of excellent luck."

"What luck was that?" I asked.

"Cholera," he replied with good cheer. "An epidemic is just the thing for rescuing the fortunes of a failing mortuary. In the case of Plumtree's, it kept the creditors from the door although the railway itself was shuttered after only a year or two. It is largely in disrepair, but I find it a perfectly acceptable means of making the journey to Plumfield swiftly. Although," he paused, surveying my smart town costume, "forgive me, Miss Speedwell, it has only just occurred to me that you might find such a mode of transportation incommodious."

I squared my shoulders and pushed him gently aside as I mounted the first car. "I assure you, nothing could be further from the truth, young Plumtree. I am a friend to Adventure and embrace her whenever I am able."

He stared after me in a sort of stupor until Stoker gave him a nudge. He recollected himself with a start and relayed a series of instructions to Stoker to help him fire the tiny engine. Together they built a blaze, warming the little machine until smoke bellowed forth and the miniature wheels began to turn, slowly and with a groan of protest at first, then faster as we drew away from the door of Plumtree's and set off into the impenetrable gloom of the tunnel beyond.

The trip was as short as Plumtree described. Not a quarter of an hour passed between our departure and the arrival at Plumfield. The air was filthy, bestowing soots and smuts upon our persons, but the novelty of the experience was unparalleled. The ground trembled beneath us which I first attributed to the slapdash condition of the little train. But after the second interlude of roaring and shaking, I realised the tunnel we were using ran quite near those of the Underground itself. Trains must have run beside us, below, above, for the sounds came from all directions. A more fanciful woman than I might have imagined we were travelling in the realm of dragons for all the thunderous upheaval. With each fresh assault on our senses, the walls shuddered, shedding clouds of brick dust which further befouled the atmosphere. It was an unholy, anarchic trip, and I was not surprised to see Stoker smiling in the gloom.

I leapt from the car, shaking out my skirts and grinning broadly. Plumtree himself seemed to have benefitted from the drive, for his pale complexion was now blooming, and his stooped shoulders, once huddled into his shawls like an old woman's, were thrown back in a posture of confidence. There was a man of action waiting patiently beneath the guise of a scholarly undertaker, I surmised. Further time spent with Stoker would only serve to encourage such intrepidness, and I made up my mind to invite the young man to dine with us once our investigation was concluded.

At the thought of the conundrum before us, I felt my spirits flag. I had been so convinced that the answer to the Beauty's identity lay within the walls of Plumtree's! The timing of the anonymous maiden pulled from Regent's Canal had fitted so exactly our needs, it seemed extravagant of Fate to have provided us with more corpses than we required. Once we had confirmed the burial of the unfortunate taken from the Canal, we would have to start over—this time with even less intelligence than we had enjoyed before. But this was no time to wallow in recrimination, I told myself firmly. Stoker and I would begin again, as we always had after difficulty. This was not the first time we had encountered disappointment, a trifling setback that would render our ultimate victory all the sweeter.

With renewed determination, we made our way out of the railway tunnel and into a sort of miniature station, a small stone edifice just large enough to permit the arranging of coffin and mourners into a procession before moving into the cemetery itself. From this shadowy little anteroom we passed into the watery afternoon light. The chill breeze that had been so concerning to young Plumtree in London was a brisk wind here, but he seemed entirely unbothered. He bounded ahead like a hound after a hare.

The cemetery itself was well-proportioned and must have been handsome when first laid out. It was not as large as Highgate but had been designed to make the most of its natural beauties. A little rockery had been left to form a view, as had a pretty river meadow. It was in this direction that Plumtree led us, through the narrow avenues of the graves. Only some looked regularly tended, and the grass of the paths was in need of mowing. Elsewhere, tired foliage had withered on leggy stems, and the wind plucked away the leaves, sending them scudding amidst the weathering gravestones. There were no grand monuments here, only a few tasteful crypts with little embellishment. Unlike the fancies at Highgate, Plumfield boasted no pyramids and only a single modest obelisk. There was not a pleurant to be found, no sign of those elegant, anonymous weeping sculptures nor any of the more florid bawling cherubs that had been so fashionable for the past thirty years. But each stone bore a heavy coat of moss, weeds grew amongst the gravel of the main avenue, and the whole effect was one of melancholy and neglect.

With an exclamation of disbelief, young Plumtree pulled up sharply. "It cannot be," he said, scratching his head in puzzlement.

"What is it?" Stoker came to stand next to him, looking where Plumtree pointed towards the edge of the graveyard.

"That is the plot listed in the ledger for the burial of the unknown lady," he explained. "But nothing is buried there."

My pulses quickened. "Are you certain?"

"Of course. Nothing *can* be buried there. That bit is adjacent to the river," he said, pointing to a narrow stream which bordered a lushly green strip of land. "It floods, you see, in the spring. It is a tributary of the Thames, and this area has never been properly drained. Grandfather didn't realise it when Plumfield was first laid out, and a rather important gentleman was buried there. A baronet," he added, sotto voce.

"Unfortunately, the next spring was dreadfully wet and—" He broke off, spreading his hands helplessly.

"You mean the grave was washed open," Stoker supplied.

Plumtree winced but nodded. "Yes. The coffin rose to the surface and burst. And it was frightfully poor timing as the widow had come to mark the first year of her mourning being finished, and she was the one to discover him in a state of . . . decay." He choked a little on the last word, and I did not entirely blame him. The scene must have been macabre indeed with the grieving widow confronted with the gruesome sight of her decomposing husband's corpse, floating gently in a puddle of rainwater.

Still, young Plumtree seemed singularly distressed, and I gave him a close look. "Forgive me, Mr. Plumtree, but perhaps Stoker is correct in suggesting another line of work. Are you *quite* certain about carrying on in this trade?"

"Oh, I am," he said with disarming cheerfulness. "At least I mean to try. You see, the only alternative is giving up the business and returning to Appleden to take up the practice of law once more. Mamma would be entirely delighted by that, but I am determined to be the master of my own fate, Miss Speedwell."

He raised his chin in what I think he must have supposed to be a noble expression. I clapped him heartily on the back. "Then you will doubtless succeed."

Stoker, who had been looking on in obvious amusement, cleared his throat. "And you are quite certain no one has been buried here since? An undesirable and unsellable plot would be a suitable place to bury an anonymous young lady whose family cannot be located to pay for the arrangements."

"Oh, no," Plumtree insisted. "Grandfather was so distressed by the experience with the baronet's corpse, he gave up the business altogether and left my uncle to the running of things. And my uncle was *most* particular that nothing of the sort should happen again. I did not recognise the numbers in the ledger—I am still learning all of the little aides-memoire my uncle employed—but standing here, I am thoroughly certain. Whatever the ledger says, the young woman pulled from Regent's Canal was most definitely not buried here."

I resisted the urge to whoop like a triumphant Viking shield maiden holding her gore-stained sword aloft. This was progress indeed, I reflected. My lowness of spirits upon reaching the cemetery had been banished in an instant with young Plumtree's revelation, and I resisted the urge to kiss him on the cheek.

"Mr. Plumtree, you have made me very happy indeed," I told him.

A crimson blush flamed his cheek and he ducked his head. "I am delighted to hear it." His expression grew puzzled again. "But I have neglected to ask, why are you so interested in the fate of this one unknown?"

I expected Stoker to dissemble. Instead, he astonished me by telling Plumtree the truth. "Because we believe she is currently in our possession."

"Possession?" Plumtree's gaze swung from Stoker to me and back again. "I do not understand."

"Simply this, Mr. Plumtree," Stoker said. "We have recently become custodians of a figure that appeared at first glance to be a waxwork. It is not. It is the corpse of a very real young woman that was preserved, very comprehensively preserved, by someone who knew exactly what he was doing."

The unorthodoxy of the situation was clearly too much for young Plumtree. He shook his head as if to clear it. "How did she come into your care?"

"It is a long and tedious story," I put in. "And not relevant to the matter at hand which is identifying the young woman and discovering if justice may be served in her demise."

"Justice? You think—you think she might have been *murdered*?" There was no one within half a mile of us, and yet this last word was issued in a thrilled whisper.

"It is possible," Stoker admitted. "But we do not know for certain. Our primary aim is to discover her identity and ensure a proper burial. At present, our only lead is the fact that her body appears to have passed through Plumtree's."

"In 1873," Plumtree finished.

"You must agree it is likely," I put in. "Surely there cannot be two such young women?"

"No, that would be too much a coincidence," he agreed. "I must admit, I am horrified to think that my family's firm might have had anything to do with such business."

But there was some new evasiveness in his manner. It was nothing obvious; no refusal to meet my gaze or reluctance to speak were in evidence. And yet I detected a sort of shrinking within him, a bone-deep dread that his relations may well indeed have got up to nefarious deeds.

On impulse, I laid a hand on his sleeve. A scalded cat could not have moved more swiftly, but I kept my fingers where they were. "Mr. Plumtree, it is nothing to your detriment if your uncle engaged in some underhanded undertaking."

His complexion, a brilliant rose pink only a moment before, paled. He swallowed hard, his Adam's apple bobbing along the column of his throat. "I confess, Miss Speedwell, I do not like to think it, but the men of my family have a sort of *laxity* with regard to what is moral. That is why my mother insisted upon bringing me up outside the sphere of their influence. She worried their weakness of character might encourage some deficiency of my own."

"I think she need not have worried on that score," I told him gently. "You are clearly a young man of great probity. And you could prove that by helping us now."

Stoker snorted, but said nothing, and young Plumtree nodded, as determined as Galahad himself to apply his might to that which was right. "Of course, Miss Speedwell. I will do anything in my power to aid your efforts to uncover this unfortunate's identity and see justice is served."

I patted his arm. "I knew we could depend upon you, Mr. Plumtree."

He blushed again, and Stoker cleared his throat before speaking. "I think another look at the firm's records is in order. The victim from the canal passed through Plumtree's, and for whatever purpose, your uncle saw fit to falsify the ledger and claim she was buried. So what happened to her after she left the Plumtree's premises, and why did they permit it?"

Young Plumtree nodded vigorously. "I will have a thorough search through all of the archives. There are other files, more private records, as well as my uncle's diaries. Perhaps some scrap of information may be found there."

I longed to search the files myself, but as if intuiting my thoughts, Stoker stepped in. "Thank you, Mr. Plumtree. Miss Speedwell and I have work of our own we must attend to, and your diligence will not be forgot."

He put out his hand, and young Plumtree shook it with an expression akin to awe. If he had been flattered by my attentions, it was nothing to the reverence with which he accepted Stoker's. It was hardly surprising. To a man of such youth and diffidence, Stoker must have presented the embodiment of all he longed to be. The notice and gratitude of such a man was no small thing.

We turned to make our way back to the city, and as we walked, I looped my arm through Stoker's. "A not altogether unsatisfactory outing," I murmured.

He grunted in agreement, and I went on. "Of course, you may be entirely incorrect in one particular." He raised his brows in silent inquiry. "You said she was preserved by someone who knew exactly what he was doing."

"That is not a point open to debate," he said assuredly. "The job was done with considerable knowledge and skill, far beyond my own."

"Oh, I will concede that point," I said with a gracious nod of the head. "But you have entirely overlooked one detail."

He stopped and turned to look at me until I met his gaze and smiled.

"It may have been a woman's work."

CHAPTER

14

The following afternoon, we were comfortably settled in the Belvedere, dogs snoring in a heap around us, the tiny tamarin—now wearing a ruffled bonnet and full petticoat—tucked under Stoker's arm as he took his tea. Upon our return from Plumtree's the day before, I had scribbled hasty notes to Mornaday and J. J. relating what we had learnt, but I expected it would be some days before we heard from either of them or young Wilfred. For the present, there was nothing more to do but enjoy a bit of refreshment and plot our next move.

"Veronica, I will not have it," Stoker said over the scones in a tone that brooked no argument. "I have considered your point and I will have no more murderesses. I think we have exceeded our quota of such unnatural creatures."

"Unnatural! What is more natural than death? It comes to us all," I reminded him as I poured. I handed Stoker his cup. "Women are as conversant with death as life," I said simply.

"But not usually the authoresses of it," he protested.

I gave him a knowing look. "You are being deliberately provocative. You, of all men, are too well acquainted with the deadliest examples of my sex to believe we are the gentle, peaceful angels of the hearth."

"Yes, that is precisely my point," he said, pausing to break off a piece of cake. He fed the titbit to the tamarin, and the monkey took it with the dainty grace of a duchess. "We have already met too many lady murderers. How many can there be? And if they are legion, then they are a bloody sight less likely to be caught than men. Women are too careful and too clever to be as easily apprehended, as we have known. Surely our experiences are unique."

I knew Stoker too well to believe him capable of any prejudices where the fairer sex is concerned. He had, through painful experience, come to understand that there is no creature on earth more dangerous than a desperate woman. The villainesses of our acquaintance had indeed proven themselves more than equal to any man, and I was just as reluctant as he to cross swords with another in the present.

"Still," I went on, "we must at least entertain all possibilities."

"We have nothing *but* possibilities to acknowledge in the absence of any real evidence," he grumbled. He fed more cake to the tamarin, who took it with delicately greedy paws.

I considered pointing out that fruit would be a more suitable addition to the creature's diet, but in the end I said nothing. Stoker was already beset by the glooms, and any constructive observations on my part might provoke an argument.

On the other hand, I considered, perhaps a good, healthful brawl was just the thing to rouse his temper and fire his blood.

"Stoker," I ventured calmly as I poured a fresh cup of tea, "I have given careful consideration to your thoughts on the contributions of Alfred Russel Wallace to Darwin's theories, and I think you are entirely mistaken."

As I had hoped, a rush of rage kindled his response. He sat forwards, upsetting the tamarin, who fled up the nearby mount of a giraffe, never stopping until it had reached the top, perching itself between the horns and peering out, chattering angrily down at us. I ignored it, and Stoker flung a piece of cake, which it caught neatly, leaving off its scolding to console itself with the sweet.

"Why in the name of seven hells would you even entertain such a notion?" Stoker demanded. "I have never heard such lunacy from an educated brain. There is no possible argument you could make which would persuade me that you seriously believe—" He broke off, colour high, chest rising and falling rapidly with the excess of emotion. "Because you do not. You are deliberately attempting to provoke me in order to amuse yourself."

"I am not," I replied. "I am attempting to provoke you in order to amuse *you*. You are prickly as an echidna these days, and I fear it will have a deleterious effect upon your health."

He lapsed back into his chair, picking at the crumbs on his plate. "I do not care," he said, staring at the outthrust tips of his boot toes. "I have little appetite for anything."

I looked pointedly at the empty plate. "For some things, perhaps," I murmured. I shifted my gaze to give him a glance from beneath my lashes, warm and meaningful.

"Well," he said, a tiny smile playing about his mouth, "some things."

He might have reached for me then, but George, the hallboy, arrived at precisely that moment with the late post. I flicked through the letters as Stoker attempted to lure the tamarin down with a bit of fly biscuit. "Come down, you bloody little vermin," he said in a sweetly coaxing voice. "I have half a mind to lock you in a cage."

I ignored this—Stoker would never confine an animal accustomed to liberty of movement—and seized upon one of the envelopes in triumph. It was written in an unfamiliar hand, the return address a neatly inscribed *W. PLUMTREE*. I tore it open in a fit of impatience, skimming the lines until my eyes fell to a name.

"Veronica, you look like Saint Paul on the road to Damascus," Stoker said as he came forwards, the tamarin now perched on top of his head, chewing gently on a lock of his hair.

I waved the letter in triumph. "Young Plumtree has prevailed. In the very first file he searched, he discovered the name of the artist commissioned to sculpt the death mask."

Stoker took the page as he resumed his chair, skimming the letter. "Julius Elyot. Who in the name of seven devils is that?"

"I do not know, but I mean to find out," I said with a grin. "Is it not a glorious thing to be embarked once more upon adventure?" I went to sit on his lap. It was not a posture I adopted often, but Stoker was always highly appreciative when I did so. He wrapped his arms about me and rested his head on my shoulder.

"Whatever did I do before you blazed into my life like a comet?"

I curled my fingers into the thick, tumbled waves of his hair and pulled his head back so I could look into his face. "I cannot imagine."

The next few minutes were spent in a thoroughly satisfactory manner until a gentle cough from the doorway drew our attention. We sprang apart, upsetting the teapot which Stoker managed to catch in midair. He settled it back onto the tea table as I leapt to my feet with genuine delight.

"Lady Wellie!" Lord Rosemorran's great aunt, Lady Wellingtonia, was a firm friend, as loyal as she was elderly, and she was, in her own estimation, older than the tombs of Egypt. She had been a frequent confidante in our earliest investigations, but one in particular had caused her to suffer from considerable disillusionment. She had taken herself off to Scotland to lick her wounds. She had travelled with her companion, an elderly, quite deaf, and amorously accomplished clergyman by the name of Cecil Baring-Ponsonby with her. Their Scottish sojourn had been followed by a tour of the Levant which was itself succeeded by a lengthy stay on one of the smaller Greek isles.

Her travels did not seem to have done her much good, I reflected sadly. She walked always with the aid of a stick now, gripped in hands grown more gnarled than they had been a year before. And her complexion—always weathered—was grooved even more harshly by the bright sun and brisk winds of the Aegean. But her eyes were the same brilliant black they had ever been, missing nothing in their sharp scrutiny like a clever bird or a watchful crocodile.

Stoker jumped to offer his chair, and she thanked him, settling herself with a sigh. "I am sorry to come among you unawares, children. I did knock," she added with a sly grin.

"Nonsense," I said briskly. "Your company is always most welcome. And unexpected! His lordship did not mention you were coming home."

"He did not know. I had no fixed plan, but a fortnight ago, I woke one morning and realised I was heartily sick of lamb, so I roused Cecil and told him to make the arrangements. I was, although I despair of the sentimentality of the word, homesick."

"You have chosen a poor time to return," Stoker pointed out. "Autumn is hardly London at its best."

She snorted by way of reply. "You tell no lies, my boy. My rheumatics started as soon as we sailed into English waters. I can hardly walk for this hip." She thumped the offending spot with her fist. "Still, it is good to be home. I have only just arrived and made my greetings to the family. I see Rosemorran still has all of those frightful children." She gestured towards the bonnet perched on the tamarin. "I suspect that is Rose's doing."

"Naturally," Stoker told her with a smile.

"As is the corpse," she added, baring her teeth at him.

"You've come to see the waxwork?" I inquired.

"Not a waxwork," she corrected. "Unless Rosemorran has the wrong end of the stick. He said you found a body inside. Show me."

We did as commanded, unshrouding the glass coffin once more. She said little, surveying the features of the Beauty for some time in perfect silence. Once, she motioned for a magnifying glass, peering through it for a long minute before handing it back to Stoker.

"I presume you have theories?"

I laid out what little we knew. "We believe she may be a drowning victim pulled from Regent's Canal in 1873. She was never identified, and there appears to be some little confusion about what became of the body."

Her gaze sharpened. "How so?"

"She was taken to Plumtree and Son, a mortuary in Chelsea where they commissioned a death mask for publication in the newspaper with a plea for information. The mask was apparently never finished and the notice never inserted."

"1873?" Lady Wellie's eyes turned heavenwards as she thought. "A Carlist War was being fought in Spain. There was rioting in Chipping Norton in favour of a group of women sentenced to hard labour for their efforts to organise agricultural workers. Schliemann discovered Troy. And in the city was a dreadful outbreak of cholera, if memory serves." It did, of course. Memory would never dare disappoint her. She shifted her attention to us. "Any of those might have proven more interesting to the editors of the newspapers than a solitary unidentified drowned girl."

"But if it were simply that," I countered, "then she ought to have been laid to rest in a pauper's grave like the rest of the unknown dead in this city."

"She was not?" Lady Wellie's brows rose in interest.

"No," Stoker told her. "The records at Plumtree's indicate she was buried in their own cemetery in Berkshire, but we have discovered that to be impossible. She simply vanished."

Lady Wellie nodded towards the coffin. "Or did she? Yes, I think you must entertain William of Ockham's principle here. One cannot have both the vanishing corpse of a drowned young woman and a well-preserved specimen with the same characteristics and no connection between them. It is too much of a coincidence to be borne." Stoker made to guide her to the chair again, but she waved him off, wrapping her hands around the knob of her walking stick. Her fingers were twisted and heavy with old, filthy diamonds of enormous size. "If I sit again, I may well never get out of that chair. One despises growing old, but"— she gestured towards the coffin—"if the alternative is that, I suppose one must be reconciled."

She turned to me. "Come with me as I unpack, child." I knew Lady Wellie enough to understand it was not so much an invitation as a command. She said "I" but the clever reader will immediately intuit that Lady Wellie stirred herself to as little labour as possible besides the handing over of presents purchased on her travels. The actual work was done by a bevy of maids, cap ribbons snapping and aprons fluttering as they dashed to and fro under her beady eye.

"That is a very rare specimen of the blue-rumped parrot, my dear girl," she told one unfortunate maid who was in danger of mishandling a stuffed trophy. "I mean it as a present for Mr. Templeton-Vane, and if you muss so much as a feather on its head, I shall send you to Borneo to fetch another."

The harried maid thrust it into my hands, and I set it aside with all due care. "How is it you have a Bornean parrot when you went no further east than Jerusalem?" I inquired.

Lady Wellie slanted me an enigmatic look. "I had it off a trader in Cairo."

"Stoker would be the first to tell you not to indulge in such extravagance on his behalf," I told her.

She flapped a gnarled hand. "It cost me not a sou, I assure you. I won it in a game of poker." Lady Wellie rootled around in one of her boxes until she emerged with a bottle. "Ah! Just what we require." Dismissing the maids, she opened the bottle and poured us each a measure of clear liquid into thin Venetian glasses no bigger than thimbles.

"Here you are, my dear. Best not to sip it. Have it down in one go," she instructed. She flung her head back and quaffed it in a quick draught. I followed her example and gasped, sudden stars streaking across the field of my vision.

"What—what—" I croaked.

"Mastika," she told me. She poured another for each of us and downed her second as swiftly as the first. I took a more gingerly approach and took a considered sniff.

"It smells of pine," I said in some surprise. I had not perceived this, the first swallow having comprised equal measures fire and regret. But there was a subtlety to the beverage, a not displeasing marriage of resin and herb, and I drank this one off with more appreciation.

"From the isle of Chios," she said. "In the north Aegean. Charming place so long as one is content to look at windmills from the back of a donkey."

"I would be," I assured her. "Although I fear the Aegean is not the most conducive spot to the study of lepidoptery. Not enough in the way of shrubberies."

"It is conducive to pondering great philosophies," she countered. "Life, death, the old gods, and one's own mortality." It was unlike her to indulge in maudlin thoughts. Indeed, amongst all my acquaintance, Lady Wellie was among the most vigorous and engaged, in spite of her advanced years. But her travels, undertaken to provide her with a change of scenery and renewal of spirits, seemed to have failed to revivify her.

I was on the point of inquiring into the matter when she shook her head and adopted a brisk tone which told me any personal queries would not be welcome.

"Have you made any progress in your latest endeavour?" she asked.

"Mr. Plumtree was able to provide us with the name of the artist commissioned to make the death mask of our unknown Beauty—a fellow called Julius Elyot." Sudden inspiration struck. "I know! I shall write to Sir Frederick Havelock." Sir Frederick, whose acquaintance we had made during the course of a previous investigation,* was perhaps England's greatest living artist. Few who aspired to earn a living by brush or chisel escaped his notice. But before I could ask for writing paper to dash off an inquiry, Lady Wellie interjected.

"Julius Elyot? Of the Rutland Elyots? With a 'y'?"

I shrugged. "Yes, that is how it is spelt, but I have no idea whence his people came. We have only just learnt his name."

"Because if it is the fellow I am thinking of," she continued slowly, "he is an artist manqué."

I sat up very straight. "Say more, I beg you."

She tipped her head, thinking, with an expression that bore a frightening resemblance to the tamarin's. "The Elyots are an old family, but not particularly distinguished by wealth or important marriages. But cleverness, that they always had in spades."

"'Had?'"

"Yes, they were never very good breeders, if memory serves. Only ever a single son and sometimes a daughter, but never more than two in any generation. Most peculiar." Her smile was one of feline contentment, and well it might be. There were enough Beauclerks to populate a series of busy villages around the country. She went on. "They did all the expected things—boys sent to good schools, girls launched into Society—but there was always the whiff of eccentricity about them." She paused to give me a speaking look. "Don't, Veronica."

I widened my eyes at her. "Don't what, my lady?"

"I can hear you thinking. Yes, the Beauclerks have more than our share of eccentricity. We may have a Galápagos tortoise in the shrub-

---

* *A Perilous Undertaking*

bery and a hermit in the garden, but that is no more than any other noble family might have."

I blinked in surprise. "Since when do we have a hermit?"

"Since I returned from my travels. I brought him with me. A Greek religious, I am told. One cannot be entirely certain since I do not speak any Hellenic dialects, and he only speaks English when it pleases him, but he does seem holy."

"Where, precisely, in the garden is he living?"

"He ought to have had the hermitage," she said with a frown, "but Rose has commandeered it for a playhouse, and Rosemorran had no wish to upset her after the loss of her wax doll, so he housed the fellow in the little folly modelled after the Scottish castle."

Within the circle of follies on the grounds of the estate, those occupied by Stoker and myself were grouped with the Roman temple which housed a convenient and comfortable bath. The others faced us across the duck pond, and chief among these was a tiny pink castle with square towers capped with witch's hats.

"It will be nice for you to have a neighbour," she said fondly. "Perhaps you can communicate with him. I believe his name is Spyridon, but I am not certain so best not to use it in conversation until you are sure."

"I will bear that in mind," I assured her. "But you were saying about the Elyots?"

"Ah, yes. Eccentric, but not in the usual way," she said with no trace of irony. "No, they were all terribly clever, the Elyots. Always tinkering with gadgets and arguing about scientific principles. I seem to remember the grandfather coming to blows with Volta after a lecture. Or was it Galvani?" She paused, then shrugged. "One hardly cares. I have known many an Italian who would have benefitted from a good thrashing. But there was some mystery about Julius, I seem to recall."

My pulses quickened. Here now was a point of inquiry. I leant forwards eagerly. "What sort of mystery?"

She thought a moment, then shrugged. "Devil if I know, my girl. That is the cruelty of old age. One forgets useful things and can remember too many trivialities that ought to be forgot. I cannot tell you any more about the Elyots, but I know what I had for breakfast on New Year's Day in 1834." I waited and she grinned. "Rassolnik. A Russian soup of sour cucumbers. I was in St. Petersburg with my uncle. Now, will you have more mastika?" She made to pour, but I rose swiftly. My head was swimming from the two small glasses I had already imbibed.

"That is the trouble with the youth of today," she grumbled. "No *bottom.*"

She waved me away but when I reached the door, she summoned me back.

"I have just remembered. Julius had a twin sister, Eliza. Must be thirty-five or thereabouts. I've heard nothing of her for years, but if you want to find her, you can do no better than to call upon Parthenope Fleet."

"Parthenope Fleet?" This was good news indeed. I did not know Miss Fleet myself, but we shared membership in the Curiosity Club, providing as it did a refuge for scientists, explorers, and thinkers of all disciplines. Miss Fleet's particular field—applied galvanics—held no interest for me whatsoever and our paths had never crossed.

But that was about to change.

CHAPTER

15

That a visit to a scientific laboratory would interest Stoker surprised me not in the slightest. But his almost indecent enthusiasm was unexpected indeed. His eyes shone, and he scarcely made a single coherent comment before dashing away as soon as I extended the invitation. He was returned within the quarter of the hour, scrubbed, polished, and fairly gleaming from hair to hem.

"I have seen you less perfectly groomed when meeting royalty," I protested. "What, pray, is the significance of this particular call that you should be as neat as a pin and fresh as the proverbial daisy?"

"Parthenope Fleet," he said, pronouncing the name with the same sort of reverence one might encounter amongst Romans when speaking of the pope.

Before I could make further inquiry, he directed me to change my own attire to something far smarter, and scrutinised me thoroughly when I had done so.

"It will suffice," he said finally. He took me firmly by the elbow and guided me along the path to the main gate of Bishop's Folly where it gave onto Marylebone Road and would provide us ample opportunity to hail a cab.

"Suffice!" I protested as we walked, the tips of my shoes fairly dragging as he bowled me along. "This is *Worth*," I reminded him. "Chosen by you and fitted by one of the master's own modistes in Paris." I might have saved my breath to cool my porridge for all the attention he paid me. He stood upon the kerb, letting several hansoms pass us by before raising his hand.

"Stoker, we might have been halfway to Shoreditch by now. What do you mean by allowing empty conveyances to pass us by?"

"We are not going in a hansom," he advised me loftily. "I do not wish to arrive besmirched by the city soots."

I stood in stupefaction, marvelling at his newfound pernicketiness, but he was not to be moved. In due course, a hackney was secured, and we climbed inside, insulated from the dirt of the streets. It deposited us where Stoker directed, outside a house in Hounslow. It was a sturdy and unhandsome building of mock-Tudor design, clearly chosen for its location. It sat in a small bit of green lawn, the grass all but obscured by a shrubbery that might have been conjured by a fairy-tale witch, all thorns and creeping vines that hung low over the windows. The door was of stout wood, and though it boasted a heavy, modern lock, an enchanted troll as a guard would not have looked amiss. We stepped onto the little porch which was shadowed by the overhanging floor above.

"It isn't very welcoming," I murmured.

"It isn't meant to be," a voice said. It seemed to float down to us, and by stepping backwards off of the porch, we saw that the casement directly above us had been flung open. A silver-white head leant out, and a pair of eyes, brilliant and sharply blue, assessed us. "Who are you and what do you want?"

"Forgive the intrusion, Miss Fleet," Stoker said, immediately doffing his hat with a sweeping gesture that would have credited any ci-devant marquis. "I am Revelstoke Templeton-Vane, and this is Miss Veronica Speedwell."

"Speedwell? Have I seen your name in the club ledger?" she demanded.

"Yes, Miss Fleet," I said, smiling ingratiatingly. "I wagered with Lady Cordelia Beauclerk upon the outcome of the Sullivan-Kilrain fight." The bare-knuckled bout in the States had been the fight of the century, lasting some seventy-five rounds, and had excited attention even in the hushed halls of the Curiosity Club.

"Did you win?" she demanded.

"Alas, no. I am afraid I wagered on Mr. Kilrain and he proved a disappointment."

She made an harrumphing noise. "How much did you lose?"

"Only a guinea."

"Only a guinea! Listen to the child. Do you know how many laboratory supplies a guinea would purchase? Tell me why I should admit such an extravagant little madam into my home."

The words were tart, and the gaze none too friendly. Stoker spoke up. "Well, you needn't, if you do not like to. We could leave her standing upon the porch like a pointer whilst we chat."

She gave a great guffaw of laughter and banged the casement shut. I regarded Stoker with some irritation, but he responded with an upraised forefinger, the universal gesture commanding patience. After a long moment, a series of thumps and bumps and the metallic thud of a bolt being drawn back announced her arrival. The door was thrown back upon its hinges, shrieking mightily in protest. Parthenope Fleet stood behind it, and for a long moment, I was so arrested by her appearance, I did not move. She was tall, her inches almost equalling Stoker's, and her shoulders were broad, giving her the elegance of a born equestrienne. Her head was held on a long, graceful neck, and her silver hair had been cropped short. The eyes were beguiling, blue as a summer sky, and she used them to great effect, permitting herself a twinkle as they rested upon Stoker.

"My god, but you're a good-looking lad," she said, gesturing for him to enter. "I might have married if I had ever found the like in my day." He made a gesture of protest which seemed to enchant her all the more. "And he blushes! Whoever thought a man alive could possess such gentility. Come in, child, and bring the flibbertigibbet behind you."

Thus encouraged, we followed her into the shadows of the house. The creepers hanging over the windows gave the rooms a shifting, aqueous light. It was like swimming at the bottom of a mossy pond, and I marvelled that a creature of science like Parthenope Fleet could inspire so many thoughts of witchcraft and enchantment.

She guided us to a room where it seemed all of the offices of domesticity were combined. A long sofa, pushed in front of the hearth, was heaped with pillows and feather quilts to create a makeshift bed. Stacks of books held discarded cups of tea and plates thick with crumbs. An elderly wolfhound reposed on a threadbare chaise, lifting its head as we entered before dismissing us as entirely uninteresting. His mistress threw him a crust of toast as she gathered up a few oddments to make a place for us to sit.

"I shall not apologise," she told us. "I do not entertain, and I did not invite you. Nor will I offer you refreshment. I will instead make you the gift of five whole minutes of my time. If I am interested enough at the end of those five minutes, I might encourage you to stay another ten. But do not expect more."

"We would not dream of imposing upon your generosity further than necessary," Stoker assured her.

"She might," Parthenope Fleet said with a nod towards me. "She looks the overbearing sort."

I opened my mouth to reply, but she waved me off. "Do not take it as an insult. It requires a forward woman to know another. Now, onto business. You have four minutes and forty-five seconds left." She glanced at the mantel clock—an aggressively ugly example of the Bavarian wood-working arts—with a meaningful look.

"We have come about the Elyots," I told her. "Julius, an artist, I believe. And his sister, Eliza. I am told you knew them."

"Told? By whom?" The narrowed gaze gave nothing away.

"Lady Wellingtonia Beauclerk," Stoker informed her.

She snorted. "That old harridan! She gathers gossip like a squirrel gathers nuts—indiscriminately and with an eye to feeding on it later."

"Is it untrue?" I challenged.

"It is not," she admitted. "I knew them."

I suppressed the flare of triumph licking through my veins. I suspected Parthenope Fleet would not give up confidences easily. She would make us earn them all, and if she wished to play games, I was content to let her do so as long as she gave us the information we required.

"What can you tell us about them?" Stoker urged.

"Why do you want to know?" She dropped a hand to the wolf-hound's head, stroking the rough fur of the creature's ears as it dozed.

"We have reason to believe the Elyots have information that could help us right a miscarriage of justice," I told her.

She did not snort in derision this time. She laughed outright. "Miscarriage of justice? Good luck to you, child. Julius Elyot was the oddest of ducks. And you are barking up quite the wrong tree in any event. He has been dead these fifteen years at least."

My spirits, so elated a moment before, plunged. "Dead? Are you certain?"

She shrugged. "I did not poke the body with a pin, if that's what you mean. But he died all the same. It was a crushing blow to Eliza, you know. She was scarcely twenty and idolised him."

"How did he die?" Stoker inquired gently.

"Accident," she replied in succinct tones. "His laboratory was burnt down, and he was unable to escape. Although there were rumours he did not especially try. Naturally, no one wanted to feed those particularly nasty notions. It gave great pain to Eliza."

"People suggested he died by his own hand?" I pressed.

"Rude people," she flung back quickly. "Unkind people."

"That must have been difficult for Miss Elyot," Stoker remarked.

Miss Fleet tipped her head, considering him a long moment. "You have an uncommon sensitivity, Mr. Templeton-Vane."

"Stoker, please."

"You may call me Parthenope," she returned. She leant forwards and put a finger beneath his chin, tipping his face towards the light. "That's a nasty scar. Amazonia, wasn't it?"

Stoker's eyes flared wide in surprise, and she gave him a knowing look. "The Templeton-Vane Expedition. I followed your travels. You were very brave. And that wife of yours ought to be fed to a crocodile."

She said nothing more upon the point, but she clearly understood the depth of the villainy of Stoker's former wife and how deeply he had been wronged. They exchanged gentle smiles, and for all they cared I may as well not have even been in the room. I almost indulged in a little polite clearing of the throat to remind them of my presence, but when I perceived the softness in her gaze, I paused. She seemed on the precipice of a confidence, and I trusted Stoker to coax it from her.

He shifted a little in his chair, moving towards her, his shoulder blocking me entirely. "You are friends with Miss Elyot?" he inquired.

"I am. She is several decades my junior, but I have always thought of her as something of a protégée. She ought to have surpassed me years ago, her intellect and originality show so much promise. But she can never seem to settle to anything, flitting from project to project. There is a restlessness in her and something of bitterness too."

"What sort of bitterness?" Stoker asked.

"Her experiments have frequently been dismissed by male scientists as frivolous and unworthy. Her speciality is in the field of applied galvanics, and recently she has been attempting to discover how the uses of electricity may be employed in the domestic sphere."

"You mean illumination for the home?"

Her mouth twisted, but the smile was not unkind. "Leave it to a man to think only of light! No, sir. I mean every manner of domestic labour. Eliza believes it is possible to harness the power of electricity to do most tasks currently carried out by the lowest drudge—the washing of clothes, the cleaning of carpets. She feels certain that devices may be invented which can liberate women from such chores."

"My god," I murmured. "What a change that would make!"

Stoker was gracious enough not to observe that my own activities in the domestic sphere were limited to the tidying, dusting, and polishing of specimens in the Belvedere which I trusted to no maid's ministrations. The rest of the washing, cleaning, cooking, and sewing of my things was carried out by a regiment of Beauclerk maids as one of the perquisites of being in the earl's employ. But I sympathised enough with the sisterhood of women to appreciate what a difference such inventions might bring to their lives. Their time could be freed for the pursuit of education or entertainment, their hours better spent in activities chosen to uplift their spirits and enrich their minds than the current dull repetitions of household drudgery.

Parthenope Fleet went on. "Naturally, male scientists see no purpose to her experiments. She has been oft-derided in professional journals, to the point she no longer submits papers or shares her research. She is resolved that whatever discoveries she makes, they can be published only after her death."

"An extreme but thoroughly understandable position," Stoker said.

"Wait a moment," I said suddenly. "You referred to Julius Elyot's laboratory. Surely as an artist he would have had a studio."

"An artist! He was no such thing," she repeated irritably.

"Forgive me, Miss Fleet, but he was listed as the artist commissioned to sculpt a death mask of a drowning victim some fifteen years ago," I persisted.

She paused to think. "He was a gifted artist, but his art was always in service of science. He was foremost a student of galvanic applications. He was Eliza's first tutor, in fact. He took her into his laboratory to serve as a sort of amanuensis. He was very protective of his work and wanted no breath of it to be discussed in the general way. Having Eliza on hand to keep records was the perfect solution. And as she showed an early aptitude for the field, he began to educate her so that she could, at times, carry out the simpler preparations for his experiments."

This was exceedingly puzzling information and not a little disheartening. If a man was supposed to have been an artist, he ought to have actually been one, I thought in some annoyance. A tiny thorn of doubt that we were on the trail of the correct Julius Elyot pricked my consciousness as Stoker and Parthenope Fleet continued to talk.

"Would you like to see my laboratory?" she asked suddenly. He accepted with alacrity, and she rose to lead him to it. I followed behind, pointedly neither included nor excluded. I had been, in short, forgot, and I had half a mind to stay and see how long it took them to remember me.

But I am always curious about the methods of other scientists, so I trailed along, listening absently to their conversation. She explained something of her work as she led him back through the hall and unlocked a stout oaken door with a key she kept pinned to her pocket.

"I permit no one to visit without an invitation," she told him.

"I shall consider myself honoured," he replied, and she smiled at him over her shoulder as she opened the door and threw a switch to illuminate the gaslights. The flickering fixtures led the way down a flight of stone stairs which gave onto a narrow stone passage. This debouched into a room of tremendous proportions, running what seemed like the entire length of the house, but it was not the enormity of the place which gave me pause. The walls were lined with shelves, many holding a vast array of jars in which unspeakable things floated. Some were simple zoological specimens, but others were far more gruesome. Organs swollen with tumours, limbs twisted with unspeakable ailments, even a malformed infant bobbing gently in a large flask. Other shelves held a collection of volumes in English, Latin, German, and Italian, whilst one wall had been fitted with racks of tools and instruments. In the centre of the room stood a wide table, large enough to accommodate a grown man, and connected to this was the greatest assembly of electrical equipment I had ever seen.

"Voltaic piles," Stoker said in a tone of hushed awe.

Parthenope busied herself retrieving one of the jars and carrying it to the table. "Everyone knows Volta and Galvani. The Italians were instrumental as pioneers in electrical studies," she said. "But it was Giovanni Aldini who brought the practical applications to England."

"I am not familiar with his work," Stoker told her, watching with interest as she spread a tidy piece of linen towelling on the table.

"He was a Bolognese," she said. "And quite accomplished in his studies. It was Aldini who theorised that it is the heart which is the engine of animation to the human body. He attempted to prove it in Italy, but he lacked a vital piece of equipment for his experiments."

"What was that?" I inquired.

She looked up in apparent surprise. I think she had forgot my existence altogether, but she answered readily enough. "A fresh cadaver. Those available for study in Bologna were dried out by the time he got his hands on them. He needed something . . ." She paused, searching for the correct word. "Something *juicy*," she finished with a smack of the lips.

Parthenope opened the jar and gently removed a hand. It was not the appendage of a lady, lacking any sort of delicacy or grace.

Parthenope noticed my scrutiny. "What do you make of her?"

I paused, studying the hand from every angle. "Young," I said finally.

"On what grounds?" she demanded. I noticed she did not catechise Stoker in the same manner, but I did not mind. I felt more than up to the task.

"On the grounds that the skin of the back of the hand is unlined and the knuckles are unswollen. It has neither the slackness of age nor the inflammation of rheumatism."

"Good. Go on." She looked coolly down the length of her nose at me. Stoker said nothing, but I could sense his amusement at her challenge.

"The broadness of the palm and bluntness of the fingers suggest the sort of exercise which comes from working with the hands. This is confirmed by the calluses on the finger and the shortness of the nails."

She nodded, pursing her lips. "Occupation?"

I paused again. "Match girl."

"And what makes you say that?"

"The jar in which you preserved the hand was in shadow before you took it down. There was a very slight greenish glow suggesting the presence of yellow phosphorus. And the only workers who consistently have traces of yellow phosphorus on their hands are match girls."

She gave me a grudging smile. "Full marks, Miss Speedwell. We will make a proper scientist of you yet."

"I think you will find that lepidoptery is—"

She flapped a hand, waving me to silence. "Butterflies and pretty bugs. They are nothing to what we are about here. Watch now."

She donned a pair of thick, dark spectacles before putting on a heavy leather apron and matching gauntlets. "Stand back," she instructed. She tinkered with the voltaic pile Stoker had noted, arranging various plates and wires as she worked. The noise was ghastly, a loud thrumming and clicking that echoed off the stone walls and floor until the reverberations filled our ears and made conversation impossible.

As we watched in horrified fascination, she touched the ends of two wires to the hand. The fingers twitched, making small, delicate move-ments, little flutters suggestive of a butterfly's wings.

Stoker and I stared in open-jawed astonishment as Parthenope Fleet increased the voltage and applied the electric current again. This time, the hand contracted as if in pain, the nails clawlike, scraping at the linen beneath. And then it began to creep forwards. It was horrible to watch, that dreadful, disembodied hand moving slowly, inexorably along, dragging itself like a living, thinking thing.

She dropped the wires and the hand gave a final shudder, surren-dering to its death throes. A shiver passed along the index finger, and it remained extended as if to point the way ahead. She snapped off the machine and removed her spectacles.

"Now, imagine that with an entire corpse," she said. "That is why Aldini came to London. Unlike the Bolognese, we do not decapitate our criminals—we hang them. Aldini wanted an intact body upon which to perform his experiments."

"To what end?" Stoker managed finally, never taking his eyes from the hand still flexing gently on the table.

"To reanimate the dead," Parthenope said. "He thought he could challenge Death, reverse the course of Fate."

"To retrieve souls from Hades itself," Stoker mused.

She shook her head. "You are a romantic, Mr. Templeton-Vane. It had little to do with souls and everything to do with bodies. Aldini wanted to create a process by which a human being could be revived."

"And your work?" I inquired.

"I have far more modest ambitions. I work with limbs that have been severed in hopes of preserving the tissues and eventually attach-ing them once more to the body. There are industrial accidents by the thousand in this country," she said. "Imagine the possibilities! Reuniting a hand or foot with its body, restoring use and purpose to those whose livelihoods depend upon their fitness for work."

"A noble ambition," Stoker told her.

"A futile one," she returned with a ghost of a smile. "I have yet to master proper preservation, and even when I manage to animate the limbs, it never lasts more than a quarter of an hour. And even if I solved those insuperable problems, how could one possibly persuade healthy tissues to accept the reintroduction of those that have been removed? No, I fear it is a folly to nurture such hopes, but I persist."

She guided us up the stairs and towards the door, our visit nearly at an end.

"Your work is fascinating," I told her with perfect truth. "I suspect Miss Eliza Elyot's is as well."

She puffed a sigh of irritation. "I cannot think of Eliza without considerable vexation. She ought to have been a name of distinction by now, but her spirit has been sorely tested. The loss of her brother was a terrible blow, of course. She was devoted to him, although I have found it best to be wary of working with men. They always seem to take the lion's share of whatever acclaim is to be had. Such is the nature of the world," she added somewhat bitterly. "In that regard, his death might have freed her to choose her own path, but she has been singularly lacking in ambition. It is as though his brilliance was a necessary spark to her own, and without him, she is groping in the darkness."

"And she never married?" he asked.

Parthenope Fleet's gaze was level. "She has not. Julius's death was very hard on her. They were terribly fond of one another." She paused, thinking. "Julius also had a partner in his work to whom Eliza was very much attached. There was a suggestion of an understanding between them, but it is not surprising that the connection was severed with Julius's death. Sometimes the pain of a shared loss can be as sharp as inconstancy." She fell silent a moment, perhaps ruminating on a failed love affair of her own before she took up her narrative once more. "Eliza has found some measure of consolation these past years. She lives with a member of our club, Miss Speedwell. I am sure you have heard of Undine Trevelyan."

"Undine Trevelyan! Indeed I have," I assured her. "Her paintings are . . . most original."

"They are *dreadful*," Parthenope Fleet said with a thin smile. "Garish colours and far too many male nudes. One can only contemplate so many scrota with equanimity. She is a forward creature. You should get along famously with her. No doubt she will be attending the tableaux vivant at the club this week. Eliza seldom accompanies her, but even if she is absent, you may apply to Undine to speak with her. Mind you, Undine is very protective of Eliza. She will most likely refuse you, and if she does, she shan't be polite about it."

I bared my teeth in a wolfish smile. "Never fear, Miss Fleet. I am impervious to insult."

She shook hands with Stoker, the pair of them exchanging warm remarks. An invitation to call again was issued—to him, not to the pair of us, I noted archly—and immediately accepted.

Stoker stopped to scratch the hound's ears in the course of our departure, and the pause gave me a moment to put one last question to Miss Fleet. I do not know what possessed me to pose it, for until that exact moment, I had not entertained the slightest notion of asking. But with a certainty borne of irrepressible instinct, I turned to her.

"Miss Elyot's suitor," I began. "The one who worked with her brother and jilted her when Julius Elyot died. What was his name?"

She looked at me in surprise. "I cannot imagine it matters now. But if you wish to speak with him, he ought to be easy enough to find. He is a marquess's son. It was Ambrose Despard. Lord Ambrose Despard."

CHAPTER

16

I waited until we were ensconced in a hackney and the driver had sprung the horses to emit a whoop of unalloyed joy.

"That utter bastard," Stoker muttered. "Despard must have known that Julius Elyot was commissioned to make a death mask for a drowning victim. And yet, he said nothing!"

"We did not put such an inquiry to him," I reminded Stoker.

"We asked about the preservation of a human body, a question which rendered him so uncomfortable he could not get us out of his house quickly enough," Stoker returned grimly. "You realise what this suggests?"

"That Julius Elyot and Lord Ambrose Despard were materially involved in the creation of the Beauty," I responded.

"We ought to have suspected him further," Stoker observed. "I never trust a man who is so thoroughly and perfectly groomed."

"As if the application of a little toilet water after shaving is an indictment on a gentleman's character," I returned. "And grime is no indicator of virtue," I added with a significant look at his cuffs. In spite of his tidy appearance when we left the Belvedere, he had acquired three new stains, one of them smelling distinctly of formalin although I knew he had been nowhere near the stuff. "It is a point of perpetual astonishment to me, your ability to besmirch yourself with apparently no effort whatsoever."

"You knew what I was when you fell in love with me," he replied. "Therefore, I would argue that it is your taste which is in question rather than my innocent befoulment."

Naturally, I took umbrage at this, and we set to quarrelling happily until we reached the Belvedere. The lamps had been lit, and a low mist was rising off the duck pond, the shreds of it hanging in the shrubbery like forgotten phantoms. The grounds of Bishop's Folly were a particular delight to me, offering so much unexpected variety in the centre of the city, but the evening was growing chill, and I shivered as we reached the Belvedere.

It was the behaviour of the dogs that first alerted me to the fact that something was amiss. They were grouped around the doorway, huddled together in considerable agitation and looking to Al-'Ijliyyah for protection. She was the most recent addition to the pack as well as the youngest and the smallest, scarcely measuring half a yard from the end of her tail to the tips of her quivering ears, but her intrepid spirit and stalwart defence of the others had led them to adopt her as their leader. Betony and Vespertine, the Caucasian sheepdog and Scottish deerhound respectively, presented a particularly ludicrous picture of cowardice as they sheltered behind her.

"What in the name of seven hells," Stoker began. He cast an eye over the pack and spoke sternly to them. "I expect this of you, Nut. You are scarcely larger than Al-'Ijliyyah, but Betony and Vespertine, you are ridiculous. And Huxley, you bring shame upon the name of bulldog."

The sturdy English fellow, the oldest of the bunch, merely slobbered in reply.

"What do you suppose has affrighted them?" Stoker asked, turning to me. But I was already pushing open the unlocked door and drawing a hatpin from my cap.

"Get behind me," I instructed him as I moved to go inside.

"I bloody well will not," came the answer as Stoker shoved past me, his booted feet crunching over a bit of broken glass. The splinters were ground to powder beneath his soles, and I was immediately glad of the dogs' collective cowardice, for their paws would have been cut to ribbons. I shut the door behind us to keep them out, and hastened to catch up to Stoker. He had lit a lamp and was inspecting the damage.

"Is there much destroyed?" I asked.

He shook his head. "Just an old Wardian case near the door. An empty one, thank god." I understood the fervour of his feelings. The Belvedere was so crammed with treasures, it did not bear thinking about what might have been lost.

"An accident? Perhaps one of the children?" I suggested.

He raised the lamp, the light playing over the harsh planes of his face as he surveyed the place. "They wouldn't dare. Not if it were locked, and it was," he added, anticipating my next question. I ought to have known better. Stoker might be careless of many things, but never the security of the Belvedere. The things he held most dear in the world—besides myself—were held within its walls.

"So we have had an intruder," I concluded. "I suppose it is not to be wondered at. There is a king's ransom housed here, and some of the valuables are quite portable. But there is nothing new—" I broke off with a cry of despair and turned on my heel, a sudden horror rising within me. The corner where the Beauty lay was still in heavy shadow, but I could see even within the gloom that she had been disturbed. The various precautions we had taken to disguise the casket had been thrown aside and the pall itself, the bit of tapestry, was crumpled on the floor.

The casket, I saw with considerable shock, was empty. I reeled back, supporting myself on a handy camel saddle. "She is gone," I said in a hollow voice.

Stoker stood, lamp raised high, inspecting the scene, but there was nothing to see, I realised. There was not so much as a fingerprint marring the glass, no telltale smudges or scratches to betray the villain's work. There was only the long satin cushion bearing the impression of a woman's body where the Beauty had once lain.

"I cannot believe we have lost her," I said mournfully. I turned to Stoker, expecting an eruption of temper or despair. Instead, to my shock, I found him smiling as broadly as a man who has just backed a winner against the longest possible odds at Epsom.

"Stoker? Dearest, if you mean to succumb to hysterics, I must warn you that I am without a vinaigrette and would be forced to slap you into sensibility."

He bent and pressed a bruising kiss to my lips. "Come with me," he ordered. He stalked away as lordly as a panther, and although I am loath to admit it, I trotted obediently behind. I tried always to maintain a dignity equal to that of any man and rejected all the niceties of female submission, but upon occasion—very *rare* occasion—I had cause to come over rather fluttery and maidenly and was content to play Penelope to his Odysseus.

I knew better than to ask where we were bound; he would not have told me. For all his aristocratic upbringing, he had a carnival barker's love of theatricality, and he relished any opportunity to play the showman. And I confess, I was more than a little excited by his air of command. So I paced my steps to his, surprised when they turned in the direction of the duck pond. He skirted the edge of the water, leading the way to the tiny Scottish castle on the far side.

When we reached the stout oaken door, he rapped smartly upon it. It was immediately thrown open by a figure draped in a sort of clerical robe. His grizzled beard was long and full as were the eyebrows beetling above dark, curious eyes. His nose was a thing of majesty, rising proudly above a set of moustaches so lavish they might have been borrowed from a Highland cow. He was smiling, his teeth very white and beautiful against the darkness of his beard, and his voice was booming.

"Stoker! You have come to see me again, my friend. And this must be Miss Speedwell. I hear such things of you, my dear, as make me very happy to make your acquaintance."

Seizing my hand, he bowed low, sweeping a courtly gesture.

"You are Spyridon, I believe," I said.

"That is what they call me," he replied. "Come in, friends. I am cooking my supper, but you will not mind this."

He ushered us into the castle folly, and I looked around in admiration. The last time I had seen the place it had been fitted out for amateur theatricals for Lord Rosemorran's children. But it had been cleared of dressing-up boxes and props and bits of scenery, swept and scrubbed until everything shone like a new pin. Spyridon's few possessions were placed with care. A series of icons in the Eastern Orthodox style were hung over the mantel, and a small shelf held a row of books in assorted languages—Greek, German, English, and French, I saw at a glance. A coverlet of rustic cloth in a bright and cheerful pattern had been spread across a narrow sofa, and a pair of carpet slippers warmed on the hearth near a pot of simmering stew. It was snug and homely, a restful and modest place. The only discordant note was a small frame on the mantel. It was enamelled and set with what looked like jewels. One might have expected a holy man to have such a thing if it held the image of the Madonna, but this was no sacred relic. Inside was a photograph of a woman dressed in some variety of formal court attire and wearing a crown.

"You have made it very cosy," I told him as he gestured for me to take the only chair in the room. "I hope you are comfortable here."

He nodded his head vigorously. "Very much, thank you." He turned to Stoker who had taken a seat on a small barrel of flour in the corner. "I think you have come about your lady?"

"I have. Is she safe?"

Spyridon grinned again, displaying those wonderful teeth. "Of course. She is in the bedroom," he said, nodding towards the closed door in the wall opposite the fireplace. "I would defend her with my life."

Such a statement from a less imposing man might have been humorous, but there was no levity from Spyridon in that moment. He spoke with a single-minded sincerity that I could not doubt, and as he moved to stir his stew, I noticed the narrow sword propped against the hearth.

"You would have made use of your sword to keep her safe?" I asked politely.

He gave me a look that was almost pitying. "I was not always a man who thinks of spiritual things."

"Indeed," I murmured, darting another glance at the photograph of the beautiful crowned woman. I turned to Stoker. "You knew someone would come for the Beauty," I said. I had not intended it to sound quite so much like an accusation, but Stoker held up his hands.

"I did not know. I merely anticipated. And when you were busy with Lady Wellie, I suggested to Spyridon that trouble might be afoot and asked him to keep a watchful eye upon the Belvedere. I did not expect that he would take it upon himself to move her," he finished with a baleful look.

Spyridon pressed a hand to his heart. "Anything for you, my friend."

"But why should you be so willing to shed blood—either your own or that of another—in this cause?" I asked. "You have only just met us."

"Just met!" Spyridon gave a shout of laughter. "I have known Stoker since he was the worst surgeon's mate on board the *Luna*."

I looked to Stoker in astonishment to find him smiling as widely as Spyridon. "I have not seen him since I left the Navy," Stoker explained. "Our vessel stopped in Corfu on our return from Alexandria. I was preparing to resign, and my spirits were not in good order."

Spyridon laughed again, slapping his knees. "Good order? My friend, when I found you, you were stark naked as the day your own mother brought you forth into this world, wearing a tea cosy for a hat." He turned to me to continue the tale. "He was so drunk, he could not find his ship. A ship. Where do you think they might have put it? It is a ship, you understand. A warship! It is not a small thing. And yet my friend misplaces it."

Stoker had the grace to blush and hurried to change the subject. "Lady Wellie wrote some months ago from Athens that she would require a guide in Corfu and recalled I knew someone who might be suited to her purpose."

Spyridon's fruitful brows rose. "Lady Wellie! There is such a lady as you seldom find in Corfu, my friends. So autocratic, so commanding! She demands to see everything on our beautiful island, and I am a good host, so I show her."

"How is it you came to return to England with her?" I asked.

He shrugged. "A man occasionally requires a change of scene," was all that he would say. But I saw his gaze flicker for the briefest of moments towards the framed photograph and back again.

"You are quite certain the Beauty is unspoilt?" Stoker asked, a trifle anxiously.

Spyridon waved a hand. "Go and look for yourself. You will not rest until you have seen." Stoker availed himself of the invitation whilst I remained with our host.

"So you have exchanged a life of holy orders for one of hermit to an Englishman?"

He grinned. "I have never taken holy orders. My habit I wear because it suits me." He flapped the skirts of his garment. "I like the breezes. Like the Scotsman and his kilt, you understand? We too have the kilt in Greece, but the linen is a little thin for this climate. I prefer the longer robes where I can move in freedom."

"So you are not a priest?"

He threw his head back and emitted a roar of laughter just as Stoker emerged from the adjoining room. Spyridon pointed to me. "This flower of a woman has just asked me if I am a priest."

"Satan would have first dibs," Stoker replied dryly, sending Spyridon into a fresh bout of laughter. Stoker looked to me and gave a short nod. "The Beauty is just as we left her."

"Excellent," I said as Spyridon sobered and wiped his eyes. I gave him a moment to finish collecting himself before I began my inquiry. "Did you see anyone enter the Belvedere this afternoon? A stranger lurking about?"

He stirred his stew as he thought. "There was a great rustling in the shrubbery that I think might be a villain, so I creep upon it, ready to do a violence. But it was merely the . . ." He paused, clearly searching for a word, before muttering in Greek. "Chelóna."

"Chelóna? Oh, turtle!" I said in sudden understanding. "You mean Patricia. She is actually a Galápagos tortoise. Very old and rather rare. She was carried to this country by Mr. Darwin himself."

"I like her," Spyridon said. "The tortoise is a very wise creature, although this one, she walks in circles making sounds like a cow." He gave a strangled *moo* and I smiled.

"She is a maiden tortoise," I explained. "She is in want of a husband."

He pursed his lips and pressed his hands together as if in prayer as his eyes rolled heavenwards. "Love is the greatest torment of all," he pronounced.

"Not always," Stoker put in with a warm glance in my direction. "Now, Spyridon. Was there anything else unusual besides Patricia?"

"A female child who set off a tiny bomb, but she is not my child, so I do not worry," Spyridon said with perfect equanimity.

"Lady Christabel," I murmured under my breath. Lord Rosemorran's eldest daughter was forever experimenting with volatile substances, and I made it a practice to give her a wide berth when she was on the trail of something potentially incendiary. The fact that explosives were once more in evidence on the estate meant that his lordship's two elder daughters had returned from their travels.

"A workman came just before teatime, after it had grown dark. Wearing rough clothes and a hat pulled very low, so I did not see his face. I saw him crossing to the Belvedere, like a fugitive. Like a fox," he added, waggling his fingers near his head in imitation of ears.

"Then what?" I demanded.

He shrugged. "Then nothing. Lady Wellie summons me to the house to take tea with her and I go."

"I thought hermits were supposed to remain in their hermitages," Stoker said.

"I am not a very good hermit," Spyridon replied without apology. "But if you worry because I left your Beauty alone, do not fret, my friend. I gave the hallboy, Giorgos, a little Greek coin to watch the folly for me. No one comes, no one goes, he tells me. And my first duty must be to Lady Wellie, my benefactress."

"How is it you know the English word 'benefactress' but not 'turtle'?" Stoker inquired.

"I know many words in many languages," Spyridon replied with a wave towards the bookshelf. "They do not always appear when I call for them."

"Back to the matter at hand," I said, "there is nothing else you can tell us? Perhaps the height of the man you saw? The colour of his hair?" I was thinking of Lord Ambrose's elegant inches and his bright gilt hair.

Spyridon tugged thoughtfully at his beard. "Average height at most. Very slightly built, like a youth, but something about the way he moved says to me he is not a very young man. The hair, I cannot see except a little just at his collar. Very dark."

I frowned. The hair might have been darkened as a disguise; indeed Lord Ambrose would have been foolish to attempt a bit of villainy without it. But he could not mask his inches or the breadth of his shoulders. A man may make himself taller or wider, but to do the opposite is a different matter.

As usual, Stoker intuited my thoughts. "Lord Ambrose would be too cautious to come himself. No doubt he hired a ruffian to do the deed for him."

"Perhaps," I said slowly. "But would a hired hand know precisely what to look for? Would he take the proper care of her? And more importantly, would a man be able to move her alone and without assistance? Particularly in her current state? She is not exactly . . ." I paused and swallowed hard. ". . . pliable."

Stoker considered, then shook his head. "Difficult, even for a man of significant strength. A body, even an embalmed one, becomes lighter after death. But the processes followed in this case seem to have added weight."

Spyridon was looking from one of us to the other, eyes bright with interest.

"Forgive me, Mr. Spyridon, but you seem to have accepted the presence of a preserved corpse in your home with remarkable sangfroid."

He made a gesture of dismissal. "It is not the first time."

I looked at him, frankly startled, and he bared his teeth in a broad smile. "I like you, Miss Speedwell."

"I like you too, Spyridon. I think you will make an excellent addition to the menagerie we inhabit here at Bishop's Folly."

He took my hand again and swept a bow. "Until we meet again." He followed this with a string of sentences in rapid Greek that caused Stoker to rush me from the little castle so quickly my feet fairly left the ground.

"Whatever is the cause for haste?" I asked him.

He stopped and turned me to face him. "Veronica, if Spyridon ever attempts to get you alone, do not permit it."

"Oh. You think he would try to seduce me." I was not entirely surprised. I had dealt with many such examples of ardent behaviour in the course of my travels, and as Stoker was well aware, I had not rebuffed all of them. But since I had given my heart to Stoker, I had no inclination to dally elsewhere. I might not believe in matrimony, but in the joys and powers of fidelity I had perfect confidence.

"No," he said seriously. "I think he will try to propose."

"Propose! Surely not."

"I have seen that look before," Stoker said.

"He has had many wives?" I asked as we resumed our walk back to the Belvedere.

"Seven, at last count. Mind you do not become the eighth."

"I shall do exactly as you advise," I told him.

He stopped dead in his tracks. "Are you possessed by a demon? Shall I summon a priest for an exorcism?"

I smiled innocently. "Can a lady not wish to defer to her inamorato?"

"Not this lady," he said, folding his arms over his chest. "And you have never deferred to anything in your life. What are you up to?"

"I must say, it is extremely offensive that you think I am up to something, as you so vulgarly describe it."

He took a step nearer, his shadow falling over my face, his breath stirring against my cheek. "Veronica."

I huffed out a sigh. "Very well. After Lady Wellie mentioned Parthenope Fleet and her connection to the Curiosity Club, I thought it might be a sound notion to purchase tickets to the tableaux vivants after all. So I spoke to Lady Cordelia this morning and secured our admission."

He furrowed his brow. "Is that all? Parthenope Fleet suggested it as a place to make the acquaintance of Eliza Elyot and Undine Trevelyan.

It was clever of you to anticipate that, but I already knew we were going to have to attend the tableaux."

"Not attend, precisely," I said. I paused, waiting for him to assemble the pieces for himself.

"Oh, no," he said at last.

"Yes. I'm afraid Lady Cordelia had no more tickets to sell. The event is quite popular, the most well-attended of all the Curiosity Club engagements of the year. The only way to gain entrance was for us to agree to pose."

"Us? We agreed to pose, did we?" Stoker could never arch his brow with the same aplomb as his elder brother, but he did a fine imitation— so fine that I found myself squirming just a little.

"We did. And you will be very pleased to know that she is placing us in tableau together. Isn't that nice?" I gave him my most cajoling look.

"In what tableau?" he asked, his eyes glittering.

"A Classical and heroic one," I told him. "You will be playing a gentleman whose physique and talents are so very like your own, it will show you to the most excellent advantage."

"In. What. Tableau." Each word was clipped and demanding.

"Samson and Delilah," I admitted finally.

"And I will be wearing what, exactly?" His tone had turned pleasant which I knew marked the most dangerous point of the conversation.

"A loincloth and a very nice belt." He turned on his heel and strode away, leaving me standing.

"And sandals!" I called after him.

A less clever woman might have made the mistake of attempting appeasement, but I had learnt long ago that a far better strategy when dealing with Stoker's tempers was to ignore them entirely. His anger, though easily provoked, was usually of short duration and handily worked out by vigorous physical exercise followed by a period of intense work upon his latest trophy.

I had expected him to be reconciled to his fate by breakfast the next morning, but this sulk proved a stubborn one, lasting through a frigid swim in the pond, a full day's work spent with his lovely owl, and the entire tray sent up by Lord Rosemorran's cook for our teatime.

"You realise you have taken all of the jam tarts? And the rock cakes?" I asked pleasantly.

"I mean to eat every one of those petit fours as well," he advised me. "And do not even look at the scones. Those are mine."

I stirred my tea and sipped contentedly. "Well, you have not asked, but I will tell you that I have had a most productive day. I finished labelling my case of Dryocampa, dusted the caryatids—they were looking frightfully forlorn—wrote an entire article to submit for the latest issue of *Modern Lepidoptery*, and I have confirmed that Undine Trevelyan will indeed be in attendance tonight along with her guest, Miss Elyot."

He gave me a look of grudging approval. "I suppose that is a small mercy." He slathered a scone in cream and jam and then added a second layer of cream. Never having reconciled the rivalry between the Cornish and Devon methods of preparing scones, Stoker had devised his own method which allowed him to enjoy the best of both. He took a large bite, encompassing half the scone, heedless of the jam dripping onto his waistcoat. "Why do they all have such unfortunate names? First Parthenope Fleet. Now Undine Trevelyan. Why do we never meet a Mary Smith? I should like, just once, to meet a Mary Smith."

"What sort of interesting things would ever befall a Mary Smith?" I demanded. "Who would stab or poison or garrote a Mary Smith? It is unthinkable."

"Not everyone of our acquaintance need be murdered, Veronica. In fact, some people find it preferable to make friends with normal folk."

"How very depressing," I said, sipping again. "I pity them their small lives."

"At least people with small lives do not have to display themselves in public in loincloths," he said darkly. He crammed the rest of the scone into his mouth and chewed with a morose air.

"I realise this is presuming upon your good nature to an unconscionable degree," I said with an attempt at contrition. "But I am prepared to make it up to you."

"How?" he asked, his gaze sharpening at once with an interest I recognised very well indeed.

I primmed my mouth. "How would you propose?" I asked innocently.

He told me. Reader, I did it.

CHAPTER
17

Thoroughly reconciled to his fate if not precisely enthusiastic about it, Stoker accompanied me to the Curiosity Club in good time for the tableaux vivants. The club had been established in a townhouse on a leafy square that received little foot traffic apart from diligent nannies with their shiny perambulators and the odd ambassador from modest governments. As ever, my spirits rose at the sight of the quiet, elegant edifice. The club maintained a discreet entrance with only a small, highly polished brass plaque next to the bell proclaiming its more formal name and motto: THE HIPPOLYTA CLUB. ALIS VOLAT PROPRIIS.

Upon entry, we were greeted by Hetty, a diminutive figure in scarlet silk and matching turban, who acted as portress but who was, in fact, the proprietress. Whether she performed the duties of portress to keep a gimlet eye upon everything that happened in the club or whether it was from an innate modesty was not entirely clear. What was apparent was her unruffled sangfroid as everyone else flapped and fluttered about her, plying her with questions about punch glasses and extra chairs and whether or not men should be permitted entrance to the smoking room as a special treat.

"Men are not allowed upstairs," Hetty reminded the querent. "I know it is a special occasion, but any gentleman who wishes to partake of tobacco is welcome to take himself outside and enjoy a little fresh air whilst he does so."

She turned to me with her customary half smile. "Veronica. Punctual to a pin, and I see you have brought Mr. Templeton-Vane. I understand you are to play Samson for us."

Stoker flushed a delectable shade of rose, and Hetty took pity upon him. "There is a robing room for the gentlemen," she advised him. The lobby where we stood had a chequered black-and-white marble floor. A carved wooden reception desk was backed by a wall of pigeonholes, each fitted with a tiny brass plaque bearing a member's name. A few chairs, tall and extremely uncomfortable, upholstered in black horsehair, were ranged along one wall. The walls themselves were hung with crimson silk, almost exactly the same shade as Hetty's gown, and more of the stuff hung draped in portieres to set off the arches leading to the rest of the club. A wide, sweeping staircase was marked off with a velvet rope bearing yet another brass plaque. MEMBERS ONLY. Hetty waved us in the direction of one of the other wings. "Veronica, after you have signed in your guest, please escort him to the robing room where he will find his loincloth and club."

Stoker very nearly bolted at that, but I simply stood, waiting out his *crise de confiance* until he recovered his nerve. I towed him down the corridor and to the designated room.

"There. Lady C. said your costume will be marked with your name. You need only get yourself into it, and I will be waiting for you right here. She wants us in position well before the first guests arrive, so mind you do not take long," I directed.

He pulled a face so ferocious, I half expected a growl to accompany it. But I merely pressed a quick kiss to his cheek and made my way to the ladies' robing room to exchange my own tasteful evening gown for something rather less English and a great deal more nude. I appeared some few minutes later in a length of pale blue silk that had been wrapped and pinned to approximate a garment of antiquity. A long scarf of darker blue was fringed in heavy gold bullion to complement the headdress and a collection of bracelets that matched the wide gold collar at my throat. My shoulders and ankles were bare, as was a good portion of my décolletage.

I emerged, neatening the drape of the scarf, as Lady C. bustled up, taffeta skirts snapping. "Quite effective, Veronica. What do you think?"

"Well, it is certainly Biblical, although rather more Salome and less Delilah than I expected," I told her.

"You are lucky I chose a modern painting for reference. If I'd selected Rubens, you'd have been bare-breasted as the Amazons," she told me, nodding towards the tribe of women clustered in a group and wearing short tunics, torsos stripped to the waist, swords and spears in hand. Curiously, they were all painted a sort of terra-cotta colour, their wigs and costumes and weapons rendered in exactly the same hue as their ruddy flesh.

Lady C. regarded them with obvious satisfaction. "A triumph! They are going to be displayed in scenes of Amazonomachy, figures silhouetted against black backgrounds such as they were depicted in ancient Greek art," she explained.

"And the rest of us?" I inquired.

"Paintings. We thought it might be an interesting juxtaposition to use modern works depicting themes from antiquity. Yours is the newest, a version by a Basque artist painted only two years ago."

"Will anyone know it if it is so new?"

"Oh, most likely not. That is why each of the tableaux will feature a small version of the art they are meant to represent on an easel just next to it. Guests will be able to compare the two—quite fun, don't you think?" She clucked her tongue. "I must dash. There is Portia, and I mean to have words with her. I have only just persuaded her to pose as Eve instead of Courbet's *L'Origine du monde*, and I want to make certain she is wearing her fig leaves."

She hurried away just as Stoker appeared. For a long moment I said nothing, for there were no words to do him justice. As expected, he was largely naked, although the drapery at his hips covered rather more than I had anticipated. This was white and embellished with a lavish cloth belt striped in coral and black and heavy with embroidery. In spite of my promise, there were no sandals in evidence, only a thick gold cuff encircling one calf. That was the extent of his costume. Everything else was left to Mother Nature, and she had acquitted herself admirably. Long, tumbling black locks, exquisitely formed limbs, a torso heavy with muscle. Not a detail was out of place.

I came to with a start, realising he was quite as distracted as I under the circumstances. He reached for my hand. "Do you think Lady C. would mind terribly if we kept the costumes?" he asked, eyes gleaming.

I did not trust myself to reply. Lady C. returned then, giving him a quick nod of approval. "Very good. Now, places, if you please."

All of the public reception rooms had been set aside for the tableaux, each according to its theme. Ours was Biblical, so she led us swiftly to the reading room where a series of daises had been erected to serve as the settings. Ours was decorated with a low divan heaped with cushions and carpets in front of a wall beautifully painted with ancient motifs. Grasses waved their plumes from a vase in the corner, and just in front of the divan lay a lion skin rug, the head in repose. As promised, a small copy of the source painting rested on an easel beside the platform, and I paused to study it. It was lush with detail, a lovers' nest of comforts captured just before the moment of betrayal. Samson and Delilah lounged intertwined, hands clasped as the hero rested upon his mistress, unaware of his fate. Her posture was more upright, stiffened, no doubt, by the tension of what was to come. Her expression was wary, lips parted in expectation, whilst his was gravely adoring. I peered at the signature in the corner and made out the word "Echena." I had never heard of the fellow, but he certainly knew which end of a paintbrush was which.

Lady C. clucked her tongue and hurried us into position, arranging our limbs this way and that, occasionally stepping back to compare with the painting. At last she was satisfied. "We shall close the doors until the guests arrive. They will be admitted to each room in turn, for fifteen minutes only. For a quarter of an hour, they will be free to peruse the tableaux. Then we will herd them along to the next gallery and close the doors once more. When the guests have seen the last, all of the doors will be thrown open for a further five minutes' return, and then every-one will vote. They have each been issued a token, and the tokens will be dropped into boxes in the refreshment room bearing the name of each tableau."

"And the purpose of voting?" Stoker asked.

"Money," was the crisp reply. "We are raising funds to support the education of a new generation of possible members, our protégées. Each token costs a penny, but further tokens may be purchased for consider-ably more, so if someone wants to scatter their vote amongst several tableaux, they must pay for the privilege. Or if they want to ensure their favourite tableaux wins."

"Wins what?" I asked.

"Glory," she said in a dry voice. "And vintage champagne from W. & A. Gilbey. They have been kind enough to donate a case for the cause. Now, I must get on." A general milling indicated the others were arriving— a spectacularly pretty Bathsheba with her wash basin, Mary Magdalene with a perfume flask, and assorted saints as well as the aforementioned Eve with a serpent. I was particularly happy to see a Judith carrying a sword and a papier-mâché head that looked startlingly like the real thing. Lady C. arranged us all, muttering and fluttering as she did so.

"Portia, you were meant to bring a serpent," Lady C. scolded mildly. "Not a pug in a snake costume." The animal in question—a portly dog of decided antiquity with patches of thinning hair and a dour expression—had been stuffed into a tube of patterned velvet with a hole for his head and a long tongue of red felted wool dangling down between his eyes. The effect was farcical, but the dog did not seem to mind. His mistress set him on the floor and he waddled about, dragging his snake costume behind.

"I couldn't leave Puggy at home," said the figure in fig leaves. "He pines."

A sudden pungency filled the air and Lady C. covered her nose. "Portia, is that dog *flatulating* in my tableau?"

"It isn't his fault," Eve said in defiance as she picked up her errant pet. "He is nervous around new people and his tummy is delicate. A little blancmange would settle it right down. Have you any blancmange?"

"I have not," Lady C. returned firmly. "Now, keep that dog in its place or I will have a fetching pug-shaped hassock for my sitting room come morning."

She swept off as Eve crooned to her pug and Judith admired her reflection in her sword. Stoker rested in my arms, one leg thrown lazily over the other.

Just then the bell sounded, interrupting my thoughts, and the doors were thrown open with a flourish. The next several minutes passed in a mild agony as we attempted to hold the positions we had assumed. The greater the stillness, the more complete the illusion, and although we had been coerced into appearing in the tableau, I had no intention of disappointing Lady C. She had always shown me great kindness; indeed, I would never have been admitted to the Curiosity Club in the first place had it not been for her sponsorship. We had become friends, intimate enough that I was the one person she chose to accompany her to Madeira when she found herself—unexpectedly and without benefit of wedlock—with child. She had concealed the identity of the father and farmed the infant out to a French caregiver, but in the end, she had not been able to bear the separation and Stoker and I had retrieved the boy under the guise of Lady C. adopting him. I am certain the ruse fooled few, but the Beauclerks possessed both the wealth and the power of an ancient name to quell any would-be scandal. Besides which, Lady C. seldom ventured into proper society, preferring the bosom of her large family and the camaraderie of the Club to endless tittle-tattle over teacups with ladies she had never particularly liked. She had been withdrawn after the little man's birth, and I had expected restoring him to his mother would cause her to bloom again. Instead, she had grown thinner and paler over the ensuing months, impatient and occasionally snappish—all qualities I should never have associated with her in the past. As the mistress of her brother's household, she had stepped into the shoes of his dead wife with good humour and common sense, and if the various demands of overseeing the staff and the education of the assorted young Beauclerks had taxed her to the limit, she had been inclined to respond with fond exasperation instead of this new querulousness. It was entirely possible her moods were simply the nerves of a new mother with too many claims upon her attention, but I feared an intrigue was afoot. If so, I could only hope she would tell me, or I should be called upon to prod her secrets out of her. Sometimes, I have noted, it is necessary to provoke people into doing things for their own good, and Lady C. was no exception. Perhaps, I mused, we could discuss matters over a stiff glass of aguardiente and a packet of French cigarettes. There are few things in life more conducive to sharing secrets than modest vices, I have found.

I made up my mind to tackle her on the subject when a propitious moment presented itself, but at present, I was straining my ears for any interesting snippets of conversation from the guests. They talked as if we actually *were* exhibitions of art, letting slip remarkably frank titbits as they lingered. My own figure was admired but it was nothing to the enthusiasm shown for Stoker's.

"Heavens, Millicent," one matron murmured behind her fan to her friend, "do you think all of that is *real*?"

"Decidedly," came the response.

"Perhaps we should touch it just to be sure," the first woman replied. She had just put out her hand when another voice, mildly reproving, joined them.

"I shouldn't if I were you. Miss Speedwell might well take offence, and I have it on good authority she is skilled in the arts of martial combat."

The pair of importunate women squawked and hurried away whilst I suppressed a smile.

"I know you are not supposed to reply, my dear, so pay me no mind, but you look ravishing," said Lavinia Templeton-Vane. "Stoker, if it consoles you, I have not dropped my gaze below your neck, so you may spare your blushes when next we meet."

There was just enough amusement in her voice to indicate she was not telling the whole truth, and I perceived the tiniest flare in Stoker's nostrils.

"My god, I haven't seen that much of you since we were boys and Nanny used to force us to bathe together," came Sir Rupert's voice. I could well imagine his moustaches vibrating in amusement as he regarded his younger brother.

"Rupert, don't tweak him. It's a lovely thing he is doing to raise money for the scholarship fund, and I've half a mind to volunteer you to take part next year," Lavinia warned him.

Without moving his lips, Stoker emitted a sound somewhere between a laugh and a snort. Rupert stepped closer. "You think I can't make as good a showing as you? My calves are just as fine, and I shall prove it." From the tail of my eye, I could see Sir Rupert beginning to tug at his trouser legs, pulling them to his knees.

"Dearest, do stop exhibiting your garters to the world," Lavinia advised. She raised her voice. "We are leaving you now, but I intend to vote for you, and I shall ensure Rupert does the same. Come along, Rip."

They gave way to a succession of other groupings, some couples, some larger parties, all of whom seemed to be having a wonderful time, sipping champagne and commenting frankly on the tableaux. "Well, they aren't quite nude, and I suppose it is for *charity*," said one inebriated voice.

Several more commented on Stoker's muscles, and one intrepid dowager duchess even got as far as poking him just inside his hip bone. "You can always judge a man by his iliac furrows, and these are most elegant. Very good indeed," she pronounced.

Just then Lady C. hurried up to guide the stragglers from the room, indicating they were to proceed to the Hall of Antiquity next door with their Amazons and Trojan heroes jostling the odd Roman empress. As soon as the door shut behind her, another bell was rung, our signal to relax for a few minutes. I rubbed out the kinks in my neck whilst Stoker looked around.

"Are you missing something, beloved?"

"My dignity," he replied dryly.

"Nonsense," called Eve from her plinth. "You're doing splendidly. Far better than Puggy and I," she added, petting her canine snake with fond exasperation. "He will keep trying to get away."

We exchanged pleasantries until the bell rang again and we resumed our poses. There were several repeat visitors—I recognised a few voices and the odd flash of a distinctly coloured gown—but we also had latecomers, one pair in particular who seemed a little rushed. They paused just in my eyeline, and I was able to study them for a moment. The taller of the two ladies had an exuberant coiffure of heavy black curls, pinned high atop her head. She was slim with a broad-shouldered, athletic build. I could well imagine her stalking the countryside in a comfortable pair of trousers, field guide in hand as she studied botany or rocks. The other was shorter, more delicate of feature, and younger. She was also very pale, with the suggestion of frailty about her, and the yellow of her frock did her no favours. It washed what little colour she might have had out of her complexion. Her hair, some indeterminate shade between blonde and brown, was limp and wan, gathered in an enormous plait at the nape of her neck. The entire effect was of a flower, once blooming and now etiolated, robbed of sun and sustenance until only the shadow of vitality remained.

"I am sorry," said the younger lady said to her companion. "If I had not lain down so long this afternoon, we would have been here on time to see all of the tableaux."

"Never mind," consoled her friend with a pat of the arm. "You had the headache and it could not be helped. I am only glad you felt well enough to come out tonight, Eliza. Now what do you think of this one?"

The pulse at the base of my throat quickened. Surely this was Eliza Elyot and her friend, Undine Trevelyan. Parthenope Fleet had alluded to Eliza's poor health and broken nerves as well as Miss Trevelyan's solicitous protection of her.

No sooner had I determined their identities than they moved away, hurriedly making their way down the row of tableaux and choosing their favourite. I waited in agony, cutting my eyes to Stoker's to find he was giving me a significant look. He had heard them as well, then, and come to the same conclusion as I. It seemed an eternity until the bell rang and we were free from our perches. I leapt to my feet and rushed from the room, Stoker hard upon my heels. Together we headed directly for the refreshment room where the guests would be gathered to cast their votes. I expected something of a crowd, but the room was absolutely *heaving* with people, all drinking champagne and conversing loudly enough to rouse a slumbering saint.

"We will never find them in this crush," I said in despair. I stood on tiptoe, trying to see above the throng, but in vain. It was Stoker who spotted them, standing by the set of double doors that gave onto the entry hall. I saw Hetty give a signal to one of the maids to fetch their wraps.

"They are leaving!" I cried.

Stoker took my arm and began to push through the crowd, but it was akin to swimming upstream against a strong current. "I feel rather like an amorous Canadian salmon," I muttered darkly.

We had gained half the distance of the refreshment room when I stopped, gasping aloud. "Stoker," I hissed. "*Look.*" I directed his attention to a gentleman standing some little distance away from the two women, watching them closely.

The fellow was oddly dressed, a heavy dark coat shrouding his figure. A black hat with a broad brim had been pulled low over his brow, obscuring his features. But it was his manner rather than his attire which caught my attention. Whilst the rest of the assembly were drinking and laughing, conversing loudly as they compared notes on the tableaux and hailed their acquaintances, this gentleman kept to the shadows of the room, his back against the windows as if he could not bear to leave himself without a means of escape. He was watchful as a cobra, his still gaze trained intently upon Eliza Elyot. His manner was curious, furtive even, and it occurred to me he might have some malign intentions towards Miss Elyot. I felt a sudden frisson at the young woman's vulnerability, watched as she was unawares. She must have felt the weight of his scrutiny then, for she turned suddenly, and her eyes locked with his.

Her eyes flared in astonishment, her mouth gaping. She made no sound of distress, no movement towards him, but stood rooted to the ground as deeply as Daphne herself, clearly overcome.

The gentleman had likewise been motionless, but he recovered more quickly. Before Miss Elyot could stir a step, he turned and vanished, only the gently wafting portieres betraying that anyone had ever been there at all. Without discussion, Stoker and I gave chase, pushing our way through the crowded assembly until we emerged through the same window into the damp night air. The window gave onto the street, and the fellow had vaulted to the pavement some five feet below. Stoker did the same, landing lightly on his bare feet before slipping onto his posterior, swearing lavishly as he did so. I saw no reason to subject myself to the same injury, so I leant as far out the window as I dared, calling encouragement.

"You managed that most athletically, my love. But you needn't get up too quickly," I advised. "He has got away."

I nodded to where a carriage was springing away from the kerb.

"Oh, in the name of bleeding Jesus—" Stoker began with a little modest blasphemy and continued on in the same vein as he picked himself up and dusted himself off. The sight of a half-naked man standing on the pavement startled more than one passing matron, and he hurried inside where I met him at the door.

"I am bloody lucky I wasn't arrested," he said coldly.

"But it was not in vain," I told him. "I saw the crest on the side of the carriage as it drove away."

His expression brightened. "Did you indeed? Who was the devil?"

"That I cannot say. The carriage was borrowed from its rightful owner," I said, drawing him to where Undine Trevelyan and Eliza Elyot still stood. "But Lord Ambrose Despard has a great deal to answer for."

Undine Trevelyan was still standing with an arm around a startlingly pale and sinking Eliza, speaking low and urgently to her, no doubt encouraging her to leave as we approached them. Before Undine could demand our business, I plucked a feather from the hat of the nearest lady and thrust it into the gaslit sconce. It flamed up, and I blew it out, wafting the smoke under Eliza's nose.

"I haven't a vinaigrette on me, but a burnt feather will do just as well," I said kindly.

Undine clutched Eliza more tightly. "We do not require assistance," she said, but even as she spoke, Eliza sagged. Without waiting for permission, Stoker swept the unfortunate young woman into his arms.

"How dare you—" Undine Trevelyan began.

"I am a former surgeon's mate with Her Majesty's Navy," he replied firmly. "This lady wants medical attention. Now, you can either accompany us to a quiet room where I will render her aid, or you will get out of my way, but you will not prevent me from helping her."

There was something overawing about him in that moment, commanding even, in spite of his loincloth—or perhaps because of it. Undine Trevelyan hesitated, and in that moment, the battle was won.

"There is a little anteroom just across the hall," I said. "We can move her there away from all these prying eyes," I added. Undine looked about and suddenly realised that although most of the crowd were excitedly discussing the event, one or two groups had begun to glance our way with obvious curiosity.

"She would not like to be the centre of attention," Undine Trevelyan admitted. I guided our little band from the refreshment room to the anteroom. Hetty used it most often for storing the tools of housekeeping but it suited our purposes perfectly. Stoker, with infinite gentleness, deposited Eliza Elyot onto an upturned bucket before beginning a cursory examination. Her eyelids fluttered, and he peered into her eyes, assessing the state of her pupils as he held one forefinger to her slender wrist.

She blinked furiously, clearly startled to find herself face-to-face with a strange man in a state of shocking dishabille. My own appearance must have done little to reassure her, but the sight of Undine's face seemed to calm her. "Undine, what has happened?"

"You had a giddy turn," Stoker told her. "Nothing more. Your pulse is a little too fast, so I would like you to sit quietly for a few moments before you attempt to move."

Wide blue eyes looked from one of us to the other. They were pretty eyes, and would have been unremarkable in another young woman, but in Eliza Elyot they carried such an expression of wariness, of tragedy even, that I could scarcely stand to meet them.

"Are you a doctor?" she asked in a thin, reedy voice. "You don't look much like a doctor."

Stoker gave her a gentle, rueful smile. "I don't look much like anything reputable at present," he admitted. "I am supposed to be Samson. But I used to be a surgeon's mate in the navy. My name is Templeton-Vane, and this is Miss Speedwell." To my astonishment, he extracted a card from his loincloth and presented it with a flourish. Undine Trevelyan twitched it out of his fingers and read it closely, as if suspecting us to be impostors.

Eliza Elyot nodded at me. "How do you do?"

"Very well, Miss Elyot."

She flinched a little, but her reaction was nothing compared to Undine Trevelyan. "How do you know her name?" she demanded.

"Really, Miss Trevelyan, there is no call for you to be pugnacious. We know who you are because we have been looking for you. In fact, we are only here tonight in hopes of making your acquaintance."

Undine flushed deeply, an unfortunate circumstance, given her freckles. She seized Eliza's hand and would have pulled her to her feet if Stoker had not put himself bodily between them.

"We are leaving," Undine said stoutly. She was tall for a woman, reaching above Stoker's ear, but she was nothing to his solidity. Her frame was bony, and I had little doubt she could hold her own if it came to wringing the neck of a chicken or wrestling a reluctant child into a bath, but Stoker could have flicked her away like so much thistledown if he'd chosen. Instead, he merely looked down his nose—an aristocratic trick they must learn in the cradle, for in my experience, anyone from an ancient family can do it, regardless of height—and waited.

Undine was an impetuous woman but not a stupid one. She knew when she was beat, and she sagged against the wall. "What do you want?"

"We wish to ask a few questions about Lord Ambrose Despard," I told her.

Eliza gave a little cry of dismay and shrank backwards. This time, Stoker stepped aside, and Undine went to her, clasping her near and petting her hair. "It is monstrous of you to torment her like this," Undine said, fairly spitting the words.

"We have no intention of tormenting Miss Elyot, but we require answers," I replied. "It is a matter of justice. A young woman has met with misadventure—possibly even murder. And we believe Miss Elyot can help us discover her identity."

"How?" Undine demanded.

"By telling us about her brother Julius," Stoker replied.

And that was the moment Eliza Elyot slipped unconscious to the floor.

CHAPTER

18

We roused her once more—resorting again to the burnt feather—but this time Undine Trevelyan thwarted us. She looped one arm around Eliza and hauled the ailing girl to her feet.

"We are leaving," she said stoutly. "And you will not stop us."

Stoker took an obliging step backwards and let them go, Eliza sagging heavily against Undine as they went. They did not return to the refreshment room but left the club altogether.

"Well, that did not go particularly well," Stoker observed.

"I don't know," I said slowly. "They are afraid—clearly and desperately so. Giving them a little time to think matters over might just persuade them that they need allies. If we present ourselves in a calmer moment, perhaps they will confide in us."

"Or Undine Trevelyan might set fire to us. I think it could go either way, honestly," Stoker said.

We quitted the anteroom to find Lady C. coming our way with all of the imperiousness of a steamship. "There you are! I have been searching for you everywhere. The votes have been tabulated and all of the participants are requested to be present for the awarding of the prizes." She shepherded us into the refreshment room again where we were made to stand next to Eve. Her erstwhile serpent, Puggy the flatulent lapdog, took quite a shine to Stoker, sitting firmly upon his feet and refusing to budge.

"Oh, he likes you! Isn't that nice," Eve remarked. She looked more closely at Stoker. "You aren't by any chance a connection of the Templeton-Vanes? Only you do put me in mind of the viscount."

"Tiberius is my eldest brother," Stoker admitted through gritted teeth. "I am Revelstoke Templeton-Vane."

"Revelstoke! And I thought my father ran mad when it came to naming his children," she said merrily. "I think as we are all half-naked, we needn't stand on ceremony. I am Lady Bettiscombe, née March."

She turned to me inquiringly and I introduced myself, shaking hands with her as the dog emitted another cloud of effluent causing Stoker to hold his breath.

"Stoker," I admonished. "This is no time to indulge in asphyxiation."

"It might be the foulest thing I have ever smelt, and I have worked on cadavers," he muttered.

With the help of Puggy's mistress, we disentangled Stoker from his new friend and gave our attention to the presentation of the prizes. We placed third behind the Amazons in second and the winner, a Mona Lisa who bore a startling resemblance to the original and turned out to be a slender youth called Edwin. He was thoroughly delighted with his prize champagne, but Stoker was not consoled with our placement.

"I was stripped nearly naked and almost suffocated by a decaying pug," he grumbled as we made our way home, fully dressed and resembling once more the respectable citizens we were. "That ought to count for something."

"Never mind," I soothed. "The evening could hardly have been more productive. We have made the acquaintance of Miss Elyot. There has been the introduction of a complication in the form of a mysterious gentleman in black, and he has a connection to Lord Ambrose, a fellow who has already engaged our suspicions."

"Up to his pretty neck in it," Stoker agreed. "I suppose you are going to insist we call upon Miss Trevelyan and Miss Elyot without delay?"

"For once, I mean to surprise you," I told him. "I think we ought to wait."

"Wait? Veronica, I had no notion that word was even in your vocabulary. You are the most impetuous, headstrong, reckless—"

"There is no call to make hurtful remarks," I cut in.

"Hurtful? I mean them as compliments. I could not endure the company of a Miss Elyot for ten minutes, fainting and swooning and giving way to fits of the vapours." He paused to shudder. "I cannot think of anything more horrifying than shackling oneself for all of eternity to a woman with anything less than your courage. You are a lioness, Veronica." I sniffed hard and he peered down at me. "My god, if you mean to weep, warn me so that I may stop the cab and leave you here upon this pavement."

"I do *not* mean to weep," I said, blinking furiously. "How lowering that you should think so. I was merely reflecting on how felicitous it is to be understood and loved for oneself—really loved, with no design to alter or diminish the object of one's affection. It is a rare thing."

"To change one hair of your head would make you something other than Veronica," he said simply.

"Stoker, do look that direction and survey the contents of that window," I said, directing him towards the inviting goods of a pastry shop whose wares had been temptingly arranged.

He did as I asked and in a very few moments I had blown my nose and wiped my cheeks, slipping my hand in his.

"I was jesting, you know," he said in a low voice. "You may weep in front of me. I do not promise to enjoy it, but I will endure it."

"I do not care to weep in front of *myself*," I told him dryly. "You may imagine how little I like it with an audience."

He squeezed my hand and we sat thus, enjoying a rare moment of calm as we surveyed the passing streets. It was early enough that the fashionable folk were still abroad, their carriage wheels ringing out as their silks swished up steps and into private houses and glittering theatres as the narrow crescent moon rose high overhead. The streetlamps lent a warm glow, causing amber pools of light to gather at the corners, and the first chestnut sellers of the season were abroad, roasting their wares over smoking braziers. The aroma of them mingled with face powder and falling leaves and the arisings of the horses waiting patiently at the kerbs. It was not a remarkable scene in any way, only the same comings and goings London had seen for centuries and would doubtless see for centuries more. We were tiny players upon that stage, I realised, called upon to deliver a short line or two before taking our bows and exiting forever. And the distance between one's entrance and one's final curtain was a short one indeed in the scope of eternity.

I said as much to Stoker, and he nodded absently. "Yes, we shall all be dead soon enough."

"How maudlin you are!" I scolded playfully. "And so melancholy about it that I have half a mind to argue the opposite and say we shall live forever."

He shrugged. "We thought of death often in the navy. The sea is so vast, it has a way of making everything else small. We planned for our deaths even. Hardly an evening passed that we did not debate whether it was better to be taken by sharks or lost in a storm or swept overboard by a rogue wave. And if the sea herself did not take you, there was always the chance of a handy bombardment to do the job."

"And what did you conclude? How would you choose?"

"I never could make up my mind," he said solemnly. "A man cannot choose to die when he has never yet learnt to live." He paused and the tightness settled behind my eyes again. But before I could respond, he went on. He put a fingertip to the heavy gold earring hanging from his lobe. "Do you know why sailors pierce their ears?"

"Boredom?" I hazarded.

A tiny smile played about his mouth. "It is so that when we are lost at sea, if our bodies wash up on a foreign shore, there is money enough to bury us. Clothes are torn off in the waves, you see. Only an earring, solid gold and of high purity, might survive long enough to ensure a proper burial. A sailor is never far from his own death. He makes friends with it the moment he sets foot upon his first ship, and he walks with it forever." He paused. "There was one lad, a young midshipman, newly come aboard. He was careless of his footing in a storm and slipped overboard. It happened so quickly, he never even had a chance to cry out. By the time we turned 'round, he was gone. We were not far off of Cyprus, and it is possible he landed there, on the rocks of the shore. But he hadn't had a chance to pierce his ear yet. I used to wonder if his body ever made it to shore, and if it did, what they would have done for him with no money to pay for a grave."

"I understand," I said, pausing suddenly to search his face. "That is why you wish to find the Beauty's identity, to lay her properly to rest. It is because she has washed up amongst strangers."

"Something like that," he said.

He might have spoken matter-of-factly about such things, but I understood that to speak of them at all meant he felt them deeply. He must have contemplated his own mortality on a daily basis aboard the *Luna*, and I was not surprised the experience had marked him forever, as indelibly as his collection of tattoos. We fell silent then, understanding one another better under the narrow glow of that cold silver moon.

When we reached the grounds of Bishop's Folly, we alighted and he walked me to my little chapel. The interlude that followed was one of unusual tenderness, slow and ardent, and all the more passionate for its sweetness. Long after, when the candles had guttered into darkness and we lay, limbs and bedsheets entangled so thoroughly it was impossible to say where one of us left off and the other began, I stroked his hair.

"Stoker?" I whispered, uncertain if he slept.

After a moment, he gave a low groan. "Veronica, I am only human. You will have to wait at least an hour or two."

"Not that. I was thinking about death again. About how sailors are always prepared for theirs, and that is why you wear your earring."

"Hm . . ." His voice trailed off and I knew he was near the precipice of sleep.

"Well, I forbid you to die," I told him. "I should not like that at all, you know. I have grown far too accustomed to you to do without you. But I do not think you should have to do without me. So I think we should make a pact. Neither of us is permitted to die without the other. What do you think?"

He wrapped his arms more tightly around me. "I promise. If I am ever near death, I vow to take you with me."

"That is not precisely what I had in mind," I began, but a soft snore told me the moment had passed. I continued to stroke his hair long into the night, reflecting that dying with him would be a very pleasant way to go indeed.

CHAPTER

19

The next day, I completed my ablutions and breakfast, preparing for a full morning's work. Upon my desk lay a half-finished illustration of an eastern tiger swallowtail—*Papilio glaucus*—that begged completion to accompany my latest piece for *The Lady Lepidopterist's Bi-Annual Journal.* I was just preparing to settle to work when George, the hallboy, appeared, a bit out of breath. This was nothing unusual—the child never walked when he could run—but the sight of the tamarin perched on his head, clinging to his curls with both little fists was a bit out of the ordinary.

As soon as the monkey saw Stoker, it gave a little squeak of ecstasy and leapt from George's head, brachiating gracefully across a series of clotheslines I had erected to dry a batch of watercolours until it dropped neatly onto Stoker's shoulder. He gave it an absent pat, fishing in his pocket for a bit of honeycomb Cook had made up fresh for him only that morning. The creature took it in its sticky paws, licking it with finicky grace.

I glanced to George, surveying him with surprise. "George, your hair is wet. Is it raining?"

"No, miss," he said woefully. "'Tis the monkey what did it."

"Oh, dear. Well, if that is the worst atrocity she has perpetrated upon your person, count yourself lucky. I hear she bit the gardener last week."

"And the auld Greek fella what lives in the pink castle," George informed me. "But he says monkeys is lucky and we oughtn't give her a good slap."

"Spyridon is quite correct," I told him firmly. "Monkeys are clever and, for the most part, clean." I glanced to where the tamarin was grooming herself, extracting the odd flea and crushing it between her nails before popping it into her mouth like a sweetmeat. I suppressed a shudder. "Have you brought the post, George? We have had the third delivery and it seems early for the fourth."

"Oh, no, miss," George said, recollecting his errand. "You've visitors like. They are waiting outside until they are sure they are welcome. A Miss Tree and friend."

"Miss Tree? Are you quite certain of the name?" I laid aside my pen and stripped off the linen sleeves I wore to protect my shirtwaist from ink and paint.

"No, miss," George said comfortably. "It were a strange name, and that is all I heard of it. There is more, but I only remember the first bit."

"That is enough," I assured him. "Please invite Miss Trevelyan and Miss Elyot inside."

In the few moments it took for George to fetch our visitors, Stoker dashed up the winding circular stair to the washroom to scrub the worst depredations of the morning's work from his person. He had been at his labour for less than a quarter of an hour and already he bore traces of sawdust and glue, although mercifully he had not yet acquired the feathers, bits of fur, ink stains, or paint smudges he was certain to be sporting by the end of the day. I smoothed my skirts and tossed biscuits to the dogs to keep them quiet. One dog is a delight; five are a nuisance. I had just got them settled when our guests appeared. Undine Trevelyan was dressed in a shade of green that made her look frankly bilious whilst Eliza Elyot, in black, was so pale as to seem translucent. Her pinned plait seemed almost too much for the slender neck, like a peony stem bowing under the weight of a heavy bloom. As she walked, she kept Undine's hand tucked firmly under her arm.

"It was not my idea to come," Miss Trevelyan said by way of greeting. "But Eliza insisted."

"You are very welcome," I told them both.

Eliza was looking about in frank astonishment. "This place is extraordinary. I have never seen anything like it."

"It is a bit of a madhouse," I said with a smile. "But it has its enchantments. Would you like a tour?"

"I should love one, but perhaps not today," she said. Her lips were bloodlessly pale.

"Of course," I told her. "If you think you can manage the stairs, it is far more comfortable in the snuggery." I gestured towards the spiral staircase at the end of the gallery and she nodded, still holding tightly to Miss Trevelyan's hand.

I followed them up the stairs, pleased to find Stoker had poked up the fire in the small tiled stove and put on a kettle. The cups were mismatched, assorted Wedgwood and Sèvres pieces from sets the Rosemorrans had long since broken. But the tea was hot and strong, the finest Assam, which I was pleased to see Miss Elyot took with two hefty lumps of sugar. She looked as if she needed nourishment, and with his instinctive courtesy, Stoker took out a tin of his favourite violet shortbread and offered it 'round. Undine seemed as if she could scarcely bring herself to accept our hospitality. She kept a weather eye upon her companion, waiting until some colour crept back into Eliza's cheeks at the steam from the teacup before she unbent a little and accepted a cup for herself.

"I wanted to thank you both for your assistance last night," Eliza began. Her voice was low and halting. "I fear we were abominably rude to you."

I was on the point of agreeing but I saw that Undine had raised her chin, clearly spoiling for a fight, so I smiled instead. "Not at all."

"We were," Eliza said with a flash of humour. "But you wanted to discuss my brother, and it's been such a long time . . . that is, it is still so difficult . . ."

She trailed off into a silence that lasted a long, painful moment before Undine covered Eliza's hand with hers. "Julius Elyot was a genius," Undine said simply. "Not as great a genius as his sister, but a genius nonetheless."

Stoker looked at Eliza. "I am sorry for your loss, Miss Elyot. I have three brothers of my own, and I cannot imagine your grief."

I choked a little on my tea. Stoker's relationship with his brothers had been fraught at best. The product of his mother's affair with an Irish painter, Stoker had been the cuckoo in the nest. The law demanded that old Lord Templeton-Vane's name was given to the evidence of his wife's indiscretion, but that had never stopped him from observing a marked difference between Stoker and his own sons. The various entangled resentments of their youth remained with them long into maturity, and it was only in the past several months that Stoker attempted any sort of rapprochement with his siblings. I liked to think it was due in part to my influence, but hearing him speak so unguardedly about his affection for his brothers, I wondered if he had harboured far greater depth of feeling for them than I had suspected.

Miss Elyot smiled gravely. "Thank you. I think. Living with Julius was complicated. And so has living without him been."

She paused again, and I broke the silence. "Parthenope Fleet agrees with Miss Trevelyan's assessment of your work, you know. She says the possibilities of applying galvanic science to the domestic sphere are remarkable, capable of reshaping society. That is very exciting."

"It would be if she could secure the proper sort of funding to carry out her researches," Undine put in darkly.

"Surely there are grants and patrons," I began.

She snorted. "Grants! Patrons! Yes, for men," she said, fairly spitting the word. "Male scientists need only click their fingers and pots of money are made available to them because they are men and because they intend to put electricity to use in ways to benefit other men—ships and trains and public lighting. But explain to a man how much more *useful* it would be for a laundrymaid not to break her back over a mangle and see how quickly he buttons up his pockets. It is maddening."

"I understand," I told her. "Many is the time I have tried to explain to a male collector that the largest butterfly is not necessarily the *best*, that one looks for symmetry and perfection of feature rather than size as the only metric of superiority. But do they listen? They do not."

"Exactly," Undine said, giving a small nod of satisfaction. She seemed to thaw a little more then, deigning to drink some of her tea as Stoker carried on his gentle interrogation of Miss Elyot.

"Your brother's work was also in galvanic science?" he asked.

"Yes," she said faintly. "He taught me everything I knew when I first started. I began as his apprentice. Apprentice! How I elevate myself." Her little smile turned wry. "He trusted no one, you see. No one but me. It was always thus. It came from being orphaned together. And from being twins, I think. The bond is an unusually strong one. Julius's genius was recognised very early. His intellect, his curiosity, they were remarkable, and suitable arrangements were made for his education." She paused, appearing to choose her words carefully. "I was much like him, if it is not immodest to say it myself. Our interests were congruent, and my abilities were not far short of his. But I was not permitted to share in his education."

There was no need for her to elaborate. Few families were willing to lavish funds and effort on the formal education of a daughter, no matter how promising. Even in our own royal family, the Prince of Wales, stolid and slow, had always been promoted above his quick-witted and clever elder sister. It was an abominable practise to hamper the development of daughters, but it was deeply ingrained. My only consolation was the growing number of young women whose talents were being fostered by organisations such as the Curiosity Club. Perhaps with time, luck, and money enough, we could effect change.

Eliza Elyot went on. "Julius understood how much I longed to join him in his studies. He brought home books, journals, papers. He made every effort to replicate the lectures and experiments he enjoyed in order to share his education with me. It was a kindness I never forgot. And when the time came for him to leave school and establish his own laboratory, he permitted me to join his work and observe his experiments."

"What sort of experiments?"

Eliza said nothing for a long moment, but the pain writ upon her face was eloquent.

"He was attempting to reanimate the dead, was he not?" Stoker suggested.

She reared back as if he had struck her; livid patches even rose high upon each cheekbone. But she nodded. "How did you guess?"

Stoker's smile was grave. "Did you see the trophies below?" he asked, gesturing towards the ground floor of the Belvedere. "Row upon row of specimen, the most interesting and complex creatures in all of the natural world. Each of them is frozen in time as it was when life departed. My work is to preserve them, to give them equal dignity in death to that they knew in life—more if possible. I oil feathers and stitch hides and sculpt their expressions, and some of them are so lifelike, one might imagine them on the point of growling or purring or roaring. But they are mere shadows of what they were. However comprehensive my talents, and I am very skilled," he added with no false modesty, "I cannot ever truly capture the spark of divinity within a living being. To do *that* would be to touch God."

Eliza Elyot shook her head, bewildered or marvelling, I was not certain which. Perhaps both. In the end, she smiled. "It is like listening to Julius speak. He believed the limits of death might be tested, the line between mortality and eternity blurred. I never quite knew if it was blasphemy or genius."

"The greatest genius often is blasphemy," Stoker told her.

"I think you must be right. In Julius's case, his genius became an obsession. He began with simple things, like frogs. All experimenters with galvanic science begin there," she said. "They all ape Volta, but Julius soon decided such things were parlour tricks, nothing more. He saw no art to making the legs of a toad twitch, but to resurrect something greater, something grander, that was his ambition. He spoke of himself in brotherhood with men like Leonardo da Vinci. There was no humility in Julius. I should like to call it confidence, but what Julius had was something more—some gift only devils in Hell know. If I believed in such things as cursed stars, I would say he was born under one, to be so single-minded in purpose, so devoted to one thing. To know such obsession is not healthy," she said, sitting forwards, thin hands clasped around her knees. The bones of her fingers shone white through the taut skin. "One must have other interests, amusements. One must love—a pet or a person. But Julius loved nothing except his work. The meanest beggar on the street may keep a cat, some poor puss with mange, grateful for a shared crust and devoted to its impoverished master. Julius had nothing and no one—except me. And Ambrose Despard."

"He assisted in your brother's work?" Stoker asked as he refreshed her cup of tea, dropping in several more lumps of sugar. She curled her fingers around the cup as if to take the warmth through the porcelain and into her pale, slender flesh.

"He did. They were at school together. Ambrose's family are famously eccentric, so there was nothing in Julius's aspirations to alarm or frighten him. He is not a clever man," she said with the cool, assessing brain of a scientist. "But he knows cleverness when he sees it. He is drawn to it, like a moth to flame, with just as disastrous a result. He was Julius' only friend. And when Julius was sent down from university for the unorthodox turn his studies had taken, Ambrose insisted upon leaving as well. They set up house together, built a laboratory, and that is when Julius invited me to join them."

"He did not trust Lord Ambrose?" Stoker inquired.

Eliza Elyot's eyes flicked to the bulldog snoring at Stoker's feet. "Your dog, what is his name?"

"Huxley."

She looked up in surprise. "After Thomas Henry Huxley? Darwin's bulldog?"

"Just so," Stoker affirmed.

"Have you had him a long while?"

Stoker cocked his head, thinking. "Five years."

"Does he bring you the spoils of his hunting?"

"Too often. Only last week, he dropped half an enormous rat into my bath. He was so proud, I hadn't the heart to scold him."

"Has he been a faithful dog?"

"None better," Stoker said, reaching to fondle Huxley's ears. One had a slightly moth-eaten look where Betony had taken to gently chewing it, and he snored so loudly he had, upon more than one occasion, driven me from Stoker's arms and into the quiet repose of my own bed. But there was no doubting his loyalty to his master.

Eliza nodded. "And yet, you must expect someday he will grow old and grizzled, perhaps a little lame. His eyes will rheum and his steps will slow, and the time will come when you will go on without him. Such is the nature of the relationship between dogs and masters. And such was the nature of the relationship between Julius and Ambrose

Despard. Julius wanted someone to sit up and take notice of him, to bring him tasty morsels, to lay at his feet and stare in admiration. Ambrose did all of those. He lauded his genius and opened his pockets and poured rivers of gold into Julius' work. Some men are born to genius. Some have a talent for sniffing it out. Ambrose is definitely the latter."

"Did he mind?" I asked. "The disparity in their abilities?"

"No. He was content to play the midwife to Julius' schemes. I think he believed standing in Julius' shadow at least meant he felt the effects of the sun. But shadows are cold things, Miss Speedwell. And nothing grows well in darkness."

It seemed churlish to point out that any number of things thrive perfectly well in darkness—bats, opossums, most species of fungi, several intriguing moths—so I said nothing and let her enjoy her metaphor, however inapt. I looked to where Miss Trevelyan sat, motionless, hands folded in her lap. She had put her teacup aside and taken no further refreshment, her gaze fixed upon Eliza's face, her own expression somehow tortured, like Moses glimpsing the Promised Land he knows he will never live to enjoy.

I turned my attention back to Eliza Elyot as she continued her tale. "We lived comfortably enough, in an unfashionable quarter of the city where no one knew us and we could afford a large warehouse to serve as the laboratory. The work was hard, but I did not mind. We saw no one, we met no one. But, again, I did not mind. I had pennies to call my own, and yet I counted myself lucky. I did not have to dress to please anyone but myself. I did not have to tat lace or découpage fire screens or learn to play the piano. I did not have to make stilted conversation with awkward young suitors as they steered me around a ballroom with sweaty hands. I was very nearly independent, at least I believed I was. It felt like freedom, Mr. Templeton-Vane, but I have come to understand it was anything but. I was as captive to my brother's demands as Ambrose. His obsession did not afflict him—it afflicted all of us, and like so many afflictions, it came on gradually. So gradually, we hardly noticed. When it all began, he was content to carry out his experiments on squirrels and cats. Then dogs and a small cow once. It was ridiculous, in a way. Almost impossible to take seriously. Until the day he brought her home."

"Her?" Stoker asked softly.

"The girl," she answered. I felt a thrill of excitement torch my veins, and it took every bit of my discipline to hold my cup steady in my hands as her small, reedy voice went on.

"What girl?" Stoker pressed.

"The one pulled from Regent's Canal, fifteen years ago," she replied. "The drowning girl he carried home and experimented upon. The one he meant to bring back to life," she finished, covering her face with her hands.

CHAPTER

20

After a moment, Eliza Elyot composed herself and lifted her face. Her eyes were rimmed in red, but no tears had fallen and her nerve seemed steady. Perhaps she had wept enough over her tortured genius of a brother.

"Tell us," Stoker urged.

She nodded. "You wanted to speak of Julius in connection with a young woman who may have met with misadventure. You can only mean *her*. The girl from the canal. It has been fifteen years, but I have forgot nothing of those days. The memories are my most constant companions. I haven't really spoken of it to anyone, not even Undine," she said with a glance at her friend.

The greatest painter would have struggled to capture the warring emotions in Undine's face. Pity and horror mingled there; a touch of resignation even as she so obviously resented what was happening. And above all, a hopeless sort of love. It was as if Julius Elyot's grave secrets lay between them, poisoning all that might have been good and pure.

Eliza swallowed hard and went on. "She drowned in February of 1873, at least that is when she was found in the canal, and she had not been dead long. She was floating there, they said. Like Ophelia, drifting amidst the water weeds."

It was on the tip of my tongue to inquire about the particulars—how she was dressed, was there anything significant about the spot she was found—but Stoker, with his exquisite perception of my thoughts, waved me off with the single flick of his forefinger. His eyes never left Eliza's face, and she seemed thoroughly oblivious to the gesture, wrapped as she was in her reminiscences.

"The police had more pressing business than identifying one anonymous girl, so they sent her to a mortuary. Julius knew the proprietor and the old fellow—Plumtree, his name was—suggested Julius sculpt a death mask of her. Julius had taken a few such commissions before, always for grieving relations who wanted a memento. They paid well, and it was a way to keep the wolf from the door when Ambrose's allowance was cut off. His father, the old marquess, was the capricious sort, never entirely comfortable with Julius, and there were times when the marquess would put his foot down and the money would be held back, and Ambrose would return to the bosom of his family. Those were the lean days, when Julius did whatever he could to earn enough to feed us both until Ambrose could find a way to return to us. And he always did return. The marquess was forever getting distracted by something or other, and Ambrose would turn up, apologetic and brimming with brass, ready to fund the next great project."

She paused, taking a little sip of her cooling tea. "This was one such time. Ambrose had been absent for some weeks and had only just returned to us. Julius was a little behind on the bills, so he agreed to look at the girl, to sculpt the death mask so she might be identified. Any artist with a modicum of talent could have done it, but we were short of money, and he was fond of old Plumtree. So he went to have a look."

She stopped again, as if to drink once more, but suddenly she seemed to think better of it and set the cup down absently. "I do not know how to describe it except to say it was a coup de foudre. The strike of the lightning bolt. I had never seen him so affected. It wasn't simply admiration for a pretty face—that I could have understood. This was some sort of dark enchantment, a bedevilment I will never comprehend. It was as though, once having seen her, he could not do without her. He returned from Plumtree's speaking like a madman, feverish and agitated. He said all of the experiments that had come before, all of the electrifying of frogs and resuscitating of bullock's hearts had been like a child playing at the thing. But he was certain he could do it properly now that he had a purpose."

"What did Ambrose say to this?" Stoker asked.

She spread her hands. "He thought it was impossible, a lunatic's dream. But he loved Julius like a brother. He believed in him, utterly. He thought it best to humour him, to give him the time and support he required to attempt the experiment. Ambrose thought it would fail, as did I. But . . ." She hesitated.

"Miss Elyot?" Stoker sat forwards in his chair just a little, his voice low and coaxing. There was an irresistible warmth to his gaze, a promise of understanding and safety that would have overpowered a stronger woman than Eliza Elyot.

"I think there was a part of Ambrose that believed he could do it. That he would do it. And I think it excited him."

"What of you?" Stoker inquired.

"What can I say to my credit? I ought to have opposed him. But I too was gripped by his ambitions. I can plead only my youth and my fondness for my brother that I was so easily led into aiding his endeavours. I worried, constantly, about the implications of what we were doing, the moral considerations of playing God. And yet I could not bring myself to leave. If Ambrose played the accomplice, then so did I. I wrote up his notes and prepared the serums and injections and chemical baths as Julius instructed. I brought him food and made up a pallet in the laboratory. He would not leave her, you see. Not from the moment he brought her to us."

"How did he manage to gain possession of her?" I asked, careful to keep my voice as neutral and soft as Stoker had done.

"He paid Plumtree," Eliza said with a shrug. "The old fellow had overextended himself by building a railway of the dead and needed the money badly."

"We have seen the railway," I told her.

She roused herself to an expression of surprise. "It still exists then? I am surprised. It was poorly built and unsound even then. But that is how Julius got her away. They thought it would be more discreet. Under cover of darkness, she was carried to the cemetery as if for burial, but once there, Julius and Plumtree, with Ambrose's help, transferred her into a cart to bring her to the laboratory. Plumtree entered her burial into his ledgers so it would appear she had been properly laid to rest, and that was the end of her existence, officially."

"And the beginning of her time in your brother's care," Stoker finished.

She nodded. "Yes. Ambrose was very involved in the work. His pet interest was in the preservation of dead tissues, and it was essential to keep her wholesome until Julius' work could be carried out." Possibly without intending to, Undine made a little face of distaste, doubtless contemplating the effects of decomposition upon the poor girl as she lay in Julius Elyot's infernal laboratory.

Eliza spoke again. "So Ambrose helped him, as did I. It would have been far simpler to remove her viscera as the Egyptians did when they preserved the dead, but Julius was adamant that she remain intact. So she was submerged in baths and injected with chemicals, foul things that had to be pumped through each of her systems—digestive, circulatory, nervous. It went on for weeks, the stuff of nightmares. I began to wonder what was real and what was illusion. We worked all hours, day and night, never resting properly. At last, the work was finished. She was, to all appearances, exactly as she had been the day she arrived in the laboratory, only better. She was perfectly preserved against destruction. And once she was perfectly preserved, the next step was inevitable."

"To resurrect her," Stoker said.

"To resurrect her," she echoed. "It was a fantastical notion, like something out of Verne. We quarrelled about it, loudly and at length. But Julius would not be swayed. He insisted that he was in the right, and nothing I said could persuade him otherwise. He cast me out, without a friend, without a penny."

She drew a deep breath, as if steeling herself. "I am not proud of what I did next, but I did not see an alternative at the time."

"Because there was not one," Undine Trevelyan broke in fiercely. Her face glowed like one of the fanatical saints bound to a pyre and awaiting the first flames. But her religion was Eliza Elyot, and I wondered how much she would suffer, how much she would endure for the sake of her beloved.

Eliza smiled, the gentle indulgent smile of a parent towards an excited child. "You will excuse me anything, Undine. A wiser woman might have found a different way. But I was young and badly frightened—not just of being sent away from my home but because of what my brother had become. There was no reasoning with him. I saw that Ambrose too was caught up in Julius' plans. He was afire with enthusiasm for the project, but I knew there was one person who would not stand by and let that happen."

"His father, the marquess," Stoker guessed.

She nodded. "Yes. I went to him and told him everything in hopes he would intervene. I only meant for him to go and speak with them, perhaps to take Ambrose away, because without Ambrose's help, Julius could never have managed. But his lordship was not prepared to limit his efforts to curbing his own son. He had a friend with the Metropolitan Police—the head of Special Branch."

"Sir Hugo Montgomerie?" I asked in astonishment.

"I cannot recollect the name, but that sounds familiar," Eliza said. "The marquess said he would enlist this gentleman's help and have my brother's laboratory raided and Julius taken up on criminal charges. You must understand how shocked I was by this," she said earnestly. "I had no idea the marquess would be willing to go so far with the matter. I thought he would fear the scandal of public denunciation when his son's involvement became known. I pleaded, but he would not be moved. He was confident he could use his influence to keep Ambrose's name out of the newspapers and out of official reports. He said he would give me a day's grace to make arrangements for my own future before he set the authorities on them." Her mouth twisted bitterly. "I was treated with as much consideration as a hunter shows his best bitch. A pat on the head and sent away to have my supper. I begged him not to do this, not to make a criminal of my brother, not besmirch our name for generations. But he would not be moved."

"You did your best in an impossible situation," Stoker said. "You were very brave. I doubt I'd have done half so well in your shoes."

She shook her head. "Do not speak kindly to me, Mr. Templeton-Vane. You have not yet heard the worst of my sins, and they are weighty indeed."

"Go on," he coaxed.

She took a deep breath, the thin chest rising and falling slowly. "I had not told the marquess that Julius had cast me out. That was my own private shame. I thought to purchase a little dignity for myself by keeping that secret, but in the end, it was the only reason the marquess delayed. Some misguided notion of chivalry, I suppose. He wanted me to have enough time to return home and collect a few things, and be gone when the police came. But I employed those few hours rather differently than he intended."

"You warned Julius," I guessed.

The eyes she turned to me were anguished. "Wouldn't you? I knew my brother, Miss Speedwell. He would have repented of his coldness to me. Indeed, by the time I returned home, he already regretted much of what he said. I think Ambrose must have reminded him of our natural affection for one another, of how it had been the two of us against the world for so long. And so I related to him what the marquess intended." She hesitated as bright tears sprang to her eyes. "I thought all of his anger had been exercised that morning, but it was nothing compared to the rage that fell upon my head when I told him. Ambrose was struck by guilt and horror that his own father meant to be the instrument of Julius' destruction. He vowed to do all that he could to help, but Julius was beyond listening. He flew at me, and if you look closely enough in strong light, you can still see the scars of what he did." She paused, her smile mocking. "But then betrayal should leave its mark, shouldn't it? The mark of Cain? That night, the laboratory was completely consumed by a fire—set, I believe, by Julius' hand. There was no police raid because there was nothing left. The fire brigade recovered a signet ring from the ashes." She touched the fourth finger of her hand where a glimmer of old gold revealed what had become of the ring. "It was our father's, and Julius was never without it. They said the fire burnt hot from all the chemicals—too hot for any trace of him to survive. So I had nothing to bury. His notebooks, his life's work, his body. Everything was lost. I might have starved if it were not for Ambrose. He kindly made me an allowance, a small amount, but enough to keep me from beggary. I took rooms and kept to myself for a long time. I had suffered too many shocks to move easily amongst people, you understand. But after some years, I grew interested in work again, and I began to attend lectures, to make a friend or two," she added with a look at Undine. "I am lucky to have such a companion as Undine to help me." Undine made no reply, and Eliza Elyot canted her head towards Stoker, her gaze sharpening. "How is it that you came to know about the girl from the canal? Of her connection to Julius?"

"We made the connection through Plumtree's," I said smoothly. "The new owner of the establishment is a recent acquaintance of ours. He was surveying the records and noted a curious thing—an anonymous young woman who was listed as buried in a spot that could not possibly hold a grave. There was a further note that her likeness had been sculpted by Julius Elyot, and so we hoped to find him to see if we could discover more about this unfortunate girl's fate." I saw no point in giving out more information than necessary, and Stoker remained silent, allowing the conversation to unspool as I wished.

Eliza stared steadily at me. "But you said there was a suggestion of murder," she pressed. "How would you know that unless you had seen her?"

"It is the likeliest explanation for a body pulled from Regent's Canal," I replied.

"Surely suicide would be more probable," Undine Trevelyan put in.

I shrugged. "It is difficult to know at such a remove. Fifteen years is a long time. Besides, how would we have seen her?"

Eliza's nostrils flared just a little, the only sign of emotion. "I believed all of Julius' work was lost in the fire. If there is any suggestion that this young woman's body survived, I should like to know it. I deserve to know it," she added fiercely.

"You have suffered a great deal in the past," Stoker said, his tone heavy with sympathy.

"And more recently," I added. "The gentleman at the club last night—"

She pressed her lips together. "I am embarrassed that I allowed my emotions to get the better of me. I lost my composure entirely."

"Why, Miss Elyot?" I asked, gentling my voice. "Was it because the gentleman you saw reminded you of your brother?"

She bit down hard upon one bloodless lip and nodded. "Yes," she said in a low voice. "God help me, he did. I thought I was losing my senses, my very sanity. To have known him dead for fifteen years, and then to see a man who resembled him so closely . . ." Her voice trailed off and Undine covered Eliza's small fingers with her own.

Stoker and I exchanged glances, and it was he who spoke, giving gentle voice to the obvious inference. "Miss Elyot, you said the body of your brother was not recovered from the fire. And this gentleman resembled him greatly. Further, he seemed to know you."

He paused, letting comprehension fall, terrible as it must.

She swallowed hard. "You think this man was Julius? That somehow he survived?"

"You must allow it is possible," I told her. "The timing of the fire was providential, was it not? Destroying all evidence against him just when the walls were closing in? You said you gave him warning of what was to come. Perhaps he saw no other way out and seized the opportunity to disappear."

"That is monstrous," Undine Trevelyan breathed.

"But possible," Stoker pointed out. He turned once more to Eliza Elyot. "Is it not?"

She nodded gravely and when she spoke her voice was a horrified whisper. "Yes. Julius would never have permitted them to take him. He was too proud. I thought he would be content to die rather than face disgrace and imprisonment. But to elude capture altogether, that would have amused him." Her mouth twisted and a harsh note sounded in her tone. "That he would have left me, believing him dead for all this time—it is unimaginable, and yet. I cannot deny it is entirely within his character. And I can find no other explanation for the man we saw last night."

"But if it is Julius, why has he come back? What does he want?" Undine demanded.

Stoker and I studiously avoided looking at one another, but I knew he had reached the same conclusion as I, the inescapable deduction that Julius Elyot had not only survived the fire but had returned for his Beauty. There were no records from the Raby warehouse to confirm the hypothesis, but it was too elegant and tidy a hypothesis to be incorrect. Julius had arranged for her safekeeping whilst he had been abroad; now that she had disappeared from her hiding place, he had returned to find her. It would not do to alarm Miss Elyot on that score, and I was searching for some bland reply to Miss Trevelyan's question when Eliza's gaze sharpened.

"She survived, didn't she? The girl from the canal? Julius' most prized experiment? Did he leave her here in London and now he has come back?" Her eyes were bright, glittering with sudden conviction. "That is it, isn't it? He would never have allowed her to be destroyed when the laboratory burnt. I ought to have known, ought to have guessed! He has returned for *her*."

Undine pressed her hands to her cheeks, clearly horrified. "But we do not know that Julius has done anything of the kind!" she protested. "You upset yourself for nothing."

Eliza went on as if Undine had not spoken, her voice gaining conviction with each syllable. "And Ambrose would have known of it—he must have. Julius could not have escaped English justice alone. But Ambrose had money. Julius could have done it with his help."

"These are wild suppositions, fantasies! You must not distress yourself," Undine urged.

"I know it is true—I feel it here!" Eliza cried, striking her breast with a fist. "He was my twin, Undine. You cannot know what that meant. He was as much a part of myself as my limbs or brain or heart. We were never divided except when he went to school. I knew him, man and boy, and I know him still. It is as though I were wandering in a fog these past years, but I see it so clearly now, his desperation, his rage. This is exactly the sort of melodrama that would appeal to him."

"But to leave his only sister to grieve his death, to starve in the streets," Undine began.

Eliza gave a sudden harsh laugh. "But he did not leave me to starve. I have had a small allowance to keep me clothed and fed, remember? And by whose hand? *Ambrose Despard's*. No, Julius crafted some diabolical plot, and Ambrose has been his henchman. If only there were proof of it!" She dropped her head into her hands with an anguished sob.

"But there is," I told her.

Eliza looked up sharply. "What do you mean?"

"Last night," Stoker said. "When the gentleman you believe to be your brother left the club, he got into a private conveyance—a carriage bearing the arms of Ambrose Despard."

For a long moment, Eliza was motionless, bloodless it seemed, all colour and vitality drained from her face. She sat, unblinking and silent, until Undine groped once more for her hand. "It is true then," she said finally. "Julius is returned. And Ambrose knows it—has known it all these years. Yet he never saw fit to tell me."

"It is unforgivable," Undine said. "To aid Julius was criminal enough, but not to warn you that he was alive and back in London—why, Julius might have killed you last night!"

Eliza flinched at this and Stoker leant forwards. "Miss Trevelyan is right. If your brother bears you any ill will from what happened fifteen years ago, then you are not safe. We can go to Lord Ambrose and speak with him—"

"No," she cut in firmly. "Mr. Templeton-Vane, I appreciate your concern, truly. But I acted precipitately once before, and my brother escaped justice. If we do not proceed quite carefully this time, he may do so once more. And this time he may be forever lost." She paused and turned to collect us all with her imploring gaze. "This has all been the most tremendous shock. I am unable to think as clearly as I ought, but I do know we must be cautious in our approach. I ask for your word as a gentleman that you will not approach either my brother or Lord Ambrose until we have spoken again and developed some plan of action when our minds are cool and rational."

"Of course," he told her solemnly. She put out her hand and he seized it in his larger one.

She moved to shake mine then to strike the same bargain, and I held hers fast. "You have my word, Miss Elyot. But I shall require yours."

Her thin brows raised in surprise. "Mine? In what capacity?"

"As you say, your brother escaped justice once before. I remind you that it was your doing. He will know you saw him last night, and he may well attempt to play once more upon your sisterly affections. I want your promise that you will not attempt to warn Julius that we are hard upon his trail."

She gripped my hand with a surprising firmness. "You have my word, Miss Speedwell."

As our callers prepared to leave, I spoke again. "One thing more. Stoker is correct that Julius may be nursing a grudge. And any man who would commit arson is an estimable foe. It might be best for your own safety to go to a friend's house to stay for a few days."

Eliza gaped at me and began to protest, but Undine proved a sudden and stalwart ally. "Parthenope. We shall go to Miss Fleet and ask her to shelter us until this madness is over."

Eliza considered this a moment, then gave a nod. "Very well. We shall go to Miss Fleet."

She took Undine's hand then, tucking it firmly under her arm as they descended the stairs to take their leave of the Belvedere. Stoker's innate courtesy would have dictated he show them out, but I put a hand to his sleeve to stay him.

"Let them go," I said. "They will be halfway down Marylebone High Street by now, and they will not thank you for giving chase."

"I suppose," he grumbled. "But I do not feel at all good about frightening that poor woman to death. Did you see her pallor? I've known jellyfish with better colour."

"It will do her no harm to be forewarned," I said, pouring another cup of tea. "She is the obvious target for Julius Elyot's vengeance if he has returned, and if she does not prepare herself for that, the consequences might be disastrous for her—perhaps even fatal."

In the end, I was mistaken. Eliza Elyot was not, in fact, the target of Julius' vengeance. But the next day brought news of an unexpected death just the same.

CHAPTER

21

The next morning I woke later than is my habit, taking my time over my toilette and lingering over a leisurely breakfast. I planned an entire programme of hard work for the day, intending to apply myself with diligence to the cataloguing of a new collection of *Hyalophora cecropia*, comely moths from North America recently acquired by Lord Rosemorran. Moths are not, as a rule, my favourite, but these were enormous creatures, seven inches at the wingspan, and beautifully coloured with crimson bodies and dark wings banded in white and khaki. I had only rarely seen such moths, and never of such variety and quality as these. I spent the day amongst them, the hours flying past as they did when I was so happily engaged. After dinner, I had just settled to finish painting my swallowtail illustration when Stoker appeared, pale under his tan and brandishing the evening edition of the *Daily Harbinger*.

"Have you gone off the *Times*?" I teased gently. "I seem to recall you saying it was the only fit newspaper for a gentleman to read after teatime."

To my surprise, he did not respond to my raillery. Instead, he thrust the newspaper under my nose. It took me a long moment to comprehend the implications of the headline, and another to skim the accompanying article.

PEER'S BROTHER FOUND DEAD IN TRAIN COMPARTMENT

"Oh, *no*," I breathed. I took the newspaper from him, reading the article a second time. It carried scant details, only informing the public in a rather breathless tone that Lord Ambrose Despard, the younger brother of the Marquess of Harwich, had died en route to Southampton where he had intended to board a ship for New York. He had been travelling alone in a first-class compartment and had apparently died of natural causes.

"Natural causes!" I rattled the paper in indignation. "They cannot be serious."

His expression was almost pitying. "You have become familiar enough with the ways of aristocracy to understand what is happening."

I blinked. "You mean they are covering this up?"

"Of course they are," he assured me. "It is the way of things for the great and good."

"And it requires no great leap of imagination to suppose who might have been responsible," I said.

He nodded grimly. "Julius Elyot."

"Ambrose Despard knew Elyot was alive—that much is proven by Elyot's use of his carriage. And it is likely Despard gave him a place to stay, perhaps even in his own house," I mused.

"My god, what fools we were! We ought to have gone straight to Despard's and confronted him as soon as Eliza left us yesterday."

"But using Despard's carriage suggests relations were cordial between the two men. How could they have fallen out so badly in less than twenty-four hours?" I asked.

"I can think of forty different reasons," Stoker said, bitterness limning his voice. "Not least of which is that Elyot is clearly in the grip of lunacy."

"If he has returned for the Beauty, perhaps he thought Despard knew something of her whereabouts and was concealing them," I suggested. "Or maybe it's to do with Eliza." I read the brief notice again. "How might Elyot have done it? It couldn't have been a bloody enterprise, or it would have been too difficult to conceal the matter."

Stoker shrugged. "The heir to the Austrian throne managed to murder his mistress by gunshot before taking his own life in January, but did you ever see a photograph of the hunting lodge where it happened? A sensational story in the newspapers? No, they concealed it as far as they were able." I had to concede the point. When the news of Crown Prince Rudolf's death finally broke, court authorities insisted he died of heart failure and didn't even mention the unfortunate girl who had died at his side, not even as a footnote. It was weeks before the whispers started and even longer before the truth was known. It had been nearly a year and still no one knew the full story of what happened at Mayerling.

"Yet Lord Ambrose did not murder anyone, so there is no sordid story for the Marquess of Harwich to cover up. And the Despards are hardly Hapsburgs," I pointed out.

"No, but they have money. And influence. To a family such as that, any whisper of foul play, even if Lord Ambrose were an innocent victim, would be anathema. They would insist upon killing the story before it even circulates. And they are well skilled in the arts of bribery," he reminded me. "They were prepared to purchase silence for Lord Ambrose's activities in Julius Elyot's laboratory."

"True enough," I admitted.

"And to answer your question, Elyot might have shot him with a very small calibre of firearm at close quarters. Strangled him. Garroted him. Poisoned him. Smothered him—" Stoker would have carried on, ticking off each grisly method on his fingers, but I held up a hand.

"Your point is made, my dearest." I turned back to the brief piece in the *Harbinger*, reading it over yet again in hopes of gleaning some snippet I had missed before. But the prose was desiccated, devoid of anything of interest and consisting only of the barest facts, such as they were. I tossed the newspaper aside in annoyance. "The question remains, what is our best course of action now?"

Stoker's expression was set as immovably as that of a pharaonic statue.

"We are going to Ambrose Despard's house and find Julius Elyot."

A re you entirely mad?" Mornaday demanded an hour later. We had summoned him with J. J., and they had responded with alacrity. As I had yet to attend my butterflies for the day, we repaired to my vivarium for our council of war. The vast glasshouse had been abandoned, subsiding into gentle decay before Stoker persuaded Lord Rosemorran to repair it and fit it with steam heat for the purpose of breeding and studying lepidoptery. Since his lordship's agreement with the plan, every broken pane had been repaired, every rib of cast iron sanded and painted gloss black. It gleamed in the lamplight, and the damp warm air was luxuriously sultry after the foggy chill of the evening without. Hundreds of tubs had been planted with the various trees and shrubs best suited to harbouring the specimens I wished to breed and to feed, and the resulting fragrance was intoxicating. Everywhere one looked was another example of verdure to soothe the senses and refresh the eye, and the occasional glimpse of flapping jewelled wings was a modest enchantment. That the vivarium remained in such good order was a testimony to my hard work—as well as that of his lordship's staff—and the standing order forbidding any of the Beauclerk offspring within its confines. It was one of only a handful of dicta laid down by the earl that was observed without fail by his children, and I was grateful as much for the peace of the vivarium as the possibilities for my work.

Leaving the duties of hospitality to Stoker, I busied myself by tying up the odd overhanging branch of buddleia and milkweed and preparing sustenance for my winged companions. As Stoker is an indifferent host at the best of times, tepid tea was poured and J. J. was given a few soft ginger nuts whilst Mornaday gazed longingly at the small plates of sliced fruits I was assembling. I laid them out in odd corners along with saucers of honey for a pretty batch of mourning cloaks before turning to my next chore. I uncovered the china bowl carried down by one of the maids, happy to find it was not cool from the larder but felt warm to the touch. When I pulled back the cloth, it gave off a gently pungent aroma which increased exponentially when I placed it onto a wooden board and began to chop.

"My god," Mornaday said, pinching his nose. "Must you feed the dogs now?"

"This is not for the dogs," I said, mincing the decaying meat into still finer pieces.

"You don't mean to say—" He broke off, looking faintly queasy.

"Yes, Mornaday. Butterflies eat meat. *Apatura iris*, the purple emperor is particularly fond of carrion. The vultures of lepidoptery, I call them," I informed him as I heaped up the gory bits and set the plate aside. Almost immediately, a large and busy specimen of that variety flapped over on indigo velvet wings, treading on the oozing pile with tiny, careful feet. He unfurled his proboscis to prod gently at the offering before condescending to feed delicately. "There," I told Mornaday happily. "As graceful as a duchess in his manners."

"There are things I have learnt in your acquaintance, Veronica, that I can truly say I wish with all my heart I had never known. That butterflies, those beautiful harbingers of spring, could eat carrion is one of them."

He returned to his tea, flopping heavily into a chair and accepting the tender ministrations of Vespertine who came to lay a kindly head upon his knee. "You're a grand old lad, aren't you? Hm? You care about poor Mornaday? Perhaps I can teach you a trick or two and we'll take to circus life. It's about all I am fit for now that I'm no longer a copper."

"No longer a copper! Have you been discharged?" I asked in real concern.

Mornaday shook his head, sunk in gloom. "No, but as good as. Sir Hugo is still away, and I thought to have a little peep at his files from the time the Beauty was retrieved from the canal."

"And?" J. J. demanded.

Mornaday rubbed Vespertine's ears. "I was caught. I heard Inspector Abbington coming and had just enough warning to close the file drawer, but I had nowhere to hide. Inspector Abbington, I might add, is not a particular enthusiast of mine," he added dryly. "He demanded to know what I was doing in the office where he has been working during Sir Hugo's absence. I couldn't very well admit I was rifling through Sir Hugo's private papers, so I told him I believed Lord Ambrose Despard was murdered."

I blinked at him. "But that is *our* theory," I told him as I gestured towards Stoker. "That is why we asked you to come here tonight."

Mornaday shrugged. "It is the obvious conclusion."

"It is not," I said, feeling unaccountably put out. The fact that Mornaday had arrived at the same theory as we had was vexing in the extreme. "But we will concede the point. We have asked you here because Stoker and I have information you do not." I paused, allowing the expectation to build.

"What is she doing?" Mornaday inquired of J. J.

"She is being theatrical," J. J. informed him. "It is a dreadful habit of hers. Do not encourage it. Veronica, speak plainly. What information do you have?"

"We have reason to believe Julius Elyot is alive," I proclaimed in ringing tones.

J. J. and Mornaday exchanged glances. "And he staged his own death when he burnt down his laboratory before travelling to the Continent where he has been living quietly ever since," Mornaday said helpfully.

J. J. took up the narrative. "Julius Elyot returned to this country three days ago under his own name but has not registered at any of the major hotels in London."

"How do you know all of that?" I cried.

"Because you are not the only one with sources," J. J. put in, looking very much like a cat who has just been at the cream pot. "Mornaday and I are every bit as capable of asking questions and developing lines of inquiry. Between the two of us, we have learnt quite a few things of significance."

"I was able to ask a favour of a friend who works at the entry point in Dover," Mornaday said, not unkindly. "He remembered the name as the spelling is unusual. The suspicion that Elyot staged his own death was recorded in a memorandum in the file in Sir Hugo's office. It was thought best to simply let sleeping dogs lie and not pursue the matter. As for the hotels, J. J. knows every desk clerk, major domo, and housekeeper within twenty miles."

"We were supposed to be investigating this *together*," I reminded them coldly.

"And we are," J. J. replied, smoothing her skirts over her lap. "Mornaday and I are here, are we not? We came to discuss the development of Lord Ambrose's death and exchange ideas about the current whereabouts of Julius Elyot."

"You are only here because I invited you," I pointed out.

"No," she said patiently, "you sent for us, which is an entirely different matter. Mornaday and I are tired of being overlooked, Veronica. You and Stoker," she said, gathering him into the conversation with a glance, "have an irritating habit of behaving as though you were the main characters in every story. But Mornaday and I have notions of our own, you know. We have things to contribute, ideas and stratagems. *Insights.*" I gaped at her, then snapped my mouth closed as she went on in a kindlier tone. "It isn't your fault. I suspect it is a matter of genetics. Royal blood has a tendency to make a person high-handed, and heaven knows Stoker has six centuries of aristocratic ancestors looking down loftily at the rest of us."

Stoker raised a brow but did not bestir himself to comment as I looked to Mornaday. "Do you feel the same?"

He tugged uncomfortably at his collar. "Well, I think given what J. J. and I have contributed to previous investigations, we might have earned a bit more of a place at the table," he said, blushing furiously and staring at the tips of his shoes.

"Very well," I said, striving for a courteous tone. "We shall bear that in mind going forward. Your contributions have indeed been valuable. But I have to say, I do think you mishandled the situation with Inspector Abbington by telling him you think Lord Ambrose was murdered. Clearly there is some sort of effort underway to conceal the fact, and you have put him on notice that you mean to ask awkward questions. Hardly discreet, Mornaday."

Mornaday's expression was outraged. "I might remind you that the Metropolitan Police are actually the ones whose responsibility it is to solve murders, not this motley crew of insufferable amateurs. Besides," he added, subsiding into sullenness, "it did no good whatsoever. Inspector Abbington was furious I even suggested such a thing. Apparently he had just finished a very cordial interview with the Marquess of Harwich who promised to stand him membership at his club if the matter could be handled quietly."

"Surely he did not admit to you that he accepted a bribe from the marquess," Stoker protested.

"Oh, no," Mornaday acknowledged. "But the implications were very clear. I was not to breathe a word of my suspicions, ill-founded and incendiary as they were. When I dared to press the matter, he began to throw around words like 'slander' and 'suspension.' I am relieved of duty until further notice," he finished darkly.

"And what did you learn from Sir Hugo's private papers?" I asked.

He shrugged. "Little enough besides the report indicating Elyot had likely escaped to the Continent. There were newspaper cuttings—a story about the fire, Elyot's obituary—and a letter."

"From the late Marquess of Harwich, presumably," J. J. put in.

"Just so. Thanking Sir Hugo for his discretion in the matter of the 'recent unpleasantness' as he put it. There were no details given. The marquess was too canny a fellow for that. He wrote in the vaguest of terms, but the dates tally. The letter was dated 1873."

"And the cuttings?" I asked.

"From the *Daily Harbinger*, a brief obituary stating the barest facts of Elyot's life with no mention of a surviving sister or how he died."

"They painted him out of his own life," J. J. mused.

"They must have been so happy to wash their hands of him," I agreed. "How very convenient for them. Did no one think it too convenient?"

Mornaday spread his hands. "If they did, there's no record of it in Sir Hugo's files."

"I suspect he would have forgot the matter entirely were it not for the marquess's gratitude," Stoker said blandly.

"How cynical you are!" I exclaimed. "Sir Hugo is an upstanding man of the most comprehensive probity. You make it sound as if he intended to blackmail the marquess!"

"Not blackmail," Stoker corrected. "But I think we all understand Sir Hugo is man enough of the world to know the worth of a marquess's gratitude."

"Hear, hear," Mornaday said, extracting a flask from his pocket and taking a deep draught.

"Have you taken to strong drink then?" J. J. inquired, her eyes bright with mischief. "Only do let us know if you can't hold it, and we will be certain to roll you home, you feckless inebriate."

Mornaday drew himself up, offended. "I will have you know it is peppermint tea, you fishwife. My stomach has been none too good these past few weeks, and ever since Abbington relieved me today, it's been positively afire."

He swigged again, muttering darkly as J. J. blew him a kiss of apology. "Save your gallant gestures. I am ended as I always knew I would be—friendless and ruined. I shall be cast on the streets and finish my days as a beggar man."

"Come now," J. J. chided. "It needn't be so dire. We shall all contribute a little and buy you a barrow. You could push it through the streets and sell muffins. Wouldn't you like to be the muffin man?"

Mornaday bared his teeth in a humourless grin. "I don't know why you are so high and mighty, Miss Butterworth. I've had it on good authority that your editor at that filthy rag of yours is none too pleased with your work after your latest failure."

"That is hardly my fault," J. J. snapped in return. "I cannot help it if Nellie Bly decided to embark upon a trip around the world in eighty days just a fortnight before I was due to depart on exactly the same voyage!"

Stoker's attention volleyed from one to the other as they bickered, but I held up my hand before J. J. could elaborate on her antipathy towards her American nemesis.

"Enough. We shall get nowhere by haranguing one another. Now, let us review what we know and what we may hypothesise. Julius Elyot staged the illusion of his demise fifteen years ago and disappeared to the Continent. At that same time, Lord Ambrose placed the Beauty in storage at the warehouse of one John Raby. When Raby died, his widow saw fit to disperse his holdings, and the consignment was sold to Lord

Rosemorran. In the meantime, Julius becomes aware of the apparent loss of the Beauty and hurries back from the Continent in hopes of retrieving her—which he first attempted earlier this week when he broke into this place. He was unsuccessful thanks to Stoker's precautions," I added with a nod to Stoker. He accepted the compliment with a little bow, and Mornaday muttered something profane under his breath. Naturally, I ignored him and carried on. "But matters have taken a decidedly deadlier turn with the murder of Lord Ambrose Despard."

"Another example of your leaping to conclusions and calling it rational, but it does seem the likeliest explanation," J. J. admitted.

I inclined my head graciously. "Thank you. And now we must test our hypothesis by going to Ambrose Despard's house and searching for clues to Julius Elyot's current whereabouts."

"When you say *going* to Ambrose Despard's house," Mornaday began.

"We mean trespassing, should the circumstances call for it," Stoker replied.

"Agreed," J. J. said stoutly. "Justice requires it."

"Requires!" Mornaday straightened, upsetting his teacup and spilling the beverage down his trousers. "No one is ever required to attend such folly, J. J. The Despard family have clearly chosen discretion over truth in disseminating the story of Ambrose's death. His brother is a marquess which makes him only slightly less important than God in this country or have you forgot the pecking order?"

"I am aware of it," she replied calmly.

"Then you ought also to be aware of the dangers of being pecked by a pecker such as that," he returned. He held out his teacup to me before recollecting I had not yet washed the traces of gore from my fingers. He shuddered again and set his cup down with a rattle. "I cannot afford any black marks against my name at present. I am *this close* to being discharged from my post altogether," he said, holding his forefinger and middle digit a scant inch apart.

J. J. leant forwards, putting her eye to the gap. "I can still see daylight, Mornaday. You can risk it if the rest of us can."

Mornaday looked at Stoker, pleading. "I know we have not always enjoyed the warmest friendship, but you must support me. Breaking into Lord Ambrose Despard's house is madness. Persuade J. J. of the folly."

"He would have to persuade more than J. J.," I put in, raising my hand. "I also vote that we go."

Mornaday thrust his hands into his hair, disordering his curls as he looked in despair to Stoker. "Come, man. Be my supporter."

With a grin, Stoker raised his hand slowly into the air. J. J. whooped as she thrust hers skywards. Mornaday groaned and dropped his head.

"Be of good cheer, Mornaday," I counselled. "There is strength in numbers, after all. Now, let me just wash the blood from my hands and we will be off. Excelsior!"

CHAPTER

22

It was the work of a very few minutes to make myself presentable. J. J. never cared much for her appearance, and Stoker had exhausted his efforts at elegance with the call upon Parthenope Fleet. He had subsided again into that peculiar combination of practicality and flamboyance which only highlighted his masculinity. I caught suppressed sighs from Mornaday and J. J. at the sight of him—for very different reasons, though. Mornaday was always conscious that, for all his winsomeness and charm, he would never match Stoker's more rustic magnetism whilst J. J. was simply responding, as most women did, to the bewitching contradiction of courtly manners coupled with an exterior that would have done a buccaneer proud. (In the interest of accuracy, I feel compelled to point out that J. J.'s appreciation of Stoker's appearance was entirely without intention. She admired his physique with the dispassionate eye of a connoisseur of art surveying a particularly fine painting. Her affections, such as they were, could best be described as "elsewhere engaged.")

For my own part, I made a great show of donning a new hat and a heavy cloak against the chill of the evening, but I saw no need to advertise to the others the fact that I had secreted rather more weapons about my person than was my custom. A pair of sharpened hatpins winked from the heart of the roses on my chapeau whilst a stout stiletto had been strapped to my calf. My cuffs were studded with minuten, and if we had had more time, I might have attempted to secure a small explosive from Lady Christabel. But the argument that would have ensued—Stoker took a dark view of things that were detonated—would have surely delayed us further.

So we set out, four against the world, or rather three with a reluctant Mornaday in tow. I half expected him to make his excuses and cry off before we reached Lincoln's Inn Fields, so volubly did he grumble, but when we arrived at our destination, he was with us still. I gave him a fond grin, for Mornaday is, in spite of his occasional lack of intrepid spirit, one of my favourite people.

We stopped to conspire in the square across from the house, considering our options. The house itself lay shrouded in darkness; no friendly light beckoned from above the front door, and no glimmer of illumination shone from any window.

"Clearly no one is about. I say we go around the back and break in," J. J. said.

"Break in? To a townhouse owned by a marquess's son? Do you wish to burn my career to ashes in a single night? You cannot turn housebreaker in the company of a police officer," Mornaday protested.

"Can you think of better circumstances under which to break into the townhouse of a marquess's son than when accompanied by a police officer?" she returned.

"She does have a point," Stoker said reasonably.

"She bloody well does not!" Mornaday's nostrils flared like a young bull's. "Very well. I see I shall have to exercise my masculine charms."

"Upon the footman?" I asked. "I suppose that might work . . ."

"Not upon the footman!" he roared. "Upon the scullery maid." He gestured to the house next door where a light shone in the area giving on to the cellar. "It is late enough the cook will have retired to her room, and you can wager your last corset string the butler himself will not be found belowstairs at this hour. No, the only creature stirring down there will be some poor young drudge with callused hands and a hope in her heart."

"How can you possibly know that?" Stoker inquired.

"Because whilst you were burnishing your brass buttons aboard one of Her Majesty's ships, I was earning an honest wage, walking the beat like any new bobby. I spent half my days in kitchens like that, gathering information from the scullery girls. They know all that happens in a house because no one pays them any attention. The family and upper servants spill any manner of secrets in front of them because they do not matter."

"As if they were wallpaper," I mused.

"As if they were *wastepaper*," he corrected. He straightened his tie and ran a hand over his unruly curls. "All right, then. Enough nattering. Let me go about my business and I will meet up with the lot of you later."

We remained in the square, leaving Mornaday to his wooing. Although Stoker was the more obvious choice if we were to dangle one of our menfolk as bait in front of a hungry maid, Mornaday was by far the less intimidating. A young woman who might find herself tongue-tied with nerves before a Stoker would be immediately at her ease with a Mornaday.

We circled the square in a desultory fashion, and after some half an hour, Mornaday appeared, looking thoroughly disgruntled.

"Were you not able to discover anything of note?" I asked. I attempted a consoling tone, but even I could detect the edge of annoyance. If Mornaday could not accomplish seducing a bit of information from a maid with few prospects of conversation beyond what the soap bubbles had to say, there was no justice in the world.

He rolled his eyes heavenwards. "What do you take me for? Of course I discovered something of note. I happen to be the only one here who is an actual detective," he reminded me in a tone of injury.

"Indeed you are," I soothed. "But you seem unsettled, and the most natural assumption is that you failed."

"Or that success came at too high a price," J. J. put in, eyes agleam with something between mischief and malice. Mornaday twitched uncomfortably, and J. J. gave a crow of exaltation. "I knew it. Tell us, Mornaday, are we to wish you joy? Are you a man betrothed?"

"Not yet," he said in considerable gloom. "But I am engaged to return on Thursday as it is her half day, and I promised to take her for a walk in the park."

J. J. crowed again, but I gave him a nod of approbation. "You would not have promised half so much if she hadn't given you considerable information. Tell us her name, to begin with."

"Minnie," he answered.

"Minnie Mornaday?" Stoker lifted a brow. "Definitely do not marry her and inflict such a fate on the girl."

"May. I. Finish?" Mornaday asked through gritted teeth. We waved for him to carry on and he did. "Minnie is sixteen and bright, brighter than she ought to be with such a job, but she is the orphaned eldest sister of five and must earn what she can to keep the younger ones in school."

"Laudable," Stoker murmured.

Mornaday carried on as if he had not spoken. "First, Lord Ambrose had no houseguests, of that she was entirely certain. Her mistress is something of a social climber and keeps a weather eye upon Lord Ambrose's comings and goings. He lives quietly, *very* quietly. Almost reclusive, to hear her tell it. Now, she says that yesterday when Lord Ambrose left, his staff had been instructed to say that he had gone to the country to be with his mother. Pig problems," he said, pulling a face. "But Minnie reckons this to be a fib because Lord Ambrose ordered the carriage to take him to Waterloo, yet he must embark at Paddington to reach his mother's house."

"Interesting," J. J. said with a grudging nod.

"Not as interesting as this: food has been disappearing from the larder at Despard's. Minnie said Despard's cook was grumbling about it to her cook and suggesting Minnie might have slipped in and helped herself."

"It wouldn't be the first time a servant has taken a crust to feed their own," Stoker pointed out.

"Ah, but it wasn't a crust," Mornaday explained. "It was a raised veal pie. And a jar of caviar, another of pickled walnuts. A French cheese of exquisite age and delicacy. Minnie denied the charge hotly and I believe her. Not only did her expression and manner ring with sincerity, what sort of Cockney girl would steal caviar or French cheese to feed her kin? No, she would take a bit of mutton or some good honest Cheddar."

"You think the thief is someone with a refined palate," I surmised.

"No, I think the thief is Lord Ambrose himself," Mornaday corrected. "Minnie observed him late one night. There is a window in the scullery which overlooks Lord Ambrose's garden. She saw him sidling out the garden door in his dressing gown with his arms full. A box from Fortnum and Mason, a bottle of port, and a few peaches, she said."

"Whatever for?" J. J. asked.

"A moonlight picnic in his own garden?" Mornaday hazarded.

"No," Stoker and I said as one. We exchanged grinning glances. "What sort of outbuildings are there in the garden?" I asked.

Mornaday paused to think. "A coal shed. I asked Minnie a few pointed questions about the layout of the grounds, and she said the coal shed is all that remains. An old summerhouse used to stand at the end of the garden, but it was falling to bits, and Lord Ambrose had it knocked down a few years back to improve the garden aspect."

"And there is no other building on the grounds? What of a garden shed?" Stoker asked, watching him closely.

"No, no other," Mornaday insisted. "I asked about the staff in resi-
dence, and there is no gardener. The fellow who takes care of Lord Ambrose's grounds comes twice a week with his own tools, and Minnie
said all of the sheds were carried away with the remains for the summerhouse. The coal stores were moved into the cellar of the house, but
the shed remained because it was supporting a creeping rose that Lord
Ambrose is particularly fond of," he said. "But as far as she knows it is
entirely empty. Not so much as a bicycle stored inside."

"Well done for inquiring so closely," J. J. remarked.

Mornaday, never one to hold on to his irritation for long—except
where Stoker was concerned—smiled in reply. "Well, I *am* rather good at
my job, you know. And there is something more."

He paused, enjoying himself immensely, I could tell, as he prolonged
the suspense.

"Mornaday, speak," I implored. "Stoker is growing impatient and I
do not think blood will clean easily out of the suit you are wearing."

Stoker gave a low growl and Mornaday shied like a pony. "Very well.
The maid saw Lord Ambrose's carriage arrive home the night before
last—carrying someone decidedly *not* Lord Ambrose. She described a
man dressed all in black with a hat pulled very low over his features."

"Elyot," Stoker said grimly.

"No doubt," Mornaday confirmed. "Lord Ambrose apparently met
him on the pavement and they spoke for a few moments, low voices, but
a heated exchange. When they had finished, Lord Ambrose returned to
the house and slammed the door."

"And the man?" J. J. asked.

"Left on foot, around that corner," Mornaday said, gesturing to the
end of the square."

Stoker and I looked at one another, exchanging thoughts as clearly
as if we had been speaking aloud. Finally, Stoker sighed. "Very well. If
we must."

Mornaday stared from one of us to the other and back again. "What just happened there? What has been decided?"

"It is that thoroughly annoying trick of theirs, demonstrating how closely attuned their minds are that they do not even have to give voice to what each is thinking," J. J. explained.

"And what, precisely, are you thinking?" Mornaday asked.

"That Lord Ambrose was carrying food to someone hid in his coal shed, someone to whom he does not wish to give hospitality of house," I said.

Stoker picked up the thread. "Someone, perhaps, who has been believed dead for fifteen years."

Mornaday's brows rose so high they nearly touched his hairline. "You think Julius Elyot is living in Lord Ambrose Despard's coal shed?"

"It is as likely an explanation as anything else." I shot the cuffs on my sleeves. "By the way, do thank your young friend for the helpfulness of her information when you see her Thursday next."

Mornaday reared. "I will not see her. I shall send a note of apology and that will be an end of it."

"You will do no such thing," I told him in my firmest voice. "You must keep your engagement. I will join you."

"Join us?" The reply came out strangled. "Why on earth would you do that?"

"The poor child probably sees little enough of the sun as it is. An afternoon in the park will air her out thoroughly and perhaps give her something better to dream of than the affections of an indifferent policeman. I shall take her past the windows of Whiteley's and show her a typewriting machine. I will explain she can hire lessons and leave domestic service altogether if she is resolute."

He opened his mouth to protest, but I held up a hand. "Now, back to the matter at hand." I looked to Stoker. "You meant what you said? You are in agreement?"

His smile was slow and knowing. "Veronica, I have learnt well enough the futility of attempting to dissuade you when you are bent upon a course of action."

"What course of action?" Mornaday demanded. "What are you talking about?"

"Trespassing into Lord Ambrose's garden and investigating his coal shed, of course," I told him.

He gave a groan and rubbed a hand over his eyes as J. J. shot him a pitying look. "You really did not deduce that for yourself? Heavens, Mornaday, it sometimes quite mystifies me how you managed to rise to the rank of detective at all."

CHAPTER

23

For such intrepid adventurers as we four, it had been the work of a very few moments to ascertain the lay of the land—to wit, that Lord Ambrose's property was bordered to the rear by a quiet mews, the division marked by a crumbling brick wall. There was a garden door for the delivery of coal and other such domestic requirements, but it was stoutly secured by a heavy, modern lock which would have taken considerable time to pick. In contrast, the wall was halfway to falling down, the gaps in the mortar offering convenient hand- and footholds for the limberest amongst us. I had, over the course of some years, refined and perfected my hunting costume and some variation of it had seen me happily from swamp to savannah and back again. I had always ordered it in tweed, serviceable and hard-wearing, but it had occurred to me that I had been remiss in not commissioning a version for town. Accordingly, I had caused one to be made out of heavy ribbed silk in a dark violet colour piped in black. A pair of flat black boots, laced to the knee, provided suitable footwear, and I was delighted to have the opportunity to put the garments to the test for the first time.

Without waiting for the others, I set the toe of my boot into a gap in the wall and vaulted myself upwards. Butterflying requires strong nerves and good balance as the best specimens are often the most elusive. Many an afternoon had I happily passed in springing over boulders or climbing up ravines, hauling myself hand over hand with the aid of a trusty vine or bit of shrubbery. I had balanced on tree limbs, hoisted myself atop outcroppings, mounted the most precarious of perches in order to secure my trophies. The experiences had left me with considerable agility coupled with strength and a good head for heights—qualities I had found surpassed only in Stoker. (His skills had been won in the service of the travelling show and Her Majesty's Navy. In spite of his position as assistant surgeon's mate, he had more than once been tasked with scaling a mast to secure the odd bit of rigging, and on one occasion his ability to face the most daunting of climbs had saved our lives and that of a prince in line to inherit the English throne.)[*]

With a very few movements, I had topped the wall, Stoker arriving a scant second behind me. J. J., with less cause to develop her athleticism, was still attempting to secure the first foothold, whilst Mornaday, with no head for heights whatsoever, kept his feet firmly on the pavement. He signalled his intention to remain there as a lookout as I reached a hand down towards J. J. She lacked some four feet of being able to grasp it, muttering furiously under her breath as she waved me on, lowering herself back to the pavement.

Wordlessly, Stoker dropped over the other side of the wall into the shifting darkness of the garden. I heard the quiet, almost imperceptible thud which indicated he had landed—doubtlessly on his feet and with the feline grace that characterised all of his movements. He gave a soft whistle, mimicking the call of a chaffinch to signal all was clear, and I followed, landing lightly next to him. We paused a moment to allow our eyes to adjust. Without the lamplight of the mews behind, the garden itself was shrouded in a midnight gloom in which the shadows rustled

---

[*] *A Murderous Relation*

with a wind that smelt of coal fires and the remnants of someone's roast supper. Above it all was the peculiar odour of autumn itself, the leaves withering upon the branches and smelling of death as they surrendered to the inevitable. One fell, brushing my cheek as it blew past, carrying the whiff of the turning seasons.

Taking my hand, Stoker nudged me towards the far corner of the garden. Crouching there in the deepest darkness of the property was the coal shed. I could just sketch its outline in the shadows, the roof low and horizontal, only two feet below the top of the wall. If we had only known it was there, we might have saved ourselves the long drop, I realised. There was nothing else of note in the area, just a few barrels stacked neatly beside the shed—for rainwater, I suspected. In all, there was nothing to excite the imagination or interest the casual visitor, yet I tightened my grip on Stoker's hand. Together, on soundless feet, we crept nearer. My pulses quickened to a drumbeat in my ears. We were forty centuries removed from the days when it was necessary to take up a spear to stalk one's dinner, and yet all the thrill of that atavistic hunt thrummed in my veins. I could sense the excitement rising in Stoker as well, the rhythm of his heartbeat matching mine as we moved as one towards the shed. What mysteries lay within? Would we indeed discover the lair of Julius Elyot? And if he had been there, would he have left traces of his fiendish intentions? Or would we find the man himself, crouched like a predator and smelling of the death he had dealt his best friend? Closer still we moved, horror rising with every step even as I resolved not to lose my nerve regardless of what abominations we might find when at last we opened the door, exposing the terrors within.

To my surprise, the door in question had been fitted with a stout new lock that gleamed against the weathered wood. Wordlessly, Stoker slipped a slender leather pouch from his pocket, extracted his lockpicks, and set to work. It was the effort of a moment to spring the lock and we

A GRAVE ROBBERY

were soon inside, surveying the interior of the shed, Julius Elyot's make-shift home these past few days.

The late roses rambling around the door lent the coal shed the air of a country cottage. Inside it was gloomy and cold, the chill having pene-trated the thin walls and settled into the bones of the place. A thin pal-let of sacking had been arranged on the floor, and there were discarded empty tins of food heaped in the corner. A bucket with a lid served what I could only assume was a necessary function, and I averted my eyes deliberately. There was no means of making a fire, no warmth to be found in that bleak and cheerless place. Nor had the inhabitant left any clue as to his whereabouts or his intentions.

"An abandoned den," Stoker said flatly. "Now the creature that lived here is afoot and we have lost the scent."

We quitted the shed, and Stoker bent to lock the door once more. All at once, from behind us, the stillness of the night air was rent by a shout. It came from the direction of the house itself, and I heard a low growl and the rattle of a chain being unclasped.

"Someone has loosed a dog!" I warned Stoker in a harsh whisper. There was no time to spare. The garden, although considerable for a London townhouse, was not large. The creature, whose size must rival that of a small pony given the crashes and poundings it made as it cov-ered the ground, breaking shrubbery and hurdling bushes as it went, would be upon us in seconds.

Stoker, whose resourcefulness is rivalled only by his quickness of action, did not drop my hand as he darted to the side of the shed where the rain barrels stood. Even before his foot left the ground, I knew what he meant to do. I braced myself as he leapt, jamming one booted foot onto the top of a barrel and using it to launch himself to the roof of the shed and thence to the top of the wall. I would have managed the same trajectory perfectly well, but it was not a matter Stoker chose to leave to

247

chance. Instead, he kept his grip upon my arm, pulling me with him as he went up.

Unfortunately, he miscalculated slightly—no doubt as a result of carrying my weight as well as his own—and exerted a touch more effort than required. In short, he did not go *up* so much as *up and over*, clearing the top of the wall by some several inches. I saw J. J.'s astonished face, her mouth round in disbelief as I sailed past her, landing neatly atop Mornaday, who crashed to the pavement under the onslaught, knocking J. J.'s feet from under her and causing her to tumble over like a ninepin.

I pushed myself to my feet, dusting off my hands. "Well caught, Mornaday," I told him. He turned onto all fours, whooping air back into his lungs. I turned to see that Stoker had caught himself at the top of the wall. He hung there by two fingers, swinging gently, until his shoulder—recently dislocated—gave way and he tumbled to the pavement. He rose, one arm hanging loose.

He surveyed Mornaday where the fellow crouched, still trembling. "What ails him?"

"I believe he has lost his wind," I said. I glanced back to Stoker. "Beloved, you have misplaced your shoulder again," I advised him.

He looked down in surprise. "So I have." With his customary lack of theatrics, he turned and slammed the joint in question hard upon the brick wall, reseating the top of the bone neatly in place. It was a manoeuvre I had seen performed so many times it no longer caused acute distress, although I will admit it took a bit of nerve to watch and still more to listen to in any measure of comfort. Whether it was the sight of the manipulation or the sound of it—a sort of animal grinding noise—Mornaday gave another great whoop and promptly vomited into the gutter.

"Well, at least he has his wind back," Stoker said genially. Whilst Mornaday finished emptying the contents of his stomach, Stoker turned and helped J. J. up, setting her neatly on her feet. "I think it best if we make a speedy departure," he counselled. "That dog sounds hungry."

"You go," J. J. said. "I will be at the Barley Mow in Dorset Street in one hour."

"We are not leaving you here," Stoker began, but he was speaking to her back. She had already set off at a trot, moving back towards the placid green square of Lincoln's Inn Fields.

"Leave her," I said. "We must trust J. J. to know her own business."

We walked swiftly down the narrow mews and through the dark streets, our way illuminated only by the occasional pools of warm light thrown by the streetlamps. A low fog was beginning to swirl about the kerbstones, muffling the sounds of any possible pursuers. We wended through Bloomsbury and into Marylebone, eventually reaching our destination at the Barley Mow. As soon as we entered, I understood why J. J. had suggested the establishment. To the left of the bar, the pub had been fitted with drinking boxes, wooden cubicles that ensured perfect privacy for small parties being completely secluded from the rest of the establishment. Drinks were handed through a hatch which opened onto the bar and could be fastened closed once libations were served. Stoker shouldered his way into an empty drinking box, rapping sharply upon the hatch to get the barman's attention. It was not the first time I had been in a public house, but the relative novelty of the drinking box lent it charm. I sipped at a genially crisp half pint of cider whilst Mornaday stared pitifully into his glass, still covered in a faint, clammy sheen.

"Stoker, do give Mornaday a handkerchief," I said. "He is decidedly moist."

Stoker handed over one of his enormous red handkerchiefs which Mornaday instantly clapped to his damp brow. He made a gesture of thanks and would have handed it back, but Stoker waved him off. "For god's sake, keep it, man."

"Who set the dog on you?" Mornaday wheezed.

Stoker shrugged. "A night watchman, most likely. Lord Ambrose would have engaged one when he shut up the house to go away. I ought to have considered it."

We sat some quarter of an hour before J. J. appeared, her colour high and her breath fast. "Drink," she said, reaching for my cider. I pushed it into her hands, and she drained half the glass before she could speak.

"Where have you been?" Stoker inquired.

"Speaking with the future Mrs. Mornaday," she said with a grin.

"Not young Minnie! The child has probably never enjoyed such popularity," I mused.

"After what she told me, I would have her crowned Queen of the May and feted through the streets," J. J. said. I realised then that her glowing complexion was due as much to triumph as it was to hurrying to join us.

"Why did you question Minnie further?" Mornaday asked sharply. It required little imagination to suppose that he resented any meddling with the witness he had taken such pains to question.

"Because something she said troubled me. She said she knew Lord Ambrose couldn't have meant to go to his mother's house because he went to the wrong station. It occurred to me to wonder how she knew which station he'd been bound for when he left his house."

"Clever," Stoker said. J. J. preened under his praise. "What did you discover?"

"That our watchful little Minnie actually saw Ambrose Despard depart for the station," J. J. revealed. "She heard him give the instructions to his driver."

"That much may be inferred," Mornaday told her loftily.

J. J.'s look was one of purely feline satisfaction. "But she told me something else, something that could not have been inferred." She paused, looking about our snug little group in silken anticipation.

"For god's sake, out with it," Mornaday ordered. "You are as bad as the pair of *them*," he added, jerking his chin towards where Stoker and I sat side by side.

Mornaday's ill-humour did not dim J. J.'s pleasure. She drank the rest of my cider, wiping her mouth on her sleeve when she had drained the glass. She set it carefully upon the table and only then did she raise shining eyes to the rest of us.

"Ambrose Despard did not leave for the station alone. Just as he entered his carriage, a woman appeared. According to Minnie, she confronted Lord Ambrose, apparently insisting upon travelling with him. She got into the carriage and they left. Together."

"Did she say what the woman looked like?" I asked. But I already knew.

"Some years past thirty, Minnie thought. Plain dress and cloak with a heavy plait of hair at the nape of her neck."

Stoker and I exchanged glances.

Eliza Elyot.

CHAPTER

24

The gentle reader must not assume I was annoyed in the *slightest* that J. J. had acted with such perspicacity. Nor that I was in *any* way vexed that she had succeeded in uncovering a vital clue entirely on her own. We had, after all, made the effort to include Mornaday and J. J. in our investigation as they had proven useful in the past, and if J. J. saw fit to undertake questioning a witness on the basis of a *hunch*—

"It is permissible for J. J. to ask questions," Stoker told me mildly as we walked back to Bishop's Folly.

"I haven't the faintest notion to what you are referring," I told him.

"Oh, I do apologise. I thought when J. J. returned in triumph from questioning young Minnie, you looked as though you'd sucked a lemon. I must be mistaken."

"Entirely," I assured him.

"And I suppose the grinding noise I can hear is not your back molars working out your indignation," he added.

"It is most certainly not," I replied. "I would never begrudge J. J. a victory, however minuscule."

"Hardly minuscule," Stoker pointed out. "We had no suspicions of

Eliza Elyot as a villainess until Minnie identified her as the woman who accompanied Lord Ambrose to the train station."

"I should hardly call that an identification," I countered. "It is an intriguing possibility, I grant you, but scarcely sufficient grounds upon which to lay a murder at Eliza's door."

"Oh?" The casualness of his tone was, I had no doubt, intended as a deliberate goad.

"There must be hundreds, nay thousands, of women in London answering to such a description," I said.

But even to my own ears, my protestations rang hollow. The hairstyle Eliza wore, low plaits pinned at the neck, was old-fashioned. And how many women of such appearance was Lord Ambrose likely to encounter?

Stoker said nothing, but I saw his lips twitching with a suppressed smile.

"Very well," I admitted. "I am perhaps a trifle concerned."

"That J. J. noted the importance of Minnie's observation?"

"No—that we did not!" I paused, turning to him. We stood in the warm, pooling light of the streetlamp that illuminated a narrow door at the far side of the garden, a discreet entrance which we often used for our more secret comings and goings. "We are scientists—observers, trained and experienced. And yet it did not occur to either of us to pursue that particular line of inquiry. We have neither of us been properly in the field for far too long. I am forced to wonder if our skills have become blunted from too much time at home. Have we become city-softened? *Domesticated?*" I shuddered at the word.

"We have most certainly not," he told me patiently. "We are as keen and observant as we have ever been."

"Do you really think so?"

"I do. In fact, I have observed something in the few seconds we have been standing here—namely, that the lock has been broken," he said. He pointed to where the plate had been wrenched away. The wooden door had been forced open and shoved back into place. To the casual observer, it would appear secure, but someone had breached the defences of the estate.

Before he could utter some nonsensical warning about staying behind him or waiting to assess the situation, I charged ahead at a dead run, issuing a fair imitation of a Zulu battle cry as I went. My intention was to flush our intruder, and the plan worked precisely as anticipated. As I flew on winged feet, crashing through shrubberies and assorted water features, a shadow detached itself from the side of the Belvedere, fleeing across the estate.

"There!" I cried, pointing.

Stoker had reached me by this point—he is nothing if not quick in his responses—and as we passed Spyridon's little castle, the door opened and our Greek friend emerged, lantern held high to discover the source of the commotion.

"Intruder!" I gasped as we ran on, keeping the shadow always in sight. Spyridon joined our chase, and to my astonishment, swiftly passed Stoker and myself, vaulting ahead of us.

The shadow turned and gave a shout of alarm as Spyridon closed the distance. I could imagine we were a fearsome sight—first Spyridon, robes flying and lantern held above his head like an avenging angel, then Stoker, head lowered with all the ferocious purpose of a charging bull. I brought up the rear, but I like to think my own contributions were not negligible, for I carried on with my Zulu cries and added a few flourishes I had learnt from a Norwegian lepidopterist of my acquaintance who had made a practice of studying the battle tactics of Vikings. These involved the baring of teeth and throwing the hands into the air to simulate a greater size in order to intimidate one's enemy. I do not claim it was this gesture which frightened the shadowy figure into submission, but I will note it was precisely at the height of my performance that he fell with a hoarse cry and did not rise again.

"Veronica, do stop waving your arms about like a demented octopus," Stoker ordered as he and Spyridon came to a halt next to the intruder.

"Jest if you like," I said, arriving breathlessly. "But I have just ensured the apprehension of this villain."

"I rather think Patricia did that," he said, pointing to the enormous tortoise lying atop the recumbent figure of our quarry. Her legs were waving gently in the air and she gave a series of piteous moans in protest at her predicament.

Together, Stoker, Spyridon, and I set our shoulders to Patricia's shell and pushed. It took four attempts, but in the end, we managed to roll her onto her feet. She lumbered away, looking back at us with an expression akin to loathing.

The figure trapped beneath her gave a low groan, and I took the lantern from Spyridon, raising it high.

"Julius Elyot, I presume," I said.

The man groaned again, covering his face with his hands.

I turned to Stoker and Spyridon. "Bring him into the Belvedere," I said. "We have much to discuss."

Julius Elyot was not a large man, but even if he had been, I suspect the combined muscular authority of Stoker and Spyridon would have suggested that any attempt at escape would be futile. He sagged between them, shoulders bowed and feet dragging as they guided him firmly inside. The snuggery was the most comfortable spot in the Belvedere, and we settled there. Stoker poked the stove to light whilst I set a kettle to boil. Spyridon kept a watchful eye from the top of the stairs, never taking his gaze from the slumped figure of Julius Elyot.

"I can go. Unless you need help with the tortures?" His tone was alarmingly hopeful, and I hastened to dispense with his services.

"Thank you, but that will not be necessary, Spyridon," I told him. "I am certain you have more interesting things to do."

Spyridon shrugged. "You call if you want me, yes, Miss Speedwell?"

"Yes, Spyridon. But I think just knowing you are nearby will be enough to keep Mr. Elyot on his best behaviour, isn't that right?" I asked politely.

Julius Elyot gave a shudder and Spyridon left us. The dogs, inquisitive as always where visitors were concerned, gathered around, sniffing at Elyot's trouser cuffs. He dropped a hand to Vespertine's enormous head, ruffling the dog's fur with his fingers.

"I had a deerhound as a boy," he said in a hoarse voice. "What is this one called?"

"Vespertine," I told him.

"A beautiful name for a beautiful fellow." He continued to stroke the dog's head whilst Stoker finished with the fire and I brewed tea. When it was finished, I assembled the tea things and brought them over, rummaging in a cupboard for some ginger nuts.

I poured out and handed a cup to Julius Elyot who took it with obvious surprise.

"I know it seems odd to offer refreshments, but it seems discourteous not to," I told him.

He accepted a ginger nut, his hand shaking a little. With more haste than dignity, he crammed the ginger nut into his mouth and I offered him another.

"You are obviously hungry," Stoker said. "Would you care for something more substantial?"

Elyot shook his head pushing away the second ginger nut. "No. I am famished, of course. But any time I try to eat anything more than a mouthful, I find I am unable. I cannot sleep either."

"A guilty conscience?" I suggested gently.

The line of his jaw hardened and he said nothing. The silence afforded me a moment to study him. The profile must once have been handsome, and I traced a resemblance to his sister. The brow was high, the hairline having receded from where it would have been in his youth, and sharp lines ran from his nostrils to the corners of his mouth. His lips were thin and his nose audacious. It was a collection of features that would have been arrogant in youth and distinguished if he had aged gracefully. But his life had been one of hardship, and the resulting depredations were easy to read in his visage.

"Are you a student of physiognomy, Miss Speedwell?" he asked, a corner of his mouth quirking into what even the most generous of souls could not have called a smile.

"You know my name?"

"I know both of you," he said in a tone of resignation. "I have been expecting to make your acquaintance these past several days, although I hoped it would be under better circumstances. I thought I might prevail upon Ambrose to introduce us, but he was unwilling."

His mouth twisted, but his hand continued to stroke Vespertine with gentleness.

"Pity he didn't manage it before his death," Stoker replied.

The effect of that simple remark was astonishing. The cup full of tea slipped from his hand, shattering on the floor. Elyot opened his mouth and closed it again, soundlessly. When he finally managed a reply, it was a gasp, a cry of anguish, and then he pitched forwards, out of the chair and into unconsciousness.

"What in the name of seven hells," Stoker began, thrusting aside his own cup.

Together we retrieved Elyot, settling him back into the chair and opening the top button of his collar. "These Elyots are a delicate family," I mused. "They faint at the slightest provocation. Do you think it an hereditary flaw?"

"I think it is damned inconvenient," Stoker said, rummaging amongst the shelves until he found a bottle with a hand-lettered label. He passed it to me, and I uncorked the bottle, waving it under Elyot's nose until he came to with a jerk, rearing back and choking.

"My god, what has happened?" he asked in a hoarse voice.

"Nothing too alarming," I told him. "A common syncope."

"What is that hideous odour?" He waved his hands in front of his face in a futile effort to dispel the fumes.

"Spirits of hartshorn, but my own receipt. I added rather more ammonia than the usual formula dictates. Most effective, but a trifle unpleasant, I will admit."

"Unpleasant! It smells as if the fires of Hell have been unleashed," he protested. I corked the bottle and handed it back to Stoker before turning my attention once more to Julius Elyot.

He had recovered himself a little; at least, his colour did not look as if he would pitch immediately back into insensibility, and I decided he was strong enough to bear a little firm questioning. But before I could speak, Elyot looked to me, his expression anguished.

"Tell me, is it true? Ambrose is dead?"

I nodded. His gaze fell to the hands clasped in his lap, and he remained thus, in a prayer-like posture, for a long moment before he looked up again. His eyes—pale blue, the tissue-thin whites mapped heavily with red—were filled with unshed tears.

"Can you tell me what happened?"

Stoker's tone was cool. "We rather thought you could tell us."

Elyot reared back in horror. "You think I know something of this? Do you suspect me of murdering Ambrose—my dearest friend in all the world?"

"You are the likeliest suspect," I pointed out calmly. "But as it happens, no. We do not think you murdered him."

Elyot drew in a sharp breath. "Thank you for that."

"Not at all," I said graciously. "We suspect Lord Ambrose's murderer was no one other than your sister, Eliza."

He went very still, his hands knotting into fists. "Oh," he whispered.

"Yes, Mr. Elyot, I am sorry to say that Lord Ambrose died aboard a train bound for Southampton. Officially, his death was attributed to natural causes, but we are persuaded the authorities are concealing the truth—that he was murdered."

Elyot nodded. "Yes, they would. Ambrose's brother, the current marquess, is as chary of publicity as their father was. He would take whatever steps are necessary to protect the family name." He looked to Stoker. "Tell me, is there evidence to implicate Eliza?"

Stoker shrugged. "Circumstantial, at present. A woman answering her description was seen entering Ambrose's carriage as he left his home."

"What of the method? The motive?" Elyot demanded.

"We are still gathering information," I told him smoothly. "But we believe the facts will support our hypothesis. Unless you can suggest another person who might bear Lord Ambrose ill will?"

He shook his head. "No. I presume you know something of our story?"

"We know that you staged your own death to escape prosecution," Stoker told him. "And that Eliza has believed you dead these past fifteen years. We supposed that Lord Ambrose aided your escape to the Continent."

"He did," Elyot confirmed. "Ambrose was the truest of friends. He helped me get to Germany and to secure employment. We have continued a correspondence, but he took care to make certain Eliza did not suspect that I survived. We believed it for the best."

"To continue this charade for fifteen years?" Stoker asked. "Do you really believe it was for the best that your sister grieved your death for a decade and a half?"

Elyot flushed to the tips of his ears. "What I did was done for the best. I believed so at the time, and I do believe so still."

"You do not seem completely surprised by our theory that Lord

Ambrose's murder may have been accomplished at the hand of your sister," I said.

"No." The voice dropped to a whisper again, faint and infinitely sad. "Ruthlessness, I am afraid, is in her nature."

"She called here two days ago," I told him. "And related a tale about your work—a very particular experiment."

"The girl from the canal. But the work was not mine. She was Eliza's experiment from the beginning. I sculpted her death mask, but it was Eliza who insisted upon preserving her, upon attempting to resurrect her. Eliza was playing God, and I feared for her."

"And you did not stop her?" Stoker asked. It was not an accusation, but Elyot's expression was pained.

"Could one harness the sun and keep it from rising? I could no more have held back the sea than stopped her. She was a force of nature, even as a girl." His eyes took on the dreamy veil of nostalgia as he began to explain. "I tumbled and stumbled, flinging myself about as all children seem to do. But Eliza *observed*—everything and everyone. She never crawled, as babies do, in preparation for walking. She simply waited until she was ready to haul herself upwards and then toddled off, serious as an owl. She did the same with speaking, reading. Nothing was attempted until she believed she understood it. Mastery was everything to her."

He paused, as much to rest his creaking voice as to gather his resolve to tell us the rest. I refreshed his tea, adding a spoonful of clover honey to soothe his voice, and he sipped, his eyes closed. When he opened them, he spoke again, stronger now.

"Her scientific studies were the same. I began them, but she soon surpassed me. Our father did not believe in formal education for girls, so she was forced to remain at home whilst I went away, but at the end of every term, I carried home my texts. She read them all in a matter of a few weeks, and I tutored her. She was a sponge, veritably thirsting for knowledge. Our mother died when we were very young, and our father followed, just after I finished school. Shortly after we established our little household, Ambrose came to live with us. He was always deep in pocket, and the additional monies were useful. They made all the difference, in fact. We were able to undertake projects of real significance. Ambrose was intrigued by methods of preservation whilst I was devoted to galvanic studies. It was Eliza who saw the potential for combining our efforts. She had been observing both of us, and it was she who first suggested marrying Ambrose's specimens to my electrical applications. "

"Did you not consider the ethical implications of what you were about to do?" Stoker inquired softly.

"Oh, no, not at all," Elyot said ruefully. "We were so caught up in the possibility of it all, the novelty, that Ambrose and I never once considered Eliza might have intended something as horrifying as her ultimate endeavour."

Stoker and I exchanged quick glances. To imagine that these two brilliant male scholars had been entirely led by a young woman was too much to swallow. They had been willing partners, of that I had no doubt, but I understood Elyot's attempt to whitewash himself of culpability. A look at Stoker's face told me he was thinking much the same. Elyot was not attempting to deceive us as much as he had already deceived himself. He was giving us the only version of events that was palatable in light of the tragedies that followed.

"So she led you into the ways of destruction," I suggested dryly.

If Elyot perceived my scepticism, he overlooked it entirely. "We were her creatures," he said simply. "I do not know how it happened, it was so slow and subtle a thing. But before I knew it, she was directing experiments and giving orders in the laboratory. We had some early successes, exciting and thoroughly innovative work. It was not until we reanimated a specimen of a squirrel that I understood what she meant to do.

It was a tiny thing, that squirrel," he said, the small smile in evidence once more. "But watching it flutter to life again, it was a miracle, something out of a mediaeval mystery play. One moment it was lifeless and still. The next, the paws began to twitch, then the limbs, waking one by one, until the eyes opened."

He paused and sipped again at his tea. "It was beyond anything I had ever imagined. Anyone who has ever worked with voltaic coils understands how easy a thing it is to give the suggestion of life. It is merely a series of electrical impulses stimulating, say, the leg of a frog to kick. When the leg moves, it appears the frog is living, but it is not. It is no more than a party trick. Galvani and Volta entertained masses with such flummery. They were attempting to illustrate sound scientific principles, and there is not a travelling show in Europe that failed to replicate the demonstration. But this squirrel—I tell you it was alive. Its eyes shone with understanding, it leapt up and ran about the laboratory. We had created *life*."

His voice dropped to a thrilled whisper, and I could see it plainly, the laboratory, the trio of young people watching in awe as their subject rose from the dead. They were conjurers as much as scientists, and the knowledge that they could ape their Creator must have been heady stuff indeed.

"What became of the squirrel?" Stoker asked.

Elyot shrugged. "It died. Again. It lived only a few minutes, and we were dismayed at the brevity of its animation. But Eliza worked feverishly to understand where we had gone wrong, and within a few weeks, she was ready to try again. This time with a dog."

I darted an involuntary look at our little family of dogs, from Huxley, the elder statesman of the group, to tiny Al-'Ijliyyah, shivering in the little jumper Stoker had knitted for her. A considerable portion of my sympathy for Julius Elyot died in that moment, but he went on.

"This time we were more successful. The puppy we used lived a fort-night. And after that it was a pig which lived two months. After that, Eliza believed she was ready to attempt something . . . greater."

"So you found her a body," Stoker said. The tone was neutral, and only someone who knew him well would have detected the distaste for what Elyot had done.

"It sounds rather grim when you put it like that," Elyot told him. "But yes. I was tasked with finding a suitable specimen. I already had a relationship with old Plumtree, a devious reprobate who would do any-thing for a coin. When he came to me with a commission for an un-known young woman pulled from Regent's Canal, it seemed a godsend, Providence itself blessing our work. I completed the sculpture of the death mask with the understanding that if the girl were not claimed, she would be turned over to us. In the meanwhile, he permitted Am-brose access to her in order to begin the preservation process. It would have all been for nothing if she had been allowed to decompose, you see."

His cup empty, he held it out for a freshener. I obliged and he gave me a smile of such charm, I could see for a moment the engaging and handsome young man he must once have been.

"Thank you, Miss Speedwell. I have met with little kindness these past years, and that meagre civility is still more than I deserve. I do not know at what point I sold my soul to the Devil, but I did. I accommo-dated Eliza's schemes—no, I aided them. I funded them and supported them, and in this, I am as guilty as she. More so, for I was her superior in status and ought to have guided her in right principles. If I speak dis-passionately about anything we did, it is only because I cannot bear to permit myself to feel. I have cut off my emotions as decisively as any surgeon hacks off a gangrenous limb, and I am left with nothing but the shell," he added with a dismissive gesture towards his body. "I have had fifteen long years in exile to contemplate my sins. They are too heavy for expiation. I can only hope that if there is a god, I will receive mercy, for if justice is meted, I am doomed."

His discourse had taken on a maudlin tone, and if I allowed him to continue, I had little doubt he would succumb to tears. (Men who claim to be beyond the grip of strong emotions are, in my experience, the very ones most likely to fall prey to them.) And since the best remedy for hysteria is a sound slap and I had little desire to strike him—if only because he was still holding his teacup and a second broken cup was simply too much to bear in one evening—I took up the narrative in a brisk tone.

"So you secured the corpse for Eliza's purposes, and Lord Ambrose accommodated by preserving her with his preparations. Eliza told us that she grew uneasy about the course of your experiments and went to the late marquess for assistance. She said that he threatened to use the full force of the authorities to bring your efforts to a halt and that in retaliation, you offered her physical violence. After this, the laboratory burnt and you with it. We perceive these are lies," I assured him as he opened his mouth to reply. "I suspect the reverse happened. Your conscience got the better of you and you went to Lord Ambrose's father yourself. What did you do? Propose to lock her in an asylum if she did not comply with your demands to stop her experiments?"

He flushed, a dull, ugly shade of red that blotched his grey complexion. "Ambrose and I had grown exceedingly worried about her. She was in the grip of an obsession, you understand. It was only when we were far into the process that I saw it for what it was—madness."

"And the cure for inconvenient females is always to lock them up," I finished dryly.

"Inconvenient! Miss Speedwell, I protest. Eliza had become a *fiend*. I tell you, I did not know her. In the thrall of this demented scheme, she was nothing like the sister I had known. All gentleness, all sober dignity were lost to her. She no longer conducted herself with anything like decorum. She ordered us about as if we were her henchmen!"

I saw then that Eliza's crime had been as much stepping out of her place as endeavouring to reanimate a corpse. I could well imagine this quiet, watchful girl, liberated by her own audaciousness to attempt what these two men could never even dream of. It would have been a heady time for her as she threw off the confines of the role into which society had forced her. How long had she bided her time, waiting to burst free like some poisonous flower, no longer in bud but fully and violently in bloom?

"So you had no choice but to hold her back," Stoker surmised.

"Exactly so," Elyot agreed, clearly relieved that someone in the room seemed to understand his motivations. But Stoker flicked me a glance of pure understanding, and I knew he intuited my thoughts.

Before Elyot could absolve himself further, I took up the thread of the narrative once more. "The marquess counselled removing her from the premises and when you told Eliza, she became violent," I suggested.

"Yes. She struck me, and before I could rouse myself to restrain her, she bolted," he said. "But not before vowing vengeance. Even now, what she said haunts me. I will remember her words, her cruel and venomous words, until my dying breath. She promised to exact her revenge upon me, and I believed her. She outlined the tortures she intended to inflict in horrifying detail, such violence and horror as only a demon in Hell could conjure." He paused, paling a little as he went on. "There were incidents when she was a child, things I had forced myself to forget. A neighbour's cat that had killed her pet canary, later a puppy that had chewed her favourite slippers. She did . . . unspeakable things. But I made excuses for her, always. It was not until she threatened me that I knew real fear. Her words struck me to my marrow, and I knew I should never be free of her."

"Was it Lord Ambrose's idea or yours to burn down the laboratory?" Stoker asked.

"Mine," he said. "I rued the necessity of it—so much knowledge lost! But I knew the only way to escape Eliza's wrath was if she believed me to be dead. And I suppose I thought if the notes and equipment were destroyed, she could never replicate the work. She had not paid close attention to Ambrose's formulae, you see. Without his preservation chemicals in precise and exacting applications, no specimen could withstand her efforts. I suppose it was an insurance policy of sorts that whatever dark path she was bent upon, she could no longer tread it." He paused, sighing. "I acted in haste, panic even. But Ambrose and I believed it to be the only possible course."

"Why preserve the Beauty if you meant to thwart Eliza's work?" I inquired.

His brows rose. "The Beauty? Oh, I see. That is what you have called her. Yes, she was enchanting, was she not? After all we had done, we could not bring ourselves to destroy her. It seemed a blasphemous thing, which I know you will laugh at, but there it is. She was so perfect, the apotheosis of our work. I could not bear to let her burn."

"She was also a human being," Stoker reminded him.

Chastened, Elyot bowed his head. "Of course. It was her humanity which ultimately made it impossible to destroy her in the end."

"Yet you did not give her a proper burial," Stoker pressed.

"How could we!" Elyot threw up his hands. "We were desperate, acting in furious haste. It seemed a miracle we managed even to secure a place for her in some grimy warehouse. I always expected we would retrieve her at some point, when it was safe for me to return."

"Yet you never did, until now," I remarked.

"Because I was a coward. You may hold as many mirrors up to my soul as you please, Miss Speedwell, and I will not flinch from the reflection there. I have been unmanly in my weakness, and yet insufferable in my arrogance. I have married the worst of conceivable flaws, and I have trailed destruction in my wake. I can only hope now to remedy my actions in a way that causes the least possible harm."

He fell silent then, and after a long moment, Stoker rose, plucking the teacup from Elyot's fingers.

"Time for something stronger, I think."

CHAPTER

25

Stoker poured a stout measure of whisky for each of us. His hospitality was finely calibrated to his respect for the person he served. Lady Wellie was always accorded the finest Scottish single malt of great maturity, whilst I had upon one memorable occasion seen him palm an importunate caller with an indifferent port thick with sediment and smelling faintly of old goat. Julius Elyot, I noted, warranted no better than a limp Irish blend. It mightn't have had the robust peatiness of its Scottish cousin, but at least it offered the virtue of being *bracing*. Elyot looked as though he could do with some propping up, and after a few sips and a vigorous coughing spell—the libation could not be called smooth by even the most charitable imbiber—a slightly healthier colour rose in his cheeks.

"Thank you," he gasped.

"Mr. Elyot, would I be correct in supposing this is not the first occasion upon which you have trespassed at Bishop's Folly?"

My tone was pleasant, but there was an unmistakable note of accusation. He flinched a little.

"My apologies, Miss Speedwell. It was badly done, but I was desperate. Your call upon Ambrose persuaded us both that you must have some knowledge of the whereabouts of the specimen." I did not care for his clinical way of referring to the Beauty, and from the immediate scowl that settled upon Stoker's features, I knew he shared my distaste. To us she was far more than a scientific project, but I said nothing and Elyot carried on, insensible to our feelings. "We were desperate to recover her."

"Why?" Stoker's inquiry was brusque.

Elyot thought a moment, sucking his teeth as he pondered. "She was our greatest achievement, even without Eliza's mad intentions. She was utterly and perfectly preserved. Ambrose and I believed it might someday be possible to present our work to the scientific community."

"To what purpose?" Stoker pressed. "Simply to say you could?"

"Perhaps," Elyot admitted with a smile. "But there are commercial applications as well."

"Commercial!" I did not bother to conceal my repulsion.

"Certainly. Consider, Miss Speedwell, the number of people who experience the loss of a beloved family member within the course of a year in this country? Those who must carry on whilst weeping for a life snatched too soon? We perfected the method by which death may be cheated, even if only a little."

"A preserved corpse is not the same as a living human!" I protested.

"No, but to a certain type of personality, one so sensitive that it suffers the most exquisite of torments in grieving, could this not be a humane and kindly tool? One has only to think of Her Majesty and the excesses of emotion to which she has been subjected since the loss of her beloved consort. More than twenty-five years and still she wears widow's weeds and has his shaving water carried in hot each morning! Would it not have been better for her, far better indeed, to have been given the consolation of seeing his cherished face?"

Given that my own parents' illicit and semi-legal marriage had contributed to the prince's death, I was disinclined to pursue that particular line of inquiry. Before I could reply, Stoker cut into the conversation.

"The queen mourns so extravagantly because she has been indulged by family members and courtiers who are willing to put up with her behaviour. She has a role to fulfil, a constitutional obligation which she has badly neglected. Surely she would have conducted herself even worse if she'd had the opportunity to sit and stare at Albert's waxen face every day," he said dryly.

Elyot shrugged. "Or she might have slowly reconciled herself to his death years ago and by now been wearing yellow and opening Parliament. I believe that grief is a thing to be faced with courage. Presenting the bodies of the dead in a state of lifelike preservation offers the grief-stricken a chance to come gradually to terms with reality."

"Or it offers them the chance to indulge in what I can only characterise as wholly unhealthy hysterics," Stoker retorted.

Elyot spread his hands. "We are not in agreement, but I will not oppose you, sir. You have been too cordial by half for me to abuse your generosity so churlishly."

"Do you still wish to retrieve her—your experiment, I mean?" I asked.

An expression of pain crossed his features. "No, I do not. I confess, I came again tonight with the same aim—securing her for my own purposes. Ambrose and I quarrelled about it," he added, his brow furrowed. "He accused me of being as obsessed as Eliza with her. He swore it was an accident that he had let the payments slip and lost possession of her, but he seemed to think it providential, as if Fate herself were lending a hand to wipe the slate clean for us." He made a moue of self-mockery. "But I am a nostalgic fool. I rushed over and Ambrose invited me to stay with him, but I refused. I was afraid if I accepted his hospitality openly, word might somehow circulate that I was returned."

"And you were afraid Eliza would discover it," I supplied.

He nodded. "You will think it unmanly that I should be so frightened of my sister, Miss Speedwell. I think it unmanly myself, so do not believe you can value my conduct any less than I do. And yet, I am wise to keep my distance."

He lifted a lock of hair from his temple, revealing an ugly, jagged scar some three inches in length. "Her handiwork as she took her last leave of me," he said. "I was lucky to escape with my life. I swore then that I would never allow her near enough to manage a second attempt." He ran his fingers through the hair, settling it back into place to conceal the disfigurement. "Ambrose at last persuaded me to make use of his coal shed, but that is as far as I would go."

"But surely any hotel would have been more comfortable," I protested.

"But far less discreet," he countered. "Oh, I admit it would have required some supernatural aid to have discovered me had I lodged in some quiet establishment. Eliza is a mere mortal woman. And yet, I cannot seem to exorcise my fears. I behave as if she were some fiend from the pits of Hell with all the attendant powers."

"You are perhaps overzealous in your caution, but not entirely unjustified," I conceded.

"Thank you for that. Ambrose and I were at loggerheads with regard to how to proceed. He urged me to forget all about our little lost lamb, and I . . . I shouted at him." He had the grace to look ashamed as he related the next portion of his narrative. "After you called upon him and I deduced you must have some knowledge of her whereabouts, I asked Ambrose to come with me to attempt to recover her. He refused, so I came alone. I was unsuccessful," he added with another of his small, self-deprecating smiles. "I promised him I would not attempt it again, at least not straightaway. So I followed you to the tableaux vivants. I thought to mix in the crowd and observe you, to glean some clue as to what your purpose might be. Imagine my astonishment when I saw Eliza! I was overcome with surprise, so much so that I forgot myself for a moment. The urge to speak with her was nearly overpowering, like some primitive call in the blood. Are such things possible, I wonder? But perhaps it was the intensity of my emotion that caused her to look in my direction and see me. I will never forget the emotions that passed over her face—disbelief, shock. And horror. That one I will remember the longest of all," he said bitterly.

"You did not give her an opportunity to reconcile herself to the reality of your being alive," I told him. "Her astonishment must have been complete."

He stared into the depths of his glass, then drained off the dregs, wincing against the harshness of the liquor as he swallowed. He set the glass carefully aside. "I cannot explain to you the instinct to flee from her, but I will say that it was as atavistic an urge as any man has ever known. I was as near to being an animal as I have ever been in the whole of my life, Miss Speedwell. I was certain my very survival depended upon fleeing her presence. Ambrose counselled me not to reveal our treachery to her. And now he has paid the price," he finished, dropping his head into his hands.

Stoker and I permitted him a moment's peace to come to grips with his emotions. When he lifted his head once more, he drew a deep breath and squared his shoulders, sitting forwards and looking us each squarely in the eye. "Miss Speedwell, Mr. Templeton-Vane, I place myself and my fate in your hands. I came here tonight with the express purpose of retrieving the only thing in the world my sister values in the hopes of removing it forever from her reach. But I have committed offences—criminal offences—and I am aware that these cannot be overlooked. Furthermore, my poor judgement has resulted in the death of my dearest—my *only*—friend. I have no will to oppose you. Do with me as you wish."

The man before us was pitiable, but he was clearly prepared to meet his fate with dignity and resignation. He offered himself up to our justice, and it would have been an easy thing to summon the earl's night watchman and have him turned over to the authorities.

But as my gaze met Stoker's, I knew we had already decided that was not going to happen. We spoke in the conversational shorthand we often adopted. It was the effect of being, as it were, souls entwined, with that perfect understanding that so often frustrated bystanders.

"You realise what this means?" I began.

He sighed, but conceded with good grace. "Mornaday. And J. J."

"Precisely." I turned to Julius Elyot. "Mr. Elyot, we are prepared to take another route. Your sins, in comparison to your sister's, are slight indeed. With your assistance, we may be able to bring her to justice for Lord Ambrose's murder. And I think I may guarantee that your efforts would go far in winning you the sympathy of the authorities."

His previous smiles had been tinged with mockery or abnegation. But the one he offered me then was so piercingly sweet, I could well understand why Lord Ambrose's loyalty had been so complete and lasted so long.

"Miss Speedwell, I deserve no such consideration, and if I am called to account for my crimes, let it be so. I will make no defence. But I will do anything in my power to aid your endeavours."

"Excellent." I turned to Stoker. "Summon the troops for tomorrow, my dearest. It is time we called a council of war."

CHAPTER

26

W e had offered Julius the hospitality of Stoker's little temple whilst Stoker spent the night with me in my Gothic chapel. Sleep proved elusive. We were eager to embark upon the next phase of our investigations, and notes had been dispatched to Mornaday and J. J., requesting their appearance as early as possible. But it was neither of them who knocked upon the door of the Belvedere as Stoker and I finished breakfasting. Stoker went to answer whilst I broke pieces of sausage for the dogs.

"Miss Trevelyan!" I heard Stoker exclaim. "What brings you to us?"

He escorted her in and urged her to a chair—none too soon from the look of her.

The creature who seated herself seemed a wraith of the woman who had called upon us with Eliza Elyot. Her hair, always untidy, had taken on a life of its own, struggling from its pins to spill down her back in a tangled snarl. Violet crescents shadowed her eyes, and her extreme pallor was the sort favoured by fashionable girls or wasting consumptives. Only her lips bore any colour, the incarnadine shade of having been gnawed in her distress. She moved, endlessly and restlessly, always plucking at her skirts or twisting her fingers together. The nails were bitten to the quick, and it occurred to me that no part of Undine Trevelyan had escaped her own depredations.

"Miss Trevelyan." Stoker spoke with the gentleness he invariably employed when faced with women in distress, but she started violently. He softened his voice further still. "I am glad you have come to us. Whatever grieves you, Miss Speedwell and I will render you aid, you have my promise."

She opened her mouth, but no sound issued forth. She swallowed hard, then tried again, managing a hoarse, rusting voice. "It is Eliza. She would not go to Miss Fleet's as you suggested. We returned to our lodgings instead, but Eliza left soon after and told me to remain there. She would only say that she had business to attend. That was just after we left you. I dare not go to the police—she told me most particularly that I must stay at home until she came, but she has not. What am I meant to do?" Her appeal was piteous as she looked from one of us to the other.

"Miss Trevelyan," I began in a soft, deliberate tone, "there is no delicacy I may employ which will make our news palatable to you."

Her eyes flared. "Eliza—you have news of her? Is she ill? Is she hurt?"

"We presume she is physically unharmed," Stoker assured her. "But she may be in some trouble. In fact, we are certain of it."

Undine clutched the arms of the chair as if they were her sole anchor to the earth itself. She swayed a little and I reached for my vinaigrette, but she shook her head. "I am all right. Tell me."

"We think she may have harmed someone else," Stoker told her.

"Ambrose Despard," she whispered.

Stoker and I exchanged startled glances. "You anticipated this?" I asked.

"No," she replied fiercely. "I did not. Never *anticipated*."

"But you do not disbelieve us," I pressed.

She shook her head, dropping her gaze to her lap. "No. I know well enough what Eliza is capable of." Slowly, deliberately, she folded back the edge of her sleeve. A narrow purple line braceleted the wrist; on the inside of the forearm, five plum-coloured finger marks stood in stark relief against the pale flesh. I thought of Undine's watchfulness during our previous meeting, the way her eyes never left Eliza's face. I had mistaken it for devotion, but perhaps it had been the wariness of a mongoose considering a cobra.

"She mistreated you." Stoker's manner was perfectly calculated to inspire confidences, entirely free of judgement or blame, and yet Undine, steeped in loyalty, hastened to defend Eliza.

"Not at first," she said faintly. "Not for a long time, in fact. We were happy together. We made a home." She shoved the sleeve down, covering the marks of Eliza's violence. "I sensed in her some strength that I lack, some talent greater than my own."

"Miss Fleet says you are an artist of great promise," I told her.

She managed something that was not quite a smile. "Perhaps once. But not for a long time. It was a question of money, you see. When we set up housekeeping—" She paused, her colour flaring high, but she held up her chin, refusing to apologise for the unconventional life she had led. "We had very little money. At first, it seemed romantic, like something from Murger's novel of Bohemian life. I remember snow falling through the roof and onto our bed the first winter and thinking it splendid to suffer together." She shuddered. "But one must eat. And a crust shared is still a crust. At Eliza's urging, I took commissions, wretched things that paid hardly enough to keep us in bread and coal. Every penny I earned, she counted and spent. Finally, a day came when there were no pennies to be had. Even the pittance Lord Ambrose paid would no longer stretch to our expenses. That is when she showed me the truth of who she was."

"And by then you could not leave her?" Stoker asked gently.

"I cannot explain it in a way that anyone else would understand," she said in sudden frustration. "How to make you see that she was a genius, tortured and brilliant? That I felt honoured to be near her? That it was a privilege to keep her fed, to feel the warmth of her attention and affection? Knowing all that she had lost made her pitiable in my eyes but also magnificent. Who else could rise, phoenixlike, from all she had suffered?"

I might have pointed out that Eliza Elyot had not risen at all save for treading on Undine's own back, but it seemed unkind. I remained silent and she went on.

"I vacillated between admiring her more than any person I have ever known and dreading the sound of her step upon the stair. I never knew which I would encounter, the friendless soul in need of succour? The frustrated scientist who longed for purposeful work? She is an ever-changing mystery to me, and that has been my greatest torment and my keenest joy. Until now."

She dropped her head into her hands for a long moment. She made no sound, but when she raised her gaze to ours, unshed tears shimmered in her eyes.

"She did not say where she was bound when she left our lodgings, but I believe she meant to go to Lord Ambrose, to confront him about Julius being alive all these years, about the lies he had told her. She wanted answers for his treachery, and she believed she deserved them."

"Did she take any sort of weapon?" Stoker inquired.

Undine paused, then nodded. "For economy's sake, I sometimes re-use canvases. When I pry them loose from their stretchers and cut them down, an awl is occasionally necessary to start a hole to fix the nail to the new stretcher. My awl was missing after Eliza left."

An awl was an inspired weapon, I thought. Light enough to be easily wielded by a woman, sharp and precise, small enough to fit into a lady's reticule.

"And it was there before she left?" Stoker asked.

"The minute before. I had it out, working a canvas," Undine confirmed.

"It remains to be seen if that is the sort of weapon that killed Lord Ambrose, but the evidence begins to mount," Stoker told her.

"Miss Trevelyan," I put in smoothly, "it may be viewed by less than cordial people that in supplying the weapon—however unwittingly—you have played the accomplice, that you perhaps had foreknowledge of her intentions."

"Never!" she cried. "I swear to you upon all that is holy, I would never have been party to such an act. Does not the fact that I have come here prove that I am speaking the truth?"

"It does," Stoker assured her. "You might as easily have kept your silence and obeyed Eliza's strictures to remain in your lodgings. It was brave of you to come to us."

And too late to be of any great use, I reflected grimly. Lord Ambrose was dead and heaven only knew what other horrors Eliza intended.

"Miss Trevelyan, it cannot have escaped your notice that by coming here, you have put yourself in danger," I began.

"Another fact which demonstrates my innocence," she said, squaring her shoulders.

"And you cannot return home, at least not until Eliza is apprehended," Stoker put in.

"I suppose I could go after all to Miss Fleet," she said.

"You cannot. It is the first place Eliza would look for you if she returned to your lodgings and found you had flown," I pointed out.

Her expression turned to keen despair. "But I have no money—"

I held up a hand. "Where I mean to send you, you will have no need of funds. Stoker, will you please offer our guest some further refreshment? I have a letter to write."

It was the work of moments to scrawl a hasty missive and fetch a warm shawl. I handed them over to Undine. "It grows cold and you have come out without a proper coat," I said, very well aware that she likely had none to call her own. "You needn't return it. The colour suits your complexion better than mine."

She turned over the letter, reading the scribbled address. "Sir Frederick Havelock. Are you quite serious?"

"Entirely," I told her.

"Sir Frederick Havelock is England's greatest living artist—perhaps Europe's," she protested.

"And he is always in need of fresh talent. He is no longer robust or young, and he will be glad of an extra pair of hands in the studio. No doubt you will be dogsbody at first, but if you impress him, you will find no better mentor for your art."

Stoker rummaged in his pockets and extracted a few coins. "It is too far and too cold to walk. You will need a cab."

She stared at the handful of largesse we offered, a letter and a few pence, but it seemed the world to her. "I do not know what to say," she began.

"For god's sake, say nothing," Stoker told her, colouring furiously. He was never more embarrassed than when his generosity was in play, I reflected as he bade Undine a hasty farewell and retreated to his owl.

I walked her to the door, wrapping the shawl tightly about her and tying the ends neatly behind her waist. "There, that ought to keep out the draughts."

She paused. "I hope you do not think I am the world's greatest fool. I suppose artists can be exceedingly stupid."

"So can people in love," I replied.

"Thank you for that, Miss Speedwell. Yes, we were in love, at least I was. And I think she loved me too. The difference is that my love has lasted, strengthened by our trials. But I think hers has worn away—or perhaps it never existed. Perhaps Eliza can love only herself." She took in a deep breath and pulled herself up to her full height. "But my love is best reserved for myself, I think. That will serve me better."

N̲o sooner had Undine left us than Mornaday and J. J. appeared, followed hard by Julius Elyot, looking refreshed after his night's sleep in Stoker's lodgings. He waited to be introduced with all the sangfroid of a baron at a ball.

"Miss J. J. Butterworth of the *Daily Harbinger*, Inspector Mornaday of the Metropolitan Police, may I present Mr. Julius Elyot, lately of Nuremberg."

If I had expected pandemonium, I would have been little short of the mark. Mornaday reached for a pair of wrist irons, and J. J. whipped out a notebook and pencil.

"Mr. Elyot, what can you tell the readers of the *Daily Harbinger* about your story? Why did you flee to the Continent and remain there in hiding for fifteen years?"

Mornaday shoved her aside. "Stand down, Butterworth. I am taking this man into custody for arson."

Stoker inserted himself smoothly between Elyot—who stood rooted to the spot, a startled expression on his face—and the importunate Mornaday.

"Stand down yourself, copper. You cannot prove he started the fire. He could easily say Lord Ambrose did."

I resumed my seat, as I expected the little fracas to be shortly concluded, settling Al-'Ijliyyah upon my lap. In any case, Stoker had matters comfortably under control. The day he could not keep J. J. and Mornaday in hand on his own would be a dark day indeed.

J. J. attempted to sidle around Stoker, but he extended one muscled arm, blocking her path. "Back. Mr. Elyot has no statement to make at this time." He turned to Mornaday. "If you do not put those restraints back into your pocket, I will use them on you."

Mornaday curled a lip. "What makes you think I cannot escape from a pair of wrist irons?"

"What makes you think I would use them on your wrists?"

Mornaday paled and leapt back like a scalded cat.

Stoker took advantage of the moment to guide Elyot forwards and indicate a chair for him to take. As Stoker played the host, pouring out a libation for Elyot, I gave him a bright smile. "Do forgive them, Mr. Elyot. We have not yet had the chance to explain everything to them, but we were just about to do so."

He murmured his thanks and took a small sip, blotting his lip with his finger. I turned to J. J. and Mornaday, who were watching him with the wariness one might extend to a lion on the loose.

"Sit down and stop looming over Mr. Elyot. He will not flee, and perhaps he will even make himself available for an arrest and an interview later," I told them.

Mornaday dropped his head in his hands, tearing at his hair as he gave a muffled groan of impatience.

"What is happening here?" Julius Elyot asked.

"I believe poor Mornaday has been pushed beyond the brink of endurance," I said evenly. "He is a sound enough investigator, and if he occasionally lacks imagination, it is not his fault. He also received some difficult news this week. He has been suspended until further notice."

Mornaday lowered his hands. His eyes were rimmed in red, and his expression so woebegone, I felt a thrust of pity for him. "Because of you," he said hoarsely. "I was meddling about in official files because of *you*. And now my career is in tatters and for what? I have a felonious firestarter sitting in front of me, and I cannot even bring him to justice because you all are mad as hatters, the lot of you."

J. J. was regarding him with her usual bright-eyed curiosity, but

Stoker's reaction was thoroughly unexpected. He sat forwards, fixing Mornaday with a level stare. "We will remedy this," he said in a voice of quiet authority. "We will catch Lord Ambrose's murderer and see that justice is done. We will not permit you to lose your position."

Mornaday's eyes lost none of their mournful look. "But—"

Stoker moved nearer still. "Have I ever once extended a hand to you in friendship? Have I ever pledged any sort of loyalty or sympathy to you?"

"None. You've been frequently hostile with occasional outbreaks of mere unlikability," Mornaday replied.

"Exactly. We may not ever be the best of friends, but I do see your worth. And though it pains me grievously to admit it, you have been helpful upon occasion," Stoker said.

"That must have cost you something," I said with an understanding smile.

Stoker's mouth curved downwards. "You cannot imagine." He turned once more to Mornaday and put out his hand. "You have my word, Mornaday. We will remedy this."

Mornaday took his hand slowly and with great caution—much as one might shake the paw of a lion.

"I appreciate that, Stoker," he said, shaking his hand only slightly from Stoker's stronger grip. "But I do hope you will not think me ungrateful if I inquire as to precisely *how* you intend to accomplish such lofty goals."

"Mr. Elyot has agreed to aid in our endeavour to bring Lord Ambrose's murderer to justice. We are in agreement that the villain was Miss Eliza Elyot."

I paused and looked around the assembled group to find them all nodding. Julius Elyot gave only a cursory nod, but I could not blame him for a certain lack of enthusiasm in naming his sister a murderess.

"We have a witness who places a lady of her description at the scene," I went on. "Furthermore, she had motive, a good one—vengeance for a perceived betrayal."

"But we do not know how it was done," J. J. put in. "The official report attributes his death to heart failure."

"I know how it was done," Mornaday said grudgingly. "I had a word with a mate who works for the police surgeon. Nothing is documented, of course, but he saw the body with his own eyes. No injuries whatsoever save a single, small entry wound. It would not bleed excessively, and death would have been instantaneous. His expert opinion is that the likeliest weapon would have been—"

"An awl," Stoker said smoothly.

"How can you know that?" The remainder of Mornaday's reaction to this interruption was volcanic. There was tearing of hair and fluent profanity until he wore himself down. When he had lapsed into furious silence, I explained about Undine Trevelyan's revelations.

"She confirmed all of our suspicions, as now has your friend who works for the police surgeon," I told Mornaday kindly.

He muttered something under his breath before turning to Julius Elyot. "You never explained how you came to be part of this menagerie of madness," he said, sketching the totality of the Belvedere with a grand gesture.

"Oh, I committed an act of criminal trespass," Elyot replied. "My second. And if you wish to take me into custody on those grounds, I entirely understand."

Mornaday gave a noncommittal grunt, but he knew perfectly well he was powerless to persecute Elyot unless Lord Rosemorran himself pressed the matter.

J. J. surveyed the group with interest. "I suppose you have a plan for apprehending Eliza Elyot?"

"Certainly," I began.

Mornaday's expression was puzzled. "We know where she lives. We can simply go and take her into custody."

"Can we?" Stoker asked mildly. "I seem to recall you have been stripped of your authority. You cannot arrest so much as an errant pig at present," he reminded Mornaday.

"Besides," I said hastily, cutting off Mornaday before he could rise to another angry retort, "at the behest of the Marquess of Harwich, the authorities have decided not to pursue the matter. Without the machinery of justice working for us we must force a confession, lure her into some further deviltry in order to catch her in the act. Hence, the plan."

I paused and looked at our merry band and, in a piece of timing so perfect, it must have been arranged by the angels, there was a knock at the door.

"Who in the name of seven hells is that?" Stoker demanded. "It's gone half ten."

"Eliza Elyot!" J. J. cried, jumping to her feet and upsetting the chessboard as she made a dash for the nearest suit of armour—German, sixteenth century, and boasting an impressive mace which she snatched up and began to swing in slow circles about her head.

Stoker grabbed it away from her. "For god's sake, give me that before you decapitate someone," he ordered.

"Yes, do," I urged. "And Mornaday, leave that revolver in your pocket. We are not Americans, for heaven's sake. Besides, it is not Eliza Elyot, I am almost certain. It is someone else entirely, and here at my invitation."

I strode to the door in perfect confidence, but—mindful that it *might* be our villainous adversary—I took the precaution of taking up my letter opener as I went. It was a Kukri dagger, old and beautifully sharp, perfect for attending to correspondence and inflicting damage on the deserving. Dagger in hand, Vespertine at my side, I completed the warrior-like image by throwing the door back on its hinges to the accompaniment of a Gaelic battle cry.

There was a shriek and a large, shambling figure dove for the nearest bush.

"Good morning, Mr. Plumtree," I called, dropping the dagger. "I apologise for the greeting, but one cannot be too careful. Do come out of the shrubbery and meet the others."

CHAPTER

27

It took a few minutes and a stiff measure of aguardiente to settle young Plumtree's nerves, but he was a sturdier fellow than I had anticipated, and colour soon flowed into his cheeks again. He took a seat on a hassock at J. J.'s feet, his gaze settled adoringly on her face as we swiftly related all that had happened thus far in the investigation. Julius Elyot, to no one's particular surprise, had no stomach for further discussion, and I urged him to the snuggery to rest.

"Thank you," he said, bowing slightly. He paused at the foot of the stairs. "I find myself entirely out of my depths in wrestling with all of this."

"I think any of us would find it an almost insurmountable challenge," J. J. told him. "You are handling it with more grace than I could summon."

He favoured her with one of his winsome smiles, and she returned it. He took himself up to the snuggery then, Huxley trailing behind.

I flicked J. J. a knowing glance. One of her usual—and invariably successful stratagems—was to befriend a potential subject for a journalistic exclusive. The look she returned to me was in no way apologetic. It was, after all, a man's world, and we understood one another well enough to condone and even admire the various tactics we had developed to survive in it.

We resumed our discussion of the case, Stoker and I painting the details for J. J. and Mornaday as well as bringing young Plumtree up to the minute. When it came to the murder of Lord Ambrose, he turned a little green. I made to pour another measure of aguardiente, but he waved me off. "No, no, Miss Speedwell, I am quite recovered, I assure you. This is fascinating, deeply fascinating. I have studied the workings of the criminal mind, you see. It is one of my little hobbies, the sort of thing I used to do to keep busy in the country. I am also fond of quilling and the accordion," he added.

"Indeed," Mornaday said dryly.

Plumtree flushed a furiously bright crimson, but Stoker gave him a kindly look. "I find a spot of macramé just the thing to occupy the hands on a cold winter's night by the fire."

"Do you indeed, sir?" Plumtree asked in interest.

"Oh, yes. That and a bit of knitting, although I'm badly out of practice. All sailors take up some sort of handcraft," he explained. "Whittling, scrimshaw. Macramé is very popular. It's to do with all the rope on board, you see."

"I do," Plumtree assured him.

"I enjoy découpage," J. J. put in. "Fire screens, usually, although I made my aunt the cleverest little table for Christmas last year."

Mornaday stared from one to the other. "Have I wandered into an assembly of lunatics? How are you all sitting there calmly discussing hobbies whilst there is a madwoman wandering loose out there?" He flung out his arms, very nearly upsetting the suit of armour again.

"It is merely a little polite conversation," I scolded. "You needn't act so aggrieved."

"Act? I do not act, Veronica. I *am* aggrieved. I have very nearly lost my job, and the lot of you promised me this case would be concluded, not just concluded but end in triumph. I confess, I do not see how a discussion of lace-tatting is going to accomplish that."

"Lace-tatting! Now that is a quick way to lose your eyesight," young Plumtree put in.

Mornaday closed his eyes. "Veronica, kindly bring this meeting back to the matter at hand, or I will do a violence to someone, and at the moment, I do not particularly care to whom."

"Very well." I sighed. "Mr. Plumtree, do forgive Mornaday. We promised to make certain he retains his employment with the Metropolitan Police, and to do so we require your assistance."

Mornaday opened his eyes to give me a suspicious stare. "How?"

I grinned. "We shall feed two birds with one apple. Mr. Plumtree is the person who can set my plan into motion. It will also require a little effort on J. J.'s part and nothing whatsoever of you, Mornaday, except to be on hand to take the credit for what transpires."

"And if it fails?" he demanded.

"Then you melt away into the night and the official story is that you were never there and had no part in it," I said. "There is absolutely no risk to you whatsoever, but there is every possibility of saving your job."

"I do like the sound of that," he admitted grudgingly.

"Perhaps, Veronica," Stoker put in, "now would be the time to explain your scheme in detail."

I smiled. "Haven't you guessed? We are going to set a trap for Eliza Elyot."

The details were sorted with astonishing rapidity. In order to attract Eliza Elyot's attention, we needed to place a story in the pages of the *Daily Harbinger*—the most crucial and difficult aspect of the entire enterprise.

"What ought J. J. to write?" Mornaday asked.

"There can be no mention of Elyot herself," J. J. said swiftly. "It will only serve to alert her to our scheme."

"Agreed," Stoker said. "The story ought to be that the body of a young drowning victim, believed lost some fifteen years ago, has been recovered in a state of curious preservation. Make no suggestions as to how it may have been done," he added firmly.

"Then say as she has never been identified, she is being laid to rest in an unmarked grave at Plumfield," I instructed.

J. J. scribbled a few phrases into her notebook. "Then what? It will seem curious there is no word from the police."

She gave Mornaday a meaningful look and he groaned. "Oh, for god's sake. In for a penny, in for a pound, I suppose. Very well. You may say that exhaustive police efforts to identify the victim were made when her body was first recovered, but since they failed, the police have nothing further to say upon the matter."

"And that is entirely true," I pointed out. "They gave up on her after Elyot was commissioned to sculpt her death mask. She was already supposed to have been buried anonymously."

"Quite right," Plumtree confirmed. The tamarin, which had been blessedly absent for some days, reappeared atop the mount of the giraffe at that moment, yawning broadly and scratching its belly. It dropped to young Plumtree's shoulder, eliciting a shriek of surprise.

"Never mind," I told him kindly. "It is only a little monkey. *Leontopithecus rosalia*. Familiarly known as the golden lion tamarin. It is a clever creature and usually continent."

"How singular," he said in a faint voice. But he put a fingertip to the creature's head and began to pet it in an absent fashion. "With that story appearing in the newspaper, it will appear that we are merely finishing what was begun fifteen years ago."

"Include the planned time of the burial at Plumfield," I told J. J.

"It ought to be as specific as possible in order to anticipate her movements."

J. J. wrote feverishly for a few minutes more, then looked up. "Tomorrow night, I presume?"

There was a chorus of dismayed reactions from the men, but J. J. and I exchanged patient looks. "It must be tomorrow night," she told them. "We already know Eliza is desperate to recover the Beauty, based upon her murderous attack upon Lord Ambrose. If we suggest she is at Plumtree's, Eliza may well break in and attack young Wilfred here."

The Plumtree in question blanched, but stiffened his spine visibly. "I am prepared to do my duty."

"But it isn't your duty, mate," Mornaday told him. "And I mean no offence, truly, but you are a country lad with spectacles and soft hands. How many times have you had call to defend yourself?"

Plumtree blinked behind his spectacles. "Well, I have read a number of very interesting books upon the subject of martial arts. There is one in particular from China that I am very eager—"

Mornaday groaned and flopped back into his chair.

"Wilfred," I said kindly, "it does you credit that you are willing to put yourself at personal risk to see this matter through. But it would distress us to no end if you were to come to any harm."

Wilfred's face was a picture of dejection until Stoker spoke up. "Books are grand for theory, but what you want is a bit of practice. I could give you a lesson or two if you like."

Wilfred brightened. "In boxing? I have read up on the Marquess of Queensberry's rules."

"Rules are for dancing, lad," Stoker told him. "If you ever begin a bout of fisticuffs with another man, make damned certain he cannot finish it. End him at once, by any means necessary."

"You mean I ought not to be gentlemanly about it," Wilfred said in tones of hushed awe.

"Slapping a fellow with your glove and marching twenty paces went out with negus punch and phaetons," Stoker said. "Do what you must and get out with your skin."

"That is quite modern. Mamma would not approve," Wilfred told him. He brightened. "But I like it. It's very robust."

I turned to J. J. before the men could raise further objections. "Mind you insert an image of the death mask. A small mention of the burial might easily be missed by Eliza, but the death mask will be impossible to overlook."

"My god," Wilfred said, eyes wide, "imagine the shock she will receive. To have been separated from her all these years and then to see the death mask itself in print with the news that her Beauty has been discovered!"

"And is about to be lost to her once more," Mornaday put in dryly. He paused, then went on in a thoughtful tone. "Although it does occur to me that she might simply wait to dig her up once Plumtree has finished the business of burying her. It would be more discreet."

Stoker shook his head. "Discreet but not feasible. Have you ever dug a grave?"

Mornaday's look was long and cool. "No. Have you?"

Stoker did not flinch. "Yes. And it's bloody hard work—too much for Eliza Elyot to undertake by herself, if you will pardon the pun."

"Indeed," Wilfred said. "We have two gravediggers on hand for each burial, and even then it takes a good five hours with necessary stops for rest. No, on the whole I think Mr. Templeton-Vane is correct. Miss Elyot would most definitely attempt to take the Beauty before she is consigned to the earth."

"Then we are in agreement," I said, looking around the little band of stalwart souls.

J. J. rose. "I must fly if this is to make the next edition."

"I will walk you to the offices," Mornaday said. "I might as well, given I have nothing better to do and nowhere better to be."

J. J. rolled her eyes heavenwards but permitted him to escort her. Young Wilfred followed soon after, and Stoker and I were left to contemplate the litter of teacups and becrumbed plates. The tamarin gave a mournful little bleat as Wilfred left, staring after him in adoration. Stoker absently fed her a few bits of cake as I tidied up.

"Veronica," he said in a tone of quiet authority, "do sit down."

I resumed my chair, Vespertine soon settling his head upon my knee, and regarded Stoker levelly. "Is there something on your mind, dearest?"

"I think we ought to discuss the rest of your plan," he said calmly. "The bit you neglected to tell the others."

"I cannot imagine why you think I omitted anything." I stroked Vespertine's head a little too casually.

"Veronica," Stoker said, his eyes brilliant in the low lamplight, "I have known you in every possible way a man can know a woman. I understand you better than you will ever admit because one cannot fully love what one does not fully comprehend, and believe me when I say I love you entirely and comprehend you completely. For all your delightful unpredictability, you are thoroughly consistent in always choosing the most outlandish, outrageous, unimaginable options in any given situation. And that is how I know you mean to take the place of the Beauty in that casket."

"Shall I explain my reasons? I assure you they are excellent," I told him.

"Oh, please do," he urged, settling back comfortably in his chair. The tamarin nestled into the crook of his arm, regarding me with an unnervingly human expression.

"Well," I began, "Eliza Elyot's most likely course of action—as we discussed—would be to waylay young Wilfred at Plumfield and retrieve the Beauty before she is buried."

"Agreed," he said, stroking the monkey's head absently. The little creature gave a squeak of pleasure.

"We ought naturally to be on hand to prevent any harm coming to

Wilfred, but someone ought to accompany him to the cemetery for his own protection—after all, Eliza has already demonstrated a propensity for violence."

"Also agreed."

"Operating on the principle that one can never underestimate the advantage of surprise, the casket seems the most logical place to hide. Now, you might offer yourself, but I think I bear a slightly stronger resemblance to a dead woman than you, beloved."

Stoker continued to scratch the monkey's head. "You might alert Wilfred to your scheme."

"He is untested in such intrigues," I pointed out. "His heart is in the right place, but there is every possibility he would trip on a spade or fall over a gravestone."

A fleeting smile touched Stoker's lips. "He does give the impression of a colt not quite acquainted with his limbs."

"Indeed. I think it very brave of you to offer to teach him the rudiments of brawling. You will no doubt be concussed for your pains."

"No doubt," he said.

I went on. "If I am in the casket, I will be in a position to help, should Wilfred have need of assistance. And should the worst happen and Eliza Elyot is successful in breaching the casket, she will not have achieved her aims. She will find a living woman instead of her Beauty. After all, one of our purposes in undertaking this investigation was to spare the Beauty any further despoliation. I cannot imagine you like the idea of dangling her as bait in front of Eliza."

"Indeed," he said again. "I notice you did not mention this part of your plan in front of the others."

"Because I expected you would object, and we had guests. There are few activities more fatiguing than watching other people's quarrels."

"Indeed," he answered.

"Stoker, that is your third 'indeed.' Two too many," I said. His hand stilled on the monkey's head and the little beast climbed up, perching atop Stoker's head to return the favour, rubbing its paws through his hair. Stoker remained silent and after a moment, I began to chafe under the weight of the stillness.

"Do you not mean to dissuade me? Point out the flaws in my plan? Express your objections with vehemence and eloquence?"

He tipped his head. "Actually, no."

I blinked in astonishment. "Are you entirely well? Have you a fever? Should I palpate something?"

He shrugged, causing the tamarin to scold him lightly. "Not in the slightest. I have never felt better."

"Then why, pray tell, are you so accommodating of the idea of my exposing myself to potential harm?" I demanded.

He put a fingertip to the monkey's ruffled hair and smoothed it gently. "Veronica, our relationship has been on an intimate footing for some time now. We have enjoyed many adventures together—hazards and perils I could never have imagined before I met you, and I say that as a person who has actually participated in naval bombardments and expeditions to Amazonia. Time and again, I have counselled patience or caution or at least a basic and sensible care for your bodily safety. And time and again, I have been ignored. You have done exactly as you pleased in the face of my objections. They have won me precisely nothing. Not an inch of ground have you given. So, I concede."

"You what?"

He fished in his pocket for one of his enormous handkerchiefs and waved it. "I know it is scarlet rather than the traditional white, but you may consider this a flag of surrender. I know when I am conquered."

I moved to snatch the handkerchief from him, but the tamarin anticipated me and reached out a greedy paw, taking the crimson cotton for itself. Within a moment, it had wrapped the fabric around its body, making a sort of drapery over its head. It looked alarmingly like the oracle at Delphi, and I stared at it a moment in fascination before turning my attention back to Stoker.

"What do you mean that you surrender?" I asked, keeping my voice level and calm. I was rather proud of the effort. There was nothing to betray the sudden churning of my insides at the idea he might have come to the end of his tether. I had pushed him, of that there could be no question. But I had always relied upon his strength, his resourcefulness, his devotion. Was it possible these were not infinite? Had I finally exhausted his affections?

I waited, breath abated, until he spoke again. He leant forward once more, taking my hands in his as the tamarin dropped to his shoulder, regarding me with eyes like ebony beads.

"Veronica, I mean that I have, at last, come to understand my role. It is not to discourage your exuberance or your audacity. How could I want to when those are the very qualities I admire most? If I have lectured or harangued in the past, it is because I am afraid. Every moment of every day, I am afraid."

"Afraid of what?" I demanded.

"Of losing that which I have come to realise I cannot live without. But I do not want a small and stifled version of you. I want you—in all your intrepid and audacious glory. I want you just as you are, the entirety of your chaos and your wildness. You are the whirlwind I did not know I needed, but now that you are here, I will not be the one to ask you to be anything different than exactly as you are. More than anyone, I ought to understand that nature cannot be denied. And your nature is tumult."

I swallowed hard against the sudden tightness in my throat. "I am not that bad," I managed hoarsely.

"No," he said with a slow smile. "You are not bad at all. If I could have created—as Eliza Elyot attempted to—a perfect woman, I could never have imagined you. But that is my failure. Not yours."

It was some time before I was mistress enough of my emotions to speak.

"Only one man in a thousand—*ten* thousand—would have answered me as you have just done."

He reached up and set the monkey gently aside. It chattered in annoyance, but Stoker ignored it as he rose and pulled me to my feet.

"Only one woman in ten thousand would have deserved that answer."

CHAPTER

28

The next morning I snatched up the first edition of the *Daily Harbinger* before I even bothered with my toast and tea. I hadn't far to look. J. J. had managed to insert the story a very few pages into the issue. The piece was small, a scant handful of lines only, accompanied by a reproduction of the Beauty's death mask. As an illustrated journal, the *Harbinger* would not print a photograph, but Julius Elyot's original sketch of the death mask was an arresting image—as were the ghoulish little drawings J. J. had provided. She was skilled with a pencil and had managed a creditable sketch of the casket as well as one of a graceful body floating in the canal. These, coupled with the mention of Plumfield, ensured that the hook was baited. It remained now only to see if the fish took the lure.

I showed the piece to Stoker who was working his way steadily through porridge, kippers, and a helping of kedgeree that would have put a farmhand to shame.

"It is ridiculous," he said as he pushed the newspaper away and reached for a fourth slice of toast. "See here where J. J. makes reference to the corpse's 'curious state of preservation'? She explains nothing. The body is fifteen years old—*how* is it meant to have been preserved?

Where has it been in the ensuing decade and a half? The editor will be inundated with demands for more information. It is nothing but vague suggestion and cryptic innuendo."

The fact that he had specifically instructed J. J. to write obliquely seemed to have escaped him entirely. But the male of the species, in my observation, is frequently irrational, and the greater the dangers we faced, the more Stoker's peevishness increased. I gave him a calm smile. "Vague suggestion and cryptic innuendo sell newspapers," I reminded him. "And her editor will no doubt be anticipating a second article tomorrow in which all is revealed."

He bit down aggressively on his piece of toast by way of reply.

Had I not a case of *Agrias claudina* to catalogue and clean, I might have spent the day in an agony of anticipation. As it was, the claudinas were delightfully distracting, not least because I read in the accompanying notes of their preferred diet of decomposing fish. Another titbit for Mornaday, I decided.

"It is time," Stoker said as I tucked away the last of the claudinas. I had no idea what he had done with himself for the day—lepidoptery being both vocation and avocation for me—but he seemed pleased with himself, if a trifle subdued. I tidied away my cases and notes whilst Stoker fed the dogs, and when we had finished, we went to the folly of the little Scottish castle where Spyridon awaited us with the understanding that Julius would join us later. We had discussed at length whether to tell him that I was to masquerade as the Beauty and decided that the fewer people who knew of it, the better. If he knew I lay in the casket, he might accidentally give away the ruse to his sister—or perhaps not so accidentally. He had joined with us to apprehend Eliza, but I wondered, if it came to a sharp end, would Elyot's loyalty lie with justice or his sister? As wiser folk have often counselled, it is good to have faith but better to have certainty.

The Beauty still rested in Spyridon's bed, and the normality of the setting only heightened the illusion that she was merely sleeping. Stoker gently untied the ribbon at her throat and secured it around mine. I made a note of her pose and the dressing of her hair so that I could impersonate her properly. These were the tasks of a moment, and yet I found myself lingering in a dark enchantment. It was a fancy, of course, but it did make me wonder how Spyridon had been able to bear sleeping only a few feet away from her.

In the corner next to the armchair, I saw a rifle, and looped about Spyridon's sturdy waist was a weathered bandolier with a few bullets. He must have seen the questions trembling on the tip of my tongue, for he gave me a broad, white smile.

"It is nice that I do not ask you about your business, is it not, missus? It's good for friends to be discreet with one another."

The smile did not waver, but there was a sternness to his eye that told me any further curiosity would be unwelcome. So I returned the smile as graciously as I could.

"Quite right, Spyridon. And do call me Veronica, won't you?'

He put a hand to his heart and bowed. He followed us to the Belvedere, where Stoker had unearthed a garment similar to the Beauty's robe in the dressing-up box. The gentlemen gave me privacy as I removed my working gown and donned the crimson frock, shaking out the stiff folds. I unpinned my hair, shaking it out and letting it tumble to my waist. When I was dressed, they returned, and Stoker helped me step up into the casket and arrange myself on the satin cushion inside. He fidgeted a little with the composition, drawing a lock of hair over my shoulder and pulling the robe down to cover my feet.

"Stoker," I said gently, "do stop fussing."

"I don't imagine Eliza will get much of a look before we apprehend her, but if she does, you must look convincing."

"Convincing! I believe all that is required of me is to lie very still," I told him.

He gave me a pitying look. "I think we can do better than that," he said as he produced a series of small pots and brushes, setting to work under Spyridon's interested eye. It seemed a trifle unfair that he was privy to our clandestine activities when he was so unwilling to discuss his own, but I decided that was a matter best left to another time.

"Do be still," Stoker ordered as he began painting my face.

"Whut ust dat?" I asked through closed lips.

"A preparation of my own invention," he told me. "I worked the better part of the day to find something that would approximate the pallor and texture Eliza achieved. I think it turned out rather well." He continued to paint, brushing on the concoction until he was satisfied. "Do not move a muscle until it sets," he instructed. He carried on, applying the mixture to my décolletage and arms, all the way to my fingertips. It was cool and the brush was featherlight, raising a delicious shiver as he worked.

"Veronica, do stop squirming," he ordered.

"Then stop *that*," I muttered, cutting my eyes to where he was drawing the brush with painstaking slowness down my throat to the neckline of the robe.

"Oh," he said, dropping the brush hastily.

Spyridon leant over and peered into the casket. "She looks good—like a very beautiful lady who is dead and also not dead."

"Thank you," Stoker replied. "That was precisely my intention."

Spyridon frowned, studying my face. "A little colour here," he said, gesturing towards my cheekbones. "The other one has a pretty flush. As though she were sleeping off a fever." Stoker agreed, applying a little waxy rouge to my cheeks.

"And to the lips. They must look inviting, as if waiting for the kiss of the prince to awaken her," Spyridon offered.

"Someday," I said, a trifle acidulously, "perhaps men will stop finding unconscious women to be an allurement."

"Some men prefer a lady who is silent," Spyridon replied sagely, "because they like to think they are smarter than their women and if she talks, he finds out he is stupid. Me, I prefer a woman to talk. It is better this way."

"I think, Spyridon, we are going to be very good friends," I told him.

"If you speak again, you are going to crack the wax, and I will not be responsible for my actions," Stoker warned. I made a noise of assent, and he applied the finishing touches, darkening my lips and adjusting the lock of hair that flowed over one shoulder.

"There," he said, stepping back and gesturing to Spyridon to look. "I think the resemblance is as close as we can make it."

Spyridon studied me a long moment before nodding his head. "Good enough to fool anyone who wants to be fooled," he said.

"Most people see exactly what they want," Stoker agreed. He bent to me. "We have modified the casket slightly by removing a small pane of the glass on the end." He gestured towards the open area I had not noticed above the top of my head. "If we had not made the modification, you might well have suffocated in there. At the very least, your respiration would have shown up as condensation on the glass."

I swallowed the curse that sprang to mind. I ought to have considered either of those—*both*, in fact—and it was a mercy Stoker had. Together, Stoker and Spyridon lifted the glass lid and settled it into place. Even with the open pane, the immediate sense of suffocation was tremendous. The wax lay heavily on my skin, and I knew I dared not move for fear of cracking it, but I was seized by an immobility far greater than that. I had put on the guise of the Beauty, and I had assumed something of her detachment as well. Sounds were muffled, and though I peeped through my lashes, my vision was veiled by the old, heavy glass.

They drew a long drapery of dark silk over the top of the casket. Stoker hesitated just as the fabric was about to cover my face. He said nothing, but he took one long, lingering look. Then a rush of silk and darkness. I knew he had arranged with Lord Rosemorran to borrow a few of the porters to transport the casket to Plumtree's, and I lay in sombre quiet as they bumped and thumped, throwing a tarpaulin over the silk shroud and lashing it into place with a series of ropes.

Just then, Elyot appeared, for I heard a new voice. "You have already covered her. I confess, I was hoping to see her again."

"Later," Stoker said shortly.

After this was a sense of movement, an awkward rocking as they conveyed me to the wagon that was to carry me on. Stoker kept up a conversation with Elyot, and although I could not make out the words, the familiar low rumble of his voice was my consolation. More than my consolation; it was my lifeline, I fancied, the only thing connecting me to the world of the living. I had the oddest sensation that I might simply float away as the Beauty had done in the canal, drifting and dreaming as everything else passed me by.

They settled the casket into the wagon with a thump. A moment later the wheels began to turn, conveying us through the darkening streets towards Plumtree's. We drove slowly, for Stoker would take no chances in breaking the casket, as the illusion would be ruined.

We had discussed at length the necessity for keeping young Plumtree as safe as possible, and he had agreed to keep well clear of the premises of his establishment until the appointed time, remaining all the while under Mornaday's watchful care. There was a chance that Eliza Elyot, upon reading the *Harbinger* piece, would assume the Beauty was at Plumtree's. If so, Eliza might preempt our plan and attempt to retrieve her trophy well before we meant to move the Beauty to Plumfield. If that happened, I would not have wagered a tuppence for Wilfred's safety, and Stoker had concurred. Mornaday, with no official work, had been only too willing to play the watchdog over our young friend. But Eliza Elyot had killed once, and I knew that to underestimate her might prove fatal. She was a desperate woman with nothing to lose except the obsession that had fuelled her existence, and it was chilling to think what violence she might employ to obtain the Beauty. I was therefore relieved when I heard Wilfred's voice as the wagon drew up to the kerb, rolling to a gentle stop at Stoker's explicit instruction.

"Hallo, Wilfred. Mornaday," I heard Stoker call.

They exchanged a few words—very few, for speed was of the essence in getting the casket off of the street where Eliza might be watching. Together the men coordinated the removal of the casket, carrying it into the mortuary. They set it down, and I heard the clink of coins as Stoker bade the porters farewell.

Suddenly, Stoker's voice came, quite near to the casket, so he must have bent near to the missing pane of glass. "Mornaday and Elyot have gone with Plumtree to see the porters out. They've put you on a plinth that will be lowered by a hydraulic winch to the floor below, so don't be alarmed when it begins to move. Give me a quick kick of your foot to let me know all is well."

I did so and heard a soft sigh. "Thank god for that."

"Mr. Templeton-Vane, is everything quite all right?" Wilfred's booming tones were audible even through the tarpaulin.

"Certainly," Stoker said, his voice more muffled now.

"Only, I thought I heard you speaking to someone," Wilfred pressed.

"Myself," Stoker returned swiftly. "Now, was there trouble today? Anything to report?"

"None," Mornaday assured him.

"Mr. Mornaday and I went to a travelling show on Hampstead Heath, and we passed the day very pleasantly indeed. They had the most interesting folk," Wilfred told him excitedly. "There was a woman who had the body of a spider. And a mermaid. And a fellow actually conjoined to his twin—" I suppressed a laugh. Mornaday had also worked for Professor Pygopagus when Stoker and I had joined the troupe as he had undertaken a clandestine investigation of Stoker as a potential murderer. I was not surprised he harboured a nostalgic fondness for the place.

Stoker's voice cut in shortly. "Good."

Just then the clock began to strike, slow, sonorous chimes of the hour.

"Our friends will be in position," Stoker told him. "Time to set the snare."

"Hang on a minute," Mornaday objected. "Where is Veronica? It isn't like her to be out of the thick of things."

"But this isn't the thick of things, is it?" Stoker asked pleasantly. "Surely the climax of our adventure will come at Plumfield."

"You mean she's gone ahead and left you to do the heavy lifting?" Mornaday guffawed. "J. J. is en route there as well. Women!"

Stoker made a noncommittal noise that might have been agreement, and after another brief silence there came the deep, protesting groan of ancient machinery as it was coaxed to life. "This really was the most advanced technology of its time when it was installed," Wilfred was explaining to Mornaday as the lift jerked into motion. We moved slowly down, down, down into the depths of Plumtree's until we came to a shuddering stop. The plinth must have been on wheels, for there came a few deep thuds—wooden blocks being kicked aside, I imagined—and then the casket began to roll. There was a rough bump as it was conveyed onto the train, then the rattle of chains as the plinth was secured.

"Right as rain," Wilfred called happily. "Tight as a parson's arse, as my father used to say."

I stifled a snort of laughter—the things men will say when they believe themselves alone is endlessly astonishing—and Stoker swiftly covered it with a cough.

"Everything all right there, Mr. Templeton-Vane?" Wilfred called.

"Just a frog," Stoker assured him.

Another pause and then Mornaday, with a note of surprise. "Aren't you coming, Stoker?"

"I will follow," Stoker told him vaguely. "Someone must function as rearguard."

"Better you than me, old son," Mornaday said, and I could hear the grin in his voice. "But it is best for the professionals to be at the sharp end of the action, and I shouldn't like for you to get in the way when I bring in a murderer."

Stoker gave a low growl and Mornaday laughed in response. "See you on the other side, Templeton-Vane!"

What followed was a pair of raps upon the casket. Just twice, the two short knocks being the signal Stoker and I had devised so that I should know when we were to be parted and I was consigned to the care of Mornaday and Wilfred. We had agreed that Julius Elyot would remain with Stoker. They would travel to Plumfield by road, arriving perhaps a quarter of an hour after our little train—enough time to execute a flanking manoeuvre and close the trap behind Eliza. She would require a wagon and a pair of porters to remove the casket from Plumfield. When I sprang out at her in surprise, she would no doubt then mean to flee, only to find her way blocked by Stoker with Mornaday on hand to apprehend her. Mornaday had long since proven himself trustworthy, but if he knew I lay in the casket, he might well be distracted, thus potentially giving away my presence when Eliza Elyot made her appearance.

If she made an appearance, I reflected grimly. There was always the possibility that she had not seen J. J.'s piece in the *Harbinger*, or—having seen it—she may well have intuited a trap and come prepared to meet with peril. A criminal is a canny creature, I had often observed, with a capacity to smell danger in the air. But I would not entertain such thoughts; I could not. I must keep myself focused upon the matter at hand, although the potential for calamity was perhaps greater than any other endeavour we had undertaken. To fail was unthinkable.

Stoker must have moved away during my reverie, for there was a murmured exchange of masculine voices and then the deep, basso profundo growl of the steam engine as it was stoked to life. I heard the scrape of the coal shovel and the roar of the fire. The little train shook with the effort of moving away from the mortuary, but after several minutes and a good deal of swearing by Wilfred, it began to inch forwards.

"We are away!" Wilfred cried happily.

Mornaday said nothing, but I heard the steady scrape of the shovel as he fed coal to the engine. We moved faster down the line, gaining speed as we left the mortuary behind and turned towards the west and Plumfield. The journey was even more harrowing than the first, for the Stygian darkness of the previous trip was nothing compared to the complete absence of light within the casket. There was an odd sensation of weightlessness as we were borne along; I felt insubstantial as a feather, drifting between worlds until at last, with a long, grinding shriek of brakes, we slackened speed to approach the little platform at Plumfield.

"Here we are," Wilfred called as the train rolled to a stop. "Jump off just there and make certain I've stopped where I ought, please."

"A little forwards," Mornaday shouted.

"Right you are," Wilfred shouted back, but the words were cut off sharply, and I heard Mornaday's exclamation of horror as a tremendous thud shook the train.

"Plumtree!" Mornaday's voice was distant now, and I realised we were moving away from the station, back in the direction of the mortuary.

Suddenly, we were gaining speed again, and I understood with dreadful and certain clarity exactly what had happened. So it was no surprise to me some minutes later when the tarpaulin was untied and the silk shroud removed and a voice spoke to me through the glass.

"At last!" Eliza Elyot proclaimed.

CHAPTER

29

S ome women, when faced with a murderous madwoman who has mistaken one for the object of her scientific obsession, might succumb to hysterics. But I was made of sterner stuff. In the short time between the sound of what I could only presume was Wilfred Plumtree's unconscious body hitting the floor of the train to Eliza Elyot's tearing away of my shroud, I realised the necessity of maintaining the fiction that I was the Beauty. That element of surprise was my only advantage in a confrontation with her, and I was deeply aware of the fact that it was not only my own safety that rested in my slender hands.

From the shouts behind us, I had deduced that Mornaday had been left behind on the platform and that Plumtree was still aboard, wounded or perhaps worse. My every instinct was to rise up and throw myself into battle, attacking Eliza and taking her unawares. In the meantime, as we steamed our way back through the darkness to Plumtree's, I considered the circumstances. J. J. was at Plumfield—although Mornaday's shouts would no doubt have roused her attention and even now they were most likely in pursuit. But the tunnel was black as a devil's heart, and the way was unfamiliar. It would be only too easy for them to mistake a turning and find themselves plunged into a maze of impenetrable gloom. I could not depend upon them for assistance, and, I reflected bitterly, Stoker was even now en route to Plumfield with Julius Elyot. He would arrive at the graveyard without knowing Eliza had anticipated our arrival and somehow concealed herself in the tunnel, leaping aboard and incapacitating young Wilfred to seize control of the little train. She had timed it perfectly, waiting until Mornaday had jumped off, leaving herself only Wilfred to deal with.

Poor Wilfred! I could not contemplate his current state with anything like equanimity. If he still lived, I owed it to him to give him whatever protection I could, and I vowed that stalwart young man would come to no further harm on my watch.

As such thoughts raced through my mind, I felt the train slowing once more. I had expected Eliza to return us to Plumtree's, but it suddenly occurred to me that she might have secured another spot to remove the casket, an eventuality that struck horror into my heart. It would be difficult enough for anyone to trace us from the mortuary, but if Eliza had some other lair, I would have no one to rely on but myself. I shuddered to think what might become of young Wilfred if much time passed before he was discovered.

I had to know where we were bound, and as Eliza must be working the controls, I ventured a glimpse, opening my eyes slowly. To my astonishment, I met Wilfred's gaze. He was holding his head, blood pouring through his fingers, shock writ upon his features. He was ghastly pale, and what little colour remained drained straight away as he looked at me.

His mouth dropped and I risked the slightest shake of the head, feeling a crack along my neck as the wax Stoker had applied so carefully gave way. Wilfred nodded once, then apparently thought better of it, wincing and sliding into a huddled heap upon the floor. He would be no help to me—and in fact would constitute a hindrance, wounded and vulnerable as he was—but I felt a surge of purpose in knowing he still lived and would be looking to me for protection.

"Almost there, my dear," Eliza called, and I realised how far she had slipped into madness to have addressed the Beauty thus. She was not, had never been, a simple scientific experiment to Eliza. The waxwork was something more, and I might have pitied her had this obsession not turned her into a monster.

The train rocked to a stop, but the screaming of the engine did not abate. In the reflection of the glass, I saw flames leaping from the open furnace. In her haste, Eliza had apparently shovelled in every last bit of coal, stoking the fire to hellish heights.

She came towards me, and with almost superhuman strength, wrenched the lid from the casket. "Finally," she said in a voice rising in triumph. For a moment, she rested her hand upon my cheek. "My god, you are warm! What have they done to you?"

She put a questing hand to my chest. As soon as her flesh touched mine, I knew the masquerade was finished. She reared back, her voice harsh as her grip tightened upon me. "You have a heartbeat," she accused. "You are not my specimen! What have you done with her?"

I opened my eyes then and with a savage thrust, drove the heel of my palm into her nose. I heard the crunch of the shattered cartilage— most satisfying—and she dropped to her knees, howling in pain. I meant to leap from the casket in one smooth motion, but the garment I wore had become entangled with my nether limbs. I fell heavily onto Wilfred, who gave a low, agonised moan of such torture, I feared his soul had left his body.

Before I could get my feet under me, Eliza reached down, blood pouring from her nose and onto my face. She clouted me once, sharply, upon the temple and more of the wax cracked, falling in shards and revealing my face.

"You!" Her voice was the snarl of a cornered cat.

I blinked, dazed, and reached into my décolletage for my stiletto. She slapped my hand away, sending the weapon skittering along the floor of the train, but before she could land another blow, I lifted my foot and drove my knee into parts unmentionable—a fiendish trick, and almost as effective upon a woman as a man. It purchased me a moment's reprieve, and I might have made an escape, but I could not abandon poor Wilfred. He lay on his back, mouth agape and making the most terrible noises I had ever heard from a human being. His eyes were unfixed and glassy.

I had little time, I realised. I was physically fit and skilled in various means of self-defence, but Eliza was driven by her mania and was desperate. She took up the poker meant for stirring the coals in the engine, and advanced, arms outstretched, lips curled back in fury.

I edged away from her, wrapping my right hand in the folds of my robe as I moved. She did not close in swiftly, meaning instead to torture me a moment with the knowledge that I was about to die.

"Where is she?" she demanded hoarsely. "If you disguised yourself to look like her, you must know where she is."

She moved a step forwards and I retreated the same distance. "If you kill me, you will never discover her whereabouts," I told her.

She flicked a glance to Wilfred's recumbent form. "I could always revive him and make him tell me. Before I kill him."

"He doesn't know." Another step forwards for her, back for me. We were moving in a dance of death, locked together, our steps patterned perfectly and Eliza always in the lead.

"You're lying," she hissed.

"I am not, as it happens. But can you afford to take that chance?" I asked. "Imagine never seeing your great experiment again, Miss Elyot. The idea of her is what sustained you all these years, isn't it? And now you've come so far. Could you really bear to lose her again?"

"You will tell me," she said. "I could force you. I *will* force you. And it will not be pleasant. You must know what I did to her. I shall do the same to you, only I imagine it will be infinitely worse if I begin the process whilst you're still alive."

It was too gruesome a fate to contemplate, and I had had enough of her games. I drove my wrapped fist into the casket, shattering the nearest pane and neatly catching one of the broken pieces before it dropped. She lunged at the same moment I brought my arm up, and I caught her just under the chin. Stoker would no doubt have claimed it a lucky blow, but I knew enough of anatomy to have chosen well. I was not fortunate enough to strike a major blood vessel; there was no fount of blood or pulsing gore to win my freedom. But there was a sudden gush of ruddy wetness and she stopped, clapping a hand to her neck and staggering slightly.

Without waiting for her to regain her strength, I raced to Wilfred, looping my arms under his and dragging him from the train. He roused under the effort—I confess, I may have, in my haste, bumped his head upon the floor a time or two—and managed to get his own feet under himself. I supported him as he heaved his bulk forward.

"Hurry, Wilfred," I urged. "We haven't much time. She is coming!"

Behind us, Eliza was on the move, hand still clasped to her neck, shirt and fingers stained with her own life's blood. It was a dreadful sight, one to strike horror in the heart, but it was not enough to stop her entirely. On she came, muttering threats in a low and rasping voice.

We had just gained the platform when Eliza staggered to us, giving Wilfred a mighty shove that drove him to the floor. Half carrying him as I had been, I would have been borne along with Wilfred, but Eliza reached out a gore-stained hand and pulled me back, wrapping one arm around my throat as she jammed the pointed edge of the poker into my side.

"Eliza!"

Halfway down the stairs in front of us stood Julius Elyot. At the sight of him, Eliza bared her teeth.

"You will not stop me, Julius," she told him. "Not this time."

"Eliza, what have you become?" he asked, his expression bereft. "How could you do that to Ambrose?"

"How could I not?" she demanded. Her grip did not loosen as she raged at him. "The pair of you took everything from me. Do you know what I could have become if it were not for you? Always thinking you knew best! But you didn't, Julius. You were nothing to me." She fairly spat the words. "You were so envious of me, you couldn't bear to see my success so you destroyed it."

"Success!" Julius descended a step. "Eliza, you were in the grip of madness. Ambrose and I did not understand it at first, and for that we are to blame. And when we did understand it, we permitted it to go on far too long."

"*Permitted.* Who are you to permit or deny me anything?"

"I admit we were dazzled by what you were achieving," he said, descending another step. "But Ambrose and I came to our senses. You were lost. You became so obsessed by your ambitions, by your unnatural attachment to that *thing—*"

"Do not speak of her!" Eliza ordered. "She would have been the greatest scientific achievement in all of history, and you ruined that."

"I thought I was saving you," he said sadly. He had reached the bottom of the steps and he paused there, stretching out his hand to his sister. "Eliza, it is not too late. Give this up now. I will speak to the authorities about Ambrose. You are clearly not in your right mind. You needn't hang for it. I will make certain they are kind to you."

She gave a short, mirthless laugh. "Even now, you think you can decide my fate for me. You destroyed my work and you kept me separated from her for years. Do you know how I have mourned since the fire? It was not because of you, Julius. I did not regret losing you. But every day that has passed, I have grieved for *her.* For the loss of what I was about to achieve. And now I discover that you knew where she was all along. You kept us apart because you are a small, small man. You could not bear my greatness."

Tears of rage spilled onto her cheeks, and the hand clasped about my arm trembled.

"Eliza, you are not well—"

"Stop saying that!" She tightened her grip upon me, shoving the poker harder against my flesh. "We are leaving, Julius. Miss Speedwell is going to lead me to her, and then I will let her go. If you are wise, you will not meddle with me further, brother."

She jerked hard upon my arm, urging me forwards.

"Not a step further!"

The shout came from behind us, next to the roaring engine of the little train. Eliza whirled, carrying me with her, and I beheld then the gladdest sight I have ever seen in the whole of my life.

"Stoker!"

He was standing beside the engine, as timely an appearance as a fairy-tale prince. He had not taken himself off to Plumfield at all. Instead he had been here all the while, waiting, preparing to mount a rescue should I require one.

And such a rescue it was! He looked like an avenging angel, a beautiful Lucifer standing with legs planted far apart, the flames playing over his face.

"Let her go," Stoker commanded over the rush and hiss of the steam.

"I think not," Eliza began, but Stoker looked at me, flicking a finger, and I understood him at once. Without a moment's hesitation, I stamped hard upon Eliza's instep, likely breaking a bone in her foot. Most opponents would have unhanded me at that moment, but Eliza only squeezed harder in her fury. In a feint, I raised my left arm as if to strike her, causing her to turn her head. As she did so, I drove my right thumb into her eye socket. She released me with a howl of pain, and I dove for the platform. I landed, again and unluckily, squarely upon young Wilfred.

Together we scrambled to our feet, allowing Stoker to guide us towards the stairs as Julius went to his sister.

He reached a hand to her. "Come, Eliza. Let me help you."

She hesitated, then took his hand, levering herself to her feet. As she did so, she pulled him off balance and onto the little train. In one smooth motion, she snatched up the poker once more and held it to his throat. "No, Julius. I will finish this."

She reached her free hand towards the brake, and as she did so, Julius made to grab the poker from her. She wrenched it away and drew her arm back, preparing to swing.

"No!" I cried.

I was too late. She swung the poker down, connecting with Julius's temple. Blood spurted from the wound, and for one terrible moment, I feared she had killed him. But he was merely stunned, giving a low moan and clapping his hand to his head, ruddy gore flowing through his fingers.

She whirled and pointed to Wilfred. "You. Bring me one of those jars," she ordered, indicating the shelves that lined the stone stairs. Wilfred hesitated and Stoker started forwards, but she brandished the poker once more.

"A step closer and I will finish him," she warned them. Stoker halted, and Wilfred blinked at her, hesitating. "Give me what I asked for," she said. "I will hit him again for every time you make me repeat myself." She raised the poker, and Wilfred leapt into action, retrieving a jar of spirits of formalin and carrying it to the edge of the platform. "Put it down and back away," she said. Wilfred did as he was told and he retreated to stand next to us in an uneasy tableau.

Stoker put up his hands to show he meant her no harm.

"Eliza, leave Julius be. You need not kill an innocent man," he said.

Her expression was scornful. "Innocent? Is that what he told you?" She gestured towards Julius with a thrust of the poker.

"He shared your story with us," I told her, placating, playing for time. "We know of your brilliance, Eliza. We know how difficult it must have been for you, always overshadowed by Julius when yours was the real genius."

"Do not pity me," she spat. "You know nothing of what my life was like, forced to creep in his shadow, yet knowing I was his superior in every way." She looked down at her brother, huddled on the floor of the train, bereft of dignity. "This is the end you deserve, Julius. And you cannot deny it."

"Why?" Stoker asked. "Because he dared to stop your experiments?"

"Stop them? He *began* them. She was our maidservant, did he tell you that?"

"You knew her?" I could not keep the note of accusation from my tone.

"Of course we knew her! Ambrose took her out of a workhouse so there would be someone to cook and clean for us. But she was more than that, wasn't she?" Eliza demanded, landing a savage kick to Julius's leg.

Julius groaned and covered his face with his hands.

"The child," I said suddenly. "Julius was the father."

Bitterness twisted her mouth. "He got her with child and then cast her out of the house. He told her she had made her bed and now she must lie on it."

"And so she threw herself into the canal," Wilfred said.

"She did not throw herself in," Eliza corrected savagely. "She ended up in the canal because *he put her there.*"

Julius dropped his hands. His face was that of Janus, half-pale as marble, half-stained with his own heart's blood. "I had no choice. She said she would tell," he said feebly.

Eliza looked at him in frank disgust, but when she spoke, it was to us. "Julius took her for a walk late one night. He came home shivering and half fainting, and the next morning her body was discovered. We knew exactly what he had done, Ambrose and I. We helped him to cover the crime."

"And you extracted the promise of the experiment as the price of your help," Stoker guessed.

"She was a workhouse maid, of use to no one anymore. Nobody would come looking for her, and Julius could be hanged for murder if someone else handled the body and realised what he had done. But she could still be useful to me. She was Julius's end, but she was my beginning. Until he *ruined* it."

"You grew too attached," Julius murmured. "There was something unhealthy about your obsession with making her live again. It had to be stopped."

"Or were you just afraid that if I did revive her, she might tell everyone the truth about what you had done?" Eliza demanded. "You never expected I would be successful, but when you realised it was possible, that I just might make it happen, that is when you destroyed it all."

"I did what I thought was best," he protested.

"And so must I," she said, straightening.

"What do you mean to do, Eliza?" I asked calmly. "You cannot think to escape justice now."

She lifted her chin, resolved. "I do not mean to escape at all."

Stoker started forwards, but she put up a hand. "My quarrel is not with you. But you cannot have him." She dropped the poker and reached for the jar of formalin, holding it aloft in front of the fiery hatch of the engine. "Go. Save yourselves."

Stoker hurled himself towards her just as she flung the jar into the engine.

There was a pause, a moment suspended in eternity, and then the explosion, the bursting, roaring, rocking of the whole world that went on until the end of time.

And then silence.

After the silence came the muffled ringing in my ears. I had been flung backwards and hit my head upon the wall during the blast. It was some minutes before I could gather my wits enough to stand. When I did, I saw that the whole of the tunnel was afire. It seemed as if the very gates of Purgatory had opened, inviting us into Hell, and I dashed towards it without hesitation. If Stoker was there, I would find him and drag him out. And if I could not do that, I would join him.

A hand grabbed my arm, and I looked back to see Wilfred, struggling to his feet and protesting. I could not hear what he said, but he was shaking his head and trying to pull me back. There was no time for polite preliminaries. I kicked him, hard and remorselessly, in a place I do not care to name. He rocked back, and I lurched forwards again, screaming Stoker's name.

Again, a hand at my arm, and I turned, my own hand curled into a fist, and landed a solid blow before I realised whose hand held me fast.

"Stoker!" I screamed the name or choked it out on a gasp for air. I could not say which. I only know it came from the depths of my soul. He pulled me to him at the same moment I threw myself on him. We landed together upon poor Wilfred who slumped into merciful unconsciousness at that point. Without a word, Stoker hoisted the fellow onto his shoulders and motioned for me to follow. Smoke was filling the tunnel, and the air was thin and harsh in our lungs, obscuring the way. I held onto Stoker's belt as he mounted the stairs. We took them, one slow, painful step at a time, upwards and into the light.

As we reached the top, a great, almighty roar surged through the tunnel, blasting rock and timbers free from their moorings. Stoker pushed ahead, carrying Wilfred to safety as I followed. We hurried through the mortuary, emerging into the street as Mornaday and J. J. dashed up in a hansom.

"My god!" Mornaday exclaimed. We must have made a terrifying sight. Wilfred was insensible, Stoker begrimed by soot which streaked him from head to heel, and my face still bore shards of wax, cracking and crumbling as I moved.

Mornaday leapt free of the vehicle to help with Wilfred. J. J. jumped out and took one look at me, shuddering. "Veronica, are you *decomposing?*"

"Wax," I told her as I plucked a piece free. "It is a very long story."

"What of Eliza?" she asked. "And Julius?"

Stoker jerked his head backwards to the mortuary and then shook it.

Before we could explain, another blast erupted, shaking the foundations of the entire street. A fireball the size of a house shot into the sky, taking half of Plumtree's with it and sending a shower of timber and bricks and glass into the street. Pandemonium ensued. A shattered piece of brick hit J. J. in the hand, breaking a finger, but that was the worst of the injuries. Neighbouring businesses emptied as spectators surged into the streets, heedless of their own safety in their eagerness to gawk at the spectacle.

"Back, all of you," Mornaday ordered. "I am an officer of the Metropolitan Police, and I am in charge here."

He began giving instructions, calling up the fire brigade and more officers and securing the street against further damage. He looked every inch in command, and as he took charge, I tore one of Stoker's scarlet handkerchiefs into strips to set J. J.'s finger whilst Stoker administered sal volatile to Wilfred to clear his head.

"That's a good lad, don't move too quickly," he counselled.

Wilfred blinked furiously, and when he spoke his voice was as hoarse and rasping as the rest of ours. "Is it finished?" His spectacles, missing both lenses, dangled from one ear.

"It is," I told him. "But I am afraid Plumtree's is rather destroyed."

He looked past me to the smouldering remains of his family business, and a wide smile cracked the sooty mask of his face.

"Most excellent," he said. "Most excellent indeed!"

The arrival of the fire brigade introduced a new element of chaos to the pandemonium, but that was nothing compared to the appearance on the scene of Inspector Abbington. A pair of uniformed bobbies opened a path for him, pushing and shoving until the inspector was stood squarely in front of Mornaday. We could not hear what was said, but it was clear the inspector was shouting. A vein stood out on his brow and he shoved his finger into Mornaday's face, wagging it imperiously as poor Mornaday attempted to explain. Whatever he said got short shrift as the inspector blazed him to silence, stepping so near their noses were almost touching as he continued to rant.

"I promised to help," Stoker said resignedly.

I touched his sleeve. "Mornaday is capable of looking after himself. He is the proverbial cat with nine lives."

"Although probably on the bloody last one," Stoker replied.

"Very possibly," I said. "We will have a word with Sir Hugo upon his return if Mornaday is still in Abbington's black books. Until then, home."

Docile as a dog, young Plumtree limped to the corner with the aid of Stoker's arm. I supported his other side, and J. J. trailed behind, already scribbling in her notebook with her good hand.

At the end of the street, I turned back to watch the conflagration for a moment and contemplate the capricious nature of Fate. The Elyots had once eluded justice by such an inferno, but now another fire had settled the score. It seemed only fitting.

CHAPTER

30

It was a subdued and disreputable little band that made its way to Bishop's Folly. Our ears were ringing, our clothes and faces stained with soot, and the stench of burning hung about us like a noxious cloud.

"J. J.," I croaked. "Come and have a bath." I made a vague gesture towards the Roman bathhouse, but she waved me off, her broken finger pointing awkwardly in the opposite direction of her palm.

"Can't," she said shortly. "This is my story, and I will have it on my editor's desk by dawn." Her face was pale under the soot, limned with pain, and Stoker put a gentle hand to her shoulder.

"At least let me set your finger properly," he urged. "And you need tea, strong stuff with plenty of sugar and whisky."

"That much I will agree to," she allowed.

The next few hours passed in a slow, painful denouement of bathing, bandaging, and consuming pots of tea. Stoker unearthed a tin of shortbread, and we slathered it with a pot of raspberry jam. It was an indifferent jam, being the fruit of Lady Rose's efforts in the stillroom and thick with pips, but it was ambrosial after the night we had endured, even if pieces of wax kept dropping into my teacup. J. J. ate with one hand, the other pecking away at the keys of the typewriting machine usually kept for the labelling of natural history specimens.

Wilfred watched her, dazed and happy, his brow wrapped in strips of linen. The bandage, coupled with the cuts from his broken spectacles, gave him a dashing air, and I saw that—like many men—he dared to entertain hopes where J. J. was concerned. He needn't have bothered. She was entirely wedded to her career, but an unrequited passion would do the lad no harm. He needed something to strive for, some bright dream to take him out of himself and spur him on to great deeds. For some men it is the image of glory or riches, for others a pair of pretty eyes. If J. J. was the spark to his daring, he might well make a habit of adventuring before he realised the futility of his hopes. And by then it would not sting quite so sharply, for he would have many other strings to his bow, I had no doubt. In the meantime, he produced a packet of cheese and chutney sandwiches from his pocket—"Mamma says never to leave home without sustenance." He unwrapped the sandwiches, sharing them with J. J. before offering one to me.

"Veronica needs attending to," Stoker told him firmly. He put a hand under my arm, levering me gently to my feet. He guided my steps towards the Roman bathhouse where he proceeded to examine me thoroughly, removing the remaining bits of wax before bathing me and dressing my wounds.

"You are very good at this," I told him as he gently probed the lump on my head.

"You will have a devil of a headache tomorrow," he promised. "But you show no signs of concussion—frankly a miracle, for you ought to have been blown to bits."

His voice broke on the last phrase, and he cleared his throat sharply. Dried blood had left a thread of crimson on his cheek, and I touched it with a fingertip. "You did not escape injury yourself. Would you like me to stitch it?"

He shook his head. "It is a scratch, nothing more. Besides," he said, a fleeting smile touching his lips, "I thought you liked my scars."

"I would rather have your scars than any other man's perfection," I replied.

He said nothing but continued to probe my person with assessing hands. "No broken bones that I can find, and I think if you were to suffer from the shock, it would be in evidence by now. Still, you ought to rest for a day or so."

He helped me to dress in fresh clothing, and as his fingers lingered on the last button, I closed my hand over his. "Thank you."

Stoker shrugged. "Little point in being a trained surgeon's mate if I cannot be relied upon to bandage a few cuts."

"I am not talking about that. I know what this must have cost you, to put your feelings aside and let me do as I pleased."

Something akin to anger flared in his eyes and died away as swiftly as it kindled. "No," he said softly. "I do not think you do know. Furthermore, I do not think you ever will. But at least you understand a sacrifice was made."

I rose on tiptoe, wincing only a little as I looped my arms about his neck. "I was perhaps overhasty in assuming I knew best how to handle Eliza Elyot," I admitted.

He reared back, astonishment writ in every feature. "Are you actually saying you were *wrong*?"

"Certainly not," I told him. "I merely miscalculated. There were many, many factors to be considered in weighing our plan of attack, and I might have given less consideration to those that proved the most important."

I leant in for a kiss, but he clasped my wrists in his hands and held me off.

"Say it," he ordered. "Just three words, but they are poetry. And I want to hear them."

"I love you," I told him, tipping my head to the side like a winsome kitten.

"Not that. Say what I *really* want to hear," he commanded.

"I don't see why—"

"Veronica Speedwell. Say. It."

"Very well," I muttered. "I was wrong."

He threw his head back and laughed, the sound of it echoing off the marble walls until the whole of the little bathhouse was filled with his merriment. "My god, I have never been so happy to hear anything in the whole of my life."

"Enjoy the moment," I told him tartly. "It will surely never come again."

B y the time we returned to the Belvedere, Mornaday was in evidence, as filthy as the rest of us had been but beaming in triumph.

"You ought to have been there!" he crowed.

"What happened?" Stoker asked as we settled ourselves. Wilfred poured out fresh tea, and Mornaday slopped half of his in his saucer as he capered around.

"Victory! That is what happened, my friend, victory."

"But how?" I asked. "Chief Inspector Abbington was reading you the riot act when we saw you last. I thought he was going to strike you."

"Oh, he did," Mornaday said, exhibiting a violet bruise upon his chin. "And just as he did, who should appear? My very own knight in shining armour—Sir Hugo Montgomerie."

"Sir Hugo! I thought he was at the seaside, nursing his gout," I put in.

"He was, but all the sea bathing seems to have done the trick. He's brown as a berry and lost half a stone. Walking like a man ten years younger," Mornaday said. "And when he saw Abbington hit a junior, he lit into him like nobody's business. Called him every name in the book and a few I've never heard, shouting that it was beneath the dignity of an officer in the Metropolitan Police to hit a fellow policeman. Abbington must have shrunk half a foot under the onslaught of it. Sir Hugo can be a fearsome man when he's in a temper," he added with a shudder.

"Well, at least Abbington has had a bit of a comeuppance," I said.

"He has had more than that," Mornaday said contentedly. "He's been discharged. Relieved of his post entirely—drummed out of the Metropolitan Police forever."

"Just for hitting you?" Stoker asked. "I am surprised someone didn't think of giving him a commendation for it."

Mornaday wagged his finger. "Even you cannot get my goat just now, Templeton-Vane, much as you may try. You are looking at the new Detective Chief Inspector."

"Mornaday! How wonderful for you!" I clapped my hands and he smiled, preening.

"I shall have a proper office now—and the wherewithal to direct my own investigations upon occasion." He propped his feet up, surveying the worn tips of his boots. "It comes with a pay rise so I can buy a new suit and a good pair of boots and that new hat I've been eyeing in the window at Lock & Co."

"I have no doubt you will look very smart," I told him.

"Well, my heartiest congratulations," Wilfred put in. He had been listening, eyes wide with interest.

"Thank you," Mornaday said graciously. "And do not think the Metropolitan Police will forget the services you rendered in the cause of justice this night."

Wilfred blushed a happy scarlet at the praise and took bashful refuge in his teacup just as J. J. wrenched a piece of paper from the type-writing machine.

"J. J., come and say hello to Mornaday. He has just been promoted," I called.

"I heard. Enough to add the perfect conclusion to my story," she said, snatching up a piece of string to confine her sheaf of untidy pages. "I described the harrowing events of the night and gave full credit of my rescue from the hands of Eliza Elyot, the fiendish murderess of Lord Ambrose Despard, to Mr. Wilfred Plumtree of Plumtree and Son Mortuary and Detective Chief Inspector Mornaday of the Metropolitan Police."

I sputtered into my tea. "*Your* rescue?"

She smiled a feline smile. "Well, I couldn't very well say it was you in the casket, could I? You shun publicity."

I opened my mouth and snapped it shut again. "Touché," I muttered through clenched teeth.

"Now I must fly to get this to my editor in time for the next edition," she said. "Wilfred, come with me and I shall introduce you. The editor might want a sketch or two of the scenes of derring-do to accompany the article."

"Oh, indeed!" Wilfred leapt to his feet.

"I should come along," Mornaday announced. "If there are illustrations to be made, the artist will naturally want to draw me as well."

"Certainly," J. J. said genially.

Wilfred paused at the door. "I shall make arrangements to retrieve the Beauty," he told us. "I have chosen a nice little plot for her on higher ground, just under a willow tree. I hope that meets with your approval."

We agreed, and he left with Mornaday and J. J., their departure taking all of the excitement and energy of the past several hours with them. A sort of deflated silence settled when they had gone, and I looked at Stoker.

"It seems young Wilfred has learnt to take initiative at last," I remarked. "Perhaps he gained something from the experience after all."

Stoker opened his arms and I went to him, settling myself comfortably on his lap and nestling my sore head against his shoulder. He quoted Keats then, the words of "Endymion" rumbling gently against my cheek. It was a particular favourite of mine, and Stoker recited beautifully, but somewhere between fair musk-rose blooms and fleecy lambs, my eyelids grew heavy. And by the time the dancing damsels tripped through the vales of Thessaly, I was fast asleep . . .

CHAPTER

31

The calendar turned its leaf to November, the gilded autumn light having given way to an early blue frost one evening when Stoker and I were settled by the fire after a satisfactory day's work. The dogs were arranged around us in a peaceful pile, the smaller ones heaped on top of the long-suffering Vespertine. Huxley snored, low and resonant and in perfect accord with the ticking of the clock that stood upon the bookshelf. It kept time poorly—the hands always stood at half past two—but it had belonged to Marie Antoinette and added a certain glamour to our surroundings. The scene was one of pleasant domesticity. I was reading the latest adventure of Arcadia Brown, Lady Detective, and smoking a small Turkish cigarette whilst Stoker mended the pocket of my favourite gown with tiny, precise stitches. The hour was too advanced for casual callers, so when the knock came, Stoker and I exchanged significant looks.

"I will go," he said, rising too quickly to permit any argument. He may have stated his intentions of supporting my more outlandish and dangerous endeavours, but the perils I had suffered at the hands of Eliza Elyot had tested his resolve, and I had been forced to concede the necessity of a strong arm at my back upon occasion. We had reached a wordless understanding that Stoker would be permitted to act the protector so long as he did so discreetly. I would accept no curtailment of my activities, but I would also happily allow him to step in when his nerves were frayed—such as the late arrival of unexpected callers to the Belvedere.

"What in the name of the oozing wound of Christ—VERONICA!" Stoker's question ended on a bellow, and I leapt to my feet to see what was the matter. The earl's porters had carried in a pair of wooden crates, each some six feet in length. Stoker had removed the lid from the first along with a drift of excelsior to reveal a glass casket. Inside was the face of a sleeping waxwork, the hair in silken blonde ringlets.

He held out the prybar accusingly. "What is this?"

"An Anatomical Venus," I informed him.

He jerked the prybar to the second crate. "And that is presumably a second one?"

"Not at all," I said happily. "It is an Anatomical Adonis. I confess, I should never have thought of it but Lavinia did inquire if such a thing existed, and I was curious."

"Why are they here?" he demanded.

"For the purposes of instruction, of course," I said promptly. "It has come to my attention that the Beauclerk children are remarkably ill-informed about biology. I mean to rectify that."

"You mean to use them as teaching aids?"

"Certainly. That is why they were created, after all," I reminded him. "And these are a particularly fine set. The Marquess of Harwich inherited his brother's collection and decided to auction them quite inexpensively."

The notion of using the models for their intended purpose seemed to mollify Stoker, and I decided it was best not to inform him just yet that whilst I promised to instruct the earl's daughters on anatomy, the tuition of the boys would fall to him.

We returned to our chairs, and Stoker brought a glass of whisky for us each.

We sipped companionably for a moment in silence before I slipped off my shoes, toasting my toes in front of the fire.

"Well, another adventure concluded, and this one most satisfactory indeed," I said. "Eliza and Julius Elyot will cause no grief to anyone ever again. Mornaday is reinstated with a promotion, and J. J. is in her editor's good graces. Even Lady Rose is happy with her tamarin," I added.

Stoker had, as a gesture of goodwill for robbing the child of her waxwork, given her the monkey. I would have laid money on the little creature fleeing from Lady Rose at the first opportunity, but to my astonishment, she was proving a devoted and responsible keeper, feeding her and cleaning her accoutrements with great care. I do not think the creature cared much for the bows she tied into her hair, but she accepted them with the same tired resignation most beings adopted when exposed to Lady Rose's ferocious energy and will.

"And young Wilfred has proven himself an excellent investigator," I reminded him. With Plumtree's burnt, our friend had been at loose ends. He recalled what Eliza had related about the Beauty being taken from the workhouse and had combed through records to find young orphan girls going into service during the time in question. It had cost him the better part of a week to learn her name, but when he had done so, he had ordered a marker for the grave he had put aside for her at Plumfield. We had gathered for her burial, laying flowers as the glass casket was lowered into the ground, consigning her to her final rest. In the spring, when the ground had settled, we would return for the laying of the stone which would be graven with her name. Mary Smith. Whether that was how she was called at birth or the name given her by the orphanage, we would never know. But I thought of Stoker's remarks upon the failure of dramatic events to happen to young women with commonplace names just the same.

"In short," I concluded, "all is well that ends well."

"I suspect Ambrose Despard would have preferred a different ending," Stoker put in dryly.

Ambrose Despard had not deserved to be murdered in a train car, I reflected. But he had conspired to keep Mary Smith's murder from the authorities as well as a dozen lesser crimes. I would not mourn him acutely.

"Still," I said, "we solved the mystery of Mary Smith's identity as well as unmasking Ambrose Despard's murderer."

"Wilfred discovered Mary Smith's name, and Mornaday and J. J. deserve more credit than we do in identifying Despard's killer," he reminded me. "In fact, we bungled this investigation so badly, you began to wonder if we had lost our detectival instincts entirely."

"Feathers," I said with an airy wave of the hand. "Even the greatest scientific minds have occasional lapses. Aristotle believed in spontaneous generation. Sir Isaac Newton conducted experiments in alchemy. Even Mr. Darwin's theories about heredity are untenable—"

"You do not really mean to suggest that you have a better grasp of scientific principles than Charles Darwin," he cut in.

"Not all of them," I replied smoothly. "But he is quite wrong about heredity, mark my words." Before he could argue the point, I hastened to change the subject.

"Isn't it curious that Mary Smith drowned and in the end came to rest amongst strangers, just like sailors swept overboard? And she has been given a proper burial." I reached out a hand to touch one glimmering ring of gold threaded through Stoker's earlobe, remembering what he had told me about the purpose of a sailor's earring.

Slowly, he slipped the ring from his ear and dropped it into my palm.

"What is this for?" I asked.

"I wore it because my greatest fear was dying alone and uncared for.

This bit of gold was my insurance that someone would give me dignity at the end." His eyes never left mine as he closed my hand around the ring. "But I know now that I will never die alone and unclaimed. I have you."

I opened my hand again and stared at the golden ring, glowing in my palm and warm still from the heat of his body. I took a silk ribbon from around my neck and threaded the ring onto it, knotting it securely before tying the ribbon back into place. The ring lay in the hollow of my throat, fitting the curve perfectly.

"Yes," I told him with a smile. "You do."

It was the first piece of jewellery he had given me, and though there would be other tokens of his affection through the years, none would ever move me quite so deeply as that slender gold ring. I promised myself I would wear it always, and I did—whether in peacefulness, passion, or peril, it was my constant companion through the escapades to come. I had no idea the day Stoker pressed it into my hand what dangers and delights lay before us, but I knew we would undertake them together and with the same indomitable spirit we faced all of our adventures. Excelsior!

AUTHOR'S NOTE

This book began more than twenty years ago when I stood in Madame Tussaud's in London and stared in fascination at the figure of the Sleeping Beauty. Her label was most likely incorrect—she is attributed to Tussaud as a portrait of Madame du Barry, but it is far likelier that she was sculpted by Tussaud's mentor, Philippe Curtius, decades before du Barry's ascendancy—but the clockwork mechanism that made her chest rise and fall gave the most perfect illusion of enchanted sleep.

The Anatomical Venuses described in this book were created as teaching aids as well as objects of entertainment and titillation. For a comprehensive overview of this phenomenon, *The Anatomical Venus* by Joanna Ebenstein is highly recommended.

The notion of a mysterious drowning victim whose beauty haunts the living was inspired by the story of L'Inconnue de la Seine, the anonymous girl plucked from the river in Paris. Although her death mask was circulated, she was never identified. Her gentle, Mona Lisa smile proved irresistible, and fashionable people hung models of her death mask on their parlor walls. She proved so popular that her face was the inspiration for that of Resusci Anne, the first mannequin used for the instruction of mouth-to-mouth resuscitation.

While the creators of waxworks and death masks worked their art in wax and plaster, others took a darker path. The story of the lavish embalming of Eva Perón's corpse is well-known, but less familiar is the monstrous effort made by Carl Tanzler to preserve the body of the beautiful young woman he had loved and lost. His obsession drove him to unspeakable and frankly unhinged lengths. Maria Elena Milagro de Hoyos was the name of the girl whose corpse he retrieved and defiled. One can only hope she at last rests in peace.

ACKNOWLEDGMENTS

First and foremost, my talented and devoted editor, Michelle Vega, who did not flinch when I turned this book in and then emailed the following morning to say, "Please, may I have it back. I got the murderer wrong." For your trust in me and our brilliant brainstorming sessions, I offer the most fervent and heartfelt THANK YOU.

To the rest of the Berkley crew—Claire Zion, Christine Ball, Ivan Held, Jeanne-Marie Hudson, Craig Burke, Loren Jaggers, Tara O'Connor, Jessica Mangicaro, Annie Odders, Colleen Reinhart, and the essential teams in Marketing, Sales, Editorial, PR, and Art, including the cover artist Leo Nickolls—I would not want to do this without you. I am the luckiest writer on the planet to have you in my corner! And thank you to all of the hardworking folks involved in the physical production of the books. Printers, packers, shippers, warehouse workers—you are the unsung heroes and I salute you.

To Amber Beard and the rest of the audio team, you conjure magic and for that I am grateful.

To Jennifer Lynes and the proofreaders on the production team, fervent thanks for the eagle eyes and incredible attention to detail. You are absolute superstars!

ACKNOWLEDGMENTS

To my agent, Pamela Hopkins, thank you for a quarter of a century (!) of riding into battle as my champion. To the Writerspace team and Paula Breen, heaps of thanks for working so hard behind the scenes.

To the readers, booksellers, librarians, podcasters, interviewers, and bookstagrammers who have taken Veronica to their hearts, thank you for spreading the love!

To my family, you are the greatest village a person could hope for.

To P, for everything and always.